THE LANCE

George Vasil

THE LANCE

iUniverse books may be ordered through booksellers or by contacting:

iUniverse
1663 Liberty Drive
Bloomington, IN 47403
www.iuniverse.com
1-800-Authors (1-800-288-4677)

Because of the dynamic nature of the Internet, any web addresses or links contained in this book may have changed since publication and may no longer be valid. The views expressed in this work are solely those of the author and do not necessarily reflect the views of the publisher, and the publisher hereby disclaims any responsibility for them.

Any people depicted in stock imagery provided by Getty Images are models, and such images are being used for illustrative purposes only. Certain stock imagery © Getty Images.

ISBN: 978-1-5320-4411-3 (sc)
ISBN: 978-1-5320-4412-0 (hc)
ISBN: 978-1-5320-4413-7 (e)

Library of Congress Control Number: 2019911587

Print information available on the last page.

iUniverse rev. date: 08/23/2019

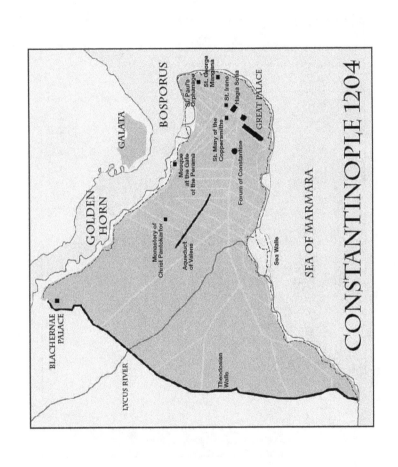

CONSTANTINOPLE 1204

GOLDEN HORN

GALATA

BOSPORUS

SEA OF MARMARA

BLACHERNAE PALACE

LYCUS RIVER

Theodosian Walls

Monastery of Christ Pantokartor

Aqueduct of Valens

Mosque at the Gate of the Perama

St. Paul's Orphanage

St. George Mangana

St. Mary of the Coppersmiths

St. Irene

Hagia Sofia

Forum of Constantine

Sea Walls

GREAT PALACE

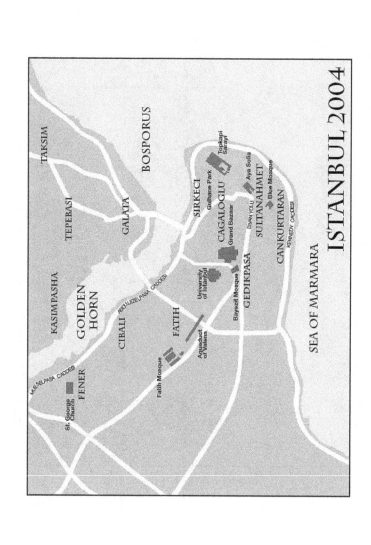

ISTANBUL 2004

TAKSIM

BOSPORUS

TEREBASI

GALATA

KASIMPASHA

GOLDEN HORN

CIBALI

ABDULIZEUPASA CADDESI

FATIH

Fatih Mosque

Aqueduct of Valens

University of Istanbul

Bayezit Mosque

SIRKECI

CAGALOGLU

Grand Bazaar

Gulhane Park

Topkapi Sarayi

DIVAN YOLU

Aya Sofia

Blue Mosque

SULTANAHMET

GEDIKPASA

CANKURTARAN

KENNEDY CADDESI

SEA OF MARMARA

FENER

MUESELPASA CADDES

St. George Church

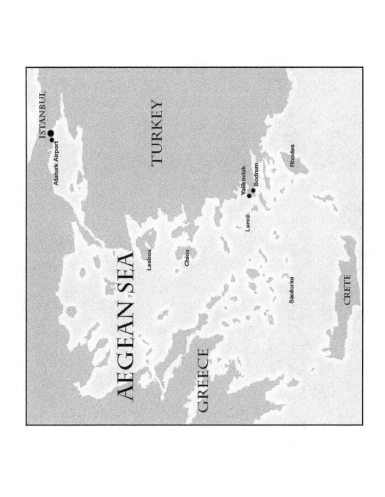

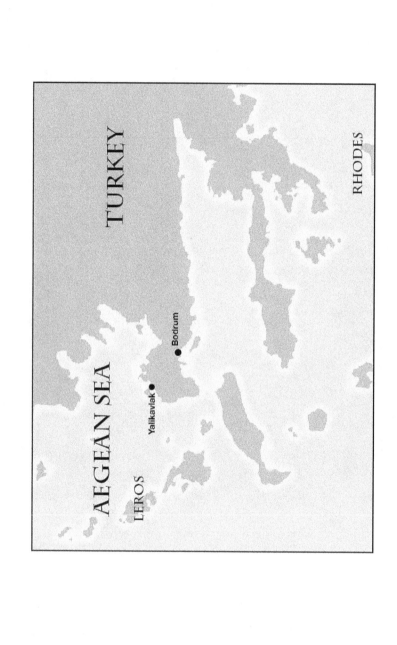

ACKNOWLEDGEMENTS

The author would like to thank the following people for their help in creating *The Lance:* Mary Hawksley for her faithful editing of *The Lance;* Jerome Petteys for his beautiful cover art and excellent maps for *The Lance;* Jeff Van Dyke for his artistic ideas for *The Lance* and his excellent cover art and maps for the author's first book, *Emperor's Eyes.*

PROLOGUE

Constantinople, April 12, 1204

"It's happening! Oh dear Christ! It's happening!" The young monk felt his heart pound frantically as he looked out of a tiny window of the Monastery of Christ Pantokrator. From his perch on the topmost floor he saw the wave of barbarian invaders disembarking from their warships in the Golden Horn and flowing through the breach in the city's walls and into its streets, like so many ants ravaging a dying animal. He ran out of his cell in search of his archimandrite but found only rampant confusion. His fellow monks rushed in and out of their cells, not knowing whether to flee or hide.

"Brother Gregory!" the monk cried as he grabbed one of the passersby. "Where is our archimandrite?"

"He's gone!" Gregory snapped back as he shook out of his comrade's grasp. Gregory lied. He had not seen the monastery's leader for many hours and had no idea where he was. *His* only interest was saving his own skin.

"Where?"

Gregory pushed his fellow monk away and ran toward the stairs. "Get out, Brother Damon! Those Frankish demons will kill you! And they'll have great sport doing it!"

Damon knew Gregory was right. He'd heard all of the stories about these unwelcome visitors. Heretics! All of them!

Since the Crusades were first declared in 1095, relations between eastern and western Christendom had gone from alliance to outright hostility. In 1203, a unique situation arose. The Byzantine Emperor Isaac II was overthrown, blinded and imprisoned by his brother Alexios, who was

1

then crowned Emperor Alexios III. In retaliation Isaac's son, also named Alexios, conspired with the western powers to oust his uncle and restore his father. In July, the westerners seized Galata across the Golden Horn from Constantinople and broke the huge chain that ran across the waterway. This huge iron barrier protected the vital channel from encroachment.

The invaders attacked the city forcing out Emperor Alexios III in the name of the deposed Emperor Isaac II and his son, Alexios, thereafter Emperor Alexios IV, who ruled with his father. All seemed to be going well for Isaac and his son but the alien armies remained camped outside the city walls awaiting the promised payment for their work: 200,000 silver marks, subjugation of the Orthodox Church to Rome and a contribution of a large military force to the upcoming crusade against Egypt. However, the clergy and people of Constantinople resented the terms of the agreement and the presence of these western hooligans. Soon the entire city erupted in riots. In January of 1204, Isaac and Alexios were deposed and murdered by a new, very anti-western emperor, Alexios V.

Rather than leave, as any civilized army would do, the westerners attacked the city on Thursday, April 9 but were thrown back. Damon knew that the power of the Christ's Holy Shroud, which the emperor hung from the walls of the Blacharnae Palace, had repelled the invaders. But the barbarians attacked again and this time they breached the walls of God's most holy city. Now they threatened to destroy the Seat of the True Faith. Damon knew that the Franks, the Venetians and their allies would drive to the heart of the city to sack the Great Palace and its churches, and his monastery was directly in their path.

"They mustn't find it!" Damon whispered under his breath as he thought of the monastery's greatest relic. He rushed to where it was kept. He knew of its power and having it fall into the hands of these heretics was unthinkable. He hoped that his fellow monks had not already found the relic and taken it from the monastery. Damon thought of his brother monks and pictured the horror of their torture at the hands of these Frankish fiends, who would stop at nothing to loot Constantinople of all of its treasures. But where could he hide it? Where would it be safe from these devils? *Saint Sophia!* Damon's heart leapt in excitement as he planned his holy mission. He had a friend who helped maintain the cathedral, Haggia or Saint Sophia, whose name means Holy Wisdom. He was certain that he remembered many places where the relic would be safe. God would not allow the heretics to violate His most sacred church and steal this holy treasure. *Emperor Alexios will retake the city, and when he does, I can reveal its location.* Damon arrived in the deserted chapel and slowly, reverently stepped through the Holy Doors of the iconostasis and prostrated himself before the altar. He quickly begged for the Savior's help and then stood up and contemplated his mystical quarry. Chills ran up his back as he examined the relic, resting serenely in its place of honor upon a porphyry pedestal in the center of the altar.

"Thank Christ!" Damon sighed as he bowed his head and extended his trembling fingers toward the reliquary. This golden casket ran only the length of his forearm and was as wide as his palm and as deep as the length of his thumb. He removed it from the pedestal and reverently kissed it. Looking deferentially at the reliquary, Damon couldn't help but admire its intricate design. He opened the hinged lid of the casket and retrieved the object of his quest, which was wrapped in luxuriant red silk. He carefully peeled away the precious wrapping and gasped, "It's still here!" His hand trembled as he felt the long, leaf-like, polished iron blade. "O treasured relic! I will see that you will be safe from these heretic barbarians!" Damon kissed the relic again, swathed it in its beautiful escarpment and laid it back upon the papyrus document upon which it rested in the reliquary. He crossed himself three times, turned away from the altar with the casket and bolted from the monastery toward the center of the city.

As Damon ran south down the hill on which his monastery was perched, he saw the massiveAqueduct of Valens. He turned east and ran through the pasture to a narrow dirt road that took him into the sprawling city. As he set foot on the stone pavement, he quickly looked over his left shoulder to see foreign flags being raised on the city walls; the ranks of imperial soldiers were melting in front of the invaders. He crossed himself again and sped eastward. There, pandemonium reigned as terrified soldiers ran into battle. Most of the citizens were running toward the center of town, praying for a miracle. Some locked themselves in their houses, hoping that the invaders would pass them by. Priests and monks dutifully patrolled the streets, reading aloud from the Scriptures, praying that God's Word would repel the heretics.

Damon soon found himself at the mosque at the Gate of Perama.

He momentarily scowled at the rounded dome and the solitary minaret. Damon wasn't happy that the emperors allowed the city's Muslim Arab traders to practice their faith. He looked up to the top of the sea wall and saw the emperor's soldiers heading toward the breach further north. "Go in God's Name, my brothers!" Damon encouraged them, "Expel these vermin from Hell!" Perhaps his trip to Saint Sophia will prove unnecessary. Surely those brave Christians would succeed but Damon had to be certain the relic would be safe. He would take no chances.

Damon turned and sprinted through the narrow streets toward the cathedral. Ahead, a panicked but immobile crowd gathered. A large wagon had broken down, blocking the course of the citizens, many of whom were carting their possessions and their children into the heart of the city. Nothing was moving. Damon backtracked and cut south down a small street.

He soon found himself in the Forum of Constantine. A giant arcade surrounded the elliptical stone plaza. In the center of this immense opening in an otherwise packed city was a tall column with Emperor Constantine the Great's statue looking down from its capital. Christ's Nail, the Constantinopolitans called it. From there he ran into the Mese, the wide, arcaded main boulevard of the city. Saint Sophia lay straight ahead.

However, Damon wasn't the only Constantinopolitan who sought entrance to the cathedral: thousands hoped for refuge in the sacred edifice, which seemed to float in the sea of humanity that surrounded it. As he approached the crowd, he begged them to let him through. After all, he was bringing a sacred relic to the cathedral but the frightened people would not listen to him. He tried to push his way through but was thrown back by two big longshoremen.

"There must be another way," he said under his breath. *The northeast side…* Damon disengaged from the crowd and headed north toward Saint Mary of the Coppersmiths. He turned east at that church and ran to the Church of Saint Irene. Another crowd surrounded that holy site as well.

Near the southeast end of Saint Irene, Damon found what he was looking for. He ran to the copse of elm trees, fell to his knees and set the golden reliquary aside. His hands busily grubbed through the soil until they found the object of their quest. He grabbed the iron ring of a trapdoor with both hands and pulled with all of his might, ripping small tears in

4

his hands, but to no avail. The trapdoor remained sealed. He withdrew his sore hands, cupped them around his mouth and blew on them, soothing them temporarily. He wiped them on his black cassock while his mind raced. How could he open the door? This was the only way he could get into the cathedral. He looked at the bough of the huge elm tree above him.

"That will work," he muttered. "I need something…a chain…a rope!" He looked around hurriedly. "Where can I find a rope?" Still crouching, he threw his hands up to his temples and closed his eyes, as if that would improve his concentration. But the answer did not come to him. He sprang to his feet and began pacing frantically. Damon pursed his lips, biting them in frustration. "How can it be so difficult to think of where to get something so simple? Dear God, please help me!"

Damon's prayer was speedily answered. "Of course!" Damon declared as the thought came to him. "The Armenian's by Saint Paul's Orphanage! He's got everything there!"

Damon scooped up the casket and sprinted east toward the acropolis of the ancient city, which lay within five hundred yards, just south of the Genoese quarter. He knew the area well, having spent many days attending to the needs of the pitiable orphans. He ran past a dozen buildings to find the Armenian busily boarding up his shop. The shop keeper hoped his shop would escape damage in the battle for the city.

"Mister Bedrosian!" Damon yelled as he ran toward the shop. "I need rope!"

Bedrosian ignored the young monk and went on with his work.

Damon grabbed his arm and pleaded, "In the name of Christ and all of his angels! I must have rope!"

Bedrosian had had more than his share of unpleasant dealings with monks in the past. It seemed they badgered him for money constantly. How was a man to make a living if the Church always had a hand in his pocket? He coolly turned to Damon. "Brother Damon, I have no rope," he lied. He quickly returned to his project.

"Where can I get some, sir?"

Bedrosian ignored him and continued his work. Perhaps the pesky monk would depart hastily.

"Where, sir? In God's name!" Damon screamed at the top of his lungs, "Where can I find some rope?"

Bedrosian scowled at Damon. There was no getting rid of the monk. In exasperation he said, "Try Kalef next door."

"Someone ask for me? What do you need?" an elderly Arab man asked kindly as he walked over to Damon. "How can I be of service to you, Brother?"

Damon shot a cold glance at Bedrosian, turned, smiled and politely asked the old Arab shopkeeper, "Rope, Mister Kalef. I need rope."

"Come with me, Brother Damon," Kalef said as he led Damon into his shop. "How much will you need?" he turned and asked, catching a glimpse of the gold reliquary Damon clutched to his breast. "May I ask what is in the gold box?"

Damon looked up as he estimated how much rope would be necessary. "Eight cubits."

Kalef, his question unanswered, muttered under his breath, "None of my business anyway." He held up three ropes of different diameters in his gnarled hands. "Which would be best?"

Damon thought carefully and then chose the one as thick as his thumb. He reached into his pocket for money and asked, "How much, Mister Kalef?"

"Consider it a donation," Kalef smiled. "It's for the Lord's service, I'm assuming."

"Yes, of course."

Kalef measured eight cubits of rope, cut it with some difficulty and handed it to Damon. "There you are Brother."

"Thank you, sir. Mister Kalef, you know that the heretics have breached the city walls and are coming this way."

"Yes. Everybody knows. That's why Bedrosian is boarding up his shop."

"Won't you do the same?"

"These hands are too old and battered to do it by myself," Kalef said as he raised his arthritic hands in front of his face. "Mister Bedrosian has promised to help me when he is done."

"Then what will you do?"

"The priest at Saint George in Mangana--"

"Father Christopher. I know him."

"Father Christopher has promised us refuge in his church. I thank the Lord Jesus Christ."

"Good. Father Christopher is a good man."

Bedrosian crossed the threshold of the old man's shop and asked, "Are you ready now, Mister Kalef?"

"Yes, my friend. I am ready."

"I must leave you then," Damon said hurriedly. He quickly looked at Kalaf and smiled. His brief glance toward Bedrosian was less than friendly. "Go with Christ, gentlemen."

"Go with Christ," both Kalef and Bedrosian replied.

Damon ran back to Saint Irene, the golden casket in one hand and the rope in the other. When he arrived at the copse of elm trees he found the trapdoor and set the reliquary down. He threw one end of the rope over the stout bough, which hung directly over the trap door and tied it to the door's iron ring. He stepped over to the other end of the rope and gave it three good tugs. He saw that the bough held strongly and the rope would certainly suit his purpose. Damon spat on his hands and pulled down on the rope for all he was worth. The stout bough sagged just a little but the trapdoor didn't budge. Damon released the rope and took several deep breaths. He pulled again with all of his might but met with the same result.

"They've entered the Forum of Constantine!" he heard someone yell from a distance. The crowd around Saint Irene raised their voices in panic. Damon could hear those at the front of the crowd pounding furiously against the church's wooden doors, but the scared clerics inside knew that not all of them could fit into the church and refused to open the doors.

Damon knew that he was running out of time. He jumped up as high as he could and grabbed onto the rope. He hung on the rope as though it led directly to Heaven and prayed silently that the trapdoor would open. Halfway through his prayer he heard groaning and then creaking coming from the trap door below him. "Yes! Thank God Almighty!" The stubborn trapdoor suddenly broke open and Damon fell to the ground, almost dropping the rope he was holding so solidly in his hands. He quickly recovered and while holding the rope taught in one hand, reached over to the trapdoor, grabbed it and opened it completely. The dank stench from within was asphyxiating. Damon turnedaway from the door and breathed deep breaths of the clean air away from the door's opening while being certain to keep the trapdoor open. He waited a few seconds, hoping the foul stench from the opening would dissipate quickly. But that was not to be. The dank smell continued to flow from the door but there was no time to waste. Damon turned his head away from the trapdoor, took a deep breath and looked into the trapdoor. He saw stone stairs that led to a lit passageway. Damon turned his head away from the trapdoor again, took another deep breath, grabbed the casket and ran down the stairs, slamming the trapdoor behind him.

Only a few people knew of this passageway. It was the Metropolitan of Selymbria who had revealed it to Damon as part of his payment for copying some ancient Greek treatises on dream interpretation.

When Damon reached the end of the damp, torch-lit passage he found another set of stone stairs, which wound upward. He figured that he had run the distance between Saint Irene and Saint Sophia and eagerly ran up the steps to another trapdoor. This one opened much easier than the first. Damon cautiously poked his head out and found that he had indeed reached his goal.

"Praise be to God!" he whispered as he climbed out of the passage and into the inner narthex.

The massive cathedral buzzed with activity. Priests, deacons, monks, government officials and army officers rushed to and fro across the stone floor of the cathedral. Damon was surprised that he came through the trapdoor unnoticed. He followed one of the priests into the nave. As he ran through the nave, he not could help but look at the spectacular beauty that surrounded him. Gorgeous icons adorned the apses and upper walls. The grain of the green marble walls had been laid so that the multiple sections appeared to be one large, intact slab of marble. He suddenly stopped. In awe he looked up at the massive dome and saw the gigantic icon of Christ Pantokrator, Christ the Ruler of All.

Damon abruptly came to his senses as he felt a strange tingling in the hand that was holding the gold casket. *Remember why you're here!* He turned around, found the ramp to the upper north gallery and ran up it as fast as he could. He ran to the mosaic of Emperor Alexander, a giant work high up on the wall, and searched for a hiding place. The last time he was in Saint Sophia, his friend, one of the keepers of the cathedral, showed Damon that the mortar around some of the bricks under this mosaic were going bad and needed to be replaced. Luckily that had not yet been done. He brushed away some of the cracking mortar, as much as he could but that was not enough to remove even one of the bricks. The bricks were laid flat and long end to long end, making the wall nearly two cubits thick.

Damon needed something hard to dig through the mortar. He looked around in desperation. Then he felt the gold crucifix around his neck. He hesitated. The archimandrite himself had blessed this crucifix. He sighed and removed the crucifix from around his neck, looked at the suffering savior laying in agony on that implement of death and kissed it. With a deep sigh Damon dug the bottom end of the crucifix into the crumbling mortar.

The crowd outside the cathedral suddenly grew louder. Damon stopped for a second. *They're getting closer!* He frantically tore into the mortar again. Soon one of the bricks was loose enough to remove. He pulled it out and set it aside on the floor of the gallery. Damon pulled at the brick next to it but it wouldn't budge. He grabbed his crucifix and quickly inspected it: the bottom end was badly bent and couldn't be used any more. He sighed and turned it over and began digging with the top end.

"They're here!" Damon heard someone scream. He looked down from the gallery onto the floor of the nave. A metropolitan was speaking to an imperial army officer and his two adjutants. The cleric pointed out the western door and soldiers ran into the narthex, gathering other soldiers in the cathedral together. "Go with God," Damon whispered as he quickly made the sign of the cross. After a few more tries the second brick from the outer layer was out, but the crucifix was now too badly damaged to use. Damon kissed it and quickly replaced it around his neck and dug at the inner layer of bricks with his fingers. He clawed at the mortar four times and suddenly withdrew his fingers: bits of brick and mortar were jammed under his fingernails, causing his fingers to bleed.

"Lord Christ, give me strength!" Damon prayed as he tried to rub the stone fragments from under his fingernails. He was only partially successful, but he'd removed enough to continue. He clawed at the inner layer of brick and mortar with renewed vigor. After just a few moments a large section of mortar crumbled in his fingers. *Praise be to God!* He grabbed the free edge of the brick and forced it to the left, then the right, over and over again until it broke loose. Damon panted as he removed the third brick. As he set it aside, he saw that the tips of all of his fingers were badly bloodied. Shards of skin were peeled away from the nails and fingertips. He wiped the blood away and remembered the many saints and martyrs who had shed their blood for the Church. He felt honored that he could now count himself among them.

"One more brick!" he hissed to himself. To Damon's surprise, the last was the easiest of all. He lay the brick down and quickly grabbed the reliquary. He quickly made the sign of the cross over it, kissed it and jammed it into its new hiding place. The casket's size approximated that of two of the bricks. *Thank God!* Damon hurriedly replaced the two exterior bricks in the hole and examined his work. *Looks like some fool is trying to hide something in there! Mortar! It needs the mortar! How in God's name am I going to fix this?*

Damon looked around frantically. He fell to his knees and cried, "My God, I have failed you! Can you forgive this miserable wretch?" He threw his hands forward and landed prostrate on the floor. "Send me to Hell where I belong, my Lord! I have failed you!"

As the monk languished in self-pity and self-abuse, a soldier burst in. "Bolt the door! They're just outside!"

Damon stopped his moaning and listened to a soft, but strong voice in his ear. He rose and looked around: nobody near him. Then he heard it again. *O Holy Christ!* He jumped to his feet and looked across the nave to the south gallery.

"Look! Look!" the voice said.

"My God, what am I looking for?" Damon muttered.

He quickly, yet carefully, scanned the south gallery, thinking that he would recognize whatever it was the voice wanted him to find. Then he saw something. He had no idea what it was but was drawn toward it like iron to a lodestone. He ran west through the north gallery, through the *Gynaeceum*, the empress's gallery at the west end of the cathedral, and into the south gallery.

Below him the confusion grew as the invaders pounded at the huge doors. The defenders prayed, cursed, or cried. Their fate was sealed.

"Good God!" Damon cried when he saw it, a bucket of fresh mortar and a trowel. "Most precious Blood of Christ!" He could see that someone had recently been working on one of these walls. He started to fall to his knees in thanks, but the voice demanded action, not adoration. He grabbed the bucket and trowel and flew back to the north gallery. He found the hiding place and quickly pulled out the two bricks, carefully placing them where he could easily retrieve them.

Damon quickly examined the mortar then the trowel. He carefully grabbed the trowel and slopped a layer of mortar over the base of the hole, making sure to use just enough for two bricks. Without thinking he grabbed a brick, applied a layer of mortar to the top and set it in place. *Blessed Theotokos,* he thought as he invoked the name of the Virgin, *this may work!* He grabbed the second brick and repeated the process. Damon thought for a brief moment and then ran the trowel over the outside of the bricks and cleaned away the excess mortar. *Finished!*

"Thank you, Lord Christ!" Damon gasped as he fell to the floor. But his ecstasy immediately vanished when the invaders broke through the door and into the outer narthex. He ran as he had never run before, down the gallery to the ramp and to the trapdoor. When he opened it two Flemish soldiers in the nave saw him and raced toward him. Damon slid into the passageway and closed the trapdoor just in time. He was ready to run down the passageway to Saint Irene when he saw the trapdoor being opened from above: they were following him! Damon jumped back, grabbed the iron ring handle to the trapdoor and pulled it down with all of his weight. As the trapdoor slammed shut, he could hear the soldiers cursing. He would have to jam the door shut…but how?

Damon looked at the burning torches on the wall as the soldiers above him tugged on the trapdoor. The commotion above him suddenly stopped. *This may be my only chance!* He jumped to the large torch just a fewfeet away and ran its handle through the trapdoor's large iron ring handle and in doing so, jammed the door shut.

The monk bolted down the passage toward Saint Irene. He remembered the trouble he had with that trapdoor and when he got there, he gave it a good push with his shoulder. To his surprise the trapdoor flew open and Damon found himself outside facedown in the dirt at the foot of a Frankish knight. He looked up slowly at the iron-helmeted soldier. Bloodstained chain mail protected his neck and cheeks.

"*Heretique Grecque,*" the knight sneered coldly as he unsheathed his sword, still dripping the warm blood of his last victim.

"No!" Damon screamed. The knight's sword pierced his chest just as the word left his lips. As the blade withdrew Damon could hear air rush into his chest. Breathing was now impossible.

Damon immediately lapsed into sleep. Now he saw them before him. Damon felt his heart sigh as he beheld them in all their glory: the Holy Martyrs. And now he was among them.

CHAPTER ONE

Aya Sofia, April 12, 2004, 7:00 a.m.

Albert Marie Boucher wiped the sleep out of his jade green eyes as he walked from the outer narthex into the inner narthex of Aya Sofia. He ran his left hand through his unkempt short brown hair. He was more than willing to sacrifice his appearance for ten extra minutes of sleep. The millennium and a half-old edifice had sustained more damage in the early morning's earthquake than it had in recent memory, although the earthquake was fairly minor. Some of the mosaics were probably cracked. That's undoubtedly why they called him at such a ridiculously early hour this morning. It was only at the insistence of his mentor, Professor Jean LeMaitre, that Albert agreed to spend the spring here in Istanbul and help his mentor's good friend Ismael Kemal, Professor of Archaeology at Istanbul University. But Albert Boucher hated the Turk. "A good archaeologist must have a wide base of knowledge," Professor LeMaitre would say. Come to think of it, Albert didn't care much for Professor LeMaitre either. When he first dreamed of archaeology, Albert imagined life as curator of the British Museum or chief of antiquities at the Louvre. He remembered watching those types on the television: glass of champagne, fancy dinner, tuxedo, limousine. My turn will come...someday, he would encourage himself when he was younger. But now his encouragement was inadequate. As he grew older, he grew more impatient. At times his impatience manifested itself as desperation.

Albert thought of his brother the wealthy banker. "I should have gone into business with Marcel," he would always moan. Then he'd have all he wanted. However, soon Albert would remember how much he couldn't

13

stand his brother and his nagging wife. Which was worse, being rich and miserable or being poor and envious? Not that Albert would ever admit regretting his career choice, but how in the hell could he afford the country estate and Peugeot his brother had on the meager wage of a budding archeologist? His khaki jacket was five years old and his brown denim pants were growing thin in the knees. His maroon knit shirt had a hole in the sleeve and his cheap brown shoes badly needed a shine.

As Albert walked into the nave, he saw that some of the scaffolding to the dome had collapsed and a small part of the ceiling had fallen to the floor. *Damn!* He knew that Kemal would have him help with the restoration. Oh, to restore a *Gothic* cathedral! At least that was tolerable and could even be fun. He briefly imagined driving up to Notre Dame de Paris, glass of Dom Perignon in one hand and a fiery redhead in the other. No, he was stuck here, in "the land of the tortoise shell domes." Istanbul's countless domes didn't impress him. To Albert, Byzantine history was static, featureless, flat. In over a thousand years, nothing happened, as far as he was concerned. Its culture was wrapped so tightly in Orthodox Christianity that it slowly suffocated itself. The Ottoman Turkish culture that succeeded it was no better: simply a Muslim version of the same thing. Their only accomplishment of note was almost conquering Western Europe in the sixteenth century.

"Monsieur Boucher!" someone called.

Albert sighed in disgust. He knew that voice too well.

"Monsieur Boucher!"

Albert looked up to the north gallery to see an excited young Turk waving enthusiastically at him. His young assistant had found him.

"Coming, Donkeybrain," he said under his breath as he waved in acknowledgement.

Albert trotted up to the gallery wondering what in this dilapidated pile of bricks and tiles could justify so much excitement. Yes, he hated Aya Sofia: the cathedral, the mosque, the museum—all of it: Istanbul, Turkey and the Turks, not just Donkeybrain. Why did he allow LeMaitre to talk him into coming to this dreadful place? "If *I* had LeMaitre's position," he would grin dreamily, "breakfast at a café near the Sorbonne, an extended lunch near the Pantheon and an evening stroll through the Luxembourg Gardens…"

"Come here quickly, Monsieur Boucher!" said the young assistant in English.

"I'm coming," Albert groaned.

The young olive-skinned assistant was about five-foot nine with thick black hair, which ran over the top of his ears. Albert noted that he wore a red cardigan, a black T-shirt, new blue jeans and impeccably maintained black leather loafers. The younger man was just beginning his studies at Istanbul University and English was the only language that he and Albert had in common: definitely not a point in Donkeybrain's favor.

Albert followed Donkeybrain, whose real name was Mehmet, toward the object of the young man's ecstasy. Last night's earthquake had cracked open the wall beneath the mosaic of Emperor Alexander. Albert could see that some of the bricks near the crack had been removed.

"Oh! Missing bricks! How exciting!" Albert said mockingly as he looked up at Mehmet, who was three inches taller. "You took these out?"

"Inside! Inside!" Mehmet pointed repeatedly at the cracked wall.

Albert rolled his eyes and stuck his hand into the hole. He looked back at Mehmet as he felt around. His eyes lit up as he felt the cold metal. *Must be a box of some kind.* He worked his fingers around the casket and gently pulled it out.

The beautiful foot-long gold casket dazed Albert Boucher.

"Same thing happened to me!" Mehmet said.

"What?"

"Same thing happened to me when I pulled it from the wall. Pretty impressive, eh?"

"You took it out and then put it back?" Albert asked sardonically. "Why didn't you keep it out?"

"I wanted you to share in my excitement."

"Idiot!" Albert muttered under his breath.

"Open it!"

"Don't tell me you've already opened it."

"No. That I leave to you."

"Thank you." Albert's exasperation was obvious. He held up the reliquary and examined the engraving. "Greek," he said to himself.

"Byzantine." Mehmet had overheard him.

Albert glared at the younger man.

"Seventh century, I'd say," the young Turk interjected.

"Who asked you?" Albert gently lifted the hinged lid and looked inside.

"Silk!" Mehmet said on seeing the contents.

"I *know* it's silk." Albert carefully grabbed the decaying red silk and lifted it by its edge out of the casket. He immediately felt something heavier inside. "Open your hands," he ordered Mehmet.

"What?"

"Open your hands. I want to set the casket down so I can see what's in it."

"Oh, yes," Mehmet said as he complied.

Albert leaned his head forward as he cautiously unrolled the moldering ancient red silk slowly and revealed its contents.

"Spear tip!" Mehmet said.

Albert looked up at Mehmet, his annoyance manifest.

"And at the bottom of the casket is a piece of papyrus," Mehmet declared.

This time the young student impressed Albert. "You're right, Mehmet," he added as he returned his gaze to the casket. Albert *never* called Mehmet by his name. "Let's go over here," he added, motioning over toward a museum display case nearby.

Mehmet followed him over to the display, his hands still outstretched and holding the casket and its contents.

Albert briefly looked over the long, leaf-like, iron spear tip that thickened and rounded off toward what would have been the shaft end. "A Roman *lancea*," he said with certainty. "Probably first century." He picked up the spear tip and examined it more carefully. "There's something engraved in the blade." Albert's heart accelerated as he read the inscription to himself. *Mon Dieu!* He gasped and then quickly recovered: Mehmet must not recognize his surprise. "I can't make it out. Spear's a bit rusty," he lied as he flipped it over and inspected the inscription on the reverse. The lancea was in very good condition for a two thousand-year old piece of iron. Another bolus of adrenaline surged through his arteries. *Merde!* His eyes grew wide as he read. "I can't read this very well either," he said with a very dry mouth. Albert carefully set the spear tip back in the reliquary and eagerly picked up the papyrus. *If this has half the value this spear does, my days of indentured servitude are over!* "This looks very old."

"How old?"

"I don't know." Albert slowly and ever so delicately unrolled the eight-inch by six-inch papyrus document. "This is in remarkably good condition," Albert remarked as he carefully studied it. He knew of the difficulties many archeologists had with ancient Egyptian papyri.

Mehmet peeked at the roll. "That's not Greek."

"No. Latin...probably ancient Roman." Albert's fingers trembled as he read the document. He read the first line written on the papyrus and then concentrated as he rethought the translation over in his mind. "Looks like an execution log and what appears to be some kind of date," he offered freely, momentarily forgetting that he wanted to keep Mehmet in the dark. Albert hurriedly read on in silence and then suddenly stopped. *Jesus-Christ!*

"Ah, there you are." The voice came from across the gallery.

Albert instinctively shoved the papyrus back into the casket with the spear and the silk. He push the casket under Mehmet's shirt. "Hide this!"

"What?"

"This is going to be our little secret! I'll explain later!"

"Monsieur Boucher!" A six-foot tall Turkish gentleman dressed in black slacks and a gray sport coat strode forward. "Good to see you getting into your work!" he continued in fluent French.

"Professor Kemal," Albert replied in French. "So good to see you sir!" He quickly glanced at Mehmet. "Sir, this is—"

"Mehmet Yakis," Kemal interrupted. "I sent him to you." The conversation continued in French. "Don't you remember? He's a very promising young student. Take good care of him."

Albert looked askance at Mehmet. "Yes sir."

"Listen, I have to leave today. My sabbatical in Paris. Do you remember?"

"Yes sir, I do," Albert lied.

"There is an American, Professor Leslie Connery, who will be overseeing my affairs here in my absence. Dr. Connery is one of the world's leading authorities on Byzantine artifacts. The professor is going to stay in Istanbul in my place for the next eighteen months. Unfortunately, she's arrived earlier than we planned, so she's staying at the Ambassador Hotel in Sultanahmet until we can get her apartment ready."

"Oh, that's good." Albert said this for lack of anything better to say. He really didn't care about this visiting professor.

"My plane leaves at ten, so I've got to rush. Come with me. I need you to get those papers you finished last week. I'll need them for my presentation in Paris." He wrapped his arm around Albert's shoulder and led him out of the gallery.

"But sir!" Albert protested. "I've got something here I must attend to now!"

"Whatever can't wait, Mr. Yakis will do." Kemal said this in English so Mehmet would understand.

Mehmet nodded vigorously at the professor.

Albert tried one last time to pull away but Kemal would not oblige.

Mehmet enjoyed watching the Frenchman's continued fruitless efforts to escape Kemal as he led him out of the museum. He waved until the two of them were out of sight.

Galata, 8:30 a.m.

"So tell me about this thing, Mehmet."

"It's quite fascinating, Osman," Mehmet replied as he sipped the Turkish coffee the waiter had just brought. Osman's bushy black eyebrows, mustache and wild black hair made this gentle six and a half-foot giant appear fearsome. But he was a Turkish teddy bear as far as Mehmet could tell, and the brown tweed jacket he was wearing lent itself to that description. He had a definite soft spot for beautiful women. "I looked at it carefully after the Frenchman left, Osman," Mehmet explained as he noticed Osman's eyes suddenly shifting to something over his shoulder. "What is it?" Mehmet asked as he turned around and searched the outdoor cafe to see what had caught Osman's attention.

"How would you like to ride the caboose on that train? Isn't she gorgeous?" Osman asked as Mehmet saw the tall young woman behind him walk across the street. "She's even more beautiful than the babe I bedded last night!" Osman sighed. "I think I'm in love!"

"Not again! Is it possible for you to take your mind off women for more than five minutes?" Mehmet growled.

"Sorry, my friend. But you must admit she'd make a welcome addition to any harem."

"Harem? You give every man a bad name. Do you know that? You're a walking barrel of testosterone!"

"I think you are jealous, my friend. I am merely following the nature that Allah has bestowed upon me."

"You say that as if you regularly answer the call to prayer," Mehmet grumbled.

A large truck roared past and Osman changed the subject. "What about this spear?"

"I examined the spear tip after the Frenchman left. Among the words on one side was the word 'Longinus' in capital Roman letters. The other side also had several words, including the word 'Dominus.' The Frenchman says it's first century Roman."

Their waiter returned and served their lamb sausage, cheese, olives and yogurt.

"Is it important?" Osman asked.

"He wants it very badly. I can tell by the look on his face as Kemal dragged him away."

"Are you going to give it to him?"

"I'd rather cut off my hand!"

"Will there be anything else?" the waiter asked.

Mehmet guessed the young man was probably Pakistani or Indian. However, his Turkish was pretty good for a foreigner. "No, thank you," Mehmet replied courteously.

"Why do you suppose he wants it so badly?" Osman asked as the waiter departed.

"I don't know the significance of 'Longinus' but 'Dominus' is Latin for Lord."

"So it belongs to some old Byzantine lord!"

"Osman! Why don't you use that thing between your ears for something other than seducing women?"

"It *doesn't* belong to some old Byzantine lord?"

Mehmet rolled his eyes. "I'll give you a clue. We found it in Aya Sofia, which used to be a church…."

The look in Osman's eyes didn't change.

"It had 'Lord' inscribed on it in Latin…."

"It's a Christian relic!" Osman gasped as if he'd discovered a chest of gold in his bedroom.

"Yes!" Mehmet replied softly, sharing Osman's excitement, "and maybe a very important one."

"Honey, gentlemen?" Their waiter reappeared from thin air.

Once they had recovered from the waiter's sudden intrusion, Mehmet and Osman declined the offer graciously. When they were certain he was out of earshot, they resumed their conversation.

"Do you have it with you now?" Osman whispered.

"No," Mehmet answered.

"Where is it?" Osman asked enthusiastically.

"It's safe!" Mehmet snapped back.

Osman briefly recoiled but then continued. "What will you do?"

"I don't know," Mehmet answered as he gazed across the Golden Horn at the greenery of Gulhane Park. A sea bus motored up the Golden Horn as two small freighters left that waterway and chugged out into the Sea of Marmara. "I would give it to Kemal, but he has left for Paris for over a year, I guess."

"Can't you give it to someone else at the University?"

"Kemal mentioned somebody…an American…staying at the Ambassador Hotel in Sultanahmet. His name is Connery…'Leslie.' I remember that. Kemal and the Frenchman were speaking in French so I couldn't understand completely but that much I got out of it."

"Some fruit juice?" The waiter again suddenly appeared without warning.

Osman choked on his coffee.

"No!" Mehmet barked. Quickly regretting his bruskness he gently added, "No thank you."

The waiter withdrew, smiling as he backed into another waiter, causing him to spill someone's breakfast on the two businessmen at the next table.

"Who but an American or a Brit would call a man 'Leslie'?" Osman chuckled. "Such a feminine name! Who is this fellow anyway?"

"An archaeologist. He'll be taking over for Kemal in his absence."

"So give him the casket."

"Technically, it's called a reliquary. You know, a place to store a relic."

"Okay, so give him the relickry."

"Reliquary."

"Right."

"Osman, this is a treasure for Turkey. I don't want to hand it to some foreigner only to have it whisked out of the country. It's not going to end up in the British Museum, the Louvre or the Smithsonian."

"Give it to another professor at the University and be done with it!"

"Who?"

"There must be somebody else."

"I don't know, Osman. I really want to give it to Kemal," Mehmet replied dreamily. He thought of Kemal and how much he admired the man. No one else could fill his shoes. No one else was worthy of such a treasure.

Aya Sofia, 10:55 a.m.

He'd better be here! Albert Boucher rushed into the museum looking for Mehmet. "Where is that goddam Donkeybrain?" he hissed under his breath as he looked furiously for his assistant. The workers were still busy restoring the damage to the ceiling. Maybe Mehmet was helping, or maybe he was still by the wall where Boucher had left him. Albert grew frantic as he could find no trace of the young Turk. He ran up the ramp to the upper north gallery and found the Emperor Alexander mosaic. "Not here!" he fumed as he wiped his sweaty brow. He ran to the wall and jammed his hand inside the hole. "Damn!" he yelled when he felt nothing but cold bricks.

Albert tried to calm himself. "Where does he live?" he whispered to himself. "Student directory!" he said aloud as a ray of hope emerged from the dark depths of desparation. He ran out of Aya Sofia to the train stop on the Divan Yolu. He would soon be at Istanbul University and then he would find Mehmet Yakis' home.

"All gigantic enterprises are worth exhaustive effort," Albert muttered to himself as he hopped aboard the westbound train. "And this is more than

I have ever hoped for." He smiled as the train rolled past the dilapidated Column of Constantine, which that emperor erected eighteen centuries ago when he named the city after himself. Albert looked up at the once proud slab, scorched by fire, standing pathetically, and only because it was braced with iron. "Christ's nail," he chuckled, remembering what the Byzantines used to call it. *And soon I will have another of Christ's possessions…and all the glory and money it will bring. My time in Purgatory is ending. Soon I will be done with this business and back in Paris…*

CHAPTER TWO

Marmara Hotel, Taksim, 11:00 a.m.

Luci Daniels sat back in her office chair analyzing the Aztec ceramic bowl she had obtained five days ago. She admired the grisly depiction of an unfortunate victim being sacrificed to Xiuhtecutli, the god of fire. "Fantastic," she mused as she ran her long, pale fingers over the god's open mouth. The depiction was strangely autobiographical. In her youth, Luci certainly identified with the god's strengths. Through sheer desire and steely determination she had always succeeded where so many had failed. She had complete contempt for any victim. Such a person was the victim of his own weakness, not the oppression of others.

Luci's father had a credo that sounded like the Protestant work ethic gone amok: "Success equals sanctity." Ironically her father was never terribly successful, but that phrase was imprinted on her from the very beginning.

Luci entered the work force ready to assert herself. Unlike most others, she capitalized on the hard lessons the business world threw her way. Her father had been right: success was measured in dollars and the ends surely justified the means. Playing by the rules was the way to a slow and mediocre success. Luci aimed higher, much higher. After a few years at various companies, she joined a small venture capital company. Luci had researched the company well, knew everything about it. She proved to be a dedicated employee, and she spent long hours studying her work. Her efforts were rewarded by success, which brought millions of dollars into the company. That soon brought her to the attention of the president, who asked to meet with her. The forty-year old man was a bright and likeable guy. He appeared strong and confident. Controlling him *could* be a challenge, but Luci knew his Achilles heel. The president had just buried his wife of fifteen years and was emotionally vulnerable. Fortunately, there were no children; that would complicate matters too much. When he extended his hand and offered her a promotion, Luci grasped it and held on as she accepted the offer and told him what an honor it was to work with him. She made certain that she praised his many accomplishments. Their meetings became more frequent. Initially, it was all business, but soon the encounters grew more and more personal. It wasn't long before they were meeting on his yacht, at his mountain cabin and later his home.

The company's business continued to boom, and Luci increased her control. She had performed exceptionally and had acquired the president's complete trust. She used that trust to maneuver into a position of power. Yet, the president and his advisors were blind to her activities. When the time was ripe, she subtly, almost subliminally, pushed the president to take the company public, which he soon did. The initial public offering was a huge success. The company grew rapidly and rewarded its workers with stock. Luci convinced the president to let her manage the issuance of stock, and she secretly gave herself one hundred times more than the president thought he was giving her. She did so by creating forty bogus stockholders, who held ninety-nine percent of the stock she had acquired. So as more stock was issued, Luci's share grew rapidly. Soon, unbeknownst to anyone, she was one of the company's largest shareholders.

The second phase of Luci's plan came two years later. She planted evidence that implicated the president and his closest associates in a huge insider trading deal. The day after the Securities and Exchange Commission jumped on the scam, Luci furtively leaked news of the company's questionable accounting practices, which she had committed in the name of the president and his chief financial officer. When the news broke, the company's stock dropped like a lead bar in a deep pond. Luci's meticulousness paid off. Nothing could be traced back to her. Six months before she dropped the SEC bomb, she began the process that slowly converted all of her shares in the company into cash that she furtively deposited in banks around the world.

As her former boss went to jail, Luci used the skills she had acquired in his destruction to acquire his old company. She knew that it was still capable of generating tons of money, so she found six wealthy, yet malleable, partners. She used their cash to buy the company's nearly worthless stock. As the value of the company grew, Luci eliminated five of her partners through scandals she had manufactured, legal prestidigitation she had organized or outright intimidation she had ordered. One managed to stay clear of the maneuvering, but he could not do so indefinitely. Eight months later, he disappeared.

Luci was now the master of the company. She changed the name to reflect her persona: Black Star International. She created the Black Division, a covert special operations team that destroyed her rivals through blackmail, manipulating corporate elections and suborning the cooperation of the authorities. Black Star's increased wealth allowed it to expand into energy production, electronics and mining for strategic minerals. Its tentacles stretched across the globe and its continued meteoric rise sent tremors through financial capitals around the world.

Luci's recalled her father's image of the trappings of success as curious. When discussing a famous billionaire, he would emphasize, "He's got three Van Gogh's" or "Her foyer looks like a Bernini exhibit." So to foster the appreciation necessary to attain such fine art, Luci's childhood was punctuated by endless trips to art museums and galleries.

Once she had the cash, Luci tried to emulate her father, but she soon lost interest after she bought her first art masterpiece. To her it was a dull, lifeless conglomeration of canvas and paint, certainly not worth the five million she paid for it. Then something happened that changed her focus. She had just acquired a new oilfield in Brazil and went to inspect it with her engineers. As she stepped out of the jeep to photograph a village near the first drilling site, the people of the village ran toward her. These naked innocents were terrified. They had lived their lives for generations, unaffected by the world around them. The arrival of these interlopers was frightening. The natives slowly, almost solemnly, approached the invaders with the only gifts they could muster. The scene was reminiscent of a tale told thousands of times in the history of humanity: the conquered surrendering to the conqueror.

A man, probably the leader of the village, held a wooden figure in both hands. He walked up to Luci, kneeled and held up what appeared to be an idol as an offering. Luci was initially caught off guard but instinct soon took over. Without displaying any reverence for the object or respect for its presenter, she snatched it from his hands and clutched it to her breast. The leader was stunned by her action and he quickly retreated to the crowd that had gathered around them. Luci held the idol in front of her and examined it. It was primitive and grotesque, but she could see that the villagers held it in the highest regard. She turned the idol toward the villagers and held it high. The natives immediately prostrated themselves and chanted something in unison.

"They have given me their god," Luci bragged to the engineers. *And in doing so, they have surrendered their lives to me.*

In time, Luci's fascination for acquiring similar relics became an obsession. With each one she obtained, she fantasized that she had assumed control of the lives of those who used to worship the relic. Soon she possessed objects from every culture imaginable: ancient Mali, aboriginal Australia, Polynesia and the Anasazi of the American southwest. The Aztec fire god she was fondling wolfishly was the latest.

"You're beautiful," she whispered to Xiuhtecutli just before she kissed his grotesque face. Her eyes shot back to the god's miserable victim. *Never again! Rewards come too slowly to those with ordinary appetites. Reach into the heavens to pluck out your star.* Luci was now Xiuhtecutli.

Luci spun her chair around toward the window. "What do you have for me, Istanbul?" She remembered the articles she'd read, the stories she'd heard, the dreams she'd had about this two and a half thousand-year old city and the great cultures it had spawned. She closed her eyes and licked her lips and saw it all: ancient Greek and Roman statues, golden Byzantine icons embellished with emeralds and sapphires, silver Ottoman daggers studded with rubies and diamonds...Luci looked back at Xiuhtecutli and smiled. After she had him for a few months she would grow tired of him. Her appetite was dynamic, always demanding something fresh. The thrill of possession was outweighed by the ecstasy of acquisition.

A high-pitched male voice on the intercom shattered Luci's reverie. "Somebody here named Osman to see you, Ms. Daniels. Something about the Aya Sofia restoration."

Luci sprang to her feet. This sounded promising. "Send him in, Roger," she replied.

In February, opportunity had knocked once again at Luci Daniel's door.

Aya Sofia, the fifteen hundred year-old cathedral built by the Byzantine emperor Justinian only to be converted to a mosque nine hundred years later by the conquering Ottoman Turks, became a museum in 1924. Through a few dark contacts, Luci had learned that the once sacred edifice was in need of limited restoration. She offered her financial assistance to the Turkish government, who gladly accepted her charity. And again Luci heard the voice of fortune call to her.

Roger opened the door and Osman walked into the suite, the best the hotel had. The giant Turk dwarfed the much smaller secretary who left quickly.

Luci held out her black-suited arm graciously. "Welcome, my friend..."

"Madam." Osman bent forward and gently grasped the five-foot five Luci's hand and kissed it. Mehmet's naïve friend had suddenly metamorphosed into a suave sophisticate. As he kissed her hand, he noticed that his employer's hips, which were seductively accentuated by her tight, black slacks, were particularly alluring. He had only seen her at the museum in the company of others, so this was his first chance to be alone with her. Osman was almost embarrassed by his own gawking at her impressive form. *She's a goddess!* His leering eyes moved upward and salivated over her supple breasts. *I can see them now: milky white, perfectly formed pink--.*

"What do you have for me, Osman?" Luci demanded curtly.

Osman recovered quickly. He smiled at her and announced proudly, "The Lance of Longinus, madam."

Luci made her disappointment certain. "The Lance of Longinus?" she asked unbelievingly.

"Yes, madam. Here in Istanbul."

"You're wrong, Osman," she growled. "It's in Vienna at the Hofburg Museum. I've been after it for years. What you've got is obviously a fake."

Osman smiled. "I have good reason to believe that the Lance in Vienna is a fake."

"What the hell are you talking about?" Luci snapped back. "That's the most ludicrous thing I've heard in years!"

Despite his boss's chafed reply, Osman kept his cool. "I have a friend--"

"We all have *friends*, Osman."

Despite her coarse rejoinder, Osman felt that his employer's appetite had been whetted. "May I sit, madam?"

Luci motioned to a pair of chairs as she scrutinized the cunning Turk and followed him at a distance. Once Osman was comfortably seated, she sat.

"May I have something to drink...tea, perhaps?"

"I have some, just made," Luci said as she stepped over to the intercom. "Roger?" she said into the intercom, "Tea."

Roger was in the room moments later pouring the hot tea. Osman thanked him and continued. "As you know, Madam," he began as he sipped the hot tea, "the Lance—oh, this is very good tea." Osman turned to Roger. "Turkish, I'm certain."

"Yes," Roger answered. He turned to his employer. "Will there be--"

"No!" Luci replied with a backward wave of her hand, which sent Roger back to his desk in the other room.

"Nothing like a good cup of tea," Osman said as he took another sip.

Osman's laggard progress was trying Luci's patience. She glared at him and crossed her arms. Her cold, dark gray eyes were a perfect fit for her alabaster skin and black hair.

"Well...where was I?" Osman took another quick sip and closed his eyes and grunted his continued approval of the tea. "Yes, the Lance belonged to a Roman centurion named Gaius Cassius Longinus. Legend has it that he was the soldier who pierced Christ's side with the Lance to expedite his death during the Crucifixion. The Jews wanted Jesus off the cross and buried before sunset, because the next day Passover began. Longinus shoved the Lance into the right chest to kill Jesus, but he was already dead."

"I've heard the story, Osman. Tell me something relevant."

Osman quickly took another sip of tea before he resumed his discussion.

"Legend has it that Longinus was suffering from a severe eye infection. When he stabbed Jesus' side with the Lance, body fluid from the wound sprayed onto his eyes and face. Thereupon, the eye infection miraculously resolved. Longinus would have gone blind had that not happened."

"I'll bet," Luci interjected derisively.

"And the Lance itself had a profound effect on Longinus. He became a Christian, and the Lance brought blessings and power to him."

"Of course," Luci added mockingly.

Osman stopped abruptly. His eyes queried his employer. *Dare I go on?* Luci smirked and opened her right hand, beckoning him to continue.

"The Lance of Longinus eventually became the possession of one Maurice, an African."

"And?" Luci asked disinterestedly.

"He was a soldier of considerable valor and a Christian. He led a Roman legion comprised of other followers of Christ, the Theban Legion, under the Emperor Maximian. In the third century they successfully squashed a revolt in Gaul. Then, in 287, Maximian ordered his troops to worship him as a god and to eradicate Christianity in Gaul. Maurice refused and was beheaded. The remainder of the Theban Legion refused Maximian's orders as well so he began to slaughter Maurice's command, six hundred at a time. The enraged emperor hoped that his severity would compel compliance, but it had the opposite effect. Eventually the entire legion was put to the sword."

"Holy shit!" Osman had Luci's attention *now*. "A legion is five thousand soldiers!"

"For the next twenty-five years the Lance was lost but suddenly turned up in the year 312 in the hands of Constantine, son of Co-Emperor Constantius Chlorus. That was just before Constantine won the decisive battle at the Milvian Bridge. Who gave it to him is unknown, but after the battle, Constantine valued the Lance of Longinus as a powerful relic, which it proved to be. With it, Constantine was unstoppable. He defeated three rivals for the throne of Imperial Rome and soon reunited under himself the empire Emperor Diocletian had divided just thirty-seven years before. Soon after, Constantine converted to Christianity."

"Unbelievable," Luci added derisively.

Osman paused until his employer reticently nodded.

"After Constantine," Osman continued, "the Byzantine emperors in Constantinople proved invulnerable while they possessed the Lance of Longinus. They entrusted the relic to a group of monks who guarded the Lance and allowed the emperor to use it when they saw fit.

"Emperor Justinian lavished gifts on the monks and his troops triumphed in battle. In the seventh century, Phocas seized the throne and treated the monks abominably. He was deposed by Heraclius and died roasting in an iron bull to the entertainment of the bloodthirsty crowd. However, later Emperor Heraclius too slighted the monks, who found his tampering with the doctrine of Orthodox Christianity most offensive and soon eastern reaches of the empire were lost to Islam. When the Iconoclasts took power, they were also hated for their impious views and were denied the Holy Lance. Under them the empire's fortunes continued to dwindle. It wasn't until 867, when Basil I established the Macedonian Dynasty and restored the monks to prominence, that the Lance of Longinus was released to the emperors again. However, almost three hundred years later, when Constantine VIII died without a son and his lascivious daughter Zoë came to the throne, the monks again retracted their favor and the empire's fortunes again changed."

"You just happen to know all of this?" Luci found the protracted history lesson boring.

"My *friend*, told me" Osman jabbed.

Luci winced at Osman's successful parry. "Your friend?" she inquired impatiently.

"Yes. He works for an archaeologist in Vienna. We've spent many evenings discussing these things over cognac."

"Vienna? Where the *fake* Lance of Longinus is," Luci simpered.

"Madam, this archaeologist is an expert in ancient and medieval metalwork. He swears the Vienna Lance cannot be dated earlier than the eighth century."

"When was Constantine VIII emperor of the Byzantines?"

"Early eleventh century."

"Then we have quite a controversy, Osman," Luci growled. "It seems that many in the archaeological community, aside from your friend's employer, place the Lance of Longinus in the hands of the Emperor Charlemagne in the eighth century. *He* was unstoppable in battle."

"Charlemagne was an excellent warrior, but he did not have the Lance of Longinus."

"Cut the bullshit, Osman. Charlemagne claimed he did and many historians would agree with him."

"Madam, there are other Lances of Longinus out there. The Armenians claim to have one. There's one in the Vatican--"

"What's your point, Osman?" Luci screeched in exasperation.

Osman recoiled, but he quickly gathered his wits about him. He politely cleared his throat and continued. "Madam, please consider this: You are a Byzantine emperor. You know the value of the Lance. Wouldn't you be absolutely certain that it stayed in Constantinople?"

"That was during the Dark Ages. Barbarians ran roughshod all over Europe. They could have seized it when they sacked the city."

"Madam, Constantinople's walls were never breached by the barbarian invasions of the fifth, sixth and seventh centuries. While the rest of Europe drowned in a sea of Huns, Goths and Avars, Constantinople remained safe."

"So you're saying that the Lance has remained here, in Constant—I mean Istanbul—for all of these years."

"Yes, Ms. Daniels."

"The Vienna Lance is a fake? The others--"

"Counterfeit," Osman declared. "Madam, Charlemagne wanted power. Pope Leo crowned him Holy Roman Emperor on Christmas Day, 800. The Holy Roman Emperor needed a holy symbol of his power. Any ruler having this powerful relic would be--"

"So someone made him a Lance of his own...." Luci interrupted. However, she hadn't quite bought the explanation yet.

"Exactly!"

"So why didn't the Byzantines show everyone the real Lance and call Charlemagne a fraud?"

"Well they *did* call Charlemagne a fraud. There could be only one Roman emperor and the Byzantines said he lived in Constantinople. They dismissed Charlemagne as a barbarian and relations between East and West never fully recovered. Did you know he needed to use a stencil to write his name?"

"So this *fraudulent* Lance, which every Holy Roman Emperor since Charlemagne held dear to his heart, and which Emperor Frederick Barbarossa carried with him into battle, was a *fake* all along."

"Absolutely! Adhemar of Le Puy, papal legate during the First Crusade, remembered seeing the Holy Lance in Constantinople at the end of the eleventh century."

"The genuine Lance of Longinus?"

"Yes, madam."

31

Osman grinned as a thought came to mind. "There is a particularly interesting story that has to do with Adhemar of Le Puy." Osman looked at his boss as if asking permission to proceed.

"Sure, go ahead," she answered hesitantly.

"During the First Crusade, the Crusaders took the city of Antioch. Soon a large Muslim army formed to retake the city. It did not look good for the Crusaders, and panic was spreading. Morale was very low, and the picture looked bleak until a Provencal peasant named Peter Bartholomew presented himself to the Crusader commander, Raymond of Toulouse, and Adhemar. Peter claimed to have seen the Lance in a vision. Saint Andrew had instructed him to find the Lance in the Cathedral of Saint Peter, which had been closed for reconsecration. With the Lance, the Crusaders could vanquish the enemy and keep the city. The Crusaders tore up the floor of the church but failed to find the Lance. As the last of them climbed out of the hole they dug, Peter jumped in and soon found a piece of metal he declared to be the Lance of Longinus."

"Another one?"

"Adhemar was furious. He had always felt Peter to be a reprobate. He had seen the Lance in Constantinople. Emperor Alexios I Comnenus had shown it to him. He knew that Peter's find was worthless, but the other Crusaders believed Peter. The enthusiasm it generated was infectious. Soon the morale of all of the Crusaders was very high. The Crusaders attacked and the Muslim army fled. Antioch was saved."

"Cute story, Osman, but what does it have to do with us?"

"Madam, I wished only to demonstrate Adhemar's certainty that he had seen the Lance in Constantinople, despite Peter's chicanery. I admit that it's a little confusing at times, but as long as we remember that any reports about the Lance of Longinus after the Crusades probably deal with Charlemagne's forgery."

Luci was suddenly very pensive. She looked away from Osman and touched her chin with her right index finger for a few seconds. "Osman," she started slowly. "I remember hearing that Napoleon tried to steal Charlemagne's Lance from Vienna after the battle of Austerlitz?"

"Indeed. It was quickly smuggled out of Vienna by the Austrians when news of the Austrian army's defeat reached that capital."

"And Hitler nabbed it when he invaded Austria in 1938."

"True, madam. He sent it to Saint Catherine's Church in Nuremberg by an armored SS train later that same year. In 1944 it was moved to an underground vault. By late April 1945, the American Seventh Army took Nuremberg. A clever American, Lieutenant Walter William Horn, tricked the Lance's SS keeper into divulging its hiding place. On April 30, 1945, at 2:10 p.m., Horn took possession of the Lance of Longinus in the name of the United States government. On the same day, at 3:30 p.m., in Berlin, Adolf Hitler committed suicide." Osman arched his eyebrows in emphasis.

"Hmmm. I wasn't aware of that." Luci wondered if she had underestimated her employee.

"However, there is a legend that the Lance that Lieutenant Horn retrieved was merely a duplicate and the original was kept by a group of SS officers who called themselves the Knights of the Holy Lance."

"Well I'll be...."

"Did you know that the Knights Templar claimed to have the Lance of Longinus at one point?"

"The Templars?" Luci asked expectantly. "You mean those guys from the Crusades?"

"Yes. A sort of *medieval* SS: true believers dedicated to the protection of the Kingdom of Jerusalem and the other Crusader states." Osman massaged Luci's newfound fascination with him. "The Templars have a fascinating history," he added with enthusiasm. "As well as being superb soldiers, they also performed almsgiving and considerable financial duties. When the Crusaders were tossed out of the Holy Land at the beginning of the fourteenth century, the Templars' military function nearly ceased, but their financial interests grew and grew. Their castles proved to be secure places for money, and many clients deposited their funds with the Templars. They also collected and dispersed funds on their clients' behalf and became the largest lenders in Europe."

"Templar Bank and Trust," Luci smirked.

"Yes. In essence, they were the first bankers in Europe. Unfortunately, many claimed that the Templars, who at their founding swore oaths of poverty, chastity and obedience, were becoming greedy and lecherous. They were answerable only to the patriarch of Jerusalem and later only to the pope. By the end of the thirteenth century, the Templars of Paris were virtually the French king's royal treasury. In 1307, Pope Clement V moved their headquarters from Cyprus to Paris. There, they held a lofty position due to their wealth.

"Now the King of France, Philip IV, was financially destitute. He soon grew to despise the Templars and their high status in Paris. They were far wealthier than he was, and they were totally immune to his authority. Many Templars took great joy in reminding Philip of this distasteful fact. Spurred on by claims of Templar idolatry, homosexuality and other anti-Christian acts, Philip arrested as many Templars as he could. Pope Clement vehemently protested these actions but could do nothing about them. At that time the popes resided in Avignon, a papal island surrounded by a sea of French territory. Finally, the Pope dissolved the Templars and conveyed their properties to the Knights Hospitaller, their chief rivals. Much to King Philip's dismay, he was still as broke as before the Templars were dissolved."

"No matter what century you're in, you've got to be careful whom you thumb your nose at." The look in Luci's eye suggested it was more of a warning than an observation.

"Indeed."

"Aren't the Templars still around today?"

"Despite the attempts of Philip and Clement to expunge them, most of the Templars escaped death or imprisonment and more or less faded into the woodwork of medieval Europe. Many of those Templars joined the Knights Hospitaller or other chivalric orders. However, any modern group claiming direct Templar ancestry is deluding itself."

"What about the Priory of Sion? I read about them--"

Osman erupted in laughter.

"What's so funny?" Luci scowled.

"I'm sorry, madam," Osman found it hard to control his laughter. "That has to be one of the most egregious examples of chicanery ever attempted." He erupted in laughter again.

Luci was insulted by Osman's flippancy. "Okay, Osman. You've had your laugh," Luci glared. "Now explain yourself."

Osman could see that his boss had had enough. "I'm sorry, madam," he said contritely as he regained a serious air. "Well, it sounds like you know something about the Priory of Sion."

"Yes…" Luci's dark eyes flashed angrily.

"You're not alone, madam. Many have fallen for the charade."

"I'm not hearing much explaining…"

"Well, the Priory of Sion claimed that in the twelfth century the Templars excavated Solomon's Temple and found documents that told of Jesus' marriage to Mary Magdalene. The Templars became the guardians of this *secret*."

"It seems plausible."

Osman rubbed his hand over his mustache thoughtfully. "Perhaps it would be best to start at the beginning."

"Whatever," Luci muttered under her breath.

"Godefroi de Boullion, Duke of Lower Lorraine, was one of the nobles who set out on the First Crusade. Once the Crusaders had conquered the Holy Land they needed a king and chose Godefroi. He, however, felt the honor was too great and agreed to serve only under the title *Advocatus Sancti Sepulchri*."

"Where are you going with this, Osman?" Luci grew perturbed.

"I'm sorry madam if I seem to be digressing, but Godefroi is important. May I continue?"

Luci hesitated but then replied. "Sure, why not." The sarcasm was obvious.

"Although there were no such claims whatsoever prior to the twentieth century, the Priory of Scion declared that Godefroi was descended from Jesus."

"Yeah, I remember this."

"According to the Priory of Sion, Jesus married Mary Magdalene, who was pregnant with his daughter at the time of the Crucifixion. When Jesus died Mary went to Gaul, which is now France, and her daughter married one of the locals. Eventually this line mixed with the Merovingian Kings of France. Godefroi was descended from the Merovingian line, which came to an end when Pepin, the first of the Carolingian dynasty, in 751, deposed Childeric. The leader of the Priory of Sion in the mid-1950's, one Pierre Plantard, claimed that he was descended from Godefroi and was therefore the rightful king of France."

"So he had Godefroi and Jesus in his family tree."

"Well, so he claimed. Plantard actually created false documents backing up his pedigree and planted them in French libraries and archives.

Within twenty years, the plot began to unravel. One of Plantard's cronies admitted to helping Plantard manufacture the false documents, including a list of past grand masters of the Priory of Sion, which included Leonardo Da Vinci and Isaac Newton. It eventually was revealed that Plantard, not surprisingly, had a criminal record for fraud. Several French books and a 1996 BBC documentary completely exposed the Priory and Plantard and left no room for doubt. Later, Plantard admitted that he really wasn't descended from Godefroi but instead was descended from Saint Vincent de Paul."

"So this con-man, Plantard, dreamed the whole thing up."

"Well, there was a Priory of Sion that was active in the late nineteenth century. It was a reactionary monarchist group that opposed representative government. Prior to World War II, Pierre Plantard made his presence known as an anti-Semite who sought to purify France. He formed a second Priory of Sion after the war."

"So there are no truly Templar groups since the Crusades?"

"Some neo-Templar secret societies do exist, but they have nothing to do with the Templars of the twelfth and thirteenth centuries."

"So this bull about Jesus—"

"Exactly, madam."

"I don't know, Osman. I still find the Priory's version fascinating."

"Pathetic, if you think about it, madam. I read better fiction when I was six-years old."

Luci was pensive. "It may not be as pathetic as you think."

"What do you mean, madam?"

"What about the Nag Hammadi documents found in Egypt in 1945… and the Dead Sea Scrolls? Don't they support this Mary Magdalene theory?"

Osman grinned like a professor who had just led his star pupil into an intellectual snare. "First of all, madam, any reasonable scholar will tell you that the Dead Sea Scrolls, though contemporary with Jesus and the early Christian Church, have little to do with them. The people of the Scrolls were a Jewish sect that happened to live in Judea at about the same time as Jesus. While their documents may shed some light on the nature of early Christianity and first century Judaism, they say little more."

"And the Nag Hammadi texts?"

"The most popular is the Gospel of Thomas. Others include the Gospel of Mary and the Gospel of Philip. Thomas is probably the oldest and dates from the mid second century."

"And the Biblical Gospels?"

"Mark dates from about 70 A.D., Matthew and Luke from some time in the eighties, and John from the nineties. The earliest letters of Paul date from the early fifties or late forties and the letters of James and Jude from 50 A.D."

"So what's your take on the Nag Hammadi texts?"

"The Biblical Gospels predate them by fifty to eighty years. And the epistles of Paul, James and Jude, which are consistent with the message in the Biblical Gospels, were written a century before the Nag Hammadi texts. Obviously the Nag Hammadi writings came from a splinter group that deviated from the mainstream, long after Jesus' death. Happens in every religion."

"You appear to be quite an authority on the subject, my dear Osman." Luci leered at him seductively.

Osman felt his loins stir. "Well, not an *authority*, madam. I have read some and, as I have said, I do have friends in the field. But one doesn't have to be a scholar to make such a determination. Given the facts, any man of reason would come to the same conclusion."

"Yes," Luci rolled her eyes. "A man of reason indeed."

"Of course, madam." Osman beamed.

Luci unexpectedly exploded. "So why are you feeding me this horseshit story about the Lance of Longinus?!"

Osman was thrown back by her sudden tempestuousness. "Madam?"

"You almost had me convinced that you knew what the hell you were talking about. Do you expect me to believe that the Lance of Longinus in the Hofberg is a fake?"

"Yes," he answered flat-footed. Luci's icy stare sent a chill up Osman's spine. "Madam I swear--"

"Answer me this, Mister *Man of Reason*. If what you're saying is true, where was the *real* Lance of Longinus from the eleventh century onward? Was it here?"

"Yes!"

"Where?"

"I'm afraid this is where my information becomes scarce."

Her chilling dark eyes blazed at Osman. "If it's been here all along, what happened to it?"

"There are only sketchy references to it since that time," Osman replied delicately.

Luci grew livid. "Don't bullshit me!"

"Madam I assure you…" Osman tried to recover his cool. "One obscure source placed it at the Monastery of Christ Pantokrator at the beginning of the thirteenth century."

"What about the Fourth Crusade?" Luci stepped forward and jabbed him in the chest, forcing him backward. "The Crusaders ransacked Constantinople and stole everything of value. They probably stole Christ's burial shroud and if they found that, wouldn't they have found the Lance of Longinus?" Luci jabbed him forcefully again. "Osman?"

Osman slowly put his hands up in front of his chest. "Not if it were well-hidden." He was still very much on the defensive.

"Do you know who the hell you're dealing with?" Luci raised her fist. "I could smash you like a roach in the middle of this city and no one would lay a glove on me!"

Osman froze as those frigid eyes ripped into him.

Luci abruptly dropped her fist and turned away. "I'm tired of your little charade, Osman. Leave now," she said coldly. "I'll mail you a check." She turned around with her eyes narrowed. "I don't want to see your sorry face again! I didn't get to where I am by chance. What the hell do *you* know anyway?"

Osman, now literally up against the wall, knew that he was risking it all by defending his position, but now he had nothing to lose. He snorted in exasperation as he directed his argument forward. "What I *do* know, madam," Osman said as he carefully raised the volume of his voice, "is that a first century Roman lancea with the words 'Longinus' and 'Dominus' engraved on it was just found in a wall in Aya Sofia. I also know that another 'Lance of Longinus' exists in Vienna, and a very reputable source says it's no more than thirteen hundred years old!" When he realized he was shouting Osman stopped. His heart was pounding. He had not only crossed the line, but he was now begging for another cup of Luci's wrath.

However, Luci Daniels was unexpectedly quiet. Osman could tell that she was thinking deeply about something. What was it? Was she reconsidering his argument or merely deciding how to dispose of his body?

Osman knew he was far out on a limb but he decided to add one last bit to his own defense. He cautiously stepped toward Luci. "Don't you see, madam? You have it!"

Luci's countenenace didn't change.

"You are free to draw your own conclusions, madam," Osman added quickly: one final effort to soothe his mistress' ire.

Luci ran her long, thin fingers over her red-colored lips. Osman's polemic, despite its thunderous volume and insubordinate tone, was hard to dismiss. *If he's right...* She quickly changed the look on her face and gently placed her hand on his.

"Find it for me, my friend."

Luci's mercurial change of heart momentarily confused the Turk. He carefully displayed a subtle, triumphant smile. "Yes, madam!" he replied zealously. "Certainly, madam!" As he turned and left her office, he couldn't help picturing her subject to his sexual caprice. He smiled discretely. *In time...in time.*

CHAPTER THREE

Golden Horn, 11:15 a.m.

Mehmet sat quietly on the ferry as it cut westward through the choppy waters of the Golden Horn from Kasimpasha to Fener. Earlier he had purchased a small white cotton bag for the golden reliquary and discreetly slipped the latter inside the former after leaving the shop. The reliquary fit perfectly. As the ferry chugged onward, he fingered the reliquary through the bag and wondered about the relic's history. *If only you could speak!* He looked around; the ferry wasn't crowded.

Mehmet daydreamed as he watched the ships cruise up and down the Golden Horn, to and from the Sea of Marmara, and he wondered where they were headed and where they'd been. To his right he saw two more ships in dry-dock, waiting for long-overdue repairs. To his left, on the Golden Horn's southern shore, he saw the cars whiz along the Murselpasa Caddesi. Just east of the road he noticed a small church. He smiled when he remembered the story of its construction. Back in the days of the Ottoman Empire, the sultan allowed some of his Bulgarian subjects to build a church on the site, provided they could do so in an incredibly short period of time. Needless to say, they succeeded.

The Bulgarian Church brought the relic back to his thoughts. Mehmet hesitated and then clandestinely pulled the casket out of the cotton bag and opened it. He gasped as he saw the Lance again. It was so simple, yet so magnificent. Its monetary value was not important, but it was truly a treasure for Turkey. Mehmet closed the casket and looked across the Golden Horn. *This find could rank among the treasures found at Ephesus!*

But to whom should he reveal his secret? With Kemal gone…there was no one. He again gently ran his fingers over the reliquary.

Kemal should get the credit. He deserved it. Mehmet opened the casket again. This time he carefully removed the papyrus and studied it. He picked out a few words he thought he might be able to decipher. *Iesus…Nazarenus…crucif--Perhaps I could fly to Paris and give it to him!* Mehmet closed the reliquary, returned it to its sack and stood up as if the plane to Paris were in front of him. Then he returned to earth and saw the foolishness of that proposal. How was he going to get to Paris? And if he were caught smuggling a valuable artifact out of Turkey, he would land in prison for certain.

Mehmet didn't know the curator of Aya Sofia, but that could be the answer. *Give it to the curator…No, no. Then Kemal would have to get in line with the others to inspect it. It must go to Kemal!* Again he realized his wishful thinking. Then he had a flash of insight. *If I can't give it to Kemal, I must give it to Kemal's American friend. Yes, I'm certain that Kemal trusts him. It would be just like giving it to Kemal!*

As the ferry neared the dock at Fener, Mehmet jumped off with his treasure and headed southeast to Sultanahmet. Taxis were too expensive for a student. The walk would do him good.

As he walked through Cibali, Mehmet tried to imagine what this American friend of Kemal's would look like. He'd watched American movies and seen American tourists, but he had never spoken to any of them. He thought of Harrison Ford in the role of Indiana Jones and chuckled. He strolled through the crowded narrow streets, past the leather goods outside one shop and the coffee, tea and spice of another. The continuous humming of the commerce around him didn't distract his thoughts from the Lance. Two women, veiled and dressed entirely in black, swept by him. Ahead the street widened. Four boys kicked a soccer ball around as a shopkeeper wheeled a cart-full of watches across the street. The street narrowed again. To his right, a fruit seller was hawking bananas and to the left, a cheese vendor announced his presence.

Mehmet's nose alerted him to his proximity to a favorite treat. He smiled as he recognized the delectable fragrance. He turned to his right and stepped into the bakery from whence the pleasant scent came. *Ah, there it is!* Mehmet smiled as he eyed the honey-soaked knitted-wheat treasures.

"*Kadaifi,*" he said to the man at the counter. He licked his lips as the man handed him the pistachio-sprinkled sweet. *Ambrosia! Pure ambrosia!* Even the most perplexing problems can't divert a man from such pleasure. The pastry didn't last long.

Once his sweet tooth was satisfied Mehmet walked onward through the myriad of stands and booths in the outdoor bazaar: vegetables, fish, TV's, CD's, clothes, hats and cameras. A spice merchant's table looked like an artist's palate: red saffron, yellow turmeric, orange paprika, gray-green oregano, tan-brown cumin and black pepper. It was impossible not to stop for a few seconds and look, but as he looked, Mehmet came to a decision. He must find this Leslie Connery and deliver the treasure to him.

Gedikpasha, 11:20 a.m.

Albert Boucher rechecked the address he had copied onto an envelope. The student directory placed Mehmet here in Gedikpasha, across from the Bayezit Mosque. With the skill of a cat burglar, the Frenchman managed to avoid the landlord and find the apartment. He had the presence of mind to knock first and when his knock went unanswered, he skillfully picked the lock and let himself in. The second-story apartment was untidy to say the least. The kitchen reeked of garlic and lamb; dishes were piled up in the sink. "*Cochon!*" Albert sneered. He made his way to the bedroom and found it a mess as well. The bed was unmade; dirty, smelly clothes were everywhere. Boucher spat in disgust, but he knew that his search had to start somewhere. He pulled open drawers, threw their contents on the floor and rifled through them. *Not here!* He lifted the mattress and threw it on the floor. *Nothing!* Albert then ran to the closet and threw all of its contents on to the mattress. *Still nothing!* As Boucher picked up and then tossed the Koran from the dresser to the floor, he suddenly heard two men come through the front door.

Merde! Albert glided to the bedroom door and saw the current residents of the apartment. One was a massive fellow in a tank top and the other, only slightly smaller, was by his side. They had just realized that they had been burgled and were most upset. *Wrong apartment!*

Albert had to get out, but there was no way of getting past the two men. He ran to the window overlooking the street below. If he timed his jump well, he could land in the back of the garbage truck that had stopped in traffic. If he missed it, he'd certainly have at least one broken leg. He pulled up on the window. It wouldn't budge. Someone had painted it shut!

Albert's struggling with the window caught the attention of the apartment's residents. They yelled at him and rushed to the bedroom door. Albert threw himself forward, caught the door and slammed it in their faces. He quickly grabbed the Koran and shoved it under the door between the bottom of the door and the floor, wedging the door closed. He grabbed a drawer from the dresser and threw it through the window as the men outside the door hastened to break it down. By the time they did so, Albert had slipped through the broken window and jumped. He landed as he had hoped, in the garbage truck, but he could not have anticipated the stench that engulfed him as he landed. He roared in disgust as he spat. The driver of the truck opened the door and yelled something at him and the men in the apartment cursed him and vowed to call the police. Albert sprang like a cat out of the bed of the garbage truck onto the street and beat a hasty retreat. He would have to go back to the University and start over.

Fatih, 11:49 a.m.

Osman stepped out of the taxi just after it passed under one of the great arches of the Aqueduct of Valens. He walked northwest another twenty yards and entered the apartment building. He remembered helping Mehmet move here last month. He waved at the landlady and trotted up the stairs to the fourth floor. He jimmied the lock and was in a flash. After a cursory look around, Osman began to dig. He threw Mehmet's books on to the floor and rifled through them. He tore open pillows and cushions with a six-inch stiletto he pulled from his jacket pocket. Osman ran to the bedroom and tore that asunder as well. Only when he was convinced that the relic was not there did he leave.

"He must have it on him!" Osman muttered to himself as he left the apartment. He ran down the stairs and waved at the landlady again as he left the building. He had a huge city to canvas, but he had to find the Lance. Where could Mehmet be? *The University? Yes, but where? The odds of finding him there are small. What did he say before I left him?*

Osman's head was swimming. He couldn't think and needed something to calm himself. He crossed the street, grabbed a table at a café and ordered *raki*. As he sipped the delicious, clear anisette, the tight knots in his mind gradually unwound themselves. He looked down into the bottom of the glass and inhaled the aromatic vapors. Soon he would remember, and soon he would have the relic.

As the alcohol penetrated his cerebral cortex, Osman couldn't help but look back on his life. He chuckled in self-satisfaction at his victories, as well as his defeats, for lessons learned from the latter increased the former. Certainly there were the women—so many women—but also the fast cars and the lavish clothes that would drain his bank account, only to lose them later to creditors. It was worth it, though. Better to have tasted the sultan's banquet and lose one's life than to never have known it at all.

The man who hurried by did not disrupt Osman's rapture. Had he glanced up from his intoxicating ecstasy, Osman certainly would have recognized Albert Boucher. In fact his rhapsody was so euphoric that he didn't hear the muezzin calling the faithful to prayer from the Fatih Mosque four blocks away.

Albert warily walked past the landlady's door. *Great! She's on the phone!* While her back was to him, he slipped past and found Mehmet's apartment. Once he got past the locked front door, Albert saw that he was too late. *Damn! Someone has been here!* He looked around the room hoping to find something. Just because someone got here before him didn't mean that the Lance was gone. Maybe they were thieves looking for money or anything they could fence—no, the television was still there. He gave up the search after just a few minutes. *It's not here. He's taken it somewhere.* Albert grabbed a chair, sat down and buried his face in his hands. "What would Donkeybrain do with it?" The answer came to him almost immediately. Albert sprang to his feet. "What an idiot!" he said of his junior associate as he ran out of the apartment.

Sultanahmet, noon.

Mehmet sat on a bench in the park between Aya Sofia and the Blue Mosque. He should have been at the Ambassador Hotel five minutes ago, but he was having last minute second thoughts. *Was Osman right? Should*

I trust this Connery with the Lance? He heard the muezzin calling over the loudspeakers of the Blue Mosque, but for the first time in his adult life he failed to heed the call. He sat with his hands wrapped around the bag that contained the casket and its treasure. He unknowingly squeezed the gold reliquary with every anguishing thought that tore at his conscience.

Galata, 12:05 p.m.

"Khalid!" the café manager yelled to the young waiter. "Take your break. You're back on at 12:30."

The young Pakistani nodded as he finished wiping down the table. He pulled a pack of Camels out of his pocket and ejected one of the cigarettes. He lit it, found a wooden chair behind the café and took a few drags. When he was certain he was alone, he pulled a cell phone out of his pocket, flipped it open and dialed a London number.

"Sir Richard?" he asked when the call was answered. "It's Khalid Muzzhar, sir. I have some information you may find very interesting."

Ataturk Airport, 12:09 p.m.

The Delta/KLMflight from Seattle via Amsterdam was longer than she had expected, and Angelique Johnson was thankful to be in Istanbul. She'd never been there before, and all she knew about Turkey was what she read in the tourist guidebooks she bought last month. Her tall, athletic figure made more than a few Turks take notice of her. She lettered in track in college and had kept herself in shape through medical school and residency. She parted her full, shoulder-length, jet-black hair on the left, and as she walked down the concourse, she unconsciously ran her slender fingers over it. Her red jacket and white pants accented her dark brown face and eyes.

"Whoa!" she heard behind her. "What's the hurry, Angie?"

Angie stopped and turned around. "Sorry, sweetheart," she answered.

Her husband struggled toward her with the lion's share of the carry-ons. "Well, slow down just a little."

"Let me take some of those, Les."

"No," he snapped back. "I can handle them."

"Honey, you always do this. What are you trying to prove?"

This tall, thin man shared none of his wife's athletic attributes. His pale beige skin demanded a grease-like sun block to avoid a nasty burn whenever he wandered into the sun. Thinning red hair covered part of his head. The rest of his scalp had lost that luxury over the past ten years. His green eyes twinkled in the bright airport lights. He wore a goatee off and on: today he was on. "Don't you appreciate chivalry when you see it?"

"Of course I do, but aren't you taking this a bit too far? Let me help."

"If you insist," Les said as he unloaded a few bags. He tried to hide his relief, but his wife knew him better than that.

As they passed through passport control and fetched their luggage, a crowd of hucksters descended upon them, each of whom could provide lodging in the city and transportation for less than anyone else could. Angie felt relieved that their accommodations were pre-paid and all they had to do was get to the Ambassador Hotel in some area called Sultanahmet.

Les hailed a taxi and opened the back door for Angie. He impatiently alerted the the driver to the luggage by pointing down at the bags from shoulder level. Once he was certain that the driver got his drift, Les walked to the other side of the cab and got in. The annoyed cabbie looked askance at him as he loaded the luggage, muttering something in Turkish as he got back into the taxi.

"Ambassador Hotel, Sul-tan Ock-Med," Les read off one of his many notes as the driver reclaimed his seat

"Sultanahmet," the taxi driver repeated. The words flowing off his his tongue like extra virgin olive oil strongly contrasted Les' rough staccato rendering on the hotel's loacation.

As the taxi peeled away from the airport, Les sighed and collapsed into his seat. "Best idea you've ever had, Angie. Great that your mom and dad could watch the kids."

"You needed a break, darling. That trial was--."

"Please, let's not talk about that."

"Okay," Angie said as she tried to get comfortable in the taxi's hard back seat.

"Doctors have better things to do than to be in court for *three weeks*."

"I thought we weren't going to talk about it."

Les went on as if she hadn't said a thing. "That damned lawyer stole three weeks of my life for nothing. *Nothing!* I couldn't work in the office: 'Have to be in court every day to impress the jury.' My patients thought I had deserted them. That damned snake-of-a-lawyer got the other two doctors to settle, but I wouldn't."

"Maybe that's because you didn't do anything wrong."

"Three weeks of harassment...I don't ever want to go through that again."

"Nobody does."

"How would you know? You've never been sued!"

Angie scowled at her husband indignantly.

"Sorry. That was out of line, Angie."

"I've never been sued, but going through it with you wasn't any fun you know!"

"I couldn't have done it without you," he said softly as he gently caressed her hand.

She smiled back at him. "You're worth it," she said as she leaned over and kissed him.

Angie had met Les as an undergraduate at the University of Washington where she went on to complete medical school and her residency in Family Medicine. Les also went on to medical school but took his residency in Neurology. They married the first Saturday after completing their training and joined a multi-specialty clinic in Everett, north of Seattle, five years earlier.

"So what's on the trip agenda?" Les asked.

"Well, let's see," Angie said as she fumbled through her handbag. "First," she announced as she pulled out a brochure, "I'd love to see the Cathedral of Saint Sophia and then--"

"More churches?" Les protested. "Jeez! Sounds just like last year in Italy. Every time we turned around we were going into a church! We spent more time in church in ten days than most Italians do in a year! You must have this complex about going into churches. Is it because we rarely attend at home that you have this strange compunction to scoot me into a church at every opportunity?"

"Take it easy, Les. It used to be a church; now it's a museum. And it happens to contain some beautiful artwork."

"You said that about Saint Peter's. The whole place is full of statues of popes! This pope and that pope, Pope Sleepy here, Pope Grumpy there…"

"Don't you have any sense of reverence?" Angie snarled.

"Only in those matters which don't pertain to religion." Les replied prosaicly. He looked out the window for a second and glanced at a truck carrying a load of cotton. "I mean I don't understand why we always do this: Paris, London, Rome. You're no churchgoer."

Angie rolled her eyes.

"What's that supposed to mean?" Les grumbled.

"Nothing." Angie turned away.

"Now, Angie," Les moaned. "What is it with you and religion? I mean it's always hovering there in the background—you're so sensitive about it."

Angie tried to ignore her husband.

"I think your folks poisoned your mind: far too many starring roles in those productions at the African Methodist Episcopal Church."

"Knock it off, Les!" Angie uncharacteristically clenched her fist as she scolded him.

Les realized he had crossed the line. "I'm sorry, babe." He leaned over and gently kissed her.

Angie had a soft spot for her husband and her forgiveness came easily. "You're a real pain sometimes. You know that?"

"I won't do it again. I promise."

Angie smiled and hugged him and gave him a big kiss. "Be prepared for the vacation of your life, Doctor Connery," Angie whispered in his ear steamily.

Sultanahmet, 12:15 p.m.

Albert Boucher was as mad as a wet hen. No taxi would stop for him so he had to walk to Sultanahmet. (He ran most of the way.) He didn't have any trouble finding the Ambassador Hotel. Most of the locals knew where it was, tucked up between a restaurant and three or four travel agencies just west of the park between Aya Sofia and the Blue Mosque.

When he arrived he put on his happiest face and very politely asked the desk clerk in English, "Doctor Leslie Connery, please. She's expecting me. I'm from the University of Istanbul, one of the archaeology graduate students."

The comely young woman at the front desk wiped her beautiful long brown hair out of her eyes as she reviewed the registry. "Room twenty-three," she said in perfect English as she motioned to the corner where the stairs and elevator were. "However, she is out. May I help you?"

"No, thank you. Can I go up to her room? I have something to give her."

"I'm sorry, no, but I can take it for you and see that she gets it."

"No, that's okay," Albert said as he backed away slowly.

As the clerk returned to her work, the front desk became very busy with newly arrived guests. Albert saw his chance and furtively followed one of the guests up the stairs; the clerk was too busy to notice. On the second floor from the ground he quickly found room twenty-three. He knocked on the door and felt relieved when there was no answer. He started to work on the door. After several minutes his efforts bore no fruit. *Merde! This isn't going to work!* He looked around, as if something nearby would help him. He ran back down the stairs and started to walk uncertainly toward the front desk. Then an idea struck him. He smiled as he realized how he would get into the room.

The young woman at the front desk was leaving and a young man, who appeared a bit less familiar with the workings of the desk than she, took over. Albert turned away from the desk toward a television set up in the lobby. He would give her a few minutes to leave and then go to work on her replacement.

When she left, Albert strutted up to the desk and declared, "Doctor Leslie Connery, room twenty-three. I believe I left my key in my room. Can you let me back in?"

In broken English the clerk tried to explain that he couldn't leave the desk.

"Perhaps you could loan me a key—I'll bring it right back."

The young man hesitated and shook his head.

Albert was losing his patience. "I must get back into my room!"

The clerk refused to release a key.

In desperation Albert pulled out his wallet and pulled out fifty million Turkish lira and showed the clerk.

The clerk smiled back and said, "Euro."

"No Euro, just lira!" Albert claimed he had no Euros.

"Euro!"

Time was of the essence. Albert slid off his shoe and retrieved a fifty Euro note. It was all he had.

The clerk grabbed it immediately with one hand and gave Albert the key with the other. "Euro!"

Albert glared at the young man and ran back up the stairs to room twenty-three. He opened the door to find four large boxes and three suitcases on the floor before him. He sighed, closed the door and started his search.

Marmara Hotel, Taksim, 12:39 p.m.

Roger Brown had worked for Luci Daniels for five years. He was a very efficient secretary and was brighter than he let on. It had only taken him twenty minutes to bug his boss's office the day after they moved in to their temporary headquarters at the Marmara Hotel two months ago.

Luci had left for lunch with her chief financial officer at noon and the cleaning crew had just finished tidying up her office. As they left, Roger smiled and bid them good afternoon. He cautiously waited a few seconds before lifting the telephone receiver and hitting "eleven" on his speed dial.

"*Herr Hugo Geissler, bitte,*" he said into the phone. "*Reinhardt Braun.*"

Sultanahmet, 12:31 p.m.

The weather was perfect for sightseeing from the taxi. A brilliant sun sparkled over the deep blue Sea of Marmara, which teemed with ships of all sizes. Traffic was good for a Saturday and within twenty minutes, the cab entered the old city. The Sea of Maramara still lingered on their right. On the left were the remains of the sea walls, twenty feet high and built over a millennium ago to defend the city from naval assault. Angie sighed as she saw bushes growing on the crumbling ruins. Fifteen minutes later, Angie and Les were at the Ambassador Hotel. To Angie it appeared to be a quiet, fairly modern place, nestled off a narrow street among restaurants and tourist bureaus.

As she stepped out of the taxi, Angie asked Les, "So Abe is sending the disc?"

"Yeah, and a jump drive, just in case."

"Why didn't he just email it?"

"He tried. Didn't go."

"Wow, how often does that happen?"

"Almost never. I'll send an email to Al Gore and tell him his internet needs some work!"

"You tell 'em, Tiger!" Angie giggled

"Anywho, my stuff was supposed to be sent DHL to the hotel. I can't believe I forgot my Power Point! Kinda hard to give a decent lecture without that."

"Absolutely, Doctor Connery," Angie smiled at him.

The woman from the front desk returned from her brief errand. The young man smiled and returned to his housecleaning chores. The fifty Euros that he had extracted from Albert would be well-spent tonight.

This conference was indeed just what Les Connery needed. Luckily, one of Angie's fellow classmates in medical school was able to help her out when she called three months ago. Angie knew that once the trial was over, despite its outcome, her husband would need a break. Her friend, a faculty member at the University of Colorado, needed a neurologist to deliver a lecture at a conference in Istanbul: a neurologist with a particular expertise in migraine headaches, which Les just happened to have. Angie's friend pulled a few strings and soon Les was on the program. Yes, this is just what he needed, a little relaxation and revalidation. Of course she knew that she would benefit from this little boondoggle, too, as would the other doctors who had come from the United States and other countries. Angie grabbed her things and followed Les into the hotel.

"Hello," he said to the female clerk with the beautiful dark brown hair. "I'm Doctor Les Connery, from the US."

"Oh, yes. We've been expecting you, Doctor."

After the passports had been inspected and Les and Angie had completed all of the paperwork the hotel required, the clerk handed them their keys. "Room forty-one."

"Thank you," Angie and Les said in unison.

"Do you know," the clerk chuckled, "there is another Doctor Connery staying at the hotel, too?"

"Really?" Les asked.

"Perhaps you will be able to meet her while you are staying with us."

"Wouldn't that be something," Les smiled. As Les spoke to the desk clerk, Angie saw one of the employees combing out the fringe of the huge Turkish rug in the entry. The young man saw her watching him and smiled back at her.

"Shall we?" Les asked as he held up a key for his wife.

"I will send someone with your bags," the clerk assured them.

The two of them barely fit into the narrow elevator.

"Wanna see some sights?" Les asked as the elevator door opened on the fourth floor.

"Sure," Angie answered.

Once in the small room they inspected the two twin beds and took a quick look at the TV, phone, the minibar in the corner and the small three-quarter bath.

"It worked out okay that there was no room at the Intercontinental," Les remarked. That was where the conference would be held. "I like this place."

"It looks nice and cozy," Angie added. "Well, where to first?"

"Surprise me," Les said as he hugged her and gave her a full kiss on the lips.

She wrapped her arms around him and the two of them tumbled gently onto one of the beds.

"That sounds like a good place!" Les smiled as he kissed her again.

Les gently moved his hand over the back of her thigh and gave her a playful squeeze. Angie opened her mouth and slowly licked the outside of his lips and then ever so sensually invaded his mouth. His reaction was predictable for her, but she loved it anyway when he shot his tongue forward, rather clumsily, into her mouth. The ensuing tongue wrestling was quite vigorous. As their passion grew, Les hurriedly slid his hand down Angie's blouse.

The sudden knock at the door froze them.

"Luggage," a cheery voice said.

"We'll continue this discussion later," Angie smiled as she got up and answered the door.

Mehmet had made his decision. He was going to find this Connery fellow and give him the Lance. No more waffling. This is what Kemal would want. If Connery were good enough for Professor Kemal, then he was good enough for Mehmet Yakis. He sprang up from the bench and made his way to the Ambassador Hotel.

Fatih, 12:36 p.m.

The *raki* was helping Osman remember. By the time he started on his second, he remembered what Mehmet had told him: Doctor Leslie Connery, Ambassador Hotel in Sultanahmet! He set the *raki* down and looked for a taxi. Within seconds he had one. He took a step toward the taxi but then turned back to the unfinished *raki* on the table. *It's an absolute crime to waste good* raki! He ran to the table, emptied the glass in one gulp. Very happy that he had not abandoned his drink, Osman ran back and jumped into the waiting cab.

Sultanahmet, 12:39 p.m.

Mehmet walked into the Ambassador Hotel, clutching with both hands the cotton bag that held the casket and its precious contents. The desk clerk was busy with guests so he looked around the lobby. On the TV news he saw a pale-skinned woman with short black hair and seemingly black eyes walking through Aya Sofia with a reporter. Mehmet walked closer to the television to hear what was going on. He heard that the woman was Lucille Daniels, a rich American, who was providing financing for the latest restoration efforts of the museum. He watched her swagger through the museum in her black suit, pointing out projects as if she were directing them herself. He could hear her speaking in English, followed by the translation into Turkish.

Les Connery ran down the stairs and pushed his way to the front desk. "We need some towels, Miss," he began. "I couldn't get through on the phone. I forgot to tell the bellman."

"Certainly Doctor," the dark brown-haired woman replied. "I'll send someone up with them immediately. Sorry for the inconvenience. Will you need anything else, Doctor Connery?"

The sound of that name yanked Mehmet's attention away from Lucille Daniels to the front desk. *Connery!* "Doctor Connery! Doctor Connery!" he shouted as he ran to the desk.

Les was taken aback. "Uh, yes?"

Mehmet smiled. *Allah be praised! It's you!* "I have something very important for you, Doctor," Mehmet said as he held out the bag.

Les eagerly grabbed for it. *My disc! All right! That's what I call service!* "Thank you very much."

"It's *very* important," Mehmet said. "Can we go to your room?"

DHL is pretty pushy! Probably wants a big tip. "I don't think that's necessary." Les tried to be polite.

A loud screech of a taxi's brakes outside interrupted their conversation.

Mehmet tried to pull back the bag without drawing any attention to them. "I need to explain something to you, Doctor Connery!" he whispered.

"What? Are you going to give me my—"

Mehmet gasped as he saw Osman run into the hotel. *What is he doing here?* Any trust Mehmet had for Osman vaporized at that instant. *He mustn't see me!* "Yes, Doctor. Here take it, sir," Mehmet said calmly as he gave Les the bag. *I can come back or call him. He'll know what to do with it.*

Les reached into his pocket for a tip, but Mehmet pulled away, warily watching Osman at the front desk. Les silently waved two one million lira notes at Mehmet, who shook his head and maneuvered his way out of the lobby and onto the sidewalk without being detected by Osman. Once he'd left, Les ran back up the stairs to the room.

"May I help you, sir?" the beautiful brunette clerk asked Osman in Turkish.

"Yes," he answered smoothly in Turkish, "I'm here to see Doctor Connery. I'm a friend of a friend."

The clerk was immediately suspicious. *Who is this Doctor Connery?* "What is your name? I can leave him a message or I can call his room."

Osman was not expecting resistance. "It's very important."

"I'm certain it is. What is your name please?"

"Professor Kemal." Osman was desperate for a name and that was the only one that made sense.

"First name?" the clerk asked as she wrote his name on a message pad.

"Ismael, Ismael Kemal."

"What did you want to say in your message or would you like me to call Doctor Connery's room now? He's just arrived."

He needed time to think. "Never mind the message. I'll just come back later. He needs to get situated. Probably hasn't eaten yet. I'll come back."

"Good-bye, Professor," the clerk said warily. "See you later."

Osman smiled as he left the hotel. He'd found Connery, but how was he going to find the Lance? He hadn't seen Mehmet around the hotel. Had he come here yet? Would he?

CHAPTER FOUR

Sultanahmet, Ambassador Hotel, 12:43 p.m.

Albert collapsed on the bed and cursed. He had opened and gone through all of Leslie Connery's luggage and boxes. He judged from her wardrobe that she was a large woman with absolutely no taste. *Typical American!* There was no sign of the reliquary or its contents. She hadn't even moved in yet. Who knew where she was: the University perhaps? Some tourist destination, maybe?

She'd probably fallen victim to the countless men in the street, all of whom have a *brother* in the Turkish rug trade. They would try to lure tourists in, saying: *Just come to look. No obligation to buy. You will like it!* Maybe she decided to grab a bite. Albert picked up one of her dresses and held it upward. *A woman of this magnitude should need to fill her belly every couple of hours!* He carefully folded the dress and replaced it in the suitcase from which it came. Then he cringed when he thought of this portly woman at a Turkish bath. *Disgusting!*

Albert's contemplation was interrupted by a sudden knock on the door. "Doctor Connery?"

Albert froze as he heard the key enter the lock. *Merde!*

"Doctor Connery? Something very important just arrived for you." It was the voice of the dark brown-haired desk clerk.

Albert slowly, silently dropped to the floor. The bed lay between him and the door. *If I can't run, I'll hide!* However, the bed stood only a few inches off the floor. He'd never get under it. Albert's heart nearly burst when he heard a key turn in the lock.

The brunette desk clerk opened the door with a Federal Express package under her arm. She walked across the room to the desk and set the package on it. As she turned to leave the room she saw Albert on the floor. She screamed immediately and ran to the door. Albert tried to calm her, but that did no good. She ran outside and shouted something in Turkish to someone who was running up the stairs. In a second the young man who had squeezed the fifty Euros from Albert just over an hour before stood in the doorway. He had a thick wooden club in his hand, and he bore it menacingly. When he saw Albert he smiled but not the kind of smile that connotes anything friendly. The smile was more typical of a lion that had just cornered a plump young zebra.

Albert looked back at him. "You have me, *batard,*" he muttered under his breath.

The young man's face then changed. He set the club over his shoulder and looked at Albert as if he were changing his attitude.

Albert didn't move. His situation was still tenuous.

"Fifty Euro," the young man said to him with a friendly smile.

"That's a fine name you have for me, my Turkish imbecile." He took a step forward.

The club suddenly shifted back to its original bellicose position. "Fifty Euro!"

It immediately became apparent to Albert that his friend was demanding another installment of money to let him go. Albert held out his empty hands. "No Euros. I have no Euros."

The young clerk swung at Albert, missing his head by a few inches.

"Jesus-Christ!" Albert hissed in French. "You Turkish --"

"Fifty Euro!" The Turk cocked the club back again.

Albert stuck his hands into his pockets and pulled out the few coins he had and put them on the desk in front of him. He retrieved his wallet and emptied that too, although all it contained was fifty million lira. When the clerk pointed the weapon at his victim's shoes, Albert obligingly removed them and revealed that they were empty.

The clerk pocketed all of the money and jabbed the club at Albert's chest. "Fifty Euro!"

"That's all I have!" Albert said while he shook his head slowly.

To Albert's surprise, the clerk motioned to him to follow. They climbed up the stairs to the fifth floor terrace, where meals were served. It was empty now. He led the Frenchman to the edge of the roof and pointed to a drainpipe that ran down to the street behind the hotel.

"*Absolument non!*" Albert protested.

The clerk raised his finger. "Police! Jail!"

Albert grimaced and then rushed forward, grabbed the pipe and shimmied down the rickety structure. Once or twice one of his pant legs caught and tore. "*Merde!*" the clerk heard him curse. Near the bottom Albert scratched his leg on a rusty bracket and he swore again. When his feet touched the ground Albert sighed but his relief was short-lived. From down the street, two big dogs ran toward him, barking loudly. He didn't have time to swear and his legs didn't wait for the command from his brain. Albert ran as if he were shot out of a cannon. Twenty feet ahead stood a six-foot wooden fence. As he approached it, he lengthened his strides and jumped as high as he could on to the fence. He hit the top of it with his midsection, knocking the wind out of him, but he recovered enough to wriggle his way over the top. To make matters worse, as he cleared the fence, he lost a shoe. Once he had flipped over the top of the fence, he fell six feet. Albert screamed as he landed flat in a huge, thorny bush.

Les opened the door and waved the bag at Angie. "The disc! Abe must have sent this right away." Les looked at the bag. "Kind of a weird container for a CD."

"That got here quickly. I'm impressed. When's your lecture?"

"First thing tomorrow morning."

"Great. Get it out of the way."

Les opened the desk's single drawer and set the cotton bag down inside. The CD's unusual packaging was no longer on his mind. "I believe we have some unfinished business…." He leered at her, raising his eyebrows as he slammed the desk drawer shut.

"Down boy! We were interrupted last time, remember? Let's try later after a nice meal…wine…."

"Oh, you're such a tease," Les said as he wiggled his hips, trying to be provocative but just looking silly.

"Let's go out and see what this town's all about," Angie said as she picked up the smaller of the guidebooks.

"Okay. Could be fun."

"Camera?"

"Rightcheer!" Les said as he snagged it off the desk.

"Let's go then," Angie said as she opened the door.

Les rushed up to her backside and gave it a pat. "You can run, Doctor Johnson, but you can't hide!"

"You're really pathetic. Do you know that?" she laughed.

"Totally beyond help, I assure you," Les answered as he closed the door and they headed out.

Fatih, 1:06 p.m.

Mehmet had wanted to return to Aya Sofia after leaving the Ambassador Hotel, but his heart wasn't in his work, so he walked home instead. Osman's appearance at the Ambassador Hotel made him very uneasy. *What in the world was he doing there?* Mehmet waved to his landlady as he entered his apartment building and climbed the stairs. As he opened the door his heart jumped into his throat.

"What in the name of Allah?" he gasped as he surveyed his ransacked room.

For two minutes he stood frozen. He ran into his bedroom and automatically began to pick things up off the floor. "Who would do such a thing?" He solemnly sat down on his bed and dropped his head into his hands. "Why?" he sighed. He thought of the Lance. Since he had found it that morning, his little corner of the world had changed precipitously.

As he picked up the telephone, he surveyed the apartment. Burglars didn't do this. His stash of money was undisturbed and his TV and iPod were still there. They wanted something specific…the Lance! It had to be that!

He thought again of Osman. Osman knew he had the Lance, but so did Albert Boucher. How well did he know Osman? He had only known him since February, when the restoration of Aya Sofia was renewed after an unexpected four-month interruption. He didn't even know if Osman were a student or not; he'd never seen him at the University. Did Osman ransack his room? It still could have been Boucher. They were the only ones. If he could just avoid the two of them…Sooner or later it would get out that the Lance was in the right hands and the issue would be moot. *Ha! Avoid the Frenchman? Impossible! Tell the police!* Mehmet shook his head as he dialed the police. He thought again of the relic, that terrible, wonderful relic that amazed him so, yet seemed to be at the center of this tumult that was just beginning to boil. He must see to its safety. He must visit Doctor Connery again. *He must be in danger, too!* When the police desk sergeant answered, Mehmet changed his mind. "I'm very sorry. False alarm." He didn't wait for a reply. He replaced the receiver and ran out the door without another thought about his apartment.

Tepebasi, 1:30 p.m.

Albert Boucher stood naked in front of the mirror of his apartment's tiny bathroom, slowly removing the many thorns that intruded into his skin after his leap over the fence. He cursed with each extraction. His walk home from Sultanahmet across the Golden Horn to Tepebasi had been long, painful and humiliating. Halfway there he threw away his only shoe: walking in one shoe is a ridiculous proposition anyway. And besides, how could he replace just one shoe? The last half of his journey, in his stockings, went fairly well. Not once did he encounter broken glass or sharp stones in his path, and he agilely had avoided a catastrophic encounter with fresh dog poop. However, his socks were shot.

Once the last of the thorns had been purged from his skin, Albert drew a hot bath and soaked his wounded skin. The thermal ecstasy not only cured his aching integument but also loosened the bonds of frustration that fettered his mind. *Ahhhh!* Now he could think.

"Donkeybrain's apartment was empty. Connery's hotel room was empty. That moron could have it with him, carrying it around like a new puppy: what a fool! Or, he may have taken it to the University, but where? Or perhaps he is cleverer than I give him credit. Maybe he has a hiding place, or an accomplice. Mehmet is the key: find him and find the treasure; find my freedom! Free myself from this wretched Purgatory! *Quartier Latin, je reviens!*"

Sultanahmet Camii (Blue Mosque), 1:32 p.m.

Osman stared blankly at architect Mehmet Aga's early seventeenth century creation. Never mind what the tour guides said; this pale gray structure was impressive. Four hemi-domes surrounded its sublime central dome and appeared to be lifting it heavenward to Allah. Six peripheral reedy minarets pointed the way. However, Osman knew the interior of the mosque was the most impressive. Four stout, yet beautiful, columns shouldered the central dome and supported the hemi-domes. Tiles with elegant blue designs covered the interior walls that were studded with stained-glass windows. Sumptuous blue rugs, made for prayer, covered the floors.

Osman dropped his head into his hands. How was he going to get into Dr. Connery's room? He'd never get past that clever desk clerk. The memory of her comely face gave birth to a momentary sexual fantasy, which Osman briefly relished. A disguise perhaps? Yes! But what? Time was of the essence. Once Connery had the Lance, he certainly would find a safe place for it. Osman glanced at his watch. Luci Daniels would be expecting him soon, *with* the Lance.

Ambassador Hotel, Sultanahmet, 1:45 p.m.

Osman wound his way through the alley behind the hotel. A rat ran under a dumpster as Osman saw something which could prove useful. He walked over to the plumber's van parked behind the building adjacent to the hotel. The alley was empty, and the back doors of the van were left open. Osman didn't hesitate. He poked his head into the back of the van and found a pair of blue overalls.

"Yes," he chuckled. "These are perfect." He pulled them on over his clothes.

"Good enough."

Osman found a few wrenches, dropped them into a toolbox and walked to the back of the hotel. He tried the door but found it locked. "Damn!" he cursed under his breath. But his luck was yet to desert him. He heard someone speaking on the door's other side and stepped backward.

"Fifty Euro" stepped through the door with the morning's trash.

Osman adroitly assumed his role. "I'm here for the plumbing…"

"Plumbing? I don't know about any plumbing problem."

"Some woman called at noon and said you had a problem upstairs."

"Did she say which room?"

"Twenty-one," Osman guessed. "Leaky faucet."

"Okay, follow me."

After climbing two flights of stairs, the young man let Osman in to room twenty-one.

"Let me know when you're done."

"Certainly," Osman agreed as "Fifty Euro" left the room and headed downstairs.

Osman quickly closed the door and locked it. He jumped over the bed and picked up the phone. "Yes," he said when the clerk answered, "I need to call Doctor Connery's room. Do you have his number?"

"I can connect you, sir." Osman's heart sank. He needed to know the room number! *All is lost!* "There you go, sir. Room forty-one."

"Thank you," Osman answered nervously. When the desk clerk connected him he immediately hung up. "Forty-one...forty-one..." He opened the door to the room he was in and inspected the lock. All room doors probably had the same kind of lock. Osman sighed and bit his teeth into his lip. High security lock: not made for picking. He looked across the hall and spotted a room with an older lock. He'd been lucky so far. Maybe room forty-one had an older lock. It was worth checking.

Osman sprinted up the next two flights of stairs and found number forty-one. The lock was the same as room twenty-one. *Shit!* In desperation he knocked. Maybe there was someone inside. Nothing.

"Do you need to get in?" Osman heard someone down the hall say. It was one of the maids.

"Uh, yes," Osman sputtered. "I'm—uh—a plumber. And—uh—there's something wrong with the plumbing in there."

"Really," the maid said. "It seemed all right yesterday."

"Just happened this morning. Can you let me in?"

"Yes," the graying sixty-year old answered warily as she fished the master key out of her pocket. "They just went out so you should have plenty of time to fix whatever it is. You're certain this is the right room?"

"Yes, this is it. I'm certain."

"Okay," she said as she opened the door.

"Thank you," Osman smiled as he stepped inside the room, bowing his head slightly, and then slowly closed the door. Osman set down the toolbox and frantically began his search. He opened one of the suitcases and rifled through its contents. Nothing! He opened and searched another and then two others with the same result. "Where is it?" he panted as he replaced the contents of the luggage and surveyed the room. The desktop was empty. He tore through the closets and then the dresser drawers. Nothing! In desperation he ran to the bathroom and scoured it as well. Osman abruptly stopped and sat down on the toilet seat. He had missed something. He couldn't think of what it was, but something kept telling him he'd overlooked something in the main room.

Osman thoughtfully paced out of the bathroom and carefully scrutinized the hotel room. He looked at each of the items he had searched: the luggage, the dressers, the closets, the desk, the beds—"Wait a minute," he said aloud. "The desk!" he said as he walked over to it. "I never looked *inside* the desk!" He grabbed the handle and slowly, expectantly opened the desk drawer.

Suddenly the room door crashed open and four policemen charged into the room and grabbed Osman.

"What are you doing?" Osman protested. "I'm the plumber!"

"He's a thief!" It was the brunette desk clerk. "Fifty Euro" scowled at Osman from her side.

"No! I'm a plumber!" he yelled as he pointed to his overalls, as if they were the only witnesses to his authenticity.

"I don't recall any pipes in that desk!" she snarled.

Osman looked back at the desk and into the drawer. He winced as the police applied handcuffs. Then he saw it, or something that could be it. Osman jerked forward to the desk and saw it again: a box of some kind in a cotton bag. *That must be it!* Osman screamed as a policeman pulled him back by his hair.

"Try that again and you'll be on the floor, dog!" the officer spat in his face.

Osman closed his eyes and imagined Luci's Daniel's fury at his failure. He was so close to bringing it to her. So close.

Aya Sofia, 2:00 p.m.

Mehmet knew that his friend Yasmin could tell him more about Osman. She was an undergraduate student visiting form Jordan, who had a great talent for restoring Byzantine mosaics. Mehmet had seen her work many times and felt lucky to assist her directly on more than one occasion. She was about five and a quarter feet tall with long black hair and deep dark brown eyes and a gorgeous figure that got her more attention than she desired. Yasmin had a good head on her shoulders and was extremely perceptive. If she didn't know each and every detail of the occurrences at the museum, she knew who did. The beautiful Arab woman pored over the tracings of the ceiling mosaic that lay on the floor in front of her. She put her hand over her mouth and extended her index finger in front of her nose. A few seconds later, she cocked her white hijab-covered head to one side.

"Yasmin," Mehmet said softly. He felt it a crime to disturb such a stunning genius at work. When she didn't respond, he increased the volume. "Yasmin."

"I heard you the first time, Mehmet," she answered, not taking her eyes off the object of her study.

"It looks very interesting," Mehmet said as he walked up to her. "Such brilliant color."

Yasmin broke her concentration, turned to Mehmet, and smiled as if she were flattered that he had taken notice of it. "Yes, it's very rich…the blue especially." Her Turkish was excellent.

"Definitely." Mehmet had to gently turn her attention away from the mosaic tracing. "Yasmin," he said after a thoughtful pause, "what do you know about Osman?"

Yasmin spun around, threw her hands on her hips and scowled. "If you mean the worthless thug with whom you choose to associate…"

"Yes," Mehmet replied sheepishly.

"I have no idea why he's here. He knows absolutely nothing about archaeology! I've never seen him in any classes at the University."

"Hmmm."

"No one else knows anything about him either."

"Is that so?"

"I have noticed one thing about him…."

"What's that?"

Yasmin looked around the room and lowered her voice. "I've worked on many restoration projects such as this one before. Never have I seen a sponsor so involved."

"Sponsor?"

"Lucille Daniels. The American. She's financing the latest restoration. I haven't seen a day go by without seeing her face here. Usually we *never* see the sponsor. He's just a name. She walks through the museum as if she owned it. And she orders the curator around like he's her employee!"

Mehmet recalled seeing her on the television at the Ambassador Hotel. "What does that have to do with Osman?"

"I've seen her speaking with Osman, more than a few times. They're usually very secretive. I don't think they knew I was watching them."

"Do you think--"

"That he's working for her? Now that you mention it, I'm certain he is. That certainly explains a lot of things."

"What else do you know about this Lucille Daniels?"

"Nothing; but I know how to find out more." Yasmin didn't wait for Mehmet to ask her what she meant. Yasmin walked away from her work. Then, just before she turned the corner, she turned to him. "Aren't you coming?"

Mehmet smiled and quickly caught up with her.

Police Station, Sirkeci, 2:57 p.m.

As the cell door clanged open, the guard burped and announced, "You're being released."

Osman poked his head up from the cot. "Released?"

"Yes," the guard snarled. "If you have anything with you, grab it and get out."

"But who--" Osman gasped.

He knew that his employer had intervened on his behalf and facing her fiery eyes was not his idea of fun. He followed the guard out of his cell and down a long corridor.

At the end, a sergeant met them. He handed Osman an envelope containing his watch and wallet. "Outside," he barked, pointing the way.

Osman exited the police station to find a black Mercedes waiting for him. One of its backdoors was open. He sighed heavily. *There she is.* Osman ran his fingers over his mustache and trudged through a varied collection of street litter to the Mercedes. He stopped at the open door and looked inside.

Luci Daniels didn't deign to offer him a glance. "Get in," she ordered, her hard face still looking forward.

Osman complied silently while the cogs and gears of his mind spun full tilt, vainly searching for a credible explanation for his failure. Finally, he ventured forth, "Madam—"

"Admit it," Luci interrupted, "you screwed up." She didn't wait for a rebuttal. "I've had enough of your bungling."

"Thank you for bailing--"

Luci turned to him and sneered. "Bail? You really are an amateur, aren't you?" She held up a one hundred Euro note. "The police were most conducive to misplacing the complaint." Luci smiled triumphantly. "Now we do things *my* way."

CHAPTER FIVE

British Airways Flight 34, somewhere over western Bulgaria, 2:07 p.m. (local time)

Sir Richard Covington-Smith sipped his Dom Perignon slowly. The stuff was "bloody awful", but he continued to force it down. After all, it was Dom Perignon. As soon as he had managed to squeeze the last gulp down his throat, Sir Richard pressed his head against the back of his first class seat and pressed the recline button at his side. He wiped the residue of the champagne from his gray mustache and let his sagging eyelids slowly droop as he drifted into half-sleep. He replayed Khalid Muzzhar's excited voice in his mind again and again: "a fantastic artifact", "a very important Christian relic", "the true spear that pierced the side of Jesus".

Sir Richard, Grand Master of the Knights of the Temple for the past fifty of his seventy-nine years, had substantially extended the wealth and power of the Order since ascending to that station. He assumed the role of Grand Master when his father, Robert, died prematurely at age fifty-two. Robert Covington-Smith had done little to expand the power of the Templars. In many ways it was but a secret society for gentlemen who needed a good reason to leave their wives on Saturday evenings. It was Richard who took the legend of the Templars to heart and expanded the society. His aggrandizement of the Order included the acquisition of millions of dollars, through various financial endeavors, and hundreds of Christian relics, most of which were kept under the most severe secrecy. By Sir Richard's personal order, to divulge the existence of any of these assets, let alone their location, would mean a gruesome death for the offender.

It was only fitting that Sir Richard be honored with the role and title. After all, his grandmother was a Plantard, one of the two French families that claimed direct descendency from the purported union of Jesus of Nazareth and Mary Magdalene. At least, that's what his cousin Pierre Plantard had convinced him. "I am only reclaiming lost family heirlooms," Sir Richard would say half-jokingly when others marveled at his determination and ability to acquire the relics. He dismissed the detractors that swore his claims were false. He knew about the BBC report and the others. However, he knew, deep in his heart, that a man of his importance must have a divine pedigree. The detractors were sadly mistaken, no matter what the evidence (and his cousin's confession) demonstrated.

The recovery of historical artifacts, however, was just an excuse to search for these puissant implements, and Sir Richard wasn't satisfied with the modern status of the Grand Master of the Knights of the Temple. He was rebuilding, however slowly, the might that the Templars had amassed in the twelfth and thirteenth centuries, when they were a wealthy, powerful nation unto themselves. The new Templars were to be a subterranean juggernaut, financial and spiritual, that would manipulate the "kings" of the earth to meet the desires of the Grand Master. It was only the wicked and despicable treachery of a jealous French king that toppled them from their virtual throne over Europe seven hundred years ago. Now Sir Richard Covington-Smith would, he vowed, re-establish the Templar Empire within his lifetime and with it, control Europe, America and, eventually, the rest of the world.

Next to Sir Richard at the window seat Kevin Meeley, his usually clean-shaven forty-seven-year-old aide of fifteen years, snored softly. Kevin had slipped into somnolence the minute the plane took off from Heathrow and had not awakened since. Then again, it was not unnatural to see Kevin in this position. As a matter of fact, it was rather unusual to see him expending any more energy than was required to keep upright with eyes open. Ambulation was a dreary chore. However, Sir Richard felt a certain attachment to the younger man. He often joked that he should examine Kevin's backside every morning to make certain he hadn't acquired any moss. Yet, Kevin had served the Grand Master and the Order loyally. He wasn't necessarily afflicted with incompetence, just lethargy. When others in the Order called Kevin Meeley lazy and demanded his replacement, Sir Richard instantly rebuked them. "No, sir! There is no substitute for

Kevin Meeley!" Those who knew the Grand Master best understood that his judgment was not to be questioned, no matter how bad it may appear.

Sir Richard smiled unconsciously as a dream brought him an image: a clear, sharp, brilliant picture of a golden lance, which he held in his hand and raised over his head as he stood miles high over the Earth. A trumpet sounded from Heaven and a booming voice announced in Latin that the Lineage of Jesus Christ had produced a new ruler, one to govern the entire globe. Sir Richard's clothes transformed into the glowing white garments of Caesar Augustus, and he shook the golden lance and roared, *"Deus et Rex!"* over the cowering billions below him. He roared again, and the masses ceased their cowering and shouted back reverently, *"Deus et Rex!"* Again and again they repeated their call, increasing their enthusiasm. Their cowering was transformed into adulation. As he savored his triumph, a white dove softly floated down from Heaven toward his outstretched hand. The people of the Earth grew silent as the bird drifted elegantly toward Sir Richard. When the heavenly creature alighted on the man's serenely extended hand, the people erupted in spontaneous applause, creating the greatest sound ever heard.

A sudden jab in his right shoulder cut short Sir Richard's endless reign. "I'm very sorry, sir," the young flight attendant said as she walked by with blankets for an old woman two rows back. "I stumbled into you. Did I hurt you?"

"Ladies and gentlemen," the captain's voice crackled over the speaker, "we are expecting more rough turbulence ahead. Please return to your seats and secure your seat belts."

"I'm very sorry, sir," the flight attendant pleaded. "I must take my seat now."

"That's quite all right, my dear," he beamed. "No way for you to know who I am."

The flight attendant wasn't sure she had heard Sir Richard correctly, but she raced to her seat and thought no more about it.

Sir Richard effortlessly returned to his reverie. Now, of course, this was no mere daydream. Of this he was certain. This was prophecy. This was the unfolding of history before his mind's eye. He saw the Merovingian kings of France gathered around him, cheering wildly. Godefroi de Bouillon and his brother Baldwin stepped forward in their royal robes and prostrated themselves before him and kissed his feet. When they arose, a line of ancestors, hundreds, formed behind them, Plantards and Saint Claires from the first century onward. They chanted his name in Latin, French, and then English. Soon their voices swelled into a gigantic wind, which blew in black clouds from the four corners of the Earth. Sir Richard stood majestically, his glowing regal raiment fluttering as the hurricane raged around him. He raised the lance again and the sky fractured into violent streaks of lightening and deafening thunder. The mortals around him, every last one of them, quaked in fear. When he saw this, the reigning Master of the Knights Templar, the man designated by God Himself to resurrect the glory of the once great Order, bellowed, "Be still!" Without hesitation, the violent tempest vanished, and the sun reclaimed the sky.

The heavens and all the Earth applauded with sweet music. Godefroi de Bouillon rose slowly, reverently, and gently clasped Sir Richard Covington-Smith's right hand, kissed it obsequiously and then shook it, like a grandfather congratulating his grandson on becoming Prime Minister.

Then, Godefroi, Advocatus Sancti Sepulchri, first ruler of The Holy Kingdom of Jerusalem, turned to the multitudes around them and spoke. "All things willed by God, no matter how strange, or how unusual, no matter how unfortunate, or how fortuitous, will come to pass. And today, my brothers, in the ninth century since the blessed excavations at Solomon's temple discovered those holy records, which demonstrate our rightful claim to be the true branches of that blessed tree conceived just before our Lord Jesus' death, the Seed of our Lord rises to power to claim our family's inheritance." Applause thundered from every quarter and it grew and sustained itself for what could have been hours.

In the eight centuries since the Knights of the Temple uncovered the sacred truth, the perfect heaven-written tale of the Magdalene and the Son of God, Sir Richard pondered, as his ears still rung with the continuing stentorian crescendo. Nine: a great and wondrous number. Nine: the highest single numeral. Nine: the product of the Trinity times itself. Nine: whose numerals of its multiples below ninety-one always add up to nine, and whose numerals of its multiples over ninety-one add up to a number divisible by nine. Nine: inducer of magical patterns. The difference between ninety and nineteen is nine more than the difference between eighty and eighteen, which is nine more than the difference between seventy and seventeen. This pattern continues and eventually ends with the difference between thirty and thirteen being nine more than the difference between twenty and twelve. Nine: the perfect number. Nine: God's number.

Was it no surprise to the world that this momentous happening was occurring at *this* time? It should not be because there was no other time for it to take place. This was the day, yea, even the hour, and even the minute that the Lord had ordained to reveal this most incredible mystery, which many over the centuries had protected with their very lives. This was the very second that the Templars, the loyal true servants of God and his bloodline, *le Sang Royal*, often mistakenly referred to as the Holy Grail, would place their king, God's king, on the world's throne.

Sir Richard, now King Richard, raised his right hand and silenced the loyal following. Then, when even the birds of the air and the animals of the land were quiet, he spoke. "The world as we have known it has passed away. Join me, my brothers, in vanquishing those wretched demons that remain in our Holy Path!"

Kevin Meeley awoke as if he had just sat on a cattle prod. "What the--" he grumbled. He could see Sir Richard's lips mouthing words and his closed eyelids quivering. "Oh, bloody hell!" he sighed. "Not again!"

Lufthansa Flight 2658, approaching Ataturk Airport, 3:09 p.m.

Hugo Geissler hurriedly licked his chubby fingers as he searched for the flight attendant. He would be back soon, and Herr Geissler had to have another wienerschnitzel or two. When Franz, the steward, finally arrived, he quietly gasped when he saw the collection of debris awaiting him.

"Zwei mehr, bitte," Hugo said pointing to his empty plate.

Franz smiled and acknowledged Herr Geissler's request. He gracefully gathered the dozen or so empty beer bottles and somehow managed to add the three plates and their flatware that crowded the passenger's tiny tray table.

As Franz departed, arms overflowing, Hugo rubbed his hands together anticipating his next delicious bite. Hugo Geissler was now seventy-eight and only twenty-five pounds overweight, despite his indulgent appetite. For nearly sixty years he had successfully maintained his identity in ironclad secrecy. First, he had fooled the British and the Americans. Later, the West German authorities would have no clue as to his covert past. Not even the Israelis caught on.

At the age of fourteen, Hugo joined the Hitler Youth. France had just fallen and to every German, 1940 appeared to be the year the Third Reich would begin its millennium of European, if not international, dominance. By January of 1944, the picture was much different. The British and Americans had erased the Axis Empire in Africa and had seized half of Italy. An invasion of France was inevitable. The Soviets had already begun their winter offensive and the German defenses were melting like butter before a hot knife. Soviet troops had entered eastern Poland.

While many boys his age had their doubts about sacrificing their lives for Hitler, Hugo was convinced that German defeats were the result of uninspired leadership and a lack of devotion to National Socialism. He joined the SS and dreamed of leading the invincible German soldier to ultimate victory and restoring the Reich. However, after a year of service on the front lines in Russia, Italy and France, Hugo had to admit that victory, while still possible, would have to be attained less conventionally.

By February of 1945, he had maneuvered his way into the upper echelons of the SS. He was often to be found at Himmler's right hand. On the fourteenth of that month Himmler named him to the Knights of the Holy Lance, the SS guardians of the Lance of Longinus. At seventy-eight, he was now the highest-ranking survivor of the Knights.

However, Geissler's rise in the SS did not stop there. On March 1, 1945, Himmler promoted him to gruppenfuhrer and introduced him to Doctor Erik Mueller, Chief of the Aryan Genetics Study Group. Mueller was seeking to preserve Aryan purity in his own unique manner. By late February, ten years after beginning his quest, Doctor Mueller stood on the threshold of the Nazism's most significant contribution to the preservation of the Aryan race. When the war ended before Mueller's dream could be realized, Geissler was ordered to smuggle Mueller's work out of Germany and restart the process once he was out of Europe.

Hugo Geissler chortled as the wienerschnitzel arrived. As he devoured the first bite, he continued his reflection on his wartime years in the SS. He thought of Mueller. "He is the future of our Aryan race!" the good doctor told him as he handed Geissler a twenty-centimeter-long tube with a three-centimeter diameter and a leather notebook. Although he did not understand what Mueller had told him, Hugo did his duty. He deftly avoided detection by the Allies after the German surrender in May, and he and the tube were out of Germany by July 1, 1945, on a Panamanian freighter bound for Uruguay.

As he crossed the Atlantic, fifty-nine years ago, Hugo agonized over the loss of the Lance of Longinus to the Americans. He would repeat to himself at least once a day that it was no wonder that without the Holy Lance, 'The Lance of Destiny', as Himmler called it, the Third Reich crumbled. One day, to divert his attention away from the tragic loss of the relic, Geissler opened Mueller's notebook. After all, he had risked life and limb to run it out of Germany.

"Genetic Engineering, *In Vitro* Fertilization, and Embryo Transfer", the title page read. It was all Greek to Hugo Geissler, but as he read on, Mueller's dream unfolded before his eyes. Mueller had completed the first two phases, genetic engineering and *in vitro* fertilization. Soon after fertilization, however, the Red Army had Berlin in a death grip, but Mueller wouldn't let his research die there. Before anyone truly knew if it were possible to cryogenically freeze living tissue and regenerate it at a later date, Mueller took the chance.

Hugo picked up the tube and analyzed it carefully. This was the sum total of Mueller's work to date. This blue-gray stainless steel cylinder that Geissler rotated nervously, back and forth in his hand, contained Mueller's cryogenically frozen embryo. It was the third and most difficult phase that would consume the next twenty-four years of Geissler's life.

After landfall at Montevideo, Uruguay, Geissler made his way to Asuncion, Paraguay. It was in the Paraguayan capital that Geissler connected with five other SS men who had been spirited out of Germany before the war's end. And with them, they had brought over ten million dollars in gold. However, none of them knew of Mueller's work or had any scientific knowledge. Mueller's project was destined to die.

Hugo Geissler, however, refused to let that happen. He had seen the SS lose the Lance of Destiny. He would not let Mueller's project tumble into oblivion. He studied Mueller's notes thoroughly. Within a year he learned Spanish and assumed the identity of a Swiss biologist. Geissler attended lectures at the universities in Asuncion, Montevideo and Buenos

Aires. He immersed himself in Mueller's work and made completion of the project his life's goal.

Embryo transfer was totally unknown, let alone *in vitro* fertilization of human ova and cryogenesis. Geissler would have to wait for technology to catch up. After 1960, he dared to visit the United States and later Europe, but his search remained in vain. In 1962 he received his degree in medicine and joined the research faculty of the Universidad Nacional de Asuncion. If the world could not show him the technology needed to complete the third phase, perhaps he would find it himself.

In 1967, Geissler bought the directorship of the reproductive studies department at the university. This was a fantastic opportunity. With dozens of researchers and government funding, he could complete his mission. He carefully screened hundreds of physicians and scientists to compose a new department, dedicated to embryology. He carefully selected only those he could trust implicitly. The screening took over two years. When the dean of the university demanded to know exactly what Geissler was researching, Hugo offered him a handsome bribe. When the dean rejected it, Geissler slashed the man's carotid arteries. The body was never found.

By early 1978, Geissler and his researchers stood at the threshold of success. Their animal research in embryo transfer was an overwhelming success. Cryogenic studies had also progressed well. He was ready to complete Mueller's phase three, but who would be the proper vehicle for this Aryan superman? Certainly none of the local women would qualify. Hugo's SS friends referred him to a contact in Munich.

"There is a woman," Hugo was told, "who will fit your needs well."

The woman arrived in Asuncion two weeks later. Her first name was Eva. Hugo never inquired as to her last name, and she never offered it. In mid July of 1978, Hugo Geissler implanted the embryo securely in Eva's womb. On April 20, 1979, what would have been the Fuhrer's ninetieth birthday, the fruit of Hugo's labor was harvested.

Hugo glanced at the passenger to his left. He savored his soul's intoxication as he surveyed the stunning six-and-a-half-foot demigod. He could barely contain his throes of rapture as he drank in this Teutonic Hercules, this zenith of Aryan manhood, this seed from which an army of Siegfrieds would spring forth to recapture the German Nation and lead it to final victory. This was the embryo with which he had left Germany fifty-nine years ago. His name? Why, Siegfried, of course! Siegfried Tapfer Geissler; Hugo promptly adopted the baby at birth. Eva, his *incubator*, as Hugo called her spitefully, was never allowed to see him. After a week of recovery from her labor and delivery, she was unceremoniously flown back to Germany.

Geissler never knew Siegfried's biological parents. As a matter of fact, they themselves never met. Mueller had seen the woman the day he extracted an ovum from one ovary, but she was under general anesthesia at the time. The only trace of the father he saw was a tube of semen. Yet, Mueller knew everything about the both of them and documented Siegfried's parentage in his notebook. Siegfried's Y-chromosome came from a young SS captain, five times decorated in battle. He was also an accomplished physicist who also held degrees in chemistry and engineering and was well-read in certain areas of philosophy (Kant, Hegel, and, of course, Nietzsche). His mother was an Olympic medalist, track and field mainly, and she held many pistol shooting titles. She had a marvelous singing voice and knew most Wagner arias by heart. Her favorite character was Brunhilde.

Young Siegfried was raised in an idyllic setting that melded the old Teutonic world with idealized National Socialism of the twentieth century. He was weaned on Goebbels and Rosenberg before he moved on to memorizing *Mein Kampf* at age five. From there he read primarily German sources, where they coincided with the party line. Jews were trash; Christians were weaklings; and Muslims, Buddhists, and whatever else weren't even human. Hugo had taught his son well. The Fuhrer would have been proud. Hugo returned to Germany with his son on April 20, 1989, the centennial of the Fuerher's birth. They settled in Munich.

Reinhardt Braun's telephone call earlier that day had electrified Hugo. The possibility of possessing the powerful relic made his heart race. At first, Hugo was indifferent to the news. After all, he knew that the Holy Lance, the Lance he had savored with his believing eyes sixty years earlier, was in Vienna. Rumors of handing the Americans a fake made the younger members of the Order feel better, but Hugo had witnessed the event. Now, the possibility of another Holy Lance, possibly the *True Lance*... After all, the Vienna Lance had produced no great victory: the Third Reich crumbled in spite of its purported power. Had the SS put its faith in a forgery? He reviewed Reinhardt's recounting of Osman's testimony to Luci Daniels regarding the Lance of Longinus. It made sense, perfect sense. Hugo beamed as he ingested the last of the wienerschnitzel. Yes, the Istanbul Lance, if it were the true Holy Lance of Longinus, the real Lance of Destiny, would give the Knights of the Holy Lance the mystical might to reshape the world in their image. This coupled with an unstoppable army of Siegfrieds.

Hugo looked back at his son. His short, almost unnaturally blonde hair, rugged, square jaw and icy blue eyes were beautiful. *He is a living legend, yet to accomplish Destiny's task.* Siegfried's face wore a permanent scowl. Hugo had never seen the corners of his son's mouth rise above the horizontal. However, Hugo knew his son well enough to know that something was eating at him.

"Siegfried," Hugo whispered, *"was ist los?"*

"Juden."

"What?" Hugo asked in English.

Franz, the diligent flight attendant, returned and gently interrupted, *"Mehr, Herr Geissler?"* he asked, pointing to the empty plate the wienerschnitzel occupied only moments before.

Hugo couldn't refuse. *"Bitte."*

Siegfried rudely turned his head away. After Franz left, Siegfried hissed into Hugo's ear, "That bastard's a damned Jew!"

Hugo responded in English. "You don't think I know that?"

"I want to strike him now, rapidly, like a cobra, and yank his throat from his neck," Siegfried growled quietly. "I would savor every second of that Jew's desperate gasping for air as his lungs fill with blood!"

"Son," Hugo held Siegfried close to him, "our time will come. For now you must be patient."

"I hate them, Father! I hate them all! I can't tolerate them any longer!"

"Son, I have been waiting over three quarters of a century. In these last fifty years I have learned patience and now Fortune has rewarded my patience. The Lance of Destiny is within reach!"

CHAPTER SIX

Ambassador Hotel, Sultanahmet, 4:00 p.m.

"What a beautiful city!" Angie Johnson sighed. "I never realized Istanbul was so fascinating!"

"Yeah. People are great. Food is superb," Les added. "Did you get a picture of me with that guy at the bakery?"

"Oh, wasn't that baklava fantastic?"

From outside their window they heard the muezzin calling the faithful to prayer over a loudspeaker.

Les looked at his watch and interjected, "He's very prompt."

"That's a beautiful sound," Angie noted. "I've got to admit it stirs my heart a little bit."

"Like church bells in Europe," Les teased.

"You're a twit. Do you know that?" Angie snapped back as she walked into the bathroom and grabbed a tissue to wipe her nose. "Darned allergies."

"Bring your meds?"

"I don't like to take that stuff. Besides, it's not that bad. Are you ready for tomorrow?"

"I was ready for tomorrow the moment I stepped off the plane!"

"Checked your disc?"

"Good idea," Les's response showed that he hadn't considered this. He picked up the cotton bag and then set it down. "How about after a night on the town?"

"Sure. Sounds great! I'll ask the desk clerk where to go. She's been very helpful."

"Yes and after that," Les announced as he seductively slid her way, "a night of torrid romance."

"With whom?" Angie cracked up when she saw the smirk on his face.

"Laugh now, woman," he roared in mock anger, "but you'll be begging for more by the time I'm through with you!"

"That quickly?"

Les quickly grabbed her around the waist and planted a big kiss on her lips. "You know you love it!"

"I do love it, Les. I love you. You're perfect."

"Laying it on a bit thick, aren't we?"

She looked deep into his eyes. "Not at all." She kissed him and held him tight. "Let's see what this town has to offer two lovesick Americans."

"Let me change and I'll be right with you." He kissed her. "I love you, Angie. Thanks for bringing us here."

"You're welcome, Les. You're very welcome."

Ataturk Airport, 4:05 p.m.

Sir Richard Covington-Smith stumbled as he walked through the airport. He would have fallen flat on his face had he not been able to grab Kevin Meeley's shoulder on the way down.

"Careful, Sir Richard," Kevin admonished his boss.

"Thank you, my boy." Sir Richard pushed his glasses from the end of his nose toward his forehead. "I daresay I could have broken my hip had you not caught me."

"All in a day's work, sir; I assure you."

"Quite."

Sir Richard straightened his black overcoat and adjusted the fedora he wore on his balding head.

"I can send for an electric cart, sir," Kevin offered as he took off his gray bowler and attempted to wave down an airport attendant.

"Nonsense! I should put a bullet in my brain if I can't walk a mere five hundred meters!"

Kevin rolled his eyes. "Sir!"

Sir Richard chuckled when he heard Kevin's reaction. "Come on!" he yelled as he lumbered toward the baggage claim.

After the obligatory half-hour wait, they saw their luggage materialize on the baggage carousel. Kevin quickly grabbed the bags and hired a man to carry them, although he easily could have managed them himself. After proceeding twenty-five meters, he urged Sir Richard to reconsider the electric cart, but again his boss rebuffed him. Sir Richard led the way to the taxi stand. Kevin followed, slowly and silently, his dirty gray overcoat slung over one arm. He silently cursed the Grand Master for walking too fast.

Siegfried's perfect body impressed nearly all of those who saw him walking out of the airport terminal. His black suit complemented his icy blue eyes. In his muscular hands he held two suitcases, each of which easily topped eighty pounds. Hugo Geissler, also in black, followed ten paces behind with cookie in one hand and a lamb kabob in the other. Siegfried effortlessly kicked the glass door open and walked out to the taxi stand. He saw a taxi approaching and raised his right arm, without putting down the loaded suitcase.

The taxi driver acknowledged him with a wave and pulled up to the curb. As Siegfried stepped toward the taxi he inadvertently collided with the dawdling Sir Richard Covington-Smith. Ironically, it was the off-balance German who fell to the ground. When the taxi's rear door opened, Sir Richard innocently stepped in and sat down.

"*Schwein!*" Siegfried fumed under his breath as he struggled to get up.

Kevin Meeley saw what had happened, quickly apologized to the battered muscle man and slipped into the back of the purloined taxi alongside his master.

Siegfried sighed in exasperation as the two Englishmen sped away in his taxi. Hugo licked his fingers and chuckled.

"What are you laughing at?" Siegfried grumbled.

"I'm wondering what you will do with England after we conquer it."

"The whole damn country will be a nuclear waste dump," Siegfried replied without emotion.

Hugo didn't laugh because he knew Siegfried wasn't joking. He'd been to England. Beautiful country. It would be a shame to destroy it.

It wasn't long before another cab pulled up. Siegfried sprang up as the driver got out, greeted them and opened the rear doors. Hugo grabbed the seat behind the driver and motioned to Siegfried to join him.

Siegfried bumped his head as he got in. *"Scheist!"* he groaned. The cabby looked back warily as he went to load the luggage into the trunk.

"Sultanahmet," Hugo announced. The yellow taxi was on the way into downtown Istanbul in a flash. Hugo removed a small address book from his suit coat pocket, found the address he needed, grabbed for his cell phone in the other pocket and dialed.

"Reinhardt," Hugo said as the person on the other end picked up. After a few pleasantries, Hugo busily scrawled several things into the address book: "Leslie Connery", "the Ambassador Hotel", "Luci Daniels", and "Osman, her Turkish flunky". *"Danke,"* he said as he tapped the "end" button.

As the taxi raced Sir Richard Covington-Smith and his young assistant to their hotel in Cankurtaran, the older man hung up his cell phone and eyed the scar on the back of his left hand. He smiled sentimentally as he remembered its creation. This self-inflicted wound of his childhood had special significance for him. He had managed to obtain a small vial of bichloroacetic acid from a friend whose father was a physician. The doctor used the noxious liquid to eradicate warts from the feet of his patients. Often times the patient would trade a wart for a scar. Young Sir Richard planned to place one drop on the back of each hand and each foot, duplicating the *stigmata* of Jesus Christ. However, so intense was the pain after one application that he passed out and never dared repeat the process.

He must have been crazy to do such a thing but then again, not really. Sir Richard lay back comfortably and recalled his family lineage. His grandmother was Olive Plantard, the only daughter of Frenchman Claude Plantard and his English wife, Nellie Jones. Olive married Lord John Covington-Smith in 1909, "joining the bloodline of the Christ and the Magdalene to the British minor nobility," Sir Richard never hesitated to declare.

He then replayed the cell phone conversation he had just had with Khalid Muzzhar, whose family Sir Richard had magnanimously helped when the Raj ruled India. The young man had provided several clues as towhere the Lance of Longinus could be. Sir Richard and Kevin Meeley would begin their search tonight.

Aya Sofia, 4:13 p.m.

"So he stole this from the museum?" the policeman asked in English.

"Yes, sir," Albert answered. Albert had just called the curator an hour before and asked to meet with the police at the museum.

The curator nervously spoke in Turkish to the other policeman, explaining that he was aghast at the news. "I had no idea this had happened this morning."

"This Mehmet Yakis, fellow?" the English speaker asked Albert.

"Yes."

"Mehmet Yakis stole this valuable artifact from Aya Sofia this morning?"

"Yes."

"Why didn't you tell the curator or call us at that time?"

"Yakis is a good fellow gone bad. I thought I could track him down and convince him to give it back and not soil his reputation. He'll definitely be expelled from the University."

"Can you describe what he stole?"

"An icon…the Virgin and Child, probably Palaeologan, fourteenth century. Very valuable."

"Do you think he has it with him?"

"Not on him. Too bulky to carry around. He's hiding it. Find him. Let me question him."

The officer's skepticism was obvious. "Why should we call you? We'll notify the curator."

"Certainly but you know I *am* the University's ranking expert on the subject, what with Professor Kemal on his way to Paris and this American, Connery, nowhere to be found. The icon will need to be authenticated: was it the one found this morning? Neither the curator nor his staff have seen it."

The policeman twirled his mustache between his fingers as he stared down Boucher. After a good ten seconds he responded to Albert. "We'll call both of you when we find him."

"I'm available twenty-four hours a day, seven days a week. I'm quite resolved to find this priceless treasure."

"Thank you, Monsieur Boucher."

The policeman turned to the curator and spoke to him in Turkish. The nervous man explained that he had told the other policeman all he knew, which was very little. The policemen said good-bye and left them both.

"This is astounding, Monsieur Boucher!" the curator shrieked. "Why didn't you tell me about this before?"

"Sir, the icon was found at 7:00 a.m. You weren't here. When I returned from taking Professor Kemal to the airport and saw that the icon was gone, I went crazy, lost my mind. I didn't think to call you, sir. I'm sorry."

The curator pulled a handkerchief from his breast pocket and dabbed the sweat from his bald head. He said something in Turkish, which didn't sound good to Albert, and strutted away.

Albert stuck his tongue out at the man as he left. "Fool!" Albert hissed. "If you only knew what was going on in your own museum." He sneered as he walked through the outer narthex and out of the museum. *The police will find Donkeybrain. And if they don't, I will.*

Marmara Hotel, Taksim, 4:28 p.m.

Luci Daniels hung up the phone and grinned at Osman, who sat to her left. Across from her sat Istanbul's chief of police and an official from Ankara. She returned her attention to them and begged their forgiveness.

"Sorry for the interruption, gentlemen."

"Think nothing of it," the two government men responded, almost in unison. Both spoke English well.

"So we have an agreement then?" Luci asked as she extended her hand to them.

The policeman waited for the other man to react first. The man from the capital grinned from ear to ear, nodded his head and answered, "Of course, Ms. Daniels." He gently took her hand and kissed it.

The police chief did the same when the other man had finished. "I shall have my men start tomorrow morning."

"Today," Luci corrected him.

The police chief was not used to taking orders from a woman and his face showed it. He wanted to put her in her place, but then he thought of the fifty thousand dollars in the envelope before him.

"Today," he reassured her.

Luci turned away. It was her way of saying she was done with them. They thanked her again and departed.

"*This* is how we will find the relic, my dear Osman."

"I'm certain we will succeed, madam. By the way, who was on the phone?"

She chuckled. "The curator. It seems that your Frenchman informed the police that Mister Yakis stole a precious icon from the museum, one that was just discovered this morning."

"So the Frenchman is after the Lance of Longinus, too."

"Yes," Luci said as she licked her lips. "He doesn't know it yet but he's working for me."

"And it's not costing you a single lira."

Ambassador Hotel, Sultanahmet, 4:48 p.m.

Sir Richard and Kevin strutted into the hotel and smiled at the pretty desk clerk.

"Good day, gentlemen," she chirped.

"Good day, madam," Sir Richard replied. "We are here to see Mister Khalid Muzzhar."

"Yes," she answered immediately. "He said you would be coming. Room thirty-three."

"Thank you," Sir Richard said as he stepped into the elevator.

"Thank you," Kevin added as he squeezed into the elevator after Sir Richard.

Muzzhar had done his work well. Only an hour before, he had called the hotel and discovered that Leslie Connery was staying there. He didn't hesitate to grab the last room the Ambassador Hotel had available.

"Sir Richard!" the young man cried with joy when he answered the door.

"Khalid, my boy!" Sir Richard replied as he bear-hugged the young man. "So good to see you again!"

"Has it been four years, sir?"

"Five, Khalid. You remember my aide, Kevin Meeley."

"Of course. Hello, Mister Meeley," Khalid said as he offered his hand.

Kevin wordlessly shook the offered hand, smiled and nodded.

"Come in! Come in! I have tea ready!" Khalid announced.

"And milk, I hope," Sir Richard added.

"Most certainly, sir!" Khalid reassured them.

As his guests were seated, Khalid presented the tea and warmed milk.

Sir Richard prepared his beverage and took a sip. "Darjeeling!" he said with delight.

Khalid nodded.

"Well done, my boy!" Sir Richard took another sip and grunted his approval. "So where is this Connery fellow, Khalid?"

"Room forty-one, sir. And he's out. I just checked."

"Well, I'd say we timed that one about right, eh Kevin?"

"Yes, Sir Richard," Kevin replied.

Sir Richard took one last sip of tea and made for the door. "Come along, Kevin."

"Yes, Sir Richard."

"Damned fine Darjeeling, Khalid! You've done your work well, my boy!"

"Thank you, Sir Richard," Khalid replied as his guests hurried out the door and headed for room forty-one.

Hugo Geissler and his son stepped out of their rented black BMW in the alley adjacent the Ambassador Hotel. Siegfried decided he couldn't bear riding in a taxi with *untermenschen*. They stopped at the first opportunity and rented the Beemer. Hugo held a twenty-meter nylon rope in one hand and a tasty *loucum* in the other.

"Fourth floor," he said to Siegfried. "Forty-one, according to Braun," he added as he popped the candy into his mouth.

Siegfried attached the end of the rope to a bolt loaded in his pistol. "Piece of cake." He fired his pistol, and the bolt lodged securely in the eave overhanging the window to room forty-one. He grabbed the nylon rope and gave it a good tug.

"Looks good," Hugo commented unnecessarily.

Siegfried grabbed the rope and swiftly executed the fifty-foot hand-over-hand climb to the window.

"There we go," Sir Richard said as he opened the door and stepped into room forty-one. "Damned handy," he added as he dropped the master key into his pocket. "Khalid comes through again."

"We're looking for a thirty centimeter-long gold casket," Kevin reminded his boss.

"Yes. Yes, must be here somewhere," the Grand Master said as his eyes scanned the room. "Check in the bath, Kevin."

"Yes, sir," Kevin said as he stepped into the bathroom.

Siegfried was now within four feet of the top. As he pulled his massive frame upward effortlessly, he imagined the reception he and his father would receive in Berlin as he presented the Lance of Longinus to the brothers of the Knights of the Holy Lance.

"Damned stuffy in here," Sir Richard growled as he wiped perspiration from his brow. He stepped over to the window and, without paying much attention, threw it open.

Siegfried saw the projectile flying toward him and jerked his head to the side, but the corner of the window clipped him in the temple, jolting him into semi-consciousness. His grip on the rope loosened as his vision went black. Hugo gasped as he saw Siegfried fall backward nearly fifty feet. However, the hood of the BMW broke the young man's fall. On impact, the car's security alarm loudly announced that its integrity had been violated.

"Siegfried!" Hugo screamed as he ran to his badly bruised son.

"Damned city is too loud," Sir Richard grumbled under his breath after the sudden activation of the car alarm below.

The phone rang suddenly, freezing Sir Richard and Kevin in their tracks.

"Pick it up, Kevin," Sir Richard ordered.

"Yes?" Kevin said quietly as he put the phone to his lips.

"Khalid here! Connery is back! You must leave!"

Kevin hung up without answering.

"Connery is back, sir."

"Blast it all, anyway!" Sir Richard hissed as he moved to the door. "We'll try again later, my boy."

Ambassador Hotel, Sultanahmet, 5:03, p.m.

"I'm sorry, Les," Angie said as she dabbed her eyes. "These allergies are killing me."

"Honey, it didn't ruin our evening. Quit apologizing."

"I don't think I've ever been this bad before," she said as she blew her nose.

"Your eyes are really red. They look like roadmaps!"

"My head feels like somebody is trying to break out of it." Angie lay on the bed and sighed.

"I'm glad you finally gave in and took something. Is it working yet?"

"It's working great: I'm ready to go to sleep!" Angie sneezed three times in a row.

"Bless you."

Les sat on the edge of the bed and kissed her forehead. "Afrin?"

"No! That stuff kills me." Angie slowly sat up. "Oh, this is great!"

"What?"

"Could—you—get—my--" she wheezed. Her words came out only with great effort.

Les sprang up and grabbed her albuterol inhaler. "Your asthma has *never* been this bad," he noted as he tossed her the inhaler.

She hurriedly took four deep inhalations—as deep as her afflicted lungs would let her--and waited impatiently for the medicine to work.

"Let me take you to the hospital."

Her wheezing was unabated.

"No! Les, I'm okay!"

"The hell you are! Did you bring any prednisone?"

"Yes, but I'm not going to use that stuff! I only brought it because you made me!"

"This might be the first time you really need it."

"No, I'm fine, really."

"I can hear you wheezing from here, Angie!"

The phone rang and grabbed Les's attention. Angie saw this and scooted into the bathroom and closed the door.

"I'm not through with you!" Les growled as he picked up the phone. "Yes?"

"Doctor Connery?"

"Yes."

"It's the front desk, sir. There's a Doctor Yakis here to see you. Shall I send him up?"

Must be a Turkish neurologist who's coming to the conference. "Yes, thank you."

Mehmet waited eagerly for the clerk.

"Doctor Connery will see you. He's in room forty-one."

"Thank you," Mehmet said as he ran up the stairs.

Albert Boucher had decided to return to the Ambassador Hotel, more out of impatience than anything else. He had to be actively looking for the Lance; he couldn't wait for the police. As he walked into the lobby he gasped as he saw Mehmet run up the stairs.

"*Zut alors!*" he hissed to himself.

He turned away quickly so Mehmet wouldn't see him. When all was clear he walked to the lobby telephone. He picked up the receiver but then replaced it. He reviewed the scenario in his mind again. Undoubtedly Mehmet had used a ruse to get past the desk clerk. A second one would be easily discovered. Let the police take him to the station. He would "visit" him and extract the location of the Lance from him with a promise of "explaining the whole misunderstanding" once he had retrieved it. Albert lifted the receiver from the cradle and dialed the police. "Inspector Gur, please." That much he could manage in Turkish.

Les was confused when he found Mehmet in front of him. "Hey buddy, I offered you a tip when you were here last time—"

"No sir!" Mehmet pleaded. He raised his hands. "That's not it at all, sir."

"Well, what is it?" Les growled.

"Have you looked at it yet?"

"What?"

"What I brought you earlier today,"

"The disc? I suppose I should. My talk is early tomorrow--"

"Disc? No, you don't understand, Doctor Connery!"

Les glared back. "What's this all about?"

"Doctor, my name is Mehmet Yakis. I am a student at the University of Istanbul. This morning a great archaeological treasure was found at Aya Sofia."

"So what does that have to do with me?"

Mehmet was stunned. "Doctor Connery, Doctor Kemal said that you were an expert in the field and--"

"Expert? I don't know what you're trying to pull here, but I'm just about ready to call the front desk!"

"No! No, please! Please, Doctor Connery, you must listen to me!"

"What's up?" Angie emerged from the bathroom, wheezing but a bit less than before.

"This young man is about to be thrown out of this hotel!" Les snarled.

"No, please!" Mehmet begged. "This matter is of the utmost importance! Please let me speak with you!"

"No!" Les roared.

"Let's hear him out, honey," Angie said to Les. "Won't you come in, Mister--?"

"Yakis. Thank you, madam. Mehmet Yakis," he answered.

"Please," Angie said, showing him a chair. She and Les sat on one of the beds.

"May I see the package?" Mehmet asked Les.

Les sprang up to respond in the negative, but before he could speak, Angie answered, "Yes." Then she turned to her husband. "Could you get it for the young man?"

Les tried to figure out what his wife was thinking as he walked over to the desk and found the cotton sack and its contents. He eyed Mehmet suspiciously before turning it over to him.

Mehmet smiled as he held the casket again. He pulled back the cotton sack and revealed the brilliant reliquary.

"That's *not* a disc!" Les barked, pointing at the reliquary as if he had been cheated.

The pieces were falling together for Mehmet. "You are not an archaeologist, Doctor Connery?"

Angie burst out laughing.

"Archaeologist? I'm a neurologist! You know, a *real* doctor! What's this all about?"

Mehmet's face showed that he was confused. *Who was Kemal talking about?*

Angie was still in stitches. "Oh, this is great!" She laughed more as Les glared at her.

"I'm glad you get it because I sure don't!" Les snapped at her.

Angie finally contained herself. "Les, honey," she began. "Les, do you remember when we arrived this morning? The desk clerk told us that there was *another* Doctor Connery staying at the hotel."

"Another Doctor Connery?" Mehmet asked.

Les replied excitedly, "Yes, that's right!" Then he started to chuckle.

"You gave this to the wrong Doctor Connery!" Angie laughed. "What do you think the odds would be on that?"

"Couple thousand to one!" Les laughed.

Mehmet's face grew pale.

"Are you all right?" Angie asked him.

Mehmet handed her the reliquary. "This is probably one of the most important archaeological finds of the last century. And now it's in great danger."

"What do you mean?" Angie asked as she opened the casket and gently lifted the Lance out.

Mehmet told them about the morning's events as succinctly as he could.

Angie carefully handed the Lance to Les.

"First century, you say?" Les asked as he cradled the Lance cautiously in his hands.

"Yes," Mehmet answered.

"You said it was in danger," Angie said as Les delivered it gingerly to her.

"There is a rich American woman, Lucille Daniels, who will stop at nothing to have it. She acquires artifacts like trinkets."

"What's wrong with that?" Les asked.

"That is the property of the Turkish people!" Mehmet objected.

Angie took note of the inscription on the Lance. "How's your Latin, Les?"

"Pretty skinny. It's been more than twelve years," Les replied.

"'The Lance of Longinus...'" Angie began.

"There is more on the other side," Mehmet interjected.

"'...which pierced our Lord's side.' Hmmmm. A relic."

"Ooooo! Sounds spooky!" Les teased.

Angie set down the Lance and found the ancient papyrus at the bottom of the reliquary. "What's this?" she asked as she gently unfolded it.

"I don't know," Mehmet replied. "I found it in there with the Lance." The Frenchmen had not revealed its secrets to him.

Angie read the papyrus to herself. "Les, come over here."

"What is it?" Les asked as he walked over to her. He noticed something different about his wife. "Angie, did you take something extra when you were in the bathroom?"

"What? For my allergies? No. Why?"

"You eyes...they're clear. And you're not wheezing," her husband said aghast.

Angie paused and took a deep breath. "Hey, I feel great!"

"Albuterol finally kicked in," Les concluded.

"No. No, it feels different somehow," she began. "Usually I feel a little better and I know that after one or two more doses, I'll be good. But now I feel like I've never had asthma in my life. And my allergies...it's like someone vacuumed all of the pollen out of the air."

"It's about time all that stuff kicked in," Les grumbled. "I'm glad you're better, sweetheart."

"Madam," Mehmet began courteously, "the papyrus?"

"Yes, of course." Angie turned to Les. "I think you might find this a little more interesting," she said as she lifted the papyrus off her lap. "It looks like the record of an execution...."

"Execution?" Les and Mehmet asked in unison.

"And not just any execution," she smiled. "'Jesus from Nazareth... executed by crucifixion...the seventh of *Aprilis*'--that's April 7—'in the seventeenth year of His Divine Majesty Tiberius Caesar.'"

"Straight from the cubicle of some medieval monk," Les snorted.

"You're saying this is a forgery?" Angie asked.

"Like a three-dollar bill." Les smiled obnoxiously.

"Doctor Connery," Mehmet said. "If I may interject something important...."

Les rolled his eyes. "Sure, why not?"

"Papyrus use in Europe fell off in the fourth century. By then, most people were using parchment or vellum. Besides, papyrus came from Egypt or Syria. In the seventh century, the forces of Islam conquered these lands. It would be very unlikely that a European monk could have obtained any after then." Mehmet smiled modestly at Les.

"That doesn't prove that it's genuine!" Les fumed. "I still say it's a--"

"Hey, listen to this," Angie interrupted. "The next sentence is very intriguing. 'The body disappeared soon after burial, despite the posting of a guard--'"

"You're not buying this are you, Angie?" Les came to within six inches of Angie's face. "It's bogus," he added deliberately.

"I'm not saying it's authentic," she replied.

"Doctor Connery," Mehmet interjected. "If I may submit an analysis of my own...."

"No!" Les growled.

"Les! Quit being such a twit!" Angie said. "Go ahead, Mister Yakis."

"Please, call me Mehmet," the young man said.

"Okay, Mehmet." Angie was warming up to him. "What do you say?"

"First, I believe I have heard this story before, but I feel I can be very objective about the relic," Mehmet began.

Les drew a breath to sling a terse retort at the young man, but his wife elbowed him in the ribs.

"You see, I am Muslim, so I have no preconceived idea, or hope, that this is real. If anything, I would be hoping that it is fraudulent. We Muslims reject that Jesus was crucified. And I am also a student, one who wants to dedicate his life to archaeology."

Les bit his lip incredulously.

"A good archaeologist must be objective," Mehmet continued.

"Yes, that's probably true," Angie encouraged him.

"Well, given the circumstances of the reliquary's discovery, the fact that the Lance probably dates from the first century and is Roman; and the execution record is written on papyrus, in a very dry way, like in a newspaper…."

"What's your point, Junior?" Les cringed as his wife's elbow crashed into his chest.

"The spear is from the first century, and the papyrus probably is too. I believe it *could* very well have pierced Jesus' side at his crucifixion, and this papyrus is a record of his execution. Again, I remind you, as a Muslim--"

"So how did it end up in Aya Sofia?" Les interrupted indelicately.

"If the man who stabbed Jesus with the spear joined the followers of Jesus after the crucifixion, he could have kept it and passed it on to others. Such an important piece of history would eventually find its way into the hands of the Christian Church."

"And the papyrus?" Angie asked.

"This Longinus was a Roman soldier, maybe even an officer. He could have stolen the record."

"Steal a Roman document?" Les growled.

"As far as the Romans were concerned, it was an execution record for a common criminal. The Roman commander may even have *given* it to Longinus. After all, the blood that sprayed from the wound Longinus had inflicted cured him. His commander wouldn't have cared about it. Jesus was just another criminal." Mehmet smiled when he had finished. He felt he had presented his case well.

Angie smiled at Les. "I think our friend here may be right.""Don't tell me—"

"Think about it Les. In the Gospel of John, the author describes that what happened after Jesus was stabbed in the chest as a flow of blood *and* water."

"Water?" Mehmet asked.

Angie turned to Mehmet. "You said *blood* from the wound in Jesus' side. But the Gospel of John says *blood and water.*"

"I still don't understand," Mehmet added.

"Crucifixion puts a huge strain on the heart, leading to heart failure, or possibly heart rupture. With severe heart failure, fluid accumulates in the pleural sac that surrounds each lung and can even fill the pericardium, the sac that surrounds the heart. This clear fluid would have been released as the pleural or pericardial sac was pierced. The blood would have been from the lung and skin tissue. If the heart were pierced, that would be another source of blood. This combination of 'blood and water' flowed out of the dead man's chest and landed on Longinus."

"Couldn't the author have known about fluid accumulating outside of the heart or lungs and cause this 'blood and water' and fabricate the story?" Mehmet wondered.

"Unlikely," Angie answered. Then she turned to her husband. She smiled because Les was losing the debate and he was going to make her final point. "Tell him why, Les."

"William Harvey didn't describe the circulatory system until the seventeenth century," Les answered begrudgingly.

"Although some Arab physicians may have known about it earlier," Angie interjected. "However, that still would have been at least a millennium after Jesus' death. And the pathophysiology behind heart failure wasn't discovered for centuries after Harvey."

"But that doesn't prove this thing is real!" Les shot back. "I still say—"

A knock at the door interrupted Les. "Doctor Connery," a voice behind the door said. "This is Inspector Gur of the Istanbul Police. Please open the door."

CHAPTER SEVEN

"They are after the Lance!" Mehmet whispered

"Please wait," Angie answered the policeman as she hurriedly returned the papyrus and lancea to the reliquary. "I'll be right there."

"You must not give it to them!" Mehmet pleaded.

"You listen here, Mister Whatever-Your-Name-Is--" Les hissed.

"Les," Angie interrupted, raising her sleek dark fingers against her husband's lips. "I believe him."

Les wanted to argue, but the look in his wife's eyes advised against it. "You're willing to let him draw us into this?" he asked nervously. "We could get in big trouble!"

"There's something about this—" Angie began as she slid the casket back into the white cotton sack.

"You're willing to let this gold box get--"

"Les, this 'gold box' is bigger than you and me."

"It's a forgery!"

"Look at my eyes! And listen to my breathing; I've never felt this good! That 'gold box'--"

"For crying out loud, Angie! You're a doctor! You sound like Oral Roberts!"

"Doctor Connery," Inspector Gur's voice boomed calmly through the door. "If you don't open this door I will have my men break it down. Now, please open the door."

"You must open the door," Mehmet said soberly. "I've looked around the room. There is no way out."

"But what about that--" Angie was interrupted by the sound of the

94

doorknob turning. She turned around to see her husband's hand pull the door open. "Les!" she screeched.

"Doctor Connery?" Inspector Gur asked when he saw the lanky redheaded American man.

"Yes, Inspector?"

The policeman extended his hand and greeted Les. "Welcome to Turkey, Doctor Connery. I'm sorry that this young man has involved you in this matter. Stealing the property of the Turkish government is a serious crime."

Les did not reply. He looked back at Angie. His face showed that he regretted his decision to open the door.

Gur turned to Mehmet. "Mister Yakis," he demanded, "you will come with me."

One of Gur's men slapped on the handcuffs and led the compliant student away.

"This isn't right!" Angie protested. "He didn't do anything wrong!"

"I wish that were true, madam," Gur said. "Who knows what other treasures this young fellow has taken from us? Speaking of which…"

Gur gently grabbed the reliquary. "I shall have to take this with me."

Angie felt her bronchial tubes constrict as Gur slowly pulled the casket out of her hands. "No!" she begged with a slight wheeze.

"Thank you for your cooperation, Doctor Connery," Gur said to Les as he shook his hand and quickly departed.

Angie's eyes begged for an explanation from Les. She wanted to speak but couldn't; she didn't need to: her eyes showed her disbelief and disappointment.

"Angie--" Les started to explain.

Angie ran to the bathroom and found the albuterol and took four big inhalations. She sneezed two or three times between the second and third puffs. "Les!" she cried, once she had enough breath to do so. "How could you do that?"

Les was amazed by his wife's sudden deterioration. He could see that her eyes were red again. The wheezing was back, and worse than before. "Let me get the prednisone," he offered. He found the medicine in his shaving kit and handed her two tablets. Angie reached for a glass but the huge doses of albuterol made her hand shake too much to grab it. Les saw this and completed the task for her. Once she had taken the prednisone, Angie took two deep breaths and walked past Les without saying a word.

"Honey," Les said. "There was nothing else I could've done."

Angie, now wheezing heavily as she stared out the window, refused to look at her husband. "We've got to help him." The wheezing was starting to make speech difficult. "Who?"

"Mehmet."

"What?"

"And we've got to get the Lance too."

"Now wait a minute. I can see getting What's-His-Name out of trouble: seems like a good guy. But I'm not about to steal an artifact from the Turkish government!"

"Then I'll have to do it myself," Angie said breathlessly as she turned around and confronted her husband.

"Angie! You're crazy! That *medieval jewelry case* has triggered a schizophrenic break from reality! I wish I had brought some haloperidol!" Les shook his head after he mentioned the anti-psychotic medicine. "Never thought I'd be using it on my wife!"

As Angie walked to the door Les stepped in her way.

"Move, Les," she wheezed.

"Angie, you won't even make it out of the hotel! You're sounding real bad again! I'm going to have the front desk call an ambulance!"

Angie gently pushed Les out of the way and reached for the doorknob. Les's hand got there first and held the door closed.

"You know better than to try to stop me," Angie warned gravely.

"Judging by your wheezing," Les retorted, "I won't have to do much!"

Angie turned to Les. The dark brilliance of her eyes--deep, dark umber--melted him. "I'm *going* to do this."

Les knew his wife well. She always did what she said she would. He called it stubbornness; she called it determination. "You can't do it by yourself," he said softly.

She smiled at him. The look in his eyes confirmed his capitulation.

"Someone's got to carry your inhaler," he quipped.

"Yeah, that's right." She kissed him fully on his lips. "Let's go," Angie added with determination.

Albert beamed when he saw the two policemen and Gur lead Mehmet down the stairs. When the men reached the bottom of the stairs, Albert hurried forward and presented himself to Inspector Gur. Mehmet glared at the Frenchman.

"I see you've got him. Very good, Inspector," Albert interjected officiously.

"Mister Boucher," Gur said as he shook Albert's hand. "Thank you for your help. I don't know if we could have found him without you. Thank you. We owe you a lot."

"Whatever service I can offer. I *would* like to question him." Albert grabbed Mehmet's arm.

"Not at this time, I'm afraid," Gur replied.

"You assured me that I would be able to question him," Albert retorted with increased inflection.

"There are a few things we must do first," Gur said. Albert's insistence grew annoying.

"Then I trust I'll be able to question him at police headquarters." Albert refused to release his grip on Mehmet's arm. "As the representative of the museum…to find the icon…."

Gur's exasperation bled through his politeness. He jerked Albert's hand away from Mehmet. "Later, Mister Boucher. Much later. Perhaps tomorrow."

Tomorrow?

The police left the hotel and Albert followed at a distance. As one of the policeman put Mehmet into the car, Gur slid the reliquary out of the cotton bag and quickly eyed it before returning it.

Albert saw this and shuddered. *Merde! They've got it!*

Angie and Les ran out of the hotel, just in time to see the police drive away.

"What now?" Les asked Angie.

"We'll never get it back!" Angie sighed.

"Doctor Connery?" a voice behind them said. It was the desk clerk. "Is something the matter?"

"No," Les snapped back. "Everything's just peachy. Just fine."

"Good. Don't hesitate to call us if you need anything," she said as she walked back into the hotel.

"Sure. Thank you."

Albert's mind whirred as he overheard the exchange. *Doctor Connery? Mehmet! The Lance!* The entire imbroglio suddenly began to unravel itself at his feet. *A second Doctor Connery, one moronic Donkeybrain and now the police!* He wasn't counting on the police finding the Lance. *How did it get here? Donkeybrain didn't have it with him when I saw him in the lobby. Did the Americans have it? How did they get it? They know something. She said, "We'll never get it back." Who else knew about it?* Whatever the answers were, the police had the Lance of Longinus now, and Albert feared he would never get it back, at least not by himself.

Sirkeci, 7:00 p.m.

Angie and Les watched the black Mercedes sedan pull up in front of the police station across the street from Café Bosphorus. They had carefully reconnoitered the station for the last ten minutes from behind the menus they held in their hands. The Americans had with them only what they could carry in their pockets: wallets, money, credit cards, passports and little else. They wouldn't risk returning to the hotel once they'd taken the Lance.

Osman stepped out of one of the sedan's back doors and ran around to open the other. Luci stepped out and wrapped a black jacket around her shoulders. The chauffeur drove the car a few blocks down the street and found a place to park.

"I'll bet she's the one," Angie said.

"How do you know that?" Les snorted.

"Call it a hunch, intuition, whatever."

Osman held the door for her as Luci entered the station.

"So now we wait?" Les asked.

"It won't be long. She sounds like the kind that doesn't like to wait any longer than she has to."

Les sipped his coffee, which had gone cold ten minutes ago. "I'm sorry."

"Sorry?" Angie's eyes didn't leave the police station door.

"All that garbage I gave you back at the hotel…the Oral Roberts crack."

"Apology accepted." Her tone and choice of words showed that she was still mad at him. Angie looked at her watch. "Okay, this is where we go to work," Angie said as she took a couple puffs of albuterol. "Do you remember what you're supposed to do?"

"Wait on the south side of the police station, catch the package when you throw it to me and meet you at the bakery where we got the baklava." Les kept telling himself this whole thing was absolute craziness, but he dared not desert Angie.

"Great. Now let's go," she commanded resolutely.

Angie set a few million lira on the table and walked to the north end of the police station as Les walked to his post.

"Don't you see her?" Sir Richard asked as he poked his head around the corner of the building. "The Negress."

At three o'clock that afternoon, Khalid Muzzhar had taken a photograph of Angie while surveilling her. Later he gave it to the Grand Master, who, with Kevin, had been following Osman for the last hour. Finding Doctor Connery's wife in the same area was quite a stroke of luck.

"Yes, sir," Kevin answered dutifully.

"Let's get into position," Covington-Smith commanded. "Bring the Rolls around to the end of that street." The Templars, too, had grown weary of Turkish taxis.

"Yes, sir."

"*Schwarze!*" Siegfried announced. His genetically-engineered body had recovered rapidly from a fall that would have killed most. His investigation had led to his identifying Doctor Connery that afternoon. On learning the identity of his wife, the Aryan Adonis appeared almost joyful as he looked across the street with his binoculars. Killing her would be a delight.

"Let me see," Hugo ordered as he set down his Turkish coffee. "So Connery's wife is a black woman," he said as he saw Angie leave the table.

"Well, this gets more interesting every moment. Come, Siegfried," Hugo added as he stood up, threw a few bills on the café table and stepped into the newly rented red Audi across the street.

"Inspector Gur," Luci smiled as she sat in the most comfortable chair in Gur's bare-bones office. "You do such fine work. And so quickly."

"It is my pleasure, madam. The Frenchman's tip was very helpful."

"May I have it?"

"Yes, of course," Gur replied as he stepped back to the wall safe behind him and opened it. He reached into the safe and fetched the cotton pouch. He quickly opened the bag, just enough to see the casket, and handed it to Luci. "Here you are, madam."

Luci's eyes widened as she held he latest acquisition. "This is so exciting!" she said as she took a couple of deep breaths. Luci set her prize on her lap and pulled back the cotton bag. She gasped as she saw the gold reliquary. "It's beautiful!" Luci slowly move her hands over the surface and expectantly opened the golden casket. She gulped when the overhead light illuminated the lancea's surface. "You're gorgeous!" Luci praised her new prize. She ran her fingers over the relic's surface and gave a sensual smile.

"May I?" Osman asked as he extended his hand.

Luci begrudgingly allowed Osman's wish, but just seconds after he touched the relic, she pulled the reliquary away and slammed it shut. "Call for the car, Osman. We'll be leaving now, Inspector Gur," Luci announced as she abruptly stood up. "Your chief of police, Mister Calik, will be seeing to your reward."

"Thank you, madam," Gur said as he stood.

"I'd like you to have a little something extra," Luci said as she pressed five one hundred-dollar bills into his hand. "In case I am in need of your services later."

"Yes, madam," Gur said enthusiastically. "Certainly!"

"Inspector," Osman asked, "What's to become of young Yakis?"

"My orders are to send him to Ankara. He may be involved in other such thefts."

Luci was glad to hear that her orders were being followed to the letter.

Angie waited, poised, one block north of the police station. She sneezed and rubbed her scratchy eyes. Her bronchial tubes wheezed with each exhalation. Angie closed her eyes briefly and concentrated. She knew that her timing would have to be perfect. The temperature had fallen with the arrival of darkness in the past few minutes and she could feel her muscles tighten. She sprinted in place for a few minutes to warm them up. It had always helped before when she ran track.

Angie's thoughts drifted to an unseasonably cold night in San Francisco sixteen years ago. By an amazing streak of luck (she thought) she had made the finals in the four hundred meters, beating out two favorites. She waited impatiently for the race to begin. It was so cold. She just wanted it to be over, but Angie felt something inside her telling her that this race was going to be like no other; and she would win. About forty-seven seconds later her victory took everyone by surprise. Angie learned something about herself that night that she never forgot. And whenever life got impossible, she remembered that night. More often than not, triumph ensued.

Angie felt that same feeling now. This was going to go right. They were going to get the Lance of Longinus back, but she couldn't say why. Her rewards when she ran track were medals and recognition. Tonight, she didn't know what the prize would be. In fact, she knew that retrieving the relic would only lead both Les and her deeper into trouble. Yet, something drove her forward. She wrinkled her forehead as she contemplated her predicament. It was as if the Lance were calling to her to save it.

Luci Daniels suddenly stepped through the door that Osman held open for her and exited the east side of the police station.

"Go!" Angie said out loud as she sprinted her hardest toward Luci.

Luci cradled the reliquary in her arms as she stood waiting for the chauffeur to bring the Mercedes around. He wasn't far away so Luci stepped toward the street.

Angie was within thirty feet when Osman stepped forward to open the door of the approaching Mercedes.

"Thank you, Osman," Luci said.

Fifteen feet.

Luci stopped and turned as she heard Angie running toward her. Osman heard her too but didn't think to react.

Six feet.

Angie's intent was obvious now. Luci threw her left arm out in front of her to push Angie away, but the taller woman stiff-armed Luci in the chest with her right arm and reached forward and wrestled the casket away with her left. Luci screamed as she fell to the sidewalk. Osman ran to her.

"Are you all right, madam?" he asked.

"Get her!" she shrieked.

Osman immediately complied. The tall black woman had a good head start, but he had to catch her. Probably some poor African just off the boat from Senegal, or some such place, who turned to purse-snatching to feed herself. She certainly had chosen the wrong person to rob.

"The black one has taken the casket from Daniels," Siegfried announced.

"Reinhardt's intelligence has been superb," Hugo smiled. "Let's get into position to intercept her."

"The African woman is running down the street with something she took from the rich woman with the Mercedes," Kevin said. "The tall Turkish fellow is chasing her."

"We'll need to stop her. Interrogate her," Sir Richard added. "Do you have the crossbow?"

"Yes, sir," Kevin replied. "Loaded with enough tranquilizer to stop a charging rhino."

"Very good."

One block south of the police station Les was in position. He heard Angie coming and readied himself.

"Go, Les!" Angie said as she tossed him the reliquary.

It thumped into Les's chest. A little heavier than he expected, but it *was* made of gold. Les ran as fast as he could for a block and then turned south. He slowed down as he took the corner and started walking, as inconspicuously as possible, back to the bakery they had visited that afternoon.

Angie turned west two blocks after she made the drop. She was surprised to see Osman a block behind her and closing fast. She turned north into an alley and then west again without looking back. At the end of the alley she turned north again into a street lined with empty bazaar booths. Angie looked back and didn't see anything, but her pursuer could be hiding among the booths. *I'm not taking any chances.* She accelerated toward the middle of the empty street.

Before Angie had moved two feet, Osman sprang forward from between two booths and tackled her. Angie winced as her shoulder slammed into the pavement. Osman quickly turned Angie on to her back and placed his knee on her chest.

"Give it back!" he demanded.

Angie didn't understand his Turkish but knew exactly what he wanted. She mumbled something back to him, as if she were going to cooperate.

Osman leaned forward and asked her to repeat herself.

Angie recognized her opportunity immediately. She introduced his left jaw to a vicious right cross that sent the big man to the pavement. Angie didn't wait for him to move, although he wouldn't for the next several minutes. She pushed his stone-still body away, jumped up and ran onward.

Siegfried, leapt out of the parked Audi when he saw Angie run by twenty-five meters ahead.

"Bring me the Lance of Destiny, my son!" Hugo Geissler yelled out the window.

Angie was wheezing heavily by this time so she stopped to use her inhaler. She took two puffs, unaware that the nearly invisible black-garbed SS man was racing toward her from behind.

"Got her!" Sir Richard whispered as he looked through the crossbow's telescopic sight and zeroed-in on Angie's chest. Sir Richard drew a deep breath and squeezed the trigger, launching the tranquilizer dart toward Angie.

Angie precipitously sprinted forward in the direction of the bakery and Les, only minutes away. Siegfried silently sped forward, just missing her. As he reached his right arm out toward Angie, Siegfried felt a sharp sting in his chest. He winced quietly as his strength left his body. He fell to his knees and then flat on his face. The look on his face confirmed that he had abruptly tumbled into mindless oblivion.

"Damn! I missed!" Sir Richard grumbled as Angie sped away. "Back to the car, Kevin! We may get another opportunity yet!" Sir Richard bellowed as the Templars jettisoned any compunction for stealth and trotted noisily back to the Rolls.

However, the whole scene had not gone unnoticed. Hugo Geissler had followed Siegfried, although from a distance, and had observed his son's fate. He caught a glimpse of Sir Richard as the Englishman looked over his shoulder at the sprinting American.

"Damn!" Hugo cursed under his breath.

The task of obtaining the Lance of Destiny just became a bit more complicated.

Les had to admit that he felt a certain exhilaration from the whole affair. He held the casket tightly with his right arm and thought of all those James Bond movies he'd watched, the ones with Sean Connery, his namesake.

"Bond, James Bond," Les said to himself.

Les sighed as he thought of all the years that had transpired since *Doctor No* was released. Sean Connery was now old enough to play Bond's grandfather. For some bizarre reason his thoughts of the venerable Connery gave birth to images of a flabby middle-ager waddling the morning away on a treadmill or a stationary bike or (*God forbid*, he cringed) a Stairmaster. *I don't know which is more ridiculous, seeing your body grow old, each part gradually losing its ability and its appeal or pathetically laboring* (the image of the Stairmaster again) *to hold on to what you've got, although this was just postponing the inevitable.*

He took the next two lefts and arrived at the front of the bakery. There was no sign of Angie. *She'll make it. No doubt in my mind. She'll be here.*

Sirkeci, 7:09 p.m.

Osman's jaw ached into his left ear. He rolled his head on the uneven pavement as he struggled to remember what had happened to him. He sat up and gingerly touched his left hand to his jaw.

"Ohhh! That hurts!"

That black she-devil had gotten him good. Osman stood, fought off the momentary vertigo, and slowly looked around. He heard someone snoring a few yards away. *Too much raki.* Osman knew that his employer would not be happy with him, especially since he had no idea where the thief had gone. Maybe he could delay his reunion with Luci Daniels. A café would still be open. Maybe some Turkish coffee. The headlights that suddenly turned onto the street were too familiar. No Turkish coffee tonight but a cup of wrath was certainly coming his way. As the black Mercedes pulled toward him and stopped, he saw the back door open. Luci jumped out and ran to him.

"Do you have it?"

"No, madam."

"Well where the hell is it?" Luci asked, her jaw clenched tightly.

"I have no idea. The woman got away."

"Get in the car."

Luci led the way and grabbed her cell phone from her jacket pocket once she was seated. She dialed in a number and closed the door. "Back to Hotel Marmara," Luci ordered the driver. "Chief Calik?" Luci said into the phone. "How did I get your home number? Why, you gave it to me when I paid you your fee…I knew you'd remember…I'm not very well at this moment…I was robbed just outside your police station in Sirkeci… Yes, the thief got the relic…I'm certain your men will find it…You may want to confer with Inspector Gur. I'm going to call him next so wait a few minutes…Good night."

Osman gently touched his left jaw and winced as Luci ended her call.

"This, my dear Osman, is how we make effective use of the local constabulary," Luci sneered at Osman.

"Yes, madam," Osman replied obsequiously.

Luci dialed another number on the phone and looked out the window at three drunken tourists stumbling out of a restaurant. "Inspector Gur? Luci Daniels…Not well at all, sir. I was just robbed outside your station… the thief has the Lance. I've informed Chief Calik…A tall black woman… Yes, a black woman…Oh, really?"

Luci's tone stirred Osman. The look in her eyes told him she was on to something.

"Thank you, Inspector. I'm sure your men will get right on it…

Good night." Luci pressed "end" on her cell and addressed her chauffeur, "Ambassador Hotel."

"Ambassador Hotel?" Osman asked.

"Yes. Inspector Gur recalled that Doctor Connery's wife is a tall black woman. They were reluctant to cooperate with him."

"You think she stole the Lance from you?"

"It's the only lead we have."

"Siegfried!" Hugo Geissler hissed as he shook the massive Nazi's dozing body. "Wake up!" He was spending valuable minutes trying to revive his son but Hugo knew that he could not seize the relic without him. He thought again of the Englishman's face. Were it not for these interlopers, the Lance of Destiny would be his!

"Angie!" Les said as he saw his wife sprinting toward him. "Baby it's good to see you!" Les kissed his wife and then held her tight. He looked behind her: not a soul in sight.

"Do you have it?" Angie asked. She was wheezing again.

"You bet!" Les pulled up his jacket and revealed the reliquary. Angie quickly grasped it and peeled back the cotton covering. Her fingers tingled as she touched the gold and her lungs shouted their pleasure. *Air! Air!*

"Are you okay?"

"We've got to get out of here!"

"What about the conference!"

One look was all it took for Angie to convey her umbrage.

"Right. Screw the conference."

"Ready?"

"Yeah, I guess so."

Angie flew down the street with Les right behind her. She cradled the casket like a football and was ready to flatten anyone who got in her way. Suddenly, they heard brakes screeching a few blocks away. As they rushed through the intersection they could see the blue police lights in the distance.

"They're at the hotel!" Angie gasped.

"What's next?" Les asked. His tone showed his undiminished faith in his wife. No more complaining. He was with her, all the way.

"The easy part's over. Now the hard part."

"Mehmet?"

Angie stopped and turned toward Les. "You up to this?"

"Are you?"

"Come *this* far."

"So how are we going to get him out of there? I've never planned a jailbreak before."

"And I have?"

"I thought you were keeping it from me."

"Yeah, right." She could tell he was joking.

Les sighed and added, "Getting into that police station is going to be next to impossible: an African woman and a man that looks as Turkish as…."

"A leprechaun?"

"You're so sensitive."

Angie uncovered the casket and held it up to a nearby street lamp. She thought of all the hard work that went in to making it as she admired its beauty. Then she turned to her husband. "Did you say something, Les?"

"No."

Angie looked over her shoulder. "Did you hear that?"

"Hear what?"

"I'm hearing something."

Les looked around. "There's no one else here, Ange."

"There it is again!"

"What is it?"

"Sounds like 'forty-four'."

"Forty-four? What's that? The winning number in the Turkish Lotto?"

"Shhhh! There it is again! 'Forty-four.'"

"I knew I should have brought the haloperidol."

"Hush! Let's walk back to the police station."

"Angie? Have you lost it completely?"

Angie thrust the reliquary into his chest and growled, "Knock it off, Les!"

Les grabbed it to push it back. "Don't do that!"

As Les pushed the casket toward Angie he stopped. He lifted the reliquary up toward his ear. "Did you just say forty-four again?"

"No…but you were touching the casket just now."

"Power of suggestion."

Les handed the reliquary back to Angie. When she touched the casket again she reacted immediately. "'Forty-four, southwest corner!'"

"What?"

"I think this thing is telling us where to go!"

"Since when do inanimate objects communicate with people?"

"Maybe it's something inside the reliquary: the Lance, or the papyrus… or something else." Angie's mouth went dry with her last words.

"Well, whatever it is we don't have much time," Les announced as he looked at his watch.

"Southwest corner, cell forty-four."

"Got it."

CHAPTER EIGHT

Police Station, Sirkeci, 7:16 p.m.

Les and Angie surreptitiously crept up to the southwest corner of the station from the poorly lit west side. They analyzed the brick exterior.

"It's crumbling!" Angie whispered.

Les ran his hand over the bricks and felt the mortar crumble as he did so. He looked at Angie and grinned. Les firmly rubbed both hands over the wall this time and the wall began to disintegrate, piece by tiny piece. Angie set down the casket and joined her husband. Soon loose bricks tumbled one by one from the wall, Angie and Les being careful to catch them before they crashed to the ground and alerted the police. Within minutes Les saw wall insulation and pulled it away vigorously. Now he was down to the drywall. He punched at it twice without result. He shook his hand in pain after his second attempt.

"Let me try," Angie said as she stepped forward. Angie analyzed the wall for a minute and then slammed her foot through the drywall.

Commotion erupted on the other side of the wall. Someone was tearing away at the drywall furiously. Les stepped in and helped Angie pull away more insulation.

"Doctor Connery?" asked the voice on the other side of the wall.

"Mehmet?"

Soon Mehmet had torn away enough drywall to see both of their faces. "May Allah be praised!" Mehmet cried.

"Shhh! Save the praising for later!" Les hissed.

"You'll need to clear away enough drywall to squeeze through," Angie said. "We'll work on the bricks."

It wasn't long before Mehmet was out.

"Let's go!" Angie whispered as she scooped up the casket and bolted.

Les and Mehmet were right behind her.

Sirkeci, 7:28 p.m.

"So what do we do now?" Les asked.

They were now a quarter of a mile away from the police station.

"Mehmet?" Angie asked.

"If we return it to the museum, that woman will have it," Mehmet replied. "And she has bought the police."

"And who knows how many other government officials," Les chimed in.

"Can we take it out of the city?" Angie asked.

"It will be difficult," Mehmet answered. "The train stations and airports will be guarded."

"We may have no choice," Les added.

"Perhaps there is a safe place in the city," Mehmet wondered.

"Like?" Angie asked.

"A church," Mehmet suggested.

"In Turkey?" Les asked. "I thought this was a Muslim country."

"It is, but before the city was taken by the Turks in the fifteenth century, Aya Sofia was the seat of the Patriarch of the Greek Orthodox Church," Mehmet answered. "The smaller Church of Saint George serves that purpose today."

"How many Greek Orthodox are there in Turkey?" Angie asked.

"There were over a million before Greece and Turkey went to war in 1922. When the war ended in 1924, 350,000 Turks from Macedonia were sent to Turkey and almost all of the Greeks in Turkey were shipped to Greece. Now there are very few here."

"So what are you saying?" Les asked.

"Perhaps we should give the Lance of Longinus to the Greek Orthodox Church. It is their relic. And that way, it remains in Turkey as well."

"Are you sure about this, Mehmet?" Angie asked.

"Yes. That Daniels woman must not have it. The Church will protect their sacred relic."

"Where is this place?" Les asked.

"Saint George's, in the Fener," Mehmet answered. "Not too far."

"Taxi!" Les yelled as a cab drove by. "I'm tired of walking."

"Why not," Angie said as the cab backed up toward them.

"Did you see that, Kevin?" Sir Richard gasped from the backseat of the Rolls Royce. "What a stroke of luck!"

"Yes, sir!" his aide replied as he started the Rolls.

They had returned to the rented car utterly dejected after the "African" had outrun them. It was Fate that she should turn up now, riding past them in a taxi.

"After them, Kevin, my boy!" Sir Richard ordered.

Cibali, 8:01, p.m.

As the taxi sped northwestward along the Abdulezelpasa Caddesi, Les scanned the red, white and green lights and listened to the chugging motors and the blaring horns from the boat traffic on the Golden Horn. He found them curiously fascinating: this chaotic cacophony in so many ways encapsulated his impression of Istanbul.

Angie held the reliquary tightly in her arms. She felt an enormous sense of relief. Soon they would leave the Lance with the Greek Orthodox Church, whom she was certain would guard and keep the cherished relic from the hands of those who would misuse it. It did her heart good to know that they were doing the right thing, in spite of the dangers before them. The taxi turned left and proceeded up a hill and turned left again.

"Almost there," Mehmet announced from the front passenger seat

Fener, 8:18, p.m.

When he saw the taxi turn left a second time, Sir Richard tapped Kevin on the shoulder.

"Go straight up this street for two hundred meters and then stop."

Kevin did as he was told.

"The Greek Orthodox Patriarchate?" Kevin asked.

"Clever idea, actually," Sir Richard replied. "However, I have planned for this contingency." The Grand Master pulled an envelope out of his coat pocket and winked at his aide.

"What do we do now, sir?" Kevin asked.

"Wait, my boy. We wait."

The taxi stopped in front of a wooden wall with a small guard kiosk out front. In front of the kiosk was a black Mercedes with small blue flags with white crosses sagging from little posts on the front fenders. Mehmet stepped out of the cab and asked the driver to wait for them. Les and Angie followed him as he proceeded to the kiosk to speak to the solitary guard.

"Kalispera," the guard mechanically greeted them.

Mehmet knew this was Greek, but he didn't speak the language. "Do you speak English?" Mehmet asked.

"Yes," the guard replied, still not having overcome his annoyance at their visit so late in the evening. "How may I help you?"

"We have urgent business with Patriarch Bartholomew."

"Urgent business? With His Holiness?" The guard rolled his eyes and demanded, "What do you want?"

"We can only discuss it with him," Mehmet answered. "Please, this is very important."

"Wait a moment." The guard picked up the phone, tapped a few numbers, and spoke in Greek to whomever received the call. Within a minute he the receiver down and made an announcement. "The Patriarch is unavailable, but Bishop Elias will see you."

"I am Bishop Elias," the cleric announced in a thick Greek accent as a deacon led Mehmet, Angie and Les from an anteroom into his office. The bishop's black beard, cassock and headpiece accentuated his pale skin. "Your business sounds quite urgent. How may I be of service?"

Mehmet looked to Angie who reluctantly agreed to present the reliquary to the bishop. "We have something that belongs to the Church," Angie said gingerly.

The bishop's eyes narrowed. "You have stolen something from this church?"

"No! No, it's nothing like that at all!" Angie answered. "We have found a relic--"

The bishop's interest was piqued, but his tone remained brusque. "A relic?"

Angie slowly slid the casket out of its cotton sheath. The gold shimmered in the dim light from the bishop's desk lamp. Angie could see the bishop's eyes widen as she placed the reliquary on his desk.

Bishop Elias crossed himself three times as he eyed the golden reliquary. "May I?" the bishop asked very politely.

Angie nodded.

The bishop slipped on a pair of reading glasses, picked up the casket and read the inscriptions on the outside. Angie could see him mouth the words he was reading. His eyes grew wide and his lips moved faster as he read on. When he had finished he slowly looked up at Angie, as if he were asking permission to open the reliquary.

"Please," Angie said.

Bishop Elias's fingers trembled as he opened the casket. He carefully pushed the decaying red silk cloth aside and gasped as he saw the relic. The bishop muttered something in Greek and he crossed himself again. Again he looked up at Angie who couldn't tell if the look in the bishop's eyes was thanking her for bringing him the Lance or cursing her for possessing such a holy relic. Bishop Elias carefully read the inscription on the exposed side of the Lance and then gently flipped it over with his finger and read the inscription on the reverse. He suddenly became aware of his own rapid breathing as he carefully cradled the relic in both hands. Bishop Elias sighed quietly and gently kissed it. When he saw the papyrus at the bottom of the reliquary, he set the Lance down in the casket, picked up the papyrus and quickly read the record of the Savior's execution.

"Where did you find it?" the bishop asked Angie breathlessly.

Angie looked at Mehmet who immediately responded. "It was found in Aya Sofia, this morning."

"Found?" Bishop Elias asked. He was not pleased by such a vague answer.

"The earthquake yesterday tore open one of the walls," Mehmet explained. "I found this hidden in one of the walls. I am a student at the University."

The bishop couldn't hide his scowl from the young Turk. The irony of the situation was most distasteful: a Muslim, and a Turk at that, had found one of the greatest treasures of Christianity. He looked back at the relic and his visage brightened instantly. Muslim, Turk, or whatever, the Holy

Lance had been returned to its protector. With that realization, Bishop Elias abruptly rose from his chair and issued a solemn pronouncement:"In the name of His Holiness, Bartholomew, Patriarch of the Greek Orthodox Church, I thank you for returning the Holy Lance to the Church." The bishop then ceremoniously extended his hand, almost as if it were an afterthought.

The bishop's suddenness startled Angie. She glanced at Les who appeared unaffected; he looked eager to depart. When she looked at Mehmet, she could see he shared her uneasiness. She rose and cordially grasped the cleric's hand in friendship. Mehmet followed suit and then Les. The deacon automatically entered the room and offered to escort the guests to their taxi.

"Again, I and the entire Orthodox Church thank you," Bishop Elias said gracefully. His eyes shifted to the deacon who responded by leading the guests out of the bishop's office.

The walk from the bishop's office through the compound and to the taxi waiting outside was disturbingly quiet. Angie's shoulders felt heavy. Something was gnawing at her neck, whispering to her that things were not right. She looked at Mehmet whose face was blank. Was he feeling the same? There was certainly no exuberance in the air. *But why not?* She had just given something for which she had risked her life to its rightful owner. Hadn't she? Why wasn't she excited? She, Les, and Mehmet should be all smiles, laughing, celebrating...

The deacon, a black-robed, bearded automaton, was silent until they reached the taxi. "Good evening," the deacon said blandly as he opened the rear door of the taxi for Angie.

"Good evening," she replied in kind as she got in.

"Good evening," Les added, happily relieved to be rid of the relic. Les slid next to his wife.

The deacon merely nodded in reply.

Mehmet opened the front passenger door himself and sat down. When the driver asked him in Turkish where to go he raised his hand and told the man to wait for his instructions. Mehmet looked back at Les. "Where to, Doctor Connery?" the younger man asked.

Les grinned. "The airport, my friend, and the next Boeing 777 out of here!"

"We can't," Angie interjected. "The police--"

"We don't have the Lance." Les smirked, "What are they going to do to us?"

"How about jail?" Angie growled.

"If we don't have the relic--"

"They will hold us until we tell them where it is," Mehmet answered.

"It has been returned to its original owner," Les argued. "The Greek Orthodox Church."

"She will not let them keep it," Mehmet predicted.

"Daniels?" Angie asked.

"Yes," Mehmet replied. "She will use the government to pressure the Church."

"That would generate an international outcry against the Turkish government!" Les protested.

"Les, you saw how small that compound is," Angie retorted. "There's no way anyone could keep the police out."

"And no one else knows that the relic exists," Mehmet added. "If the police raid the Patriarchate and take it, there's no way for us to prove it ever existed."

"And you forget that we broke a police prisoner out of jail," Angie continued. "That's a matter of pride to the police and that's not going to settle well with them."

Les sighed and frowned. "So where do we go?" he wondered

Mehmet broke the momentary silence. "I have an idea." Mehmet ordered the driver to proceed.

"Where are we going, Mehmet?" Les asked

"To a safe place, for now."

Sir Richard looked carefully at the taxi driving toward them. "They're leaving!" He shook Kevin to awaken him as he saw the taxi pull out of the street that led to the Patriarchate.

"Shall we follow, sir?" Kevin asked with a yawn.

"No, no!" Sir Richard snapped. "We are going to the Patriarchate!"

"The Patriarchate?"

"We're going to collect the Lance of Longinus, my boy!"

"But don't they have it, sir?"

"My boy, didn't you see the look of relief on their faces? They've the weight of the world off their shoulders now and that can only mean one thing."

"Yes?" Kevin uttered expectantly.

"That they've delivered the Lance of Longinus to a safe place, dear Kevin! Can't you see?" *Well of course not. You're not of the bloodline. Poor sap. Makes a damn fine cup of tea though and his Yorkshire pudding…absolute heaven.* "On to the Patriarchate now."

The Rolls gracefully glided into reverse and then forward. When the guard kiosk was ten feet away, Kevin slid the car against the curb and got out to open Sir Richard's door. Sir Richard alighted and adjusted his overcoat. As he did so, he automatically thrust his chin outward and his head back. He marched over to the guard kiosk; Kevin followed a respectful step behind his master. When he reached the kiosk, Sir Richard smiled at the guard and leaned forward into the kiosk, resting his elbow on the windowsill.

"*Kalispera,*" rolled easily off Sir Richard's tongue.

"*Kalispera,*" the guard answered.

Remembering the three visitors who had just left, the guard examined these new visitors carefully. The situation was bizarre, to say the least. The hour was late and here where two more visitors, two more unusual visitors. The typical guest was Greek Orthodox and wanted to see the headquarters of the Church. Most other Christians had no idea the Patriarchate was here. And now, within twenty minutes, two Americans, a Turk and two Englishmen had approached him.

"Might we talk in English, my good man? My Greek has lost some of its luster over the years," Sir Richard explained. "You do speak English?" he asked, lowering his head and raising his eyes.

The guard restrained himself. His job was to protect the Patriarch, not to teach rude Englishmen manners. "Yes, sir," the guard replied begrudgingly.

"Splendid. Were there three people here, not more than a few minutes ago? Two Americans, a young Turk?"

Ah, the English pig needs help from this lowly Greek! The guard savored the moment. "Now, sir, why would a Turk care to visit the Patriarch?"

Sir Richard looked over his shoulder at Kevin who then stepped forward and pulled a one hundred euro note from his coat pocket. He then gently placed it on the counter.

"Three people, here…" Sir Richard continued.

The speechless guard could not take his eyes off of the crisp new bill.

Sir Richard turned to Kevin who instantly produced a second one hundred euro note and placed it next to the first.

"Were those three people here?" Sir Richard asked patiently.

The guard looked over to Kevin who looked back to Sir Richard. Upon receiving a nod, Kevin produced a third bill, exactly like the others and this time he handed it directly to the guard.

"Do you remember now?" Sir Richard asked seductively.

"Yes!" the guard gasped. "Yes, they were here."

The guard turned to Kevin and raised two fingers. The guard's eyes sparkled again as Kevin smiled and handed him two notes this time.

"May we enter now?" the Grand Master inquired.

"Yes, yes! I'll call someone immediately!" The guard grabbed the phone and impatiently informed the bishop's assistant in coarse Greek that Sir Richard easily recognized.

Ah, the value of pretty paper! Sir Richard was very pleased.

"He will be here shortly, gentlemen," the guard said with a very large smile that betrayed his poor dentition.

As the deacon arrived to escort these newest visitors, he scowled at the guard, who ignored him. "Please, come with me," the deacon beckoned the new arrivals graciously. When they arrived at the anteroom before the bishop's office, the deacon bade them wait. "Bishop Elias has asked not to be disturbed for just a few more minutes. He is finishing some very important business, I believe."

"We are happy to wait, sir," Sir Richard's voice boomed as he removed his fedora.

As the deacon left the anteroom, Sir Richard beamed at Kevin Meeley. There was no need for conversation. For once, Kevin could read his master's thoughts. The Lance of Longinus was here, probably on the other side of that door ahead. Soon it too would be added to the many treasures of the Templars. Not that he understood Sir Richard's obsession with Christian relics and his precious "royal bloodline". Strange man, Sir Richard, but, as far as Kevin was concerned, the work was easy and the pay was much better that any other job he could possibly hold down. Kevin stretched, yawned and then looked at his watch. At the same time, the muezzin announced the final call to prayer. Almost nine o'clock.

Bishop Elias slid the reliquary into an oversized desk drawer. What a wonderful gift God had bestowed upon him this fateful evening! "I'll be made metropolitan, at least!" Elias whispered as he envisioned becoming the Greek Orthodox equivalent of archbishop. "The man who returned to the Church the Holy Lance, lost for eight centuries." The bishop imagined an icon, with his image: Saint Elias, holding the Holy Lance and offering it to the Christ. *I have arrived! God be praised! I have arrived!*

The sudden knock on the door was most unwelcome.

"Yes?" Bishop Elias growled.

The deacon entered and announced, "Two gentlemen here, Your Grace. They say they have urgent business."

"This seems to be an evening full of urgent business," the bishop replied, exasperated.

"Yes, Your Grace," the deacon answered patiently.

"Well," the bishop paused as he stood to greet his guests, "Show them in."

"Sir Richard Covington-Smith?" Bishop Elias asked after the elder Englishman introduced himself and extended his right hand forward. Elias had heard the name before. But where? As Sir Richard pumped the bishop's hand, it came to him.

"Yes, now I remember!" the bishop snapped as he jerked his hand out of Sir Richard's grasp. "You're the Grand Master of the Templars!"

Sir Richard's jaw dropped. "How did you--"

"Your society is not as secret as you would like!"

"But where did you--"

"There are those of us who keep vigil against heretics..." Bishop Elias sneered at Sir Richard and said, "The leader of those who plundered this city eight hundred years ago and stole everything of value: holy relics, gold, silver, precious stones!"

"That's not true, Your Grace," Sir Richard answered calmly.

"You lie! How dare you lie! And here in the center of the Orthodox Church that you and your kind tried to destroy!"

"We stole nothing from the Church, Your Grace--"

"You lie again!" the bishop shrieked. "How else could you have obtained the Holy Shroud and the countless other relics?"

"Your Grace, it was the French, the Venetians, the Flemings...they sacked your city, stole your relics--"

"And sold them to you! To you, Templar!" Bishop Elias roared. After a brief pause he caught his breath and slowly calmed down in the pervading silence. "Now leave," he added calmly.

"Your Grace," the composed Grand Master of the Templars began, "you are correct. Buying stolen articles is tantamount to theft. I will admit that."

"Leave, please," the exhausted bishop pleaded softly. "You have profaned the Patriarchate. Now go."

Sir Richard sat in the chair opposite the bishop, leaned forward and looked the man in the eye. "The relics are still holy, no matter who possesses them," Sir Richard began. "And jewels and gold can always be replaced." The Grand Master stopped and reached into his coat pocket and procured an envelope.

The bishop looked warily at Sir Richard. "What is this?"

"Open it, Your Grace," Sir Richard smiled as he handed the envelope to the bishop. "At one time, God provided for your church well. He has also provided me well. And what He provides, He sometime takes away."

Bishop Elias wasn't really listening to Sir Richard. He slid a finger into the open envelope and looked inside. Only with difficulty did he successfully hide his surprise. *There must be ten thousand euros in here!*

"And sometimes He provides..." Sir Richard added as he produced two more envelopes and laid them on the bishop's desk. "...when we least expect it."

"What do you want?" the bishop asked suspiciously.

Sir Richard moved his chair closer to the bishop. "Three people just left here. They left something with you..."

Bishop Elias backed away. "I don't know what you're talking about."

"They left you a gold reliquary that contains the Lance of Longinus, the very Lance that pierced Our Lord's side while he hung on the cross at Golgotha."

Bishop Elias said nothing.

"And a Roman execution log..."

Bishop Elias remained silent.

"I wish to buy them from you," Sir Richard added as Kevin laid two more envelopes on the desk. "This makes fifty thousand euro."

The bishop's eyes darted wildly from envelope to envelope. Sir Richard could palpate the cleric's anguish. The trial of Judas: how much would it take for you to betray everything you care about?

"Why don't you kill me and take it?" Bishop Elias asked.

"Killing's a sin…and is far too messy." Sir Richard sat on the desk. "How about a million?" he ventured.

"What?" Bishop Elias sat openmouthed.

"A million euro. Something magical about that number: one million. Once you've got a million, you're pretty well set, unless you're greedy."

The bishop dropped his head into his hands. *Resist! Resist!*

"Are you a greedy man, Your Grace?" Sir Richard knew he had the upper hand. He could hear the bishop sobbing beneath his hands. "It's all right, your grace. No one will know." He reached into his vest pocket, retrieved a check and placed it on the bishop's desk alongside the envelopes. "Here you are, Your Grace. It's right in front of you."

Bishop Elias uncovered his wet eyes and looked at the check. One million euro. A check for one million euro with the addressee left blank. He cautiously looked up at Sir Richard.

"It's good; I assure you." Sir Richard palpated the bishop's agony. "No one will know," the Englishmen promised him.

Bishop Elias slowly opened the desk drawer and extracted the casket in its cotton sack. He winced as he set it on the desktop. He did not look up at Sir Richard.

"Thank you, Your Grace," Sir Richard said as he gently placed his hand on the cleric's shoulder. "Thank you." He patted the black cassock a few times and added, "The bills are yours as well, my friend."

Bishop Elias, his head still looking no higher than his desktop, looked away and said nothing.

"Come along, Kevin," Sir Richard said without looking to his aide.

"Yes, Sir Richard," Kevin replied automatically as he awakened from his nap.

CHAPTER NINE

Fener, 8:48 p.m.

"I can't believe you sometimes, Angie!" Les groaned. "We're on our way out of this disaster and you slam on the brakes and throw us right back into the thick of it!"

"Les! How many times do I have to tell you? Something's gone wrong! Terribly wrong!"

Mehmet pointed the cabdriver toward the Patriarchate and added, "We must be certain the Lance is safe, Dr. Connery!"

"Hey we did our part! We got it here! That doesn't mean that whenever Angie hears an SOS, we're the ones to answer it!"

"Who else will, Les?" Angie pleaded. "You just don't get it! Do you?"

"Who the hell anointed us 'keepers of the golden box'?"

"I did!" Angie was practically nose-to-nose with him. The taxi stopped. "Now get out!"

Les rolled his eyes as he stepped out of the car. "I hope you remember how ridiculous you're being when this is over! That is if we survive your little mission!"

Mehmet asked the taxi to wait as he followed the others.

The guard stepped out of the kiosk and raised his hands. "Christ and Mary! What a night!" he muttered to himself in Greek. He recognized the trio and declared in English, "You can't go in!"

Angie was not about to let him stop her. When the shorter guard tried to block her, she straight-armed him, knocking him back against the kiosk. When he recovered, Mehmet and Les rushed by, forcing him against the small building again.

"Hey! You mustn't go in there!"

Angie knew where she was going. The deacon sprang from his desk outside the bishop's anteroom as he realized she was there, but she was too fast for him. In five seconds, she was at the door to Bishop Elias's office and in two more she was inside.

"Where is it?" she demanded.

Bishop Elias looked like the Archangel Gabriel had just burst into his room. He held ten thousand euro in each hand. "My God! Where did you come from?"

"I tried to stop her, Your Grace!" the deacon pleaded as he entered the room. Mehmet and Les were right behind him.

"What have you done with it, Bishop Elias?" Angie roared.

"NOOOOOO!" he screamed as he rushed to the window.

Angie beat him to the window. "Where is it?" she growled. "It's gone, isn't it? Isn't it?"

Bishop Elias collapsed on to his knees and wept uncontrollably, "Oh, God, forgive me!" he cried as he unconsciously wiped his eyes with his wads of money. "Oh, God, please forgive me!" he wailed inconsolably. "What have I done? Dear God forgive me!"

"Where is the relic?" Angie yelled in the bishop's face.

Bishop Elias took no notice of her. He continued his pathetic blubbing on his knees, as if he were before the Throne of Heaven itself at the Last Judgment.

"Do you think he knows where it is?" Les asked.

"No," Angie replied. She glared at Elias brieflybefore adding, "Let's get out of here."

As the others left, the deacon stared in disbelief. Before him was a holy man he had admired and revered for over five years, in a state of total collapse, surrounded by hundreds of euro notes. "What in the name of Heaven is happening?"

Cagaloglu, 9:07 p.m.

"It's beautiful, my boy!" Sir Richard declared as he shone the flashlight on the Lance of Longinus, which lay in his lap. It sparkled as it reflected light to the ceiling of the Rolls Royce.

"Yes, Sir Richard, it is." Kevin lied. He was not impressed.

"Indeed! It's wonderful!" Sir Richard cried as he embraced the relic. He kissed it and then tried to read the engraving in the blade. The Rolls' jerking through the uneven traffic made this impossible. "Damn!" he groaned. "Can't read a thing with all this jossling, Kevin!"

"Sorry, Sir Richard," Kevin apologized.

"Pull over and park!" Sir Richard ordered. Kevin obeyed, turned onto the Tarakcilar Cadessi and parked across from the Nuruosmaniye Mosque. Sir Richard held the Lance up in one hand and held the flashlight with the other. He quietly mouthed the words as he read the inscriptions on both sides of the blade. "Oh, dear Father!" he whimpered. "I have it! I have it!"

Good! Kevin thought. Now we can get out of this godforsaken place and back to London!

"Father, look!" Siegfried shrieked, as he jammed on the Audi's parking brake. The vehicle screeched to an abrupt halt. "Look out of my window!" he bellowed as he frantically tapped the glass.

The man driving the car behind him immediately slammed on his brakes and leaned hard into his horn, as did the others further behind.

Hugo Geissler flew forward with the Audi's sudden forced stop as he shoved the last piece of lamb kabob into his mouth. He choked briefly on the meat before looking to his left, past Siegfried, and into the Rolls Royce parked at the curb. "*Mein Gott!*" he coughed. "My son, you have found the Lance of Destiny! Or perhaps it has found us!"

Siegfried didn't wait for his father's instructions. He threw open the driver's side door and slowly walked up to Sir Richard's window. He momentarily watched the Englishman fondle the relic. However, the enraptured Briton took no notice of the giant Teuton outside of his car window until Siegfried's massive fist smashed through the window and snatched the Holy Lance from Sir Richard's hand.

"What in God's name!" Sir Richard grumbled as he realized that his prize was gone. Before he could react a second hand stretched through the broken window and grabbed the reliquary, which he had just replaced in its cotton sack. "Thief! Thief!" he cried helplessly.

Siegfried ran back to the Audi and tossed the treasures, one at a time, to Hugo Geissler. With a broad smile he disengaged the parking brake and slammed the car into gear. The Audi was nothing but a red blur as it streaked into the night.

"I've lost it, Kevin! I've lost it!" Sir Richard screamed as he sprang to his feet outside of the Rolls Royce.

Kevin opened the driver's door and stood up, despondent. The return to London was just postponed, indefinitely. Maybe Sir Richard would consider giving up this quest.

"I've lost it, Kevin," Sir Richard announced again. "But as I live and breathe, I will not return to England without it!"

Kevin's heart fell through the asphalt under his feet with the Grand Master's declaration.

"We have it! We have it, Siegfried!" Hugo Geissler chimed as the massive Teuton drove the speeding car away. Hugo held up the blade and gasped. "We have the Lance of Destiny!"

"Shall I drive to the airport, Father?"

"Do we have the case?" He was referring to a stainless steel, false-bottomed briefcase brought specially to smuggle the relic out of Turkey.

"Yes, Father, in the trunk."

"Ser gut!" Hugo chuckled and slapped Siegfried on the shoulder. "You made it look so simple, Siegfried. So easy. After all we've been through… you and your sharp eyes. You just grabbed it and now we have it!"

"Yes, Father!" Siegfried flipped on his right blinker as he rolled to a stop, passing the Egyptian Bazaar on his right.

"No, don't turn here."

"Why not? We're going to the airport."

"Yes, but not immediately. Our good fortune calls for a little celebration. Don't you agree?"

"But Father, we can't waste time! We must leave now!" His eyes mirrored his impatience.

"Nonsense. There's always time to celebrate! Turn left. There's a little restaurant a block or two away that is perfect."

"If we must," Siegfried sulked angrily as he parked the Audi where Hugo instructed. As he got out he moaned, "Why don't we celebrate at the airport or on the plane? Why here?"

Hugo chuckled. "Because no one makes rice pudding like the fellow that runs this place."

"Why do you enjoy these people and their food? *Untermenschen!*"

"Tell me that after you've finished your dessert!" Hugo laughed out loud as he slid the Lance back into the casket and the casket into the cotton sack. "Come," he said as he held the golden reliquary in his left arm and started toward the restaurant, "enjoy yourself!"

"But Father, The Lance of Destiny…shouldn't we put it in the briefcase?"

"Siegfried, I agree that this city is full of nothing but thieves," Hugo replied as he neared the entrance. "But which will attract more attention, this cheap cotton sack or a stainless steel briefcase?"

"You are right, Father," Sigfried said begrudgingly as he stepped into the restaurant.

The two Germans sat at a table as a waiter greeted them. Hugo set the reliquary on the table and ordered the rice pudding. As the waiter departed, Hugo tousled his son's blond hair and teased him about his unease. The older man's peals of laughter could be heard all over the little restaurant.

One patron in particular was quite annoyed by the over-jubilant Germans. "German pigs!" Albert Boucher whispered into his Turkish coffee. He scowled at the men fifteen feet away. "So obnoxious! Why don't you goosestep your way back to Berlin, *boche cochon?*" He looked away in disgust and downed the last of the coffee. Just after Albert saw his waiter and hailed him, the older German let out another thunderclap of laughter and left the table for the men's room. And when he did, Albert saw the cotton sack.

"Yes, sir?" the waiter asked as he responded to Albert's signal.

"Uhhh," Albert was caught off guard.

"Sir?"

"Another coffee," Albert blurted out.

"Certainly," the waiter said as he walked away.

Albert looked back at Siegfried. *Is that really it? Mon Dieu! I thought the police…No, no. That's got to be it! I'll get closer.* Albert slowly got up and casually walked past Siegfried's table, his eye on the cotton sack. *That's it! Merdre! Le voila!* Once he was twelve feet beyond the table, Albert innocently inspected the poster on the opposite wall. A quick glance backward: *Who is that boche? How did he get it from the police?* Albert's mind raced furiously. His future was a mere twelve feet away. He mustn't lose sight of it. *Almost mine!* He saw Siegfried's massive hand rest on the reliquary. *Zut! That giant could squash me like an ant. Zut alors! Here comes the other one.*

Hugo Geissler laid a beefy hand on the casket and patted it as he sat down. "Smile, my son! Our journey is near the end."

Albert sized up Hugo. Aha! An opportunity, perhaps? *Yes, my fat fellow. You are the weak member in that pair.* He turned and walked by the Germans, his eyes wishing the casket into his hands. He slowly took his seat as the waiter arrived with his coffee.

"Your coffee, sir."

Albert startled at the sound of the waiter's voice. "What? Oh, thank you. Thank you."

"Anything--"

"Just leave me now!" he grumbled quietly. "Sorry. No. Nothing."

Sirkeci, 9:15 p.m.

"Mehmet," Yasmin asked in Turkish, "who are these people?" She viewed the visitors with suspicion.

"Friends," Mehmet reassured her. He turned to Angie and Les. "Doctor Johnson and Doctor Connery," he said in English, "this is my friend Yasmin."

"Thank you for your help," Angie said. Les nodded uneasily.

"Yasmin?" Mehmet reminded his friend.

"Hello," Yasmin answered curtly. She turned away from these unwanted guests and with narrow eyes reverted to Turkish. "Friends, Mehmet?"

"Yes, friends." He spoke to her in his native tongue. "Friends who need our help."

"What are you talking about?"

"I can't explain it all now, but I promise I will later."

"The African is beautiful."

"Please listen. I need your complete trust. You must promise me that you will tell no one."

"What is this? Are you in trouble?"

"Yes."

"Mehmet! What have you done?"

"Do you remember Lucille Daniels? The woman on the Internet."

"Of course, the sponsor."

"She has the police working for her now and they're looking for us."

"Why?"

"I found something at Aya Sofia this morning. A priceless relic."

"Relic? What are you doing with such a thing?"

"I found it."

"Found it? Just lying around the museum?"

"Yasmin, please. I don't have time to explain. Remember what we read about her? How she collects artifacts from all over the world? I know she is trying to take this relic out of Turkey to keep for herself. She used the police to get it from me."

"But surely the police will help to keep such a valuable thing in Turkey--"

"She owns them, Yasmin. She has bribed every high official she needs to get what she wants, and she wants the relic."

"*Baksheesh.*"

"Yes, *baksheesh*," Mehmet replied, confirming that in Turkey, *baksheesh*, whether blackmail or bribery, was a way of life. For the right price...

"So, she has it now?" Yasmin said in English, asking Angie and Les.

"No. We stole it from her," Mehmet interjected.

Yasmin was confused. "So where is it?"

"We took it to the Greek Orthodox Patriarchate, thinking it would be safe there. However, somebody took it from them."

"Who?" Yasmin asked in English. "The Daniels woman?"

"Possibly, but I don't think so," Angie interjected. "It wasn't that long ago that we got it back. I don't think that she or the police were able to follow us."

"Who else knows about it?" Yasmin asked. She continued in English.

"The Frenchman," Mehmet replied.

"Boucher?" Yasmin asked.

"Yes, but it is very unlikely that he has it," Mehmet answered. "There is no possible way for him to know that we took it from the Daniels woman."

"So how do we determine which of them has it?" Angie asked.

"I know a way," Les said with a grin.

"You?" Angie asked incredulously. "Oh this I gotta hear!"

Les's tongue darted out at his wife as he narrowed his eyes. He turned to Mehmet. "Call the police and tell them you found the relic."

"That's it?" Angie laughed.

"Doctor Connery is right," Mehmet countered. "I will call the chief, Calik is his name, I believe."

"Good idea," Les interjected. "Some desk sergeant isn't going to know anything about this."

"Yes," Mehmet continued, "I will tell him I have the Lance. If the police or Daniels don't have it, he'll be interested in getting it from me."

"Well," Angie sighed, "it's a long shot, but it's all we've got."

"There is a pay phone on the street," Yasmin suggested.

"Good idea," Mehmet said.

"I'll come with!" Les volunteered.

"This is Chief Calik," the voice on the other end of the phone said.

Mehmet nodded excitedly to Les, confirming that he was speaking to the chief of police. "Chief Calik," Mehmet said through three pieces of toilet paper, "something of great interest to you has come into my possession."

Calik sighed in disgust. In his mind he cursed his aide for letting this prankster through. "Don't ever call me again or you'll find yourself in Turkey's worst prison!"

"I have the relic," Mehmet said, just as Calik pulled the phone away to hang up.

"What?" Calik asked excitedly.

"I have the relic. The one the Daniels woman wants."

"Who are you?" Calik pressed a button on the side of his desk, which summoned his aide.

"Do you want it?" Mehmet answered.

Calik pointed to the phone as the aide walked in. The younger man immediately left the room to trace the call. "Yes, yes! Very much!"

Mehmet quickly hung up.

"The police don't have it," Les guessed.

"No" Mehmet answered. "That leaves the Frenchman."

Cagaloglu, 9:46 p.m.

Albert watched the manager scold the young waiter for the second time in ten minutes. It was obvious the fellow was new to the trade. Thus far he had dropped a half-dozen or so dishes, each with a freshly prepared meal on it.

The Germans were still there, the fat one inhaling another piece of baklava. The cotton sack had not moved, nor had the giant. But not for long. The Turkish coffees the blond Hercules had been drinking for the last thirty minutes had had their affect on his big German kidneys, necessitating a trip to the men's room.

This is it! Albert's eyes darted to and fro as his mind raced. How could he get—The waiter! The clumsy waiter! Perfect timing too, because the unlucky fellow was now carrying a large bowl of hot soup. In three seconds he'd been in the perfect place! Albert shot out of his chair toward the waiter. The poor man never saw it coming. Albert's left shoulder crashed into the waiter, sending the hot soup into Hugo Geissler's lap.

Geissler stood and screamed as the soup burned his thighs. The waiter grabbed Siegfried's napkin from the tabletop and tried to dab away the molten mess he had dropped on Geissler. He succeeded only in making matters worse. Geissler screamed again and then collapsed into his chair. The manager ran forward. In one breath he was begging Geissler's forgiveness and in another, he was berating the hapless waiter.

Siegfried heard the commotion and ran out of the men's room to the table. "Father, are you all right?"

Geissler's lap was now clear of soup and the burning was gone. "I'm fine, Siegfried. Fine. Just a little accident."

Then Siegfried noticed the cotton sack was missing. "Where is it?" he thundered as he searched under, around and on top of the table.

Geissler knew immediately what Siegfried meant. "It's gone!" He sprang up and quickly surveyed the restaurant. "It's gone!"

Sirkeci, 9:48 p.m.

"The Frenchman?" Yasmin asked. "You think the Frenchman has it now?" Her face reflected her doubt.

"He's our only lead," Mehmet answered. "The police don't have it."

"So Lucille Daniels doesn't have it," Les added.

"That leaves Boucher," Mehmet concluded. "We need to find out where he lives."

"What makes you think he went home?" Les asked.

"This is a huge city," Mehmet replied. "We've got to start somewhere."

"Right," Angie added.

"Tepebasi," Yasmin said, handing Mehmet a piece of paper with Albert Boucher's address on it. She had just retrieved the address from the university's on-line student directory.

Mehmet smiled at her. "Thank you, Yasmin," he said as he took the paper. "One day I will tell you all about this."

"Be careful," she said softly in Turkish.

"I will," he answered in kind.

Sultanahmet, 10:00 p.m.

Albert Boucher closely cradled the contents of the cotton sack. He rocked sideways as the nearly empty streetcar turned north in front of Aya Sofia. White spotlights dramatically illuminated the museum. The shadowy minarets stretched into the night ski. *Au revoir, mon vieux*, Albert thought as the museum went by. He would leave the streetcar at the end of the line, by the New Mosque. From there he would walk across the Galata Bridge and make his way back to his apartment; Albert needed money and his passport to leave the country. He had not expected to find the Lance so quickly. Ah, Paris was but a few hours away! He would fax his resignation to the University of Istanbul from Paris. LeMaitre would be furious, but who cared about what he thought.

Albert looked down at the cotton sack. Dare he open it? He slowly pressed his fingertips into the sides of the reliquary. "Yesterday," he mused in a low whisper, "I was one of millions of graduate students in the world. With any luck, my efforts would land me in some dull teaching position at a ramshackle college deep in the recesses of France. Tomorrow, I will possess wealth and fame beyond my wildest dreams and lead the life of *my* choosing!"

"Where do you suppose he is?" Les asked as he looked around from outside Albert Boucher's apartment building.

"I don't know," Mehmet responded. "I don't associate with him socially. He could be anywhere."

"Maybe he has a girlfriend?" Les ventured.

"Maybe he's already out of the country," Angie suggested, voicing what each of them hoped wasn't true. "Are you sure you rang the right room?"

"I had the manager do it for me the last time," Mehmet replied. "He's not answering."

"Should we try to break in?" Les wondered.

"The manager wouldn't let me through the security gate." Mehmet sighed. "If he comes back to his apartment, or if he leaves it, he will have to come through this door."

Angie examined the apartment building's street front. "We'd better hide somewhere."

Mehmet noticed a narrow alley separated the apartment building from the butcher shop just to the west. "Over here," Mehmet ordered.

"This could be a long night," Les sighed as he followed Angie into the alley.

"Yes," Mehmet agreed. "You two should rest while I keep watch."

Angie and Les squatted on the cold pavement. "Thank you," she said to her husband.

"For what?"

"For doing this. I know you don't really…"

"We're in it up to our eyeballs now, Ange. There's no turning back."

"We're going to get it back. I'm as certain of that as the red hair on your head."

"What makes you so sure?"

"He's coming!" Angie sprang up and hurried over to Mehmet. "Do you see him? He's coming, I know it!"

"Nothing yet, Doctor Johnson," Mehmet answered. "I don't see anybody."

"He's getting closer. *It's* getting closer."

"The relic?"

"Who's that?" Angie whispered pointing at a man coming toward the apartment.

"It's Boucher!" Mehmet gasped. "Doctor Connery!" he whispered as he waved at Les.

Boucher trotted up the steps jauntily, holding the reliquary close to his body with his left hand. He found his keys when he reached the top step and inserted one into the lock. He turned the key and pulled the door open only to have it slammed closed from behind him.

"Hand it over, Frenchie!" Les growled.

Albert pushed the good doctor out of the way only to find Mehmet and Angie waiting behind.

"I should have known that you had something to do with this," Albert snarled at Mehmet.

"The reliquary, Monsieur Boucher," Mehmet asked, hand extended.

Albert abruptly thrust the casket into Mehmet's chest, knocking the wind out of the young Turk. Still clutching the cotton sack, he pushed Angie away and sprang toward the street. At the last minute he felt something catch his foot and he tumbled to the sidewalk. As Albert got to his hands and knees, Les landed on him and slammed his head against the concrete. All went black.

Les turned Albert's motionless body over. "He's out cold."

Angie grabbed the cotton sack and felt a rush of gentle warmth into her fingers. "It's here," she beamed.

"Where to now?" Les asked Mehmet.

"I don't know. We must get off the street." He scratched his head. "Back to Yasmin's."

CHAPTER TEN

Sirkeci, 10:46 p.m.

Mehmet pulled the reliquary out of its cotton sack and showed it to Yasmin. Les and Angie had just begun a meal that Yasmin had prepared for them.

"Oh my!" Yasmin said in Turkish. "It's beautiful!"

"I found this hidden in a wall in the museum this morning. Yesterday's earthquake revealed where it had been hidden."

"For how long?"

"Who knows? Maybe centuries."

"What's in it?"

"Open it," Mehmet encouraged her.

Yasmin slowly ran her fingers over the front of the casket. "The engraving is beautiful." She carefully examined the engraved image of Jesus sitting on a heavenly throne. Then Yasmin slowly opened the reliquary and inspected the Lance with her keen eyes. She took particular interest in the inscription. After a brief hesitation Yasmin ran her fingers over its length, as if she were reading the inscription with her fingers. She gently lifted the relic out of its reliquary and carefully turned it, examining every aspect.

"It is the Lance that pierced Jesus' side on Calvary," Mehmet said. "That papyrus you see is the Roman record of Jesus' execution."

Yasmin looked as if she hadn't heard a thing. The two thousand year-old spear entranced her. To Mehmet, she looked as if she were in another world. Mehmet watched her face, not knowing what she was experiencing.

"It's fascinating," Yasmin finally said.

"Isn't it, though?" Mehmet added as he wondered how he felt about the relic. Was this spear an instrument of divine goodness? For Doctor Johnson, the Lance was a blessing, but she is a Christian. What effect could such a thing have on one of the True Faith? Was this a devilish idol sent by Satan himself to lead Muslims away from the True Path? Yet, he had seen what it did for her. Was this a revelation from Allah or a deception by the Master of Darkness? Or was it neither blessing nor idol? Was it simply a piece of iron that coincidence and circumstance had turned into a magical talisman? Doctor Johnson said it helped her find him at the police station. Or was it simply an archeological treasure and nothing more? His mind's examination of the possible explanations confused him all the more. Mehmet sighed. Well, whatever it is, it must not fall back into the hands of the Daniels woman.

As Yasmin set the Lance back in the casket, Mehmet asked her, "Do you think it is really what I told you it was? Do you think it pierced Jesus' side?"

Yasmin didn't answer for a few seconds. "I don't know."

The answer surprised Mehmet. He was expecting a definitive "no" and could have accepted a "yes" but not "I don't know".

Yasmin's face grew more solemn. "I know what my father would say: 'What are you doing with these Christian things?'"

"Your father must be a good Muslim."

"Yes, very devout," Yasmin replied thoughtfully. Mehmet could see her grow unsettled.

"Something's bothering you, Yasmin." She didn't answer. "Is it the relic?"

"Perhaps my father is right." Yasmin looked away. "Jesus was a great prophet, but he did not die on a cross. As Muslims, we are taught that from a young age."

"Yes…"

Yasmin turned around and looked at Mehmet with her beautiful dark brown eyes. "If that is true, then this Lance of yours is a fraud. So why are you mixed up with it?"

"Yes, what you say is true." Mehmet decided to try another tack. "Why not look at it as a piece of history, as I do? It is part of Turkey's magnificent past."

"Mehmet," Yasmin began solicitously, "Do you know what bothers me about it the most?"

"No. What is it?"

Yasmin racked her brain to find the words to express her true thoughts. "When I touched it," she began uncertainly, "it felt like…"

"Yes?" Mehmet eagerly anticipated her answer.

"Well, it has a presence…"

"Yes, I agree, but I've experienced something like that too. Last week… when I examined some ancient Hittite artifacts--"

"No, no. This is different." Her face reflected the anguish of her uncertainly. *How does one express herself when all one feels is an emotion that defies verbal expression?*

"Yasmin?" Mehmet inquired softly.

There was a brief pause.

She feels something, too! Oh, Great Allah! Can the Lance truly be a deception of the Devil? "So Yasmin, you think it's…"

"I don't know. It's just different. I'm sure my father would not approve of my thoughts about your relic." Yasmin reached out and grabbed Mehmet's hands. "You must get rid of it, Mehmet."

"What?"

"Just leave it somewhere, anywhere! Why do you still have it?"

Yes, why do I still have it? Is Allah guiding me? "Yasmin, listen to me. I don't know for certain what the Lance is, but I know that it is one of the greatest archaeological treasures to be found in this country. That the Daniels woman will get it unless I get it to safety out of Turkey!"

"So give it to the museum curator!" Tears were forming in her eyes.

"She owns him! You know that, Yasmin!"

"Mehmet, this relic will only bring you sadness. Let the Americans take it!"

"And how will that help to get it out of Turkey?" Mehmet shot back. "I am going to take it out of the country with Doctor Johnson and Doctor Connery," he added resolutely.

Yasmin saw the determination in his eyes. She wiped a few tears away from her own and smiled at Mehmet. "Where will you take them, Mehmet?" she asked gently.

"I don't know."

"You are right about one thing," Yasmin admitted. "The relic belongs in Turkey but as long as that Daniels woman is here it won't stay in Turkey for long. As much as I hate to say this, I would rather see it in the British Museum than in her possession."

"We must leave."

Yasmin smiled at him tenderly. "The police will have the airports well-guarded."

"Yes, I know. The bus and train stations will be dangerous, too."

"Your friends," she chuckled as she looked at them, "don't blend in very well."

"True," Mehmet admitted, "but I have an idea. My uncle has a ship. He runs freight from Istanbul down the Anatolian coast and to Syria."

"Will he take you?"

"I don't know. I can only ask and hope he agrees. He is a rascal though. He is not above smuggling, although he has never been caught."

"Do you know how to contact him?"

"That might be a problem. I haven't spoken to him in three years. I remember where his office is, or at least where it was three years ago."

"Are you certain he's still around?"

"Not really."

Yasmin sighed in frustration. "Is there any other way?"

"No. Not that comes to mind." Mehmet looked her in the eye. "It's all we have to go on, Yasmin. Time is running out. We're desperate!"

"I wish I could help you more."

"You have helped more than you know. Thank you."

"Mehmet," Yasmin began, "I don't want to seem forward. It's something that a good Muslim woman shouldn't do...."

"Yes. What are you saying, Yasmin?"

"When you come back, please come see me."

Mehmet smiled and said, "I will be back, and you are the first one I will come to see."

Mehmet found his uncle's business in the telephone book and called his Uncle Murad's office. He was surprised to be speaking directly to his father's youngest brother.

"Uncle," Mehmet began after reintroducing himself, "I have a special favor to ask."

"I don't hear from you in three years, and suddenly I'm your favorite uncle!" His tone was good-natured. "What do you want? And why are you calling so late?"

"Uncle, this is of the greatest importance to me. Will you help me?"

The older man softened a little. "What do you want, Mehmet?"

"I need to get to the Asian side."

"Take a taxi over the Bosphorus Bridge."

"No, Uncle. I need to go a bit further south."

"How far?"

"Quite far."

"You may be in luck. I'm leaving tonight for Bodrum. Will that help?"

"Yes, it will!" Mehmet was amazed at how everything was lining up so well. *Was this the hand of Allah?* He looked at the Americans and smiled hopefully. "When do you leave, Uncle?"

"Eleven-thirty."

"Forty minutes. That's perfect."

"Mehmet, why do you need to leave Istanbul? What about your studies?"

"This does concern my studies, Uncle. I'm doing a great favor for Professor Kemal."

"Fine. One more person onboard isn't a problem."

"How about three?"

"Three? Who are they?"

"American professors," Mehmet lied. "Very prominent archaeologists." Yasmin rolled her eyes when she heard this.

"Can they work if I need them to?" Uncle Murad inquired.

"I'm certain they'd do anything to repay you."

"Where are you now?"

"Sirkeci."

"Perfect. My ship's anchored off Sarayburnu. We finished loading an hour ago. I'm waiting for my navigator to download some new software onto the ship's computer. I'll pick you up in my skiff at the ferry docks by the Galata Bridge. Be there in twenty-five minutes. Can you manage that?"

"Yes, Uncle. We'll be there."

"Well?" asked Yasmin when Mehmet hung up.

"We need to go very soon," Mehmet said in English. "We are to meet my uncle at the ferry docks by the Galata Bridge in twenty-five minutes."

"That doesn't give you much time," Yasmin said in English. She rushed into her tiny kitchen and brought out some bread, meat and cheese. "You must eat. Bodrum is a long way, especially by ship. There's probably no decent food aboard."

"Thank you," Mehmet said.

"Mehmet," Yasmin said in Turkish, "while you were on the phone I did a quick internet search on this Lance of yours. The Lance of Longinus sounds like a bit more than a valuable artifact."

"What do you mean?" Mehmet inquired, continuing the conversation in Turkish.

"Byzantine emperors claimed it made them invincible when they carried it into battle. Somehow Charlemagne obtained it; you know how large his empire was—"

"Yasmin--"

"Napoleon Bonaparte wanted it and Adolf Hitler had it in his possession. Mehmet, this thing you have is no mere talisman! This is a diabolical source of unstoppable power! That is why the Daniels woman wants it!"

"More the reason to get it out of Turkey, Yasmin!" Mehmet declared dutifully. "The Lance of Longinus was not meant to fall into the hands of---"

"You're a fool, Mehmet!" Yasmin interjected passionately. Then she smiled with a tear in her eye. "A very brave fool."

Mehmet joined Les and Angie in the next room. They were finishing the meal Yasmin had prepared for them. As Mehmet handed Angie the reliquary, now back in its cotton sack, his face showed the heavy burden he carried.

"Are you okay, Mehmet?" Angie asked.

"I'm fine, I assure you Doctor Johnson," Mehmet said with a less than convincing smile. *Should I tell them? Doctor Johnson knows that there is something special about the relic, but I can hear Doctor Connery scoffing now. Do they need to know that they are in more danger than they thought?* A lump formed in his throat as he watched the Americans eat. *No. They know the Lance must leave Turkey and that's all they need to know. But what will we do with it once we've left the country?*

Yasmin brought water and tea. "Drink quickly and then you must go. Take the bread with you," Yasmin suggested. "That will keep the longest."

"Thank you. Thank you so much," Angie said to Yasmin.

"Yes, we appreciate this very much," Les added.

"You are friends," Yasmin replied. "Go quickly. Be safe."

Angie stepped outside the apartment with Les. She held the casket tightly with both hands.

"Any messages?" Les asked, half-teasing.

"No," Angie smiled back. "Nothing since the last one."

Inside, Mehmet looked at the beautiful woman in front of him. "Thank you, Yasmin. You didn't have to do this."

She rushed forward and pleaded, "Come back to me, Mehmet. Just come back." "I will," Mehmet replied as he stumbled out the door. "I will."

Marmara Hotel, Taksim, 11:16 p.m.

"The airport is sealed," Chief Calik said. "The bus stations, train stations and sea bus ports too. We've sent descriptions of Yakis and the Americans to every car rental agency in the city." He had all but dismissed the mysterious phone call he had earlier. Was he speaking to those whom he sought?

"We've even ordered the taxis to look out for them," Inspector Gur added.

"If they can't leave Istanbul," Osman noted, "then they must hide here."

"I have one hundred men looking for them," Calik said. "We will find them."

"Try two hundred," Luci snarled. "Have you notified Ankara, Chief Calik?"

Calik was taken aback. "No. There is no need. They will not get out of Istanbul."

Luci handed him the phone. "Call Ankara. I'm taking no chances."

The Bosphorus, 11:20 p.m.

The skiff shuddered as it chopped through the cold water. Angie looked at the freighter anchored four hundred yards ahead. The air was chilling. She held Les tightly. The reliquary rested between them.

Mehmet sat next to his Uncle Murad and watched the captain as he guided the skiff over the waves. He was a tall man with a lantern jaw, thick black hair and a salt-and-pepper mustache. He cut a rugged figure. His captain's cap rested easily on his head. Mehmet chuckled. He was a far cry from Mehmet's father: bald, weak chin, short, stubby legs.

Murad turned to his nephew and smiled. "This will be a good experience for you, Mehmet," he shouted over the roar of the engine. "Real man's work. Your cousins have learned a great deal working with their father."

"I'm looking forward to it, Uncle," Mehmet answered, convincing himself that at least part of what he was saying was true. He looked up at the bow as they drew closer to the ship. Persephone, *interesting name: daughter of the goddess Demeter kidnapped by Hades and forced to spend six months of every year in Hell.*

By eleven thirty-five the freighter was underway. Mehmet watched from the bridge as helicopters flew over the strait every few minutes.

"This is most unusual," Uncle Murad noted. "I've never seen so many helicopters in one place before."

Mehmet knew why they were there. The Daniels woman was exercising her newly acquired authority well. He had left his American friends in the ship's galley. Evidently Yasmin had been wrong about the ship's food supply.

"Captain," the radioman said as he walked over to Murad, "Bodrum wants to know when to expect us."

"Have them read the manifest we faxed them yesterday," Murad replied coolly.

"They are concerned because we left later than expected, sir."

"Tell them to read the manifest. We'll be there when we are supposed to be there."

"Yes sir."

Murad turned to his nephew. "I've been a sea captain for two decades and the harbormasters still treat me like a child."

Mehmet smiled back.

"Tired?" Murad asked.

"Yes," Mehmet replied.

"We're down a few crewmen. Go down to B-deck. Find rooms seventeen and eighteen. Those are for you and your friends. They're small, but you can sleep and have some privacy. If you need anything, I'm usually right here, if I'm not in my bunk."

"Thank you, Uncle Murad. I'm sorry about the late hour and the sudden--"

"Yes. This is very unusual, but I've had stranger requests. Don't worry about it. Glad I could help you, Mehmet." Murad smiled and slapped his nephew on the shoulder. "I always thought you had a bit of the sea in you, boy," he chuckled.

"Perhaps we all do, Uncle," Mehmet responded with an uncertain smile as he headed for the galley. He wondered if the prospect of a bed sounded as good to the doctors as it did to him.

"This food's not bad," Les declared.

"How can you eat after all you had at Yasmin's?" Angie asked.

"Have you tried it?"

"Don't want to."

"How's your friend?"

"The Lance is fine," Angie answered with a scowl.

"Pity about the conference. I feel bad for letting them down."

"I'm sure Trudy will understand."

"Think she'll ask me next time?"

"Yes," Angie chuckled, "I'm sure she will. Trudy is a very gracious person."

"How's the food?" Mehmet inquired as he entered the galley.

"Pretty good," Les replied.

"My uncle has quarters for us."

"I could use some sleep," Angie yawned.

"Yeah, it's been a long day," Les ageed.

"A very long day, but an important one, I believe," Mehmet said.

"I couldn't agree more," Angie added.

"You realize we're attempting the impossible," Les interjected. "I mean just think of what we're trying to pull off. We've got the Turkish authorities looking for us in a country we don't know, whose language we don't have the foggiest idea how to speak."

"But you have me, my friends," Mehmet assured them as he smiled uneasily.

"And we have the Lance of Longinus," Angie added soberly.

Les rolled his eyes.

Mehmet couldn't help but stew about the new information Yasmin had revealed to him. As he watched them debate, Mehmet couldn't help feeling a deep concern for them. Should he tell them? But wouldn't that be adding unnecessary concern? They had plenty to worry them. They needn't know more about something they couldn't control.

"It hasn't steered us wrong yet, Les," Angie retorted.

"We're steaming toward the coast of Asia because an ancient spear told us to."

"Haven't you figured it out yet, Les? Something...someone is guiding us through the Lance."

Les laughed. "So now it's God's telephone!"

"Les--"

"Hello Angie? God here. How about getting that box out of Turkey for me?"

She didn't let his teasing bother her. "There have been too many coincidences--"

"We live in a world of coincidences!"

"What about my asthma, Doctor Connery?"

"It's the *prednisone*, Angie," Les retorted.

"It never works that fast. You know that, Les," Angie countered.

"Humbug!"

"Just supposed, for a minute, that there is something to this, Doctor Scrooge."

"Explain."

"The Lance that pierced the side of the Son of God—" she turned to Mehmet, "I don't mean to offend your religion."

"None taken," Mehmet responded with a smile.

"The Lance," she continued, "that pierced the Son of God *may* have, I said *may* have, certain *powers* associated with it."

Les giggled. "Such as squelching asthma attacks and channeling God's messages--"

"Les!"

"Okay, okay. How about 'receiving'? So it's a heavenly receiver with certain medicinal capabilities." Les sounded halfway serious.

"Sure."

"Come on!"

"You've seen it work. Why can't you believe in it?"

Les rubbed his forehead as he wrinkled his nose. "Angie, you have no proof. How do you know?"

"Why not?" Angie asked.

"Because things like this don't happen!" Les roared.

"I believe that fits the definition of the term 'miracle!'" Angie countered.

"Angie--"

"Explain to me what has happened over the last fifteen hours. And what the heck are we doing on this freighter headed for some place we've never heard of?"

"I can't!"

"Then why did you come with us?" Angie shouted.

"Because I love you!" Les replied in greater volume. "And I'm not going to stand by and let this thing destroy you!"

"Les," Angie added tenderly, "it's not going to destroy me."

"I can't accept that. Look at what's happening to you."

"Les--"

"You're a brilliant, *rational* person. And now you're hearing things—"

"You heard it too!"

"That's what scares me the most! You're believing in fairytales and I'm following right behind you!"

"Les, I haven't lost my mind," Angie answered with a soothing voice. "What I'm hearing and feeling are as real as anything I've ever experienced." She turned to Mehmet. "What do you think?"

"I don't want to get involved in a family argument," Mehmet protested after a brief hesitation.

"It's not an argument," Angie said. "It's a discussion. Right, Les?"

"Whatever," Les snarled.

"Well," Mehmet began cautiously. "Although some of what you are saying is quite contrary to what Islam teaches, I have noticed several things that are very difficult to explain."

Les yawned loudly. When he realized the disruption it caused he apologized, "Sorry."

"If I may continue…" Mehmet said.

"Please," Angie encouraged him.

"I find it difficult to explain Doctor Johnson's speedy recovery from her ailments when she is in contact with the Lance. I'm not a doctor--"

"Bingo! No, you're not, so your opinion in that matter carries very little weight!" Les interjected. "I still say it's the prednisone."

"Les!" Angie retorted, "Let him finish!"

"Yes, well, my lack of expertise in the medical field may very well diminish the weight of my opinion on that point, as you say, but there are other questions that cannot be explained away so easily." Mehmet looked at Les as if he were allowing him a rebuttal. When none came he continued. "First of all, how did you determine my location at the police station? How did you know the wall was weak there? Usually the corner of a building is the strongest structurally."

"Coincidence and dumb luck," Les answered.

"We lost the relic, found it, lost it and, against heavy odds, found it again. Now, on very little notice, we're on the ship of my uncle, whom I haven't spoken to for three years, and he happens to be going to a place where we could easily hide without leaving the country. We've escaped the city right under the nose of the police. There must be ten helicopters flying over the Bosphorus right now. How did we get away? Why is everything going so well for us?"

"And why aren't we sitting in first class on a 747 headed for London?"

"Les!" Angie snapped.

"More dumb luck," Les continued. "Your argument has done little to sway me, Mister Yakis."

"Doctor Connery, this part is difficult for me to say because I am Muslim and my understanding of Christian theology is incomplete. However, that Lance could very well have pierced Jesus' side and may have acquired certain powers in doing so. We Muslims acknowledge Jesus as a great prophet, but he was not the son of Allah. And we do not believe he died on the cross."

"I believe you mentioned that before."

"Things are progressing in such a way--"

"So you're saying that God is using it to guide us out of Turkey?" Les asked.

"It would appear so, Doctor Connery."

"Why doesn't he just tell us? Why is this "relic" so important to God?"

"I have no idea, but look at what has happened to us and ask yourself why?"

"But you are a Muslim. You said yourself that this whole Lance of Longinus story doesn't go with your religion."

"Well, let's remove any religious association this Lance may have. Let's think of it as belonging to...."

"Abraham Lincoln?" Les chuckled.

"Les!" Angie hissed.

"Very well," Mehmet answered, "it belongs to this Mister Lincoln."

Les giggled.

"Look at what Mister Lincoln's Lance has done for us?"

Les stopped giggling. "What?"

"Doctor Connery, I have removed all religious associations with the Lance, made it totally 'religion-neutral', if you wish to say it that way," Mehmet responded. "Does that make it easier for you to believe in it? I mean all of these coincidences we have been through seem to revolve around the relic."

"Can we talk about this tomorrow?" Les asked. It was obvious he was avoiding the question.

"Just say 'yes', Les," Angie ordered.

Les set his head down on the table. "I'm too tired," he moaned like a five-year old.

"Well while you're sleeping, chew on this," Angie began. "This thing is real. I know it, Les. I feel it deep within me. I've never felt anything like this."

"You obviously didn't experiment much with drugs in college," Les joked.

"Believe it or not. I'm ignoring you, Les."

"That's too bad."

"I believe this thing is what it's advertised to be," Angie declared. "It is the spear that pierced Jesus Christ's side at his crucifixion, it has supernatural powers and now it's leading us to--"

"Where?" Les demanded. "Where?" he asked more quietly when there was no reply to his first inquiry. "Where does it want us to take it?" Les scoffed. "How about Rome, New York, about a few weeks on the Riviera?"

"It's gotten us this far!" Angie replied sharply. "It *will* tell us when the time is right!"

Les did not answer, but he laid his head back on the table.

"You know, from an historical perspective," Angie mused, hoping to spur Les' interest, "that papyrus is probably more significant than the Lance."

"How?" Les asked disinterestedly without raising his head off the table.

"All that science can do is to confirm that the spear comes from the proper time period and is of Roman origin. It may even tell us the blood type of anyone who was cut by it, but it will not tell us that this Lance pierced Jesus' side at the crucifixion."

"Where are you going with this, Angie?" Les asked, his head still on the table.

"Just listen. The papyrus mentions Jesus *by name.*"

"So? Somebody carved something about Jesus on the Lance too."

"No, they engraved the word '*Dominae*', Lord, not Jesus. That was obviously done after the fact, once Jesus' position as the Son of God had been confirmed by his resurrection. The papyrus mentions Jesus as a matter of fact, just like any other criminal: name, where he came from, and when and how he was executed. Nothing ethereal there. The papyrus could be the earliest documentation of Jesus' death by crucifixion."

"The papyrus is fake, too," Les rejoined, as he raised his head off the table. "Carbon dating could place it in the fifth or sixth century, before Egypt's papyrus became less accessible to Europe."

"True, Les, but again the nature of the text is so...."

"Clinical."

"Yeah, that's right, even insipid."

Les yawned. "I'm still not convinced."

"And probably never will be."

"'I think, therefore I am.'"

"Why does the papyrus mention that the body was missing? Why does it mention the temple guard sent to secure the tomb?"

Les lifted his head off the table again. "Angie, we went over this all when we were at the hotel," he moaned.

"Yeah and you still don't get it!" Angie retorted. "Why is the papyrus--"

"Because some sixth century zealot wrote it that way!" Les replied angrily. "How many fake Christian relics are there out there? There are enough pieces of the 'True Cross' to make ten of them!"

"Actually," Mehmet interjected, "a French scientist determined that all the existing splinters of the True Cross would add up to about a third of--"

"Who asked *you*?" Les growled at Mehmet.

"Les!" Angie countered, "Quit being such a jerk!" Les stared back at Angie silently. "I'm not saying all relics are genuine, but I am saying that this one could very well be."

"Could very well be?"

"Okay, IS!"

"You really believe that?"

"Yes, I believe that."

"And you believe that Jesus Christ rose from the dead on Easter morning?"

"Well, yeah, I guess I do. And I believe that his resurrection changed the world--"

"Angie," Les said as he rubbed his forehead again, "I've know you over fifteen years and you've never said anything like this before. Hell, we only go to church on Easter and Christmas, and even then maybe half the time. And that's only because you insist on it. It's like it's a social obligation of some sort. I've never seen you open a Bible, let alone read one. I married you because you're a levelheaded thinker (and outstandingly beautiful). And now you believe in myths! What's happened to you?"

"*Happened* to me?"

"Yeah, who gave you this sudden massive infusion of Sunday School?" Angie didn't answer.

"Do you see where I'm coming from?" Les asked. "I love you, and when I see this...*radical* change in you, it scares me."

"Radical change?" Angie sighed. "Les, what are you talking about? I haven't changed."

"Yes. You have."

Angie paused thoughtfully. "Maybe I have." She wiped a tear from the corner of her eye. "I wish I could explain it to you…so you could understand."

"Angie? Angie, I'm sorry."

"I'd better head for bed," Angie said as she scooped up the relic.

Mehmet stood up. "Let me show you to your bunks."

"Do you want me to come with you, Angie?" Les asked.

"No, you don't have to do that. Come when you're ready to sleep," Angie replied.

Mehmet led Angie to B deck and offered her a choice of bunks. Across from the bunk she chose was a small safe. Murad had given Mehmet the combination, which he shared with Angie. He opened the safe and set the casket inside. Angie jumped into a bunk and didn't bother to take down the bedding. It appeared to Mehmet that she was asleep soon after her head hit the pillow.

In the galley, Les sat quietly, thinking about what his wife had said to him. He shook his head a few times. "Angie…"

Mehmet returned quickly. "Doctor Connery, you have quite a wife, if you don't mind my saying so."

"Thank you. I couldn't agree more."

"You are not a religious man."

"No."

"Are you an atheist?"

"No, agnostic," Les answered.

"What's the difference?"

"Well…" Les faltered. *Why am I talking to this guy about religion? Twelve hours ago I didn't know he existed!*

"Were you raised in a Christian church?"

"Roman Catholic."

"When did you quit going?"

"I wouldn't say I've quit."

"You said that you and Doctor Johnson don't go the church much; you're pretty inconsistent."

"I'd say I began to lose interest since I left home, college."

"Why do you still go at all?"

"Angie, I guess. I'm willing to sacrifice a few hours a year to keep her happy. And I suppose it's just something that you've got to do every now and then…with a family, you know."

"Why?"

"Why? Because—because that's what you do—ah, crap; I can't explain it."

Mehmet waited patiently for an answer.

"When I was a kid, my folks went, not every Sunday, but they went. So, as a husband…I go, sometimes."

"You go to a church to worship something you are not certain even exists."

"I don't go to worship."

"You go to make Doctor Johnson happy."

"I guess. I don't know why."

"Why do you go if you don't know why you are going? Would you attend a rally for a political party you disagreed with?"

"I don't *disagree* with Christianity."

"So you believe in Jesus' divinity. You believe he is the Son of God."

"Well, no."

"Then you are not a Christian. So it is kind of silly for you to go."

Les's face reflected that he'd never thought about that before. "I don't know. Well maybe I am. Maybe I do believe."

"You don't sound too certain."

"You're right. I really don't know. Some days I don't even know what my name is."

"So it is a medical problem."

"What? No, no!"

"You said you had memory problems."

"That's not what I meant."

"What *did* you mean?"

"I meant that sometimes pressures and stress from everyday life are so great that I don't have time to sort out the important stuff, let alone religious or philosophical questions."

"Some would say that that *is* the important stuff."

Les didn't respond.

"It sounds like Doctor Johnson has begun to understand that."

Les thought for a few seconds and then smiled at Mehmet. "Yes, it does sound like Doctor Johnson has begun to do that."

"And you, Doctor Connery?"

"I'm not there yet. I don't know if I'll ever be there." Les dropped his head in his hands and sighed.

"Well, it's been a long day." Mehmet yawned. "I think I'll retire now. Good night, Doctor Connery."

"Mehmet."

"Yes, Doctor Connery?"

"Thank you."

"Doctor Connery?"

"For talking with me."

"You're welcome. Good night, Doctor."

"Good night, Mehmet."

CHAPTER ELEVEN

"Wake up! Wake up!"

Les slowly raised his weary head. "What?"

"Leslie Connery, wake up me boy!" The speaker carried a strong Irish accent. Les quickly wiped the sleep away from his eyes. When he saw who was in front of him his jaw dropped.

"What's wrong, Leslie?"

"Father Flaherty?" Les guessed.

"Good to see you still recognize me after thirty years."

"What are you doing here? This is a ship! We're in the middle of the Aegean Sea!"

"Well, not the middle."

"This isn't real! This isn't happening!" Les said as he looked around. He repeated himself two or three times, each time with a little less emphasis until it appeared that he had finally convinced himself. Then he looked up at his visitor. "You died ten years ago," Les declared with unquestionable certitude, only to buckle at the last minute. "Didn't you?"

"Fifteen."

"So you aren't real! This is just a dream!"

"Call it what you like; I'm here nonetheless."

"So why I am dreaming about you?"

"It's *your* dream, Leslie."

"Well in that case, go away."

"I can't."

"I thought you said this is *my* dream."

"It certainly isn't mine."

Les groaned when he realized he couldn't make the priest vanish.

"I see your exasperation, my boy," the priest said. "Why don't we have a little talk?"

Les bowed to what seemed to be the inevitable. "Yeah, why not? You're not going away, and I'm not waking up," he conceded with a surly grin.

"Do you go to Holy Mass, Leslie?"

Les chuckled. *What else would a priest ask?* "Eh, no."

"Why not?"

"The wife," Les answered after a brief delay. "She's a Protestant."

"That's good."

"*Good?* It doesn't bother you that she's not Catholic?"

"'All who call on the name of the Lord shall be saved.'"

"How ecumenical of you."

"Time is a great teacher. So, you go to services with your wife?"

"Sometimes."

"Oh, then sometimes you go by yourself?"

"No."

"You don't go much at all, do you?"

"Hardly ever."

"I can see why not."

Les felt strangely impressed by Father Flaherty's compassion. "I'm glad you understand."

"You're a very wise and important man, Doctor Leslie Connery. You have acquired the knowledge of the centuries and more wealth than your father ever knew."

"What are you driving at?"

"You're a strong, self-made man. You have everything you need because of your own hard work. Never needed anyone's help. You're truly a rich man, Leslie."

"I'm not a *rich* man," Les retorted. "Well... I'm not a *poor* man."

"Maybe you are a poor man."

"What do you mean?"

"A rich man has all he needs, be it money, happiness, love. A poor man is needy."

"Needy? Yeah, he needs money."

"Maybe. Or maybe he needs something else. Maybe the man or woman with the most money is among the poorest of all."

"That's deep," Les said mockingly.

"How about a story?"

"A story?"

"You seem pretty bored with the course of this dream so far so let's liven it up a little."

Les cringed. He remembered oh-too-well the torture of sitting through one of the good father's endless yarns.

"Once there was a man, not unlike yourself, Leslie--"

"Of course," Les said as he rolled his eyes.

"Let's call him Leslie, for the sake of convenience."

"Sure."

"Now Leslie was a shepherd."

"A shepherd?"

"Yes, a shepherd. He was a very bright shepherd, perhaps the brightest of all. He had a large flock of sheep. They were beautiful, and they were his pride and joy. Leslie lived in a valley with other shepherds. It was a lush, green valley with the sweetest grass that any sheep could ever want to eat. The shepherds worked hard, but they loved their work.

"One day it became known that a wolf had come to the valley. One of the shepherds, we'll call him Larry, lost three of his sheep. He did not see the wolf take them, but he found sheep's blood in the grass and the paw prints of a wolf nearby. Larry's father had told him how dangerous a wolf could be. Larry remembered that his father bought a dog to protect his sheep, so Larry went out to inquire as to how to obtain such a valuable animal.

"Larry soon found that a dog, though very helpful in keeping the wolf away, did not come without a cost. The dog had to be fed, brushed, worked with and attended to. He had less time to play cards with his fellow shepherds and less money for wine and roast, which he loved, but he soon got over that when he saw how happy his sheep were.

"Now Larry's neighbor--uh, let's see, what's a good name for him?"

"Hank," Les blurted out. He was eager for the story to end.

"Good name, Leslie. Very well, Hank came to Larry and told him that he was losing a sheep a day. He'd noticed that Larry hadn't lost a sheep for several weeks. 'What's your secret?' Hank asked. 'It's my dog,' Larry began as he told Hank all about everything his dog was doing for him. 'I think

I will get a dog,' Hank declared. 'Now the dog will require your time and money,' Larry warned Hank. Then he told him all about his dog's other requirements. 'I've seen the difference it's made for you, Larry,' Hank said. 'Any cost the dog may bring is certainly worth it.'

"Soon Hank found himself in the same situation as Larry. His flock flourished, but his investment in them grew. At times he wondered if he made the right decision, but one look at the face of his sheep convinced him that he had. Word soon got around to the other shepherds. Many chose to do as Larry and Hank had done, but not all of them.

"Leslie--" when Father Flaherty said Les's name, Les found himself thrown into the bucolic scene in which the good priest had set the story. "Leslie had always had more sheep than the others." Les was suddenly surrounded by dozens of sheep. He could hear them, even smell them. "No wolf had ever made its presence known among his flock and Leslie did not believe one ever would.

"One day Leslie received a visitor." Les saw a short man walk up to him. "'I'm Larry,' the visitor said." Les shook the man's hand when he offered it. Les could feel the lanolin and grit on the shepherd's hand. "'I'd like to talk to you about protecting your sheep.'"

"That won't be necessary," Les heard himself say to Larry.

"'Haven't you heard of the wolf? He has destroyed many a flock in the valley. Those of us with dogs, who have followed the advice of my father and his father before him, have saved our flocks; not that the accursed wolf has not tried.'"

"Have you seen this wolf?" Les heard himself say. "Did you see him steal your sheep or those of your neighbors?"

"Larry rubbed his head a bit before he answered. 'No I haven't, but when my sheep have disappeared, I've seen the blood of the sheep mingled with the paw prints of the wolf.'"

"That doesn't prove anything," Les heard himself say.

"'Why have those with dogs seen their flocks flourish while those without have seen their flocks diminish?'"

"Poor stewardship on the part of those shepherds, obviously," Les heard himself say.

"'Not the lack of dogs?'"

"Precisely. I've lost no sheep, and I have no dog."

"Leslie," Father Flaherty continued, "was so impressed with himself at dismissing Larry's argument that he went to some of the neighbors who had obtained dogs to show them the foolishness of their decisions."

Les found himself walking down a country road talking to others about their dogs and the unlikelihood that the wolf had taken their sheep.

"Many felt his counsel wise and chose to believe him and abandoned their dogs," the priest continued. "Some, however, chose to believe Larry and kept their dogs."

"One day Leslie had a visitor. He had never seen this person before, but he soon took a liking to him. Leslie's new friend was tall with a pointy nose, big ears, pearly white teeth and fluffy white hair on his head. The new friend brought roast and wine, and he was quite good at cards. Leslie enjoyed his company immensely. When their time together was finished the new friend asked Leslie for a favor. 'Might I have one of your sheep,' he asked. 'I have none of my own and surely you could spare just one.' Leslie was not about to see his friend go away unhappy, and he graciously let him choose one of his sheep to take with him. 'Thank you so much,' said the visitor. 'May I call on you again tomorrow?'"

"Yes, do come," Les heard himself say as he showed his friend out.

As Father Flaherty continued, Les saw that his dream was becoming more and more lifelike. He was definitely *in* the story: he moved around like a puppet, not at all under his own volition. He could smell something different about his hairy new friend, but he couldn't quite put his finger on it. He seemed like a nice fellow.

"Leslie and his new friend met every day. They enjoyed the roast and the wine that the friend brought and the card games were absolutely tremendous."

Les could taste the smooth red wine and the succulent roast beef. They were quite delicious.

"Again the friend asked for a sheep and Leslie was only too happy to oblige him. The friend returned the next day and the day after that and the next day as well. Each time, Les offered a nice plump sheep for his gracious friend.

"Soon the news of Leslie's new friend spread throughout the valley, much of it because Leslie was only too happy to tell his fellow shepherds, those without dogs, about his new friend. Soon others asked the new friend to their houses. Such a wonderful time was worth a sheep or two.

"One day Larry came to Leslie's house with Hank. Leslie was entertaining his new friend and had gone outside to pick out a good sheep for his guest to take home that day. 'Leslie,' Larry said, 'Hank and I feel that you are in great danger.'"

"How so?" Les heard himself say.

"'Your flock has dwindled to almost nothing and your new friend, well, look at him,' Hank said as he pointed at the big window in the front of Leslie's house. 'He's the wolf!'"

"Don't be ridiculous!" Les heard himself say.

"'Look at him!' Larry said."

Les could see inside of the house. The visitor did look a little unusual. His face had become hairier, his nose more snout-like and his ears a little longer. And to make things even more curious, he appeared to have grown an appendage at the end of his spine, the *tail end*.

"He looks perfectly normal to me," Les heard himself say. *Hey, Leslie, or whatever your name is, that's a wolf!* "He's an ordinary person." *Hank and Larry are right: that's a wolf! Why can't you see that? I can and you're supposed to be me!*

"'Let me bring my dog over here. He'll be able to tell if you're friend's a wolf. Dogs are good at that,' Larry said."

"No need," Les heard himself say. "Now if you'll excuse me." He grabbed the last plump ewe of his flock and carried it into his house. *What are you doing? That's a wolf, you fool! Can't you hear me? Why can't you hear me?* "Here you go friend," Les heard himself say as he presented the ewe to what now there was no mistaking was a six-foot tall white wolf with a bushy white tail and pearly white fangs. *Can't you see that's the wolf? Let me out of here! Why can't I move? I want out! Father Flaherty! Why isn't this ending?*

Les felt the warm breath of the wolf on his neck. The wolf was right on top of him now. He felt the wolf wrap his giant jaws around his neck. *Run! Run you fool!* A second later he heard the delicate vertebrae of his neck crumble under the awesome crunching force of the giant carnivore's massive jaws.

"Nooooo!" Les screamed as he jumped to his feet, grabbing his neck as he did so. Wide-eyed, he looked all around. He was back in the galley. No sign of Father Flaherty! Certainly no sign of a wolf! "God!" he panted. "Jesus Christ! What the hell happened?" He looked around again. "A dream! A dream!" he panted. He grabbed his head and sat down. "Oh, boy! Wooo! Haven't had one like that for a while!"

Les rubbed his hand over that spot on his neck the wolf had bit in the dream and felt something warm. "What the—" He withdrew his hand quickly and examined it closely to find a small drop of fresh blood.

"Les!" Angie screamed as she ran into the room. "Les! Are you all right? I heard you yelling from down the hall!" She ran to him and threw her arms around him.

"I'm fine," Les declared as he looked over her shoulder and scrutinized that strange drop of blood. "It was a dream, Angie, just a dream! I'm okay!" He looked at the blood again. "Really! I'm fine!" If she could have seen the look on his pale face, Angie would have known better.

"That must have been some dream," Angie said. "I've never heard you scream like that before. What did you dream about?"

"I don't remember," he lied. "I remember falling asleep here and then waking up screaming." Les wrinkled his forehead as he contemplated his recent reverie. *That was weird! And so realistic! And the blood…what about the blood? I must have scratched myself or something. Yeah, that's it.* He looked at his fingernails: no blood. His eyes quickly scanned the room again. He felt a chill go up his spine when he thought of what he had been through. *What the hell is going on here? It's the relic! It has to be that damned Lance of Longinus!*

CHAPTER TWELVE

Cankurtaran, April 13, Midnight

"Sir Richard," the voice said gently.

"Yes, yes," the Grand Master of the Knights Templar said dreamily as he rose from his slumber.

"Sir Richard, I've finished my search," the voice said again.

"Capital, Quincy! Absolutely capital!" Sir Richard cheered as he rose from his hotel bed. "You boys at MI-6 do wonderful work!"

Jasper Quincy was a pale thin man with thinning black hair. "So you say that this tall blond fellow stole something from you?"

"Yes. German-looking sort of chap. Funny thing is I think I shot him with my crossbow yesterday evening!" Sir Richard chuckled.

Quincy let this new information go. "Based on your description, I was able to come up with three men." He opened his briefcase and retrieved three photographs. "Do you recognize any of them?" he asked as he set each one on the bed.

"That one! That's him!" Sir Richard exclaimed. "Wouldn't forget that bastard's face!"

"You're certain?"

"No doubt, Jasper! No doubt!"

"I thought as much. He's Siegfried Geissler. Part of a Neo-Nazi group of some kind. We don't know much about them."

"Bloody MI -6 doesn't know much about him? I find that impossible to believe!"

"We do have our limits, Sir Richard. What exactly did he take from you?"

"Jasper, how long have you been a Knight of the Temple?"

"You know, sir. My father was a Templar and when I came of age…"

"So how long then?"

"Well, thirty-seven years, Sir Richard. Why do you ask something you already know?"

"Sit down." When Quincy had complied, Sir Richard began. "Have you heard of the Lance of Longinus?"

"Hasn't every Templar?"

"What if I told you that I was holding the genuine article in my hands when this Hun bastard stole it from me?"

"I thought it was in Vienna."

"I assure you that what I held in my hand was the very same spear that pierced the side of my blessed ancestor."

"Good Lord!"

"Now you know why I called you."

Quincy's face went pale. "That may explain why Siegfried Geissler stole it from you, sir."

"What?"

"His father Hugo was the keeper of the Lance of Destiny for the SS. Some say there is still an organization of SS men who worked with Geissler."

"But how did the bloody SS find out about its discovery yesterday?"

"That's not important. It's bad enough that they have it now. I'll get as many agents as I can on this without attracting too much attention. I will find Geissler for you sir."

"Let me know as soon as possible, Jasper."

"Will you need help getting it back, Sir Richard?"

"No. Just find him for me."

Marmara Hotel, Taksim, 5:00 a.m.

"It's Chief Calik," Osman said as he handed the phone to Luci Daniels.

"How does he sound?" Luci asked.

"Excited," Osman smiled.

"About time." Luci took the phone from Osman. "Good morning, Chief Calik. Do you have something for me?"

"Good morning Ms. Daniels. I am happy to say that I do."

"Excellent!" Luci smiled and looked at Osman who smiled back.

"My men have been working all night."

"Do you *have* it?" The tone of her voice made her impatience known.

"No, but--"

"Chief, I'm rather disappointed. For what I'm paying you, I'd expect the relic gift wrapped with a pretty bow sitting at my front door."

"We are not so lucky, madam."

"You're inept is what you are!"

Calik was silent. "We may have found out where Yakis is."

"May have?" Luci growled. "I don't want 'may have'!"

"Please, Ms. Daniels. This could be very important."

"So what is it?"

"Yakis has an uncle who owns a freighter."

"So?"

"It's on its way to Bodrum as we speak."

Luci motioned to Osman to bring her pen and paper. "Bodrum, you say?" she asked as she wrote it on the pad of paper. "What's the name of the ship?"

"*Persephone.*"

"Chief," Luci crowed, "you may have just redeemed yourself. Good day," she added and hung up. "Osman, there's a bottle of Dom Perignon in the fridge."

"A cause for celebration, madam?" he asked as he uncorked and poured the champagne.

"We have them, Osman," she said as he handed her a glass. "This calls for a toast: to victory!" Luci said as she slowly sipped the sparkling wine.

"To victory, madam," Osman repeated as he lifted his glass and then took a sip. "Where are they?"

"Bodrum," she answered with a smile. "Have Roger call for the helicopter. When they get there, we'll be waiting."

"Yes, sir," Roger Brown said after receiving the order from Osman. He acted surprised, but he had heard the news through his hidden microphones before Osman called. Roger called the helicopter pilot and informed him of the news as Luci and Osman left her office. He waved good-bye to them and then hung up. He found his cell phone in his desk drawer and dialed another number.

"*Herr Geissler? Reinhardt Braun*...Bodrum," he continued in German. "The Lance is on its way to Bodrum on a ship called *Persephone*...a young Turk named Yakis and two Americans...one a tall *schwarze* the other an Irishman...*Bitte, mein herr.*"

Cankurtaran, 6:58 a.m.

"Telephone, sir," Kevin Meeley said as he handed the phone to his master.

"Covington-Smith here," Sir Richard declared.

"Jasper Quincy, sir."

"Jasper! Any news?"

"Your German friend has booked a flight for Bodrum--"

"Bodrum? Why the devil is he going there?"

"I don't know, sir, but he's taking his father with him."

"Well I'll be buggered!"

"Turkish Airlines Flight 112 leaves at 10:35 a.m. I took the liberty of purchasing you two tickets on another flight, 104, which leaves at 10:00."

"First class?"

"No, I'm sorry. Coach was all they had."

"Any other flights?"

"Only if you want to arrive after they do. You'll lose them for certain then sir."

"Blast! Well, we all have our crosses to bear."

"Yes, sir."

"Good work, Jasper! Call Kevin on the cell phone if you need me."

"Yes, Sir Richard. Good day, sir."

Sir Richard hung up without replying. "Pack up, my boy! We're off to Bodrum!"

Eastern Aegean Sea, 7:06 a.m.

Angie sat with Mehmet in the galley as they sipped coffee. Les had retired seven hours earlier and was still sawing logs on B deck.

"Is Doctor Connery okay?" Mehmet asked.

Angie looked the young man in the eye. "I've never seen him like this before," she began slowly. "He's never awakened from a dream like that. Not since I've known him."

"Now he is exhausted."

"Yes. I wonder if his exhaustion…" Angie began as she looked away from Mehmet and stared at a stack of dishes in the distance.

"What are you thinking, Doctor Johnson?"

"Nothing really." Her stare was unbroken.

"I'm going up to the bridge to speak with my uncle. I'll ask him how much longer until we reach Bodrum."

Angie turned to Mehmet. "Thank you, Mehmet. I'd like to know."

As Mehmet left the galley Angie's thoughts returned to Les. *Something got to him. Was it the argument? No, we've had worse before.* Angie ran her hands through her hair. She worked the coarse black strands through her fingers as if she were teasing fine sand out of cashmere yarn. *But never about this.*

We don't ever talk about that kind of stuff…about…God…church… magical reli—Stop! Angie wiped a tear from her eye. *Now, that's all I want to talk about. What is happening to us?* She bowed her head and clasped her hands together, like a four-year old does when she says grace. *God, what are you doing?* She sniffed back a few tears. *Why me? Why Les?* Now she was angry. *What are you doing? You throw two good people together in an impossible situation and tear their marriage apart! Ha! That's assuming we live through this!*

Angie suddenly felt a small ache in her heart: an ache that one might feel when a lifelong friend leaves for a very long time. She swallowed hard and took a deep breath. *It's not fair! I don't want this thing! Leave me alone! Leave both of us alone!* For some reason she thought about Mehmet. She lifted her head. *Mehmet, yes Mehmet!* A wide smile appeared on her lips. *We'll let Mehmet take care of the Lance of Longinus, wash our hands of it!* As she thought this Angie felt a crushing pain in her right wrist. She screamed in anguish. She had never experienced such pain in her life. Then it left only to return a few seconds later. "Oh, God!" Angie screamed in absolute agony. It happened a third time, without pause, and the pain threw her to the floor. She quickly thought of every possible medical explanation, but none of them made sense. "My God, why is this happening?" Angie cried. Her right hand throbbed incessantly as perspiration dripped from her forehead. She groaned and felt her throat tighten. "Oh my God!" She had never experienced such torment.

Then the anguish suddenly departed and Angie's vision blurred for a second or two. When it returned she thought she saw something. She squinted and saw that it looked like a human form, but she had never seen anything in this way before. Angie couldn't convince herself that she was seeing *anything,* but there was something there. She could feel its presence. The figure raised his, or her, she couldn't tell, right hand. When the limb reached its zenith the pain returned to her right wrist, but this time it was much less intense and lasted only a second or two. Then Angie suddenly felt a similar sensation in her left wrist and a second later simultaneously in both ankles. Angie gasped. She couldn't endure the pain again were it to return in its previous severity, yet the limb pains ebbed without incident.

Angie sighed. *It's over!* However, a lightening bolt into her right side fractured the apparent respite. "My body," she heard, "broken for you."

Angie felt her fingers tingle, then her toes. *I must be hyperventilating!* But this was a most unusual tingling. She likened it to the way her body felt when she crossed the finish line in first place, how she felt when she learned that she had finished first in her class at medical school and the feeling she had as she and Les exchanged vows at their wedding. This was how she felt when Les' and her first child was born. She held her breath, but the tingling progressed. Her arms, her face, her legs and then, all at once, her entire body felt it. The sensation consumed her: it was all of these wonderful feelings together and more. It gave new meaning to the word "ecstasy".

"Be still!" Angie heard, "and know that I am--"

"God!" Angie gasped.

The formless figure faded into the milky light from which it had come, but Angie still felt its presence. She stood and felt strong, renewed, rejuvenated, even better than she had ever felt when she was at the peak of her training. She looked at her wrists, and for a brief second Angie swore she saw a scar over each one, but the image failed to persist.

Angie ran out of the galley and up to B deck. Les was still sleeping. She smiled as she watched him snore. She walked over to the safe, opened it and slowly removed the casket. That same beautiful, dreamy feeling returned all over her body: rapture, ultimate and complete. Angie set the reliquary by her side and slowly dropped to her knees.

"I'm sorry!" Angie said under her breath. "I'm sorry I doubted you!" she said, as if she had disappointed her very best friend. The ecstasy slowly grew. She closed her eyes as she felt the warm waves wrap around her. "How wonderful! How magnificent this feels, God!" Then she slowly opened her eyes. "But I still don't understand. Why me? Why Les?" Angie felt a twinge of pain in her heart as she asked. When she touched her breast to soothe the ache, Angie thought she heard a whisper in her ear. She couldn't understand what was said, but she felt strangely satisfied, although she couldn't tell why. "I will do as you wish, God," she said, almost resignedly. "But please protect my husband and me." Angie stood, and as she did so, she added, "And please let him know, someday, this beautiful thing you showed me today."

CHAPTER THIRTEEN

Police Station, Sirkeci, 7:10 a.m.

Albert Boucher watched the police scratch their heads in confusion. They had studied every aspect of their building's southwest corner. It was inconceivable that the nearly-new building's corner had disintegrated as it had.

How did Donkeybrain escape? Albert shook his head in disgust. His dream was evaporating before his eyes. He had come to police station hoping that Mehmet had been caught again or that the police were on to him, but he doubted that these Turkish morons were up to the task. Albert walked into the police station. "Inspector Gur," he said in passable Turkish to the desk sergeant.

The sergeant pointed to an office at the end of a long corridor and said something that Albert didn't understand. When Albert failed to respond, the sergeant encouraged him toward the office.

Albert approached the door quietly. From inside he could hear Gur yelling at someone. Albert couldn't hear anyone else in the room and surmised that Gur was on the phone. He pressed his ear to the door and listened. Of course he couldn't understand most of what the inspector was saying, but he did catch a few words that were familiar. Among them were "Yakis" and "Daniels", obviously referring to Mehmet and this Daniels woman, whom Albert knew as the patron of this most recent effort to restore Aya Sofia. The frequent allusions to Mehmet were understandable, but the repeated references to Lucille Daniels seemed bizarre. Since when did a wealthy museum donor garner so much attention from the police?

Gur's conversation on the phone continued during the entire five minutes of Albert's eavesdropping and showed no sign of stopping. Albert left the police station. *I'm not going to find out what I need to know here.* He ran over to Aya Sofia to find the curator.

Aya Sofia, 7:16 a.m.

"Did you know that the police found that thief Yakis yesterday?" Albert asked the nervous curator as soon as he arrived at the museum.

"Yes, I heard," the curator answered without looking Albert in the eye. He was far too busy looking over the museum's financial records.

"Well, Yakis has escaped."

The curator froze and looked Albert in the eye. "What?"

"Gone. Escaped through a hole in the wall of the police station." Albert savored the fearful expressions that flashed across the curator's face.

The curator hastily called an assistant on the phone. Again the conversation was unintelligible to Albert, except for one word that recurred with curious regularity: Daniels. The curator hung up and looked at Albert as if his continued presence were irritating to him. The curator wiped his brow again and tried to assume some resemblance of normalcy. "Will you be working in the gallery again today?"

Albert hesitated momentarily. "Certainly, sir," he lied. "However, it seems that I have left an important tool at my apartment. I'll have to go get it."

"Very well," the curator said as he turned away from Albert and nervously picked up the phone again.

Albert ran out of the museum. *Lucille Daniels! She is the key!*

Marmara Hotel, Taksim, 7:42 a.m.

Albert Boucher bolted out of the taxi and ran into the Marmara Hotel. He ran to the front desk and pushed his way to the front.

"I am Jean Ternier, Vice-President of European Operations for Black Star International. Please direct me to Ms. Daniels's office."

The tall black-haired woman behind the desk examined his casual dress. "You are a vice-president?" she asked incredulously.

Albert was ready for her. "The airline lost my luggage. I've come all the way from Iceland."

She smiled back at him. "Penthouse, top floor, Monsieur Ternier. Do you need assistance?"

"No thank you," Albert said as he raced for the elevator.

Within minutes Albert was at the penthouse. He slowly swaggered up to Roger Brown's desk and introduced himself. "I'm Jean Ternier. The Paris office sent me to review the LeClerc account with Ms. Daniels."

Roger moused through several screens on his computer. "I don't--"

Albert saw that he had only one chance. "This is ridiculous! I haven't come all this way to be detoured by an errand boy!" He shot around Roger's desk and hurried to the door to Luci's office.

"Wait! You can't!" Roger screamed.

"Ms. Daniels, I'm Jean Ternier," Albert said as he flew into the office. "Paris is very concerned--" He stopped when he found the room empty.

Roger rushed in after him. "I'm calling security! I don't care who you are!"

Albert coolly raised his hand to silence the irate secretary. "She's gone," he noted, confounded by missing her.

"I could have told you that!"

"Where?"

"I'm not about to tell you! Now get out!"

Albert's eyes shot across the room. He needed to find a clue, anything. The uncorked champagne bottle grabbed his attention. He casually walked over to it and lifted it off the table. It was more than half full! "1994." He smiled at Roger. "Ever have some? It's the best."

Roger had never indulged in expensive champagne. He jettisoned his characteristic toadiness and hurried over to the door and closed it. "Good, huh?" he asked as he walked back to Albert.

"It will make your entire body tingle." Albert sat down and encouraged Roger to join him. As the secretary approached, Albert raised his finger. "We're going to need glasses. Have to do this right, you know."

Roger smiled. He was beginning to like this Frenchman. "Sure thing. There's a wet bar across the way."

While Roger was gone, Albert's eyes scoured the table for anything. He saw the used notepad and picked it up. He saw the imprint from two words written on the previous page. Albert carefully pulled a pencil out of his jacket pocket and shaded the imprint on the first page. "Persephone," he whispered to himself as he read to top line. He shaded the next line. *Bodrum.*

"Glasses!" Roger announced as he walked in, champagne glasses raised high.

Albert stood up. "My friend," he said as he threw his arm around Roger's shoulders, "if we're going to enjoy this absolutely perfect champagne, let's add something equally perfect and make this a real party!"

"What do you have?"

"In my room downstairs I have some of the best hash you ever smoked." Roger's eyes glowed. "All right!"

"I'll be right back, my friend! Go ahead and pour yourself some champagne!" Albert cajoled as he ran to the elevator. With any luck a taxi would be out in front of the hotel, and he could be on his way to the airport and from there to Bodrum.

Eastern Aegean Sea, 7:31 a.m.

Angie had fallen asleep with her knees on the floor and her waist bent over the bed. Her hands were still clasped in prayer and her face possessed a tranquil grin. Some may have thought Les's snoring capable of peeling the paint off the walls, but even that couldn't rouse her. However, something suddenly startled her. Angie jumped away from the bed. Her eyes were wide open, pupils dilated. Something had heightened her sense of alarm. It almost felt as if there were a third person in the room. She spun her head around and looked at the floor where she had left the relic. She looked at the cloth bag hesitantly. The Lance was there, beckoning to her. Angie vacillated. She couldn't help but be overwhelmed by a pervasive air of dread that filled the room. Something was up. Angie bent down opened the bag cautiously, as if it were electrified, placed her hand on the reliquary.

As Angie touched the casket her fears were confirmed. Her forehead ached. As she closed her eyes to mollify the pain, she saw someone taking the reliquary away from her; Les's lifeless body lay crumpled on the ground and Mehmet was slowly dying from a gunshot to the chest. Angie opened her eyes and gasped. She instantly knew what this meant. "We can't land at Bodrum! They're on to us! Les! Les! Wake up! Where's Mehmet? Les, wake up!"

"Are we sinking?" Les screamed as he precipitously emerged from his sleep.

"We've got to get off this ship! We can't go to Bodrum!" Angie grabbed the casket and ran out of the room to Mehmet's cabin next door. She frantically pounded on the door and called his name. When no answer came from the room, Angie turned and ran toward the bridge. Les had fallen back asleep.

Angie found him on the stairs on the way to the bridge. "Mehmet!" She grabbed him and hugged him tightly.

"Doctor Johnson?" Mehmet was flabbergasted by Angie's greeting. "What is the matter?"

"We can't go to Bodrum! "We've got to land somewhere else!"

"Why?"

Angie held up the casket. She didn't have to say anything else.

"I see," Mehmet said soberly. He thought for a second and added, "Doctor Johnson, there is something I must tell you."

"What is it, Mehmet?"

"Yasmin told me that the Lance of Longinus is more than just an artifact."

"You already knew that."

"No, I mean something even more significant."

"Like?"

"The Lance of Longinus has been considered a source of great power by kings and emperors since ancient times."

"Do you mean that Daniels--"

"It's more than just another trinket to add to her collection."

Angie sighed heavily.

"She's a very powerful woman who obviously isn't satisfied with what she has," Mehmet added.

"Oh dear God," Angie muttered. "What have you gotten us into?"

"Come," Mehmet interjected. "We must speak to my uncle."

Uncle Murad was very busy on the bridge. Mehmet hated to interrupt, but the urgency was paramount. "Uncle," he said calmly, "I must discuss an emergency with you."

Murad hid his alarm well. He took Mehmet and Angie to an empty corner of the bridge. "What is it?" he whispered.

"We must leave the ship, immediately. Trouble awaits us in Bodrum," Mehmet replied.

"We'll be there in less than four hours. How do you know--"

"I'm sorry I can't explain it to you now, but we must leave. How can we get ashore? It's a matter of the greatest urgency, uncle."

Murad scowled back.

"I swear it! You must get the three of us off this ship as soon as possible! Please, Uncle. I beg of you!"

Murad walked over to a map and consulted with the navigator. "Prepare one of the boats," he said to one of the mates. He turned to Mehmet. "Come here." Murad thrust his finger at a point on the map as Mehmet joined him at the map table. "Yalikavak. We'll be there in two and a half hours. I'll take you and your friends ashore." Murad sensed unease and added, "It's the best place to leave you."

"Yes, Uncle. Thank you." Mehmet nodded and walked back to Angie. "Uncle Murad is going to take us ashore at Yalikavak, about two and a half hours from now."

Angie held the casket by her fingertips, hoping for a revelation: nothing. "I guess that's okay. I'll tell Les." She returned to B deck to find her husband life-jacketed and ready to abandon ship.

"Well are we sinking or not? None of the crew seemed the least bit concerned," Les whined.

Angie chuckled and gave him a big hug. "I love you, Les." She kissed his lips.

"My guess is we're not sinking."

"Right. Let's go sit and talk."

Les removed his lifejacket and followed Angie back to their bunks.

"We're going ashore in a couple of hours," Angie began.

"Bodrum already?"

Angie hesitated. "No. There's been a change of plan."

"How so?"

"Bodrum isn't safe. We'll go ashore further north."

"Mehmet's uncle decide this?"

Angie was silent. How could she explain to Les what Mehmet had told her just minutes ago?

"What's up, Angie?" Les asked innocently.

Angie sighed. "We've had a rough time the last ten hours. I don't want to fight with you again, Les."

Les gently put his hand on her cheek. "It's the Lance, isn't it?" he asked softly.

Angie didn't answer.

"Sweetheart," Les said as he gently ran his fingers over her lips. "It's okay. I understand."

Angie looked longingly into his eyes. "What do you mean, baby?"

"I've done a lot of thinking since the last time we spoke."

"About...."

"Everything."

"Everything? What do you mean?"

"I guess I mean the Lance... and all the other stuff we fought about...."

"Go on."

"I think I owe you a giant apology. I can't believe I was treating my best friend like that."

"Les--"

"Honey, let me finish, please. The last twenty-four hours have been the most bizarre in my life."

"Mine too."

"But I've learned something. I've learned something about you. I see what this relic is doing to you--"

"Les--"

"Please, let me finish," Les said as he raised his hand. "You know how highly I think of you, not just as my wife but as a doctor, as an athlete, as a human being. If you say that there is something special about this Lance, then I believe there is."

"You're not just humoring me?"

"No. No, I'm not." Les looked away, bit his lip, then turned back to Angie. "I think, last night the Lance spoke to me, too."

"*Spoke* to you?"

"Maybe that's not the right word."

Angie inched closer to him and laid her hand on his. "What is it, Les?"

"I had a dream--"

"When you were screaming."

"Right, when I was--well, you remember. Angie, that dream..."

"Pretty weird?"

"Weird's not the right word."

"Was it about the Lance?"

"No. It was something else. Something *parallel,* let's say."

"What was it?"

"That's not really important." Father Flaherty's visitation was too embarrassing to discuss at the moment. "What is important is that he helped me to realize that you're right...about the relic, I mean." He meant to say that she was right about more than just the Lance, but pride was too large an obstacle. He knew that the Lance was just the beginning, and he reasoned that whatever spoke through it, maybe it was God, had touched him as it must have touched Angie. Les felt a sort of hunger, a curious yearning, to explore this *feeling* that the Lance had given them. He had never felt anything like it before, and something deep within him wanted more. This strange fragment of history, this iron artifact, had turned Angie's and his comfortable life upside down, and he had to know why. They were intelligent, well-educated people. Relics were the epitome of superstition. Or were they? This one was certainly not.

Angie gently grasped his hand. "I knew you'd come around. Thank you." She kissed him and then hugged him tightly. "I have this overwhelming sense of obligation—it's hard to explain."

"I think I'm feeling that too: we've got to see this thing through."

"God willing," Angie interjected, uncertain that Les wouldn't chafe at her invoking the Almighty.

"God willing," Les said back to her without wincing.

Bodrum, 9:38 a.m.

"Thank you, madam," Osman said as he grabbed a few more figs from the basket between Luci Daniels and himself. The Mercedes limo they had taken from the airport rode smoothly over the freshly paved road.

"I can have the driver stop if you need something else," Luci suggested.

"No, I don't want to slow down. We have a relic to collect!"

"You've been a great help, Osman." Luci placed her hand on his knee. "When we get our treasure, my friend, you will have your reward." She winked at him and then looked out the window at the fourteenth century Crusader castle near the harbor.

Most of the castle had been made from the ruins of the great Mausoleum, built by King Mausolus in ancient times to house his wife's remains. In its time, everyone considered it one of the Seven Wonders of the World. Now the Mausoleum was but a story in a history book, obliterated, torn asunder; its fragments now scattered throughout this crude castle.

Ataturk Airport, 10:09 a.m.

"You need to relax more, my son," Hugo Geissler said with a chuckle as he hugged his son. He sat in a chair in the waiting area for Flight 112 and stretched out his legs. "Sit, Siegfried." He took a bite from a roll and looked around. "Soon, we will find the Lance of Destiny--"

"And this time we will not lose it!" Siegfried steamed.

"Yes, my son," Hugo agreed sheepishly. "This time we will not lose it. Come, they are boarding the plane."

Turkish Airlines Flight 104, 10:10 a.m.

"We'll be landing soon, Sir Richard," Kevin Meeley yawned after awaking from a brief nap.

"It won't be too soon!" Sir Richard groused. "Damned cattle car!" Up to this point he had been a stranger to coach class.

"Just think, sir," Kevin said in a rare moment of insight, "you will soon be holding the Holy Lance again."

"In *one* hand," Sir Richard growled as he looked at the picture of the giant German that Jasper Quincy had provided him. "And in the other hand, this bloody German bastard's head!"

CHAPTER FOURTEEN

Eastern Aegean, 10:32 a.m.

The rubber dinghy bounced rhythmically over the waves of the harbor at Yalikavak. Angie and Les sat in the bow, holding hands tightly as they leaned forward and watched the Asian shore draw nearer. Angie glanced at her husband and noted his childlike gaze locked on the docks. She remembered the first time she met him, at a party in their college dormitory. She was standing with some of her fellow track teammates, and this gangly, redheaded boy introduced himself and offered her a beer. As she accepted his gift, Les stumbled and her libation became a shower.

Angie looked away, smiled and giggled inside as she remembered that first meeting. *And now here we are, risking our lives to save a two thousand-year old spear. But maybe to save more than an ancient piece of iron.* She looked at Les again. *He seems convinced that we're doing the right thing.* She glanced back at Mehmet who sat amidships, cradling the casket easily in his hands. *What will You have us do next?* Angie remembered singing a spiritual in church when she was six, "Children, go where I send thee...."

Angie looked up at the sun in the sky. *You've finally reached me after all of these years.* A big smile formed on her face. *You really have a way of getting a person's attention!* She remembered the feeling she had while Les slept on the ship earlier that morning: the excruciating pain and the indescribable ecstasy. She replayed the entire episode in her mind two or three times. *Yes. I understand now.*

At the stern, Uncle Murad spoke with the harbormaster by walkie-talkie as he guided the craft forward. He had informed the authorities that *Persephone* was having engine trouble, and he would like to come ashore to meet a mechanic and bring him aboard. This ruse was his idea. Before they had left the ship, Murad had called a friend in Yalikavak. Once they were ashore, Mehmet and the Americans would meet him and plan their escape.

Mehmet probably understood the reliquary and its contents as well as Angie. He hadn't directly experienced any of power Doctor Johnson claimed it had. At least, not yet. But the Lance had an indescribable presence about it that he couldn't neglect. It was if it were speaking to him in a language he couldn't understand. One thing he knew for certain: he had to do his best to keep it from Lucille Daniels. At first it was a treasure, a treasure of his country, a treasure that deserved a better end than to sit in the dark vault of a woman of questionable character. However, if what Yasmin had told him about the Lance were true, and he had no reason to doubt her, it was his obligation as a Muslim to keep such a fantastic weapon, for lack of a better word, from someone as evil as the Daniels woman. He re-examined what he'd said in his discussions with the Americans. *If this Lance is genuine…am I helping the Christian cause? Is that wrong?* He shook his head disapprovingly and looked down at the casket. *It has never spoken to me…only to Doctor Johnson…but I have felt* something! He squeezed it gently and thought of his last conversation with Yasmin. *Is this an idol? To be destroyed so it does not mislead the faithful?* He closed his eyes. *My heart says "no" but my mind knows it to be true.* He looked down and sighed. *If I destroyed it, the Daniels woman could not have it, and it could not mislead the true believers. I could just drop it into the sea! Right now and be done with it!* Then he wondered if Angie were right: would destroying such a precious relic with such wonderful powers bring down the Almighty's wrath upon him? *Allah, you make life so complicated!*

Les appeared to be entranced with the harbor ahead, but his mind couldn't have been further away. Father Flaherty, the dream, the blood on his neck: the images refused to leave the forefront of his mind. He was frozen and didn't move. He didn't want to, as if staying perfectly still would reveal why all of this was happening. Les had told Angie that he believed her and he did. The Lance of Longinus was something fantastic, something that touched the flesh of God. It had to be! He couldn't deny that anymore. *Why would God…*He closed his eyes briefly, thinking that would clear his head. *I don't know what's happening, or why. Angie's right. Angie's right.*

Murad cut the engine and steered the dinghy into the dock. "You must go now," he said to Mehmet. "At the end of the wharf a taxi is waiting. The driver's name is Arslan. He is a friend of mine, and he will take you wherever you need to go. Don't worry about money; he owes me."

"Uncle—" Mehmet began.

"You must go now," Murad barked. "Thank me later." He motioned to Les and Angie to disembark.

"Thank you, sir," Angie said. "We owe you our lives."

"Yes, thank you—" Les began.

"Go," Murad said gently in halting English. "You go now."

"Good bye, Uncle," Mehmet said in his native tongue as he hugged Murad. "Thank you!"

Murad helped each of them on to the wharf, Mehmet last. "Remember," he said to his nephew, "Taxi; Arslan."

"Yes, Uncle."

At the end of the wharf, the yellow taxi waited. An old man in abrown tweed jacket leaned against the driver's door, smoking a cigarette.

"Mister Arslan?" Mehmet asked uncertainly in Turkish.

"You are Murad's nephew?" Arslan asked.

"Yes!" Mehmet answered. "Yes!"

Arslan eyed Angie and Les.

"They are with me," Mehmet added.

Arslan stepped to the rear door and opened it for Angie and ushered her into the cab.

"Thank you," she said.

Les went around to the other rear door to open it but Arslan would have none of it. He shooed Les away from the door and then opened it for his guest.

"Thank you," Les smiled.

Arslan quickly stepped to the front passenger seat once Les was in and opened it for Mehmet. "Mister Yakis," he began, again in Turkish, "be so kind as to have a seat in my taxi."

"Thank you. You're very gracious, sir."

Arslan chuckled. "Your uncle is the gracious one, young sir. He has helped my family and me many, many times. He's a good man."

"I thank you for your kindness anyway."

Arslan trotted around the front of the taxi and quickly examined his headlights. In ten seconds he was in the driver's seat turning the ignition. "Where may I take you, Mister Yakis?"

Mehmet was dumbfounded. He looked back as Angie and Les. "Where should we go?" he asked them.

"I don't know," Les replied. "Angie?"

"I never thought of that," Angie answered. "Well, I'm open to any ideas," she added looking at Mehmet.

Mehmet handed Angie the reliquary. "Do you think it may help?"

"Maybe." Angie smiled and accepted it.

"Anything?" Les asked after waiting a few seconds.

Angie looked down at the cotton bag and slid her fingers inside. She gently pressed them onto the golden reliquary. "Nothing." She looked up at Les. "Nothing."

"What should we do then?" Les asked.

Arslan said something in Turkish to Mehmet. Mehmet replied and turned to the Americans. "Mister Arslan says he knows of many nice hotels two or three kilometers from here."

"That's a good thought," Angie said. "Pending any other ideas," she glanced down at the casket, "we need to figure out what to do next."

"I could use a bite," Les said.

Mehmet said something to Arslan and the taxi rolled forward toward the town.

Bodrum, 11:05 a.m.

"He says that he expects the *Persephone* at this dock at 11:30," Osman said to Luci.

Luci looked over the Bodrum police chief, a short, nervous man with a gray mustache and wire-rimmed glasses, who was very happy to tell them everything about his city's harbor whether they asked or not.

The police chief scanned the harbor and informed Osman that the traffic was particularly light today. He mentioned that he had taken care to enlist the harbor patrol with its dozen speedboats and four helicopters. The chief expected their arrival at any minute.

Luci's response to Osman's translation was cool. "I don't care if he has the whole damned Turkish Army here. As long as we get what we're after."

Bodrum, another part of the harbor, 11:16 a.m.

"I don't think this idiot knows where he is going!" Siegfried growled.

"We're at the harbor, Siegfried. We still have time before the *Persephone* docks," Hugo retorted.

When the cab stopped, Hugo paid the man and then joined Siegfried, who was questioning harbor workers as to where their quarry was to land. Siegfried saw Hugo come up behind and signaled him to follow.

"There they go, Kevin!" Sir Richard screeched, rousing his slumbering companion from his reverie in the back seat of the cab. "Damned Nazis!"

"Yes, sir," Kevin replied, wiping his sleepy eyes. "I'm right on them, sir!"

"Wait! Give them a little more room," Sir Richard warned. "We've tailed them all of the way from the bloody airport. We don't want to spook them now."

"Yes, sir."

Yalikavak, 11:19 a.m.

Arslan had found a little outdoor restaurant that overlooked the water. They sat on old painted wooden chairs around a round table, just big enough for the four of them. Of course Arslan knew the owner so only the best food was offered.

"These are absolutely incredible!" Les declared as he swallowed the last dolma on his plate. "Is that cinnamon I taste?"

"Nutmeg," Mehmet answered after conferring with Mister Arslan.

"They are quite good," Angie added as she took a sip of white wine made in a village near the ruins of Ephesus. "Now that we've had lunch, anyone have an idea what we do next? It won't be long before they find out we're not on the ship."

"Where can we go?" Les asked. "Are we going to spend the rest of our days running around Turkey, one step ahead of the police?"

"That certainly is not sustainable, Doctor Connery," Mehmet answered.

"Can we hide the Lance?" Angie asked.

"Where? Whom can we trust?" Les asked. "Anyway, if they catch us with or without the Lance, we'll go to prison for sure."

"I know many people who would be willing to hide it for us," Mehmet answered, "but I am not willing to endanger their lives. This Daniels woman would stop at nothing to have the Lance; I am certain of that."

"Turkey's a big country," Les said. "There's got to be some place it will be safe."

"But where?" Angie asked Mehmet.

Mehmet became very quiet and his face betrayed a deep sadness.

"Mehmet?" Angie asked. "What's wrong?"

"Perhaps," Mehmet began softly and slowly, "Perhaps it is best that the Lance is taken out of the country."

"But you have said so much about how this is a great treasure of the Turkish people," Les protested.

Angie put her hand on Mehmet's shoulder. "We know how much this means to you."

"Thank you, Doctor Johnson--" Mehmet began.

"Please. It's about time you called us by our first names," Angie said.

"Very well," Mehmet replied. "Angie, Les," he began uncertainly, "I have come to realize that I would rather see the Lance in another country, out of Turkey and safe, than in the hands of that woman."

"I think we all agree on that," Angie said.

"But where? British Museum, Smithsonian?" Les asked.

"I fear that even those places would not be safe enough," Mehmet said.

"It should be *hidden* in another country?" Les asked.

"It has been hidden for centuries already," Mehmet replied.

"Mehmet, I agree that it may be best to get the relic out of Turkey," Angie said, "but hiding it?"

"It must be safe!" Mehmet raised his voice.

The table was suddenly silent. Angie's heavy sigh was followed by gentle words. "Yes. You're absolutely right."

"So what's our next move?" Les asked.

"Getting it out of the country, I suppose," Angie answered.

"What's the closest country? Syria? Iraq?" Les asked. "Those both sound delightful," he sneered.

"Greece," Mehmet said with certainty.

"Greece?" Angie asked. "We'd have to fly--"

"There are many small Greek islands a short distance off the coast," Mehmet interjected.

"We gonna swim there?" Les chuckled.

"We can hire a boat," Mehmet answered. "Once we are in Greek territory we can make our way west."

"What if we're caught on the way?" Angie asked. "The Turkish authorities have secured all of the borders."

Mehmet asked Arslan something in Turkish. The older man laughed and replied to Mehmet and then smiled at the Americans.

"What's he so happy about?" Les asked.

Mehmet was smiling as well but not as widely as the older man. "Mister Arslan and Uncle Murad used to smuggle...certain items...between here and the Greek islands."

"And now he wants to relive the old times?" Les asked disapprovingly.

"Les," Angie interjected, "he can be a big help to us. If he knows how to get past the border patrols, let him help."

"Suppose we make it to Greece," Les wondered, "what guarantee do we have that the Greek authorities won't hand us over to the Turks?"

"You are not very familiar with the history of relations between Greece and Turkey," Mehmet interjected.

"What do you mean?" Les asked.

"They don't get along very well," Angie interjected. "It's a centuries-old feud."

"So the Greeks wouldn't cooperate?" Les asked.

"At least not immediately," Mehmet answered. "However, you must also realize that if the existence of this relic became known, the Greeks would claim it as their own. The Greeks still refer to Istanbul as Constantinople. It was the holy city of the Greeks before the Ottoman Turks took the city in the fifteenth century. Aya Sofia was a Greek Orthodox cathedral--"

"So let's give it to the Greek government and that will be the end of it," Les interrupted.

"It still would not be out of the reach of that woman," Mehmet replied. "She has corrupted the Turks. There is no reason to believe she could not do the same to the Greeks. You remember Bishop Elias..."

"So beyond getting it out of Turkey, we still haven't decided what we're doing with it," Angie said.

"We must take one step at a time. Perhaps the answer will come later," Mehmet hoped.

The waiter came with the bill and Arslan and Mehmet held a friendly discussion as to which of them would have the honor of being the host of the other.

Les leaned closer to Angie. "Have you, uh, you know?"

"What?"

"The Lance..." Les said as he held out his hands as if he were holding it.

Angie slid the golden casket out of its cotton pouch and held it with her fingers spread. "Nothing," she whispered to Les after a few seconds.

"What do you think of their plan?" he whispered.

"It's all we've got. I say we go with it."

"Okay," Les said calmly.

"You're sure?"

"Yes."

Mehmet grabbed for the check when it arrived, but Arslan reminded Mehmet of all Murad had done for him and paid the tab. Mehmet thanked the older man and they continued their discussion. Arslan's sudden increased animation and Mehmet's obvious receptivity led the Americans to believe that the subject had changed.

"What do you suppose that's all about?" Les asked Angie.

"It looks positive, whatever it is," Angie answered.

"Mister Arslan tells me he knows someone who can help us," Mehmet announced. "He said the best time to go is at night. This man knows the way; he has made the trip many times."

"So we lay low in the meanwhile," Angie said.

"Lay low?" Mehmet asked.

"We just wait here and stay out of trouble until tonight," Les answered.

"Right," Angie said.

Arslan said something to Mehmet who replied and then spoke to the Americans. "Mister Arslan and I will go talk with his friend in the meanwhile."

"Where's his friend?" Les asked.

"Do you see that older gentleman down by the pier with that little boy?" Mehmet asked.

"Kinda old. He looks like he helped build the Parthenon," Les smirked.

"He's old, but Mr. Arslan says he knows these waters very well," Mehmet added.

"So does the little boy drive the boat?" Les remained sarcastic.

"That's his grandson," Mehmet replied. "I don't believe he has anything to do with the operation. He is only five-years old."

"Mehmet," Angieinterjected, "thank you. We couldn't do this without you."

"And I couldn't do this without you two either," Mehmet said.

As the two Turks departed Les slowly squeezed Angie's hand. She turned and held him.

"I love you, Angie."

"I love you, too."

"Do you think this will work?"

"Know it will."

"Me, too."

CHAPTER FIFTEEN

Bodrum, 11:27 a.m.

Luci Daniels looked at her watch and then picked up the binoculars and scanned the Mediterranean beyond the harbor.

"Anything?" Osman asked.

"You must have more patience, dear Osman," Luci said as she set down the binoculars. "The *Persephone* isn't due for another thirty minutes at least."

"I have good news!" the Bodrum police chief announced as he ran up to them. "A helicopter reports that the *Persephone* is en route and should be here in twenty-five minutes."

"You see, Osman," Luci said with a distinct air of condescension. "Patience is a precious attribute. Try to acquire some."

"Yes, madam," Osman replied. *Patience, yes. I must be patient with you and your attitude: so demeaning! Ah, but I will be patient counting my money on the side of a bed on which I have just had my way with you when this is all over!* He looked her over as she scanned the harbor with the binoculars again. Her short black hair glistened in the morning sun. As Luci set down the binoculars, Osman stole a peek at her face. Her sensuous eyes sent a surge of lust through him. *Such a beautiful body, despite her rudeness. Are you as much of a tigress beneath the sheets, or not? Is your passion restricted to acquiring precious treasures? I think not! You're hot-blooded through and through! And I'll bet I'll make you whimper before you purr, purr like you never have before! You are not cold like a snake but hot and passionate. And a warm-blooded creature is more easily tamed.* He ran his fingers over his mustache as he scanned her perfect nose and cheekbones. *You have managed to keep me at arm's length for now. But I will be patient as you ask and, eventually, no matter how long it takes, I will tame you, tigress!*

The police chief's assistant noisily ran up to his boss and disrupted Osman's reverie. He handed the chief a written message and went on to tell him what the message said before the police chief had unfolded the paper.

Osman did not hear what the assistant told the chief, but he heard the police chief's response. *Yalikavak?*

The police chief read the message as if his assistant were not reliable. "Yalikavak."

"Something wrong, sir?" Luci asked the police chief.

"Excuse me, madam," the police chief replied as he dismissed his aide. "It appears that three people were taken to shore from the *Persephone* to Yalikavak about two hours ago."

"Was it they?" Luci asked. "The ones who stole the Lance?"

"We don't know," the chief answered.

"It must be!" Luci hissed. "Damn!"

"They could still be onboard the ship, madam," Osman suggested.

Luci silently assessed the situation as she locked her fingers together. "Have your men meet the ship," she ordered the police chief.

"Yes--"

"Search her! Find the thieves!"

"Yes--"

"Good!" Luci abruptly turned to Osman. Her business with the police chief was completed. "You and I must get to Yalikavak. Call for the helicopter, now! And tell the pilot I'm flying!"

"Yes, madam," Osman said as he grabbed the radio-telephone.

Luci turned back to the police chief. "Don't forget: search the ship and find them if they are on it!"

"Yes--"

"Osman!" Luci snapped. "Helicopter?"

"They haven't picked up—yes, meet us at the heliport immediately... Yes, our destination is Yalikavak...Out." Osman set the phone down. "The pilot will be there in ten minutes."

Luci looked back at the police chief. "Understand?"

The chief nodded.

"Osman," Luci said under her breath, "make certain that twit understands. If they're not at Yalikavak they mustn't slip away here. I'm calling Roger," she added as she grabbed the radio-telephone. "He'll keep the Istanbul cops in the loop."

Osman confirmed with the police chief in Turkish and returned to Luci, who had just hung up with Roger Brown. "He understands."

"To the heliport then."

Yalikavak, 11:34 a.m.

"Mehmet back yet?" Les asked as he sat up on the bed. Arslan had arranged for them to stay at a small hotel next to the restaurant while they awaited the passage to Greece. Both were owned by the same man.

"No," Angie answered. "Did you have a nice nap?"

"Delightful. A good meal, a good little nap...I'm ready for anything now."

"I don't see how you can nap at a time like this."

"Another one of my many talents, my dear."

Angie sat next to Les and kissed him. "Another reason I love you so much."

"Why? Because I can nap on demand?"

Angie chuckled. "Your sense of humor, my dear, is indefatigable."

"Whoa! That's a mighty big word to be throwing around--and in Turkey of all places."

Angie jabbed his ribs playfully and then hugged him tightly.

"Thanks, Angie."

"What for?"

"Always being there for me."

"You're always there for me," Angie said as she released him and looked him in the eye.

"Yeah, but you never complain about it."

Angie erupted in laughter and hugged him again. "Silly boy!"

"Ouch!" Les cried as he placed his hand over his chest.

"I didn't squeeze that hard!" Angie chortled.

Les suddenly became very quiet.

"Oh my God! You're not having a heart attack are you?" Angie asked.

"No, no. That's not it."

"What is it?"

"All of the sudden I feel like something horrible is going to happen!"

"Are you having an anxiety attack?"

"I never—ouch! Geez, that smarts!"

"The Lance?" Angie asked as she went to pick up the reliquary. "I don't feel anything!"

Les's breathing accelerated.

"Les?"

Les stood up, as if he were awakening from a nightmare. "They're coming! They're coming here!"

Angie didn't have to ask whom he meant.

"They'll be in Yalikavak very soon!" Les announced.

"We need to find Mehmet!" Angie said as she led Les out of the room. "We may have to make that trip to Greece sooner than we expected!"

Bodrum, 11:36 a.m.

"What the hell is going on down there?" Albert Boucher whispered to himself as he saw the police interviewing the crew of the *Persephone* from their ship. The chief of police was there with several of his junior commanders and a dozen-or-so officers. A man who looked like he was probably the ship's captain argued vociferously with one of the junior commanders. The phlegmatic policeman met the captain's wild gesticulations calmly. The officer's underlings paid no particular attention to the irate seaman as they updated their superior with their investigation's lack of progress.

Albert knew he couldn't approach the police chief. Perhaps one of his inferiors could be more pliable. Albert accosted one of them as he walked away from the chief.

"Sir," Albert said in Turkish as he gently placed his hand on the officer's shoulder. "Sir, if I may...."

"What do you want? Interfering with a police officer in the performance of his duty carries a stiff penalty!" The officer eyed Albert closely. "You are not Turkish. Italian perhaps? Never mind. Get out of my way!"

"Sir, I am French." Albert's Turkish was reaching its limits.

"*Francais!*" the policeman proudly revealed his knowledge of the language.

Albert greeted this revelation with a smile and a mental sigh of relief. He continued in his native tongue. "I represent a company who had goods aboard this ship, the *Persephone*—"

"So," the policeman snapped back.

"If the captain or his company is involved with any illegal dealings, we would want to terminate any relationship with them immediately. Do you see my concern, sir?"

"Perhaps, Monsieur…."

"D'Alambert."

"Monsieur D'Alambert, the captain had fugitives aboard; we are certain of that."

"He is denying it?"

"Of course, but we know that they were onboard."

"What sort of criminals?"

"Thieves. Stole something from a museum. The whole country's looking for them."

"They're gone now?"

"Yes, gone."

"Did they hide what they stole onboard?"

"We can't find anything. The captain, the crew…they deny everything."

"Will the captain be arrested?"

"We don't have enough to charge any of them yet. We'll keep him in jail for a few days, maybe scare something out of him."

"So where are the fugitives?"

"We heard reports earlier that they may have gone ashore at Yalikavak."

"*Yalikavak?*"

"Due north. On the other side of this peninsula."

"Will I be able to speak to the captain? About our cargo."

"Wait a few days. He and your cargo are not going anywhere."

"Yes. I'll do that," Albert agreed as he walked away. "Thank you for your help," he added as he waved to the policeman.

"*Certainement!*" came the reply.

Yalikavak! Albert left the wharf and headed into town. *Yalikavak! Car would be best. Bus would be cheaper.* He pulled his wallet from his pocket and opened it. *Bus it is.*

Bodrum, 11:53 a.m.

"Geissler," Hugo answered his cell phone. *"Ja, Reinhardt...Yalikavak! Scheist! Ja, ja. Danke."* He yelled to Siegfried, who was six meters away, *"Yalikavak!"*

"Yalikavak!" Siegfried shrieked. "How the hell are we going to get there?"

"I'm certain there is a way," Hugo replied calmly. "They're going by helicopter. Maybe we can hire one, or a plane. Let's start asking." The two Germans split up, each one inquiring of any official he could find.

"He said Yalikavak, sir!" Kevin panted breathlessly. He had overheard the Germans from his camouflaged surveillance position fifteen meters away from them. He then ran three hundred meters back to Sir Richard.

"What the deuce!" Sir Richard threw open a map on the ground. "Here it is!" he declared, pointing to a town on a peninsula several miles north of Bodrum. "I imagine they're going by air."

"Yes, sir." Kevin was still panting. "Said something about a helicopter or a plane."

Yalikavak, 12:35 p.m.

Mehmet grumbled and put his hand to his forehead as he walked back twenty feet from his conversation with the smuggler. Arslan had gone to visit his brother in a nearby village and there was no time to look for him. In desperation Mehmet, Angie and Les went to the old smuggler to see if he would take them across the water as soon as possible. They found him where they had last seen him, on the beach in front of the restaurant. His grandson remained at his side.

"What's wrong?" Les asked.

"He says he won't take us; not in the daylight," Mehmet answered.

"No!" Angie protested.

"Tell him if he doesn't we'll do something outrageous!" Les growled as he watched the old man play with his grandson.

"Les--" Angie began.

"Such as?" Mehmet asked.

"I don't know…beat him up, burn his house down, shoot his donkey, kidnap his grandson…how should I know?"

"Les, that's ridiculous!" Angie retorted.

"I don't think there's any chance of intimidating him," Mehmet reasoned. "And we must leave as soon as possible."

"There must be some way he can help us," Angie said.

"Maybe he'll let us use the boat," Les suggested.

"We don't know how to get there!" Angie interjected.

"Maybe he could point us in the right direction--"

"Les!"

"No, no. Doctor Connery may have a point," Mehmet noted.

"What do you mean?" Angie asked.

"I'm convinced he will not take us. No other way of making the crossing presents itself at this time," Mehmet explained.

"It couldn't hurt to ask, Ange," Les said.

"Okay, why not," Angie conceded.

Mehmet returned to the smuggler who became very animated when Mehmet presented the proposition. The old man gesticulated wildly and laughed and then scolded the young man loudly, wagging his finger as he did so. The little boy mirrored his grandfather's actions.

Mehmet paused thoughtfully and then suggested something else to the smuggler. The older Turk's countenance suddenly became more agreeable. He smiled, and the Turkish words that flowed from his lips seemed strangely honey-sweet. Then he grasped Mehmet's hand and shook it energetically and said something that sounded very conclusive. The grandson repeated the act. The smuggler stepped over to Les and shook his hand and said that same word again.

"What's goin' on, Mehmet?" Les asked suspiciously.

"Well…" Mehmet began slowly.

"Yes," Les said expectantly.

"He will let us use the boat--" Mehmet continued.

"All right!" Les interrupted.

"For two thousand dollars," Mehmet concluded his statement.

"What?" Les fumed.

"And he will also show us how to get to one of the islands he used to smuggle to," Mehmet continued.

"Do you know how to operate a boat?" Angie asked Mehmet.

"I have before," Mehmet answered.

"How many times?" Angie asked.

"Only once," Mehmet replied.

"That's great," Les interjected in feigned calm.

"It will have to do," Angie concluded.

"Now wait a minute!" Les argued.

"Do you have any other ideas?" Angie asked incisively.

Les didn't answer. He suddenly became very cool. He swallowed hard and said solemnly, "They're almost here."

"Tell him we accept his offer," Angie said to Mehmet. "How much money do you have?" she asked as she turned to Les.

Les pulled his money belt up from beneath his trousers and rifled through it. "Two hundred American…about three hundred fifty million Turkish lira…fifteen hundred dollars in traveler's checks."

"I've got about two hundred million lira," Angie added.

"I have one hundred million lira," Mehmet volunteered.

"Sounds like enough," Angie said to Les.

"That should leave us a hundred fifty American," Les added after completing his calculations.

Angie and Mehmet handed their cash to Les who presented it to the smuggler. The older Turk picked out the dollars and traveler's checks and then started waving his hands and shaking his head.

"What's wrong?" Les asked.

"He's refusing the lira," Mehmet answered. He said something to the smuggler who quickly snapped at him. "He said two thousand *dollars* and that's what he wants."

"Tell him this is all we have," Les said.

"I did," Mehmet replied. "He wants the two thousand or we can forget about the boat."

Les jerked the money belt out of his pants and opened it. He removed the remaining traveler's checks and said to Mehmet, "Tell him we're shy of two thousand, but that's all we have."

Mehmet complied and the smuggler smiled as he thumbed through the newly presented traveler's checks. He said something to Mehmet and then smiled at Les.

"What did he say?" Les asked.

"He said that if you give him your watch you've got a deal," Mehmet responded.

Les scowled indignantly at the smuggler and then turned to Angie.

"Go ahead, Les," Angie said. "We have to."

"Is the watch special to you?" Mehmet asked as Les removed the watch.

"I gave it to Les for his birthday last year," Angie answered. "There's a message engraved on the back."

Mehmet stepped forward and took the watch from Les. "May I?"

"Sure."

Mehmet read the back of the watch. "'Yours through all time. Love, Angie.' That's beautiful," he added as he handed the watch back to Les.

"Something tells me it won't mean as much to him as it does to me," Les growled as he handed over the watch to the smuggler.

The smuggler didn't waste any time fulfilling his part of the bargain. He led them to the dock where a wooden boat in need of a decent paint job bobbed up and down with the Aegean's waves. She was far from what Les had imagined, hardly fifteen feet long, but she looked seaworthy. Barely. She was open, no roof, with two threadbare bench seats, which looked reasonably comfortable, and a cracked windscreen.

As Les signed the traveler's checks, the smuggler quickly explained the craft's operation to Mehmet, asking him every few seconds if he understood. Mehmet didn't disappoint him. The older man slapped the younger on the back in encouragement and then pointed out to sea. His finger zigzagged back and forth across the horizon, turning this way and that. He would suddenly break off and point to the craft's instrument panel and then back out to sea where the zigzagging began all over again. Finally, he dropped his hand by his side and asked Mehmet one last question. When the young Turk replied in the affirmative, the smuggler looked to Angie and Les and hurried them onto the boat.

As Les boarded the smuggler pointed to his newly acquired watch and nodded excitedly. He went to the back of the boat and removed the gas cap and set it on the wharf. The smuggler proceeded to a shed near the wharf and one by one hauled out four five-liter fuel cans. As he set the last one on the wharf, he said something to Mehmet.

"What did he say?" Les asked.

"We can leave as soon as he fills the tank and checks the engine one more time," Mehmet answered. "He said he was sorry, but he wasn't expecting us to leave until this evening."

"Great!" Les fumed. Any further delay could be fatal.

Yalikavak, 12:49 p.m.

"The Daniels woman is still in there," Hugo said as he simultaneously chewed some Turkish delight and scanned the tiny airport concourse with his binoculars from their car's passenger seat.

From Bodrum Sigfried had driven the rented Ford Escort at eighty kilometers per hour to make the twenty-six minute eighteen kilometer drive in fourteen minutes. There were no collisions with other cars, but there were plenty of gestures of contempt from the irritated Turks.

"How can we follow her if she's airborne?" Siegfried moaned as he watched through binoculars. "I can't believe there were no aircraft available for us!"

"Patience, Siegfried," Hugo belched. "She hasn't gone anywhere yet. And remember, Reinhardt said that she's chasing three people who are most likely traveling by land. There are plenty of taxis around."

"Here she comes!" Siegfried said, dropping his binoculars to his side. "Turkish fellow's still with her."

"They're getting into the helicopter!" Siegfried cursed as panic set in.

"Keep watching. Keep watching."

"They're taking off! Father we've got to do something!"

Hugo chuckled. "We are doing something, Siegfried."

Siegfried bolted toward the airport.

"Wait! Come back, Siegfried!"

"They're getting away!"

"No they're not," Hugo said as he pulled a locating device out of his pocket and held it up.

Siegfried ran back. "When did you—"

"When you went to take a leak across the way. I walked right up to the helicopter…"

"*Ser gut! Ser gut!*"

"What's Jerry up to now, Kevin?" Sir Richard asked. Miraculously the Grand Master's questionable driving skills had allowed them to keep their rented Anadol close to the Nazis without their quarry's knowledge.

"They're both just sitting there talking," Kevin replied. "The old one has something in his hand he keeps looking at."

"Don't lose them. I'm on my way to the loo."

"I won't fail you, sir."

"Damn well better not!"

Eastern Aegean, 12:50 p.m.

The old boat progressed slowly over the choppy water. The old smuggler's boat hadn't been out for a while and was due for more than a few adjustments. When Mehmet saw that they had cleared the pier he opened her up. Much to his delight her outward appearance was nothing like her capabilities. Her engine roared as she made short order of the waves ahead of her. The smuggler had prepared his vessel very well.

Before the old man let them go, he had his grandson fetch a clear, watertight container for the casket. The old smuggler had seen how Angie carefully cradled the reliquary and surmised that this object was very important. Since they were headed out to sea, they were at risk for losing this treasured item. The casket fit the container with only a little room to spare.

Les still didn't appreciate his latest acquisition. He looked her over and snorted. *No life jackets? For crying out loud!*

Angie gripped the casket in her hands. She had taken it out of its watertight container and its cotton sack to feel the cool metal reliquary. *Do you have anything to tell me?* She waited a few minutes. Nothing. Angie placed the reliquary back in the cotton sack and then into the watertight container. She convinced herself that the container was superfluous but put the casket inside to please the old man and his grandson. She smiled as she looked out over the turquoise-blue sea. *It's so beautiful!* She felt the warm breeze on her face, intermittently punctuated by cool spray from the sea. *The relic will soon be out of Turkey. From Greece, who knows where it will end up. One step at a time.*

Yalikavak, 12:59 p.m.

"She's circling. She keeps circling around the town," Hugo announced.

"But why?" Siegfried asked.

"I don't know. Wait a minute. She seems to be spending a lot of time over the sea now. Her circles are getting tighter and tighter."

"Daniels has found what she's looking for?"

"Maybe." Hugo sprang to his feet. "Down to the pier, *schnell!*"

"They're up and running, sir!" Kevin announced. "Toward the pier!"

"They're up to something! I know it!"

"Shall we run, sir?"

"Don't be bloody ridiculous." The Grand Master turned toward the stree and raised his hand. "Taxi!" The cabby screamed to a stop at Sir Richard's feet. "Come along, Kevin!"

"Circles are getting smaller," Hugo reported. "She's found something!"

Siegfried paid the fee to the rental agent and hopped onto the nineteen-foot wooden boat. "Come, Father!"

"They're going by boat!" Kevin said. "Out to sea!"

"Take us to the pier!" Sir Richard barked to the cab driver.

"Any change, Father?" Siegfried screamed over the roar of the engine.

"Still circling."

Siegfried chafed at the lassitude of their boat's engine. "This thing's as slow as a barge!"

"She'll get us there."

"I'm going to take a look at the engine; see if I can get her to move faster."

"A submarine, sir?" Kevin cried out in disbelief.

Sir Richard paid the fee and climbed aboard. "*Two-man* submarine!" he chimed with relish. "I called ahead to make sure they had one. She's a beauty! Reminds me of my days in the Royal Navy!"

"But sir, isn't it a bit slow?"

"Pish posh! She gives us the element of surprise. We can sneak right up on them! Come along now, Kevin!"

CHAPTER SIXTEEN

Eastern Aegean Sea, 1:20 p.m.

The sparkling blue sea mesmerized Angie. Dolphins popped up every now and then and ran with them for a while. Les dozed on the bench while Mehmet handled the controls. The young man turned and quickly looked at the Americans. All was well. The Lance of Longinus was on its way to Greece. Mehmet reviewed the old smuggler's instructions in his head and saw that up ahead he needed to turn thirty degrees to starboard.

Suddenly the windscreen disintegrated. Mehmet intuitively turned hard to port as glass flew into his face.

Les heard a high-pitched scream rocket past his left ear and then his right. "What the—" he screeched as he poked his head up and looked behind. As Les protested this intrusion, a helicopter roared overhead, from stern to bow. As it passed he saw a gunman positioned on the starboard skid. "Trouble!" he yelled in Angie's direction.

Angie had seen the intruder before Les did and was already prostrate on the deck, beckoning him to do the same. After the helicopter had passed she sprang up and went to Mehmet. "You okay?"

"I'm fine," Mehmet answered as he returned the boat to her previous course.

"We've got to find some protection," Angie yelled over the noise of the engine.

"Where? We're in the middle of the ocean!" Mehmet retorted.

By now the helicopter had turned and was making a second pass. "I'm going to try something," he told Angie.

As the helicopter bore down on the boat's bow, the gunman opened up.

Bullets at first flew into the bow but then zipped over their heads and into the water behind them. Mehmet responded by turning forty-five degrees to port and then ninety degrees to starboard. Angie looked back and saw that the trail of bullets was missing the mark.

"It's working!" she yelled in Mehmet's ear.

Les rolled from side to side in the stern, the victim of Mehmet's continuing evasive maneuvers. He groused at Mehmet's actions, but when he saw its success he was immediately forgiving.

"I'll get lower!" Luci Daniels yelled to Osman as she turned the helicopter back toward its prey. Osman nodded and reloaded. As Luci completed the turn she decreased her altitude. She gave Osman a thumbs-up. Osman nodded and lifted the machine gun into firing position. As they drew nearer to the boat he squeezed and his weapon responded. A stream of bullets ricocheted across the narrow fantail.

"Geeze! He's getting close!" Les screamed. The latest burst of fire from the helicopter forced him to move toward the bow.

Mehmet turned thirty degrees to port as the helicopter passed overhead. "Take the wheel!" he yelled to Les.

"What are you doing?" Les protested.

Mehmet pulled Les forward to the wheel and instantly began to search for something under the console.

"She can't be more than a kilometer away," Hugo yelled to Siegfried as he examined the locater. Siegfried's efforts with the old engine had borne fruit, increasing her speed by thirty percent.

"Can you see her?" Siegfried yelled back.

Hugo raised his binoculars. "*Ja! Ja!* I see her!" Hugo replied pointing dead ahead.

"Dead ahead, Kevin! She's only a hundred forty meters ahead of us!" Sir Richard said from the periscope. The sub was five feet below the surface of the water and was, for all intents and purposes, invisible to the Nazis.

"I've got her at top speed, sir." Kevin was amazed that they had been able to keep pace with the Germans.

"This sub was not such a bad idea after all, eh, my boy?" Sir Richard laughed.

"What are you looking for?" Angie yelled over the engine noise.

Mehmet didn't answer but continued his quest. He stopped suddenly, as if he had just convinced himself of something, and went to the other side of the boat.

The helicopter turned and started its fourth approach. Luci brought the bird lower and slowed her down to improve Osman's aim. When the chopper was a hundred yards in front of the boat, he opened up again.

As the bullets landed around him, Les dropped his head below the console, keeping his hands on the wheel and steering blindly. He felt something warm on his right shoulder and touched it with his left hand. *Blood!* He pressed hard into his shoulder. *No pain. Must be superficial.* Then he realized he had no feeling in his right shoulder at all. *Damn!* Part of his right hand was numb, but he had no trouble steering.

"Aha!" Mehmet yelled as the helicopter flew past.

"What?" Angie asked.

Mehmet raised a flare gun and smiled.

"Thank God!" Angie groaned.

"Now all I need are some flares."

"What?" Angie had hoped that they were ready to combat the deadly menace. When she heard the helicopter returning, she quickly joined Mehmet in a desperate search for the flares.

Les had no idea which way the boat was going. He remained below the console, maneuvering the boat blindly with his hands at the wheel. His right shoulder was bleeding, but he didn't feel faint. He checked it again: still numb; very little blood.

The helicopter approached from the stern. Bullets riddled the stern and skipped forward over the rear seat, sending Angie and Mehmet to the deck. A solid stream of lead sliced through the bench and moved toward Les, who jumped out of the way, leaving the wheel unattended. The boat spun out of control to starboard, sending its occupants rolling to the port side.

"The helicopter's shooting at that boat," Hugo yelled over the engine noise. "They must be the ones with the Lance of Destiny!"

Siegfried smiled and produced an Uzi from under the boat's console.

"Steady as she goes, Kevin!" Sir Richard ordered. *Wonder what she's after?* Sir Richard turned the periscope through one hundred eighty degrees of arc. "A helicopter! A bloody helicopter!" He turned the periscope around some more. "Ah, there's the prize!" he reported as he saw the old smuggler's boat. "Bloody chopper's blowing her out of the water!"

"We've got her now!" Luci yelled to Osman. "Kill them and I'll set you down to get the relic!"

Luci brought the helicopter down slowly, closer and closer to the whirling boat. Osman looked back at Luci and stuck his thumb up. Luci nodded back and smiled. *Now I have you!* The helicopter crept to within one hundred yards of the boat and Osman sprayed the deck. The circular motion of the old smuggler's boat didn't do much to impair his aim, each turn being very predictable. Osman jerked out the spent clip, tossed it inside the helicopter, inserted a new one and sent a torrent of the deadly metal into the old boat again.

The wheel was now but a tenuous stick. Holes appeared by the dozens in the starboard side and the boat rapidly took on water. Les saw that Angie and Mehmet continued their search despite the hail of bullets. "What are you doing?" he yelled.

"Flares!" Angie shouted back. "We found a flare gun!"

"I'll help," Les yelled as he crawled over to join them. However, two of Osman's bullets found their mark. "Ahhhh!" Les screamed. "My leg!"

"Les!" Angie shrieked as she moved toward her husband.

"No!" Mehmet yelled as he tried to pull her back, but he was too late.

Angie shot toward Les and grabbed his left arm. "I'll get you!" She pulled him toward her with all of her strength. "I'll get you, Les!"

"Turn to port! Ninety degrees!" Hugo ordered. "Stay with the boat!"

"That chopper's making mincemeat out of that old boat!" Sir Richard announced. "She's headed to the bottom for sure! We need more speed! Bring her up to a foot below the surface and keep her forward, Kevin!"

Another burst of bullets flew into the old smuggler's boat. As one whizzed by Angie's ear, she hugged the deck. A second bullet grazed her scalp. "Owww!" she screamed. She let go of Les's arm and grabbed her head. As she did so she saw the reliquary, not six feet away, under the rear bench. "The Lance!" Angie gasped as she crawled toward it. Machine gun fire fell over the boat again, but this time she was oblivious to it. Les screamed. He was hit again, but Angie's attention was fixed on the reliquary. Seawater was slowly leaking onto the deck. Suddenly the watertight container became a brilliant idea. Angie stretched toward it with her right arm, elongating that upper extremity one joint at a time. "Got it!" she heard Mehmet shout just as she touched the casket. Angie pulled the reliquary toward her and held it with one hand while she pulled Les forward with the other.

Mehmet loaded the newly discovered flare into the flare gun and sprang up to fire it at the helicopter. When he saw Osman sitting in his sights, he hesitated. *Osman, I'm sorry!* But before Mehmet could send the blazing flare to the helicopter, Osman squeezed the trigger of the machine gun. Mehmet fell back without a sound. The flare gun flew out of his hand and landed next to Angie. When she saw the young Turk's motionless body hit the deck she shuddered. She turned toward Les. He wasn't moving either. *My dream! Oh my God! It's coming true! No! No! Why God? Why?* Another burst of machine gun fire slashed another section of the port side away from the hull. Seawater now rushed in.

Angie felt the cool water on her skin. *This is it, Angie! Do or die!* Almost in a single motion she released the reliquary, grabbed the flare gun with both hands, sprang up from the deck of the foundering boat and fired at the helicopter.

Seeing the blazing missile speeding toward him, Osman leaned away from the oncoming incendiary, lost his balance and he and his machine gun fell twenty-five feet into the sea. As his body slapped against the waves, his machine gun sank into the sea.

The flare continued into the open cabin and richoceted off the glass canopy toward Luci. Before she could react, the flare lodged against her jacket, spewing combusting nitrates throughout the cabin. She swatted at the flare but only knocked it on to the control console, which immediately caught fire. Luci had to choose between incineration and jumping to what may be certain death. She didn't wait long. In a second she sprang out of the burning helicopter and fell into the sea.

To Angie, the helicopter seemed to float, suspended in the sky for a few seconds, before it dropped laggardly from the heavens. Steam shot over the water as the red-hot remains of the helicopter splashed into the cool sea. She watched only for a second. The old smuggler's boat was headed toward the bottom.

"Lucky shot!" Hugo roared. "Bring her around to the wreckage," he ordered, circling his left arm out and away from his body.

"Well I'll be skewered!" Sir Richard bellowed as he watched Angie shoot down the helicopter with the flare gun. "She shot down the helicopter! Amazing, Kevin!"

"Amazing," Kevin yawned.

"Now let's see what our German friends are up to," Sir Richard said as he turned the periscope around, looking for the other boat. "Oh, God!"

Before Sir Richard could say another word, the submarine collided with the Germans' boat. The wooden keel snapped the periscope off the conning tower and the sub began to take on water.

"Abandon ship! Abandon ship!" Sir Richard screamed.

"What the hell was that?" Siegfried yelled as both Hugo and he felt the collision with the sub.

Hugo felt water through his shoes and looked down. "Whatever it was, it tore a huge hole in the hull!"

"Can we bail it out?"

"It's coming in too fast!"

Siegfried ignored his father, grabbed a bucket and started to bail. Hugo turned around to find another bucket. As he walked aft to get it, the boat suddenly broke in half.

CHAPTER SEVENTEEN

Except for their shallow breathing, Les and Mehmet remained motionless in the rising water. Angie quickly tucked in her shirt, grabbed the reliquary in its watertight box and slid it against her chest. Mehmet's body began to float as the water continued its dilatory conquest of the vessel. Angie looked at Les and then Mehmet. *No way I can swim both of them to shore!* She speedily surveyed the waters around them. In the distance she saw what looked like land, but was it? And if it was, which island was it or was it the Turkish coast they had just fled?

Angie looked about the disintegrating vessel. "Raft!" she panted. She kicked a large section away from the top of the bullet-riddled rear bench and slid it under Mehmet, so his chest was centered in the middle of the large section. She clutched the casket against her chest as she felt for the pulse in Mehmet's neck. It was present but very weak. *Dear God! Mehmet, you've got to pull through!* Angie watched as her creation floated steadily away from the sinking boat. *This is going to work! Good! Now one for Les!*

The boat suddenly lurched as the weight of the incoming water proved too much for her shattered hull. The aft section dropped away slowly into the depths, taking Les with it.

"Les!" Angie screamed as she dove toward the sinking stern. She hit the water and swam straight down toward Les. However, she then felt the reliquary slip out of her shirt and sink slowly into the blue depths. Angie instinctively reached for the casket, but its descent was too rapid. She swung her head around toward Les and the sinking stern. She summoned every last ounce of strength she could muster and struggled toward her husband. Angie stretched forward and seized his arm to pull him toward her, but instead she found herself sinking with Les and the boat's afterdeck.

What? Angie calmly pulled herself toward the sinking mass and discovered the problem: Les's pants were snagged on a jagged edge of machine-gunned decking. Her pulling him upward had only worsened the problem. *Got to get him free!* She realized that trying to undress him while he was attached to the foundering section was futile. Angie pulled herself toward Les, brought her feet to the deck and lifted him by his belt as she braced her legs against the deck. *Not working!* She braced her legs again and pulled. *Oh, God!* Angie felt her throat constrict as her mind blurred. Oxygen levels in her blood plummeted and her brain faltered as she almost let go of her husband. Then Angie mustered the last of her ability. *God! Please!*

Angie saw darkness, which was abruptly shattered by an intense white light. *This is the end.* She'd heard all of the stories. Soon she'd see her grandmother who died, too young, when Angie was eight. *See God at the end of the bright tunnel?* Her head was swimming in confusion. *Sleep, peaceful sleep, come to me.*

The bright light suddenly intensified a hundred-fold, burning, searing her vision painfully. Les was cold and blue. Angie's feet were still planted on the sinking deck, and her husband was still in her grasp. "Pull!" she heard the voice thunder in her ears. Her muscles didn't wait for her brain to digest the message. The sinewy musculature of her arms, shoulders and legs contracted mightily in a sudden, intense explosion of energy.

Angie immediately sensed her success as her burden lightened precipitously. *Now up we go, Les! Not too much further!* But the surface could not come fast enough. She saw the darkness beginning to return as her ascent progressed too slowly. She struggled to keep the dark away, but her vision was obliterated in a matter of seconds. Her mind again sunk into that same sullen nothingness, unaware of anything around her.

Her life had been good. She had surpassed most of those in her profession, excelled in her athletic endeavors, served her community well. She had a loving husband for whom she would do anything, even die in an unknown corner of the world. And it wasn't painful, as she always thought it would be. Rather serene, tranquil. It was the supreme irony: death claims the doctor, one who spent her professional life laboring to cheat that undefeatable villain. Wasn't it all just a matter of putting off the inevitable?

Death always claimed its prize in the end, be it after one hundred seconds or one hundred years, or in her case, somewhere in-between.

Death's invitation was suddenly revoked by bright sunshine at the water's surface. Angie heard Les coughing in her ear and then heard herself gasping for air, as if she had run a mile while holding her breath. Her chest ached with every exaggerated excursion of her diaphragm. She coughed as wavelets of ocean water leapt into her open mouth. She looked at her right arm which, as it worked its way forward and back through the water, behaved as if it were independent of her brain's dictates. Angie felt her legs ache, as they were in league with her right arm, independently treading water beneath her. Les coughed and spit out seawater at the end of her left arm, her fingers grasping his shirt with all of their worth.

"Made it!" Angie gasped between lung-filling breaths. "Made it!"

"Angie!" Les moaned quietly. "Angie!" His recovery was shaky.

"It's okay, Les!" she whispered quietly into his ear. "We're gonna be okay!"

Angie spotted a six-foot section of the hull drifting close by and swam them to it. "Les! Hold on!" she ordered as she set one of his arms, and then the other, over the top of the debris. Once he was secure she threw her arms over it and laid her weary head on its surface. *My God! My God we made it!*

When Angie felt the hard wood of the hull resting against her chest, an image of the Lance flashed in her mind. *Oh no! It's lost! After all we've been through, it's lost!* She sighed deeply. *But we're alive! Thank God for that! We're alive!* Her heart warmed with those thoughts, despite of the loss of the great treasure she had, until but a few minutes ago, held in her hands. God had brought them there to lose the golden reliquary and its precious Lance. Perhaps the world wasn't ready for this relic yet. Eight hundred years of seclusion was not long enough. Angie sighed and slowly opened her eyes. The empty sea before her eerily created precipitous alarm.

"Mehmet!" Angie screamed as she frantically searched around her. "My God! Mehmet! Save him, dear God! Save him!"

In an instant the young Turk's hand broke though the surface grasping the reliquary in its watertight container.

"Mehmet!" Angie cried. "How did you? Oh, Mehmet! Thank God, you're alive!" she screamed as she reached out to him.

"Doctor Johnson! Doctor Johnson!" Mehmet cried back, "I've got it! I've got it!"

Angie pulled Mehmet to her and hugged him tightly. "You're safe! Oh thank God, you're safe!" Her sobs evolved into peals of laughter. "Mehmet!"

"How is Doctor Connery?"

"He'll be fine. He'll be good. Just needs some rest." Angie noticed the blood on Mehmet's chest. "Mehmet! They shot you!"

"Doctor Johnson, I'm really okay--"

"But Mehmet," Angie exclaimed incredulously, "they shot you in the chest! Your pulse was very weak--"

"Yes, yes, Doctor Johnson. They did but I'm all better--"

"The reliquary! How did you get it?"

Mehmet calmly smiled at Angie. "I remember looking Osman in the eye and hearing the machine gun. The next I knew a surge of energy shot into my body and I was awake. I saw you struggling to free Doctor Connery as the boat sank. I dove in after you and saw the casket fall away from you. I am sorry to say that the only thing I could think of at that point was retrieving the reliquary." His face betrayed his shame. "I didn't think at all of helping you and Doctor Connery."

"Mehmet," Angie reassured him, "Les and I are here. We're well." Her smile grew. "And you saved the Lance!"

"The Lance!" Les cried as he overcame his wounds and awakened. "Do we have it? Do we have it?"

Angie turned to Les, saw his searching eyes, and held him tightly. "Yes, Les! We have it, and we're all here!"

"Doctor Connery!" Mehmet added as he set his hand on Les's back. "This is truly a miracle!"

"Mehmet! Angie!" Les cried. "My God, this is all like a dream!" Father Flaherty's face popped into his mind and Les's voice grew more sobered. "Just like a dream."

Eastern Aegean, 2:57 p.m.

"Three o'clock," Angie whispered to herself as she glanced at her watch. She was amazed it still functioned. Les and Mehmet had drifted off to sleep clinging to the makeshift raft. She rested her hand on the casket, squeezing it every now and then to make certain it was still there.

The unseasonably hot weather kept the sea a bit warmer than usual, but the unbroken sunshine dried her parched lips. Angie thought about the wounds Les and Mehmet had suffered. She had counted two wounds in Les's left shoulder, one in his right thigh and one in his right shoulder. All of them were now healed or were healing rapidly. Mehmet had two wounds to the chest, but he was none the worse for it now. It was inconceivable that, with those wounds, they were alive at all, let alone conscious. How could Mehmet dive into the water after her with his wounds? Angie again removed the casket from the watertight box, peeled the cotton sack away and looked deeply at the casket, as if a scrupulous inspection of the relic would answer her questions. Soon Angie's fatigue overcame her and she realized that she would eventually have to surrender to her exhaustion. She steadied herself on the makeshift raft, checked Les and Mehmet and closed her eyes. Sleep is a more valuable staple than water.

Bodrum, 3:15 p.m.

Albert impatiently watched the passengers load from his seat in the front of the van. The Turks call these small, crowded vehicles *dolmus,* which means stuffed, and they deserve the moniker. Albert counted eleven, exclusive of the driver and himself. The close quarters could mean trouble if someone detected the revolver he had just purchased. He had just enough money for the weapon and five bullets and he loaded them into the weapon just before he lined up for the bus.

However, the driver wasn't satisfied with only a dozen passengers. Anyone along the route need only raise his arm as the van approached, and the driver would be only too willing to offer a lift. Albert swore that at one point the vehicle was carrying sixteen people. Of course there were also those who had reached their destination: the intersection of a narrow dirt road or in the middle of a tiny village or the other side of a stone barn. Some got out at no particular place, bidding the driver good bye as they paid him and continued their journeys to oblivion by foot.

CHAPTER EIGHTEEN

Eastern Aegean, 4:00 p.m.

"Angie! Angie wake up!"

"Les?"

"Look! Land!"

"Land?"

"Yes, land!" That voice was Mehmet's.

Angie's head shot up and saw Mehmet and Les pointing at the horizon. "Land! Land!" she sobbed.

The men dropped into the water and kicked the raft toward the island.

"How far would you say that is, Angie?" Les inquired.

"I don't know. Couple of miles or so, maybe," Angie answered as she joined them in propelling the raft.

"At least that," Mehmet chimed in. "But it is land nonetheless!"

"And that way's west!" Angie added as she looked left at the sun in the sky. "It's got to be one of the Greek islands!"

"All right!" Les screamed.

"Praise be to Allah!" Mehmet added.

"Yeah!" Angie cheered as she closed her eyes for a second and thought of the last two days. Then she opened them and looked at the reliquary, which sat directly front of her on the raft. "Amen!"

Yalikavak 4:31 p.m.

It was over an hour later that the *dolmus* pulled into Yalikavak.

"An hour," Albert grumbled to himself, "to go twenty-five kilometers!" He handed the driver the fee and stepped out of the van. *Turkish sardine can!*

Albert looked at the city around him. Where could they be? Since they had arrived by ship the docks were the best place to begin. He guffawed when he imagined his chances of finding *another* longshoreman who spoke French, or even English. He cursed this Asiatic backwater as he found a chair at a café and sat. He sighed as his back rested up against the wooden chair's hard back. "If you've got any hunches," he murmured to himself, "now is the time."

There were but two patrons in the café who were sitting close by. They chattered away in Turkish and Albert paid no mind. He had more important things to think about, but as the two men continued their conversation, its volume steadily rose. Albert grunted in disgust and silently recited all of the reasons he hated Turkey. Yet, the conversation suddenly began to interest him. He didn't know much Turkish, but four words he could extract from the old men's conversation suddenly became relevant: black, woman, red and hair. *Mon Dieu! Donkeybrain et les Americans!*

He nonchalantly looked at the two men. He didn't know that he had been listening to the last two Turks to speak to Mehmet and the Americans: Mister Arslan and the smuggler. Within minutes the two men rose from their table and bid each other goodbye. Arslan slipped into his taxi and sped toward the main highway and the smuggler started toward his house. Albert stealthily followed the second man the half-mile to his house.

As the old man approached, his grandson ran to greet him. The smuggler scooped up the little boy and hugged and kissed him. He set the boy down and rubbed the top of his head. The boy grabbed his grandfather's hand and led him down to the dock and pointed excitedly at one of the boats.

Albert felt the pistol in his coat pocket and smiled as a plan materialized in his brain. He sneaked down to the dock and watched. As the little boy sat in the cockpit, turning the wheel to and fro, his grandfather sat down next to an old boat motor with a screwdriver in one hand.

Perfect! Albert sprang up from his hiding place and ran to the boat. Upon seeing this, the old man dropped his tool and ran to the boat, but he was too late. Albert grabbed the boy and yanked him out of the seat.

In a second he spun around toward the grandfather, pulled out his pistol and jammed it in the little boy's neck. The smuggler froze in his tracks as his grandson screamed.

"Don't harm him!" the old man pleaded in Turkish.

Albert nodded his head to try to reassure the old man, although he had no idea what he had just said. When the old man calmed down, Albert began his interrogation in broken Turkish. "Black woman," he began. "Red hair," he added a few seconds later. The old man looked confused. "Black woman, red hair!" Albert shouted more loudly. The old man said something that seemed to reflect his continued uncertainty. Albert cocked the pistol and forced the barrel deeper into the boy's neck. The child screamed for his grandfather. "Black woman! Red hair!" Albert repeated. The old man threw up his hands and nodded. He spoke rapidly and pointed with his finger at the sea. Albert followed the smuggler's finger as it darted left and then right and then pointed straight three times.

Now we're getting somewhere! Albert loosed his grip on the little boy but still held him close. He pointed to one of the two old boats the smuggler kept in the dock and then at himself. He repeated himself and then pointed out to sea. "Yes," the smuggler said in Turkish. "Yes." He fumbled in his pocket and produced a key. He walked down the pier to the boat he had selected, inserted the key in the ignition and turned it. The engine chugged two or three times but then sprung to life. The old man smiled and beckoned to Albert.

Albert didn't loosen his grip on the little boy as he walked down the pier. As he stepped out of the boat, the smuggler pointed to the wheel and the dials and buttons on the control console as if Albert could understand him. Albert nodded just to get the old man to stop. *What could be so hard about driving this boat?* He stepped onboard as he released the smuggler's grandson. The little boy ran to his grandfather and cried in the old man's chest. The old man untied the lines holding the boat in the dock and pointed out to sea again, making the same motions with his finger. He nodded twice and put his hand up as if to wave. Albert pushed the throttle lever forward and the boat left the dock. He turned and waved at the old man and his grandson who smiled at him as they faded into the distance. Little did Albert know that the smuggler had chosen this boat especially for him. A closer inspection of the boat's starboard fantail would have revealed a small defect in the hull three inches above the waterline.

Eastern Aegean, 6:26 p.m.

Despite their efforts the island drew closer, but slowly, oh so slowly.

"What time is it, Angie?" Les asked. "It's starting to get dark."

"Almost six thirty," Angie answered as she checked her watch.

"The island still is far away," Mehmet noted.

"But it's closer. It is closer." Angie's insistence was more for her own reassurance than for the others. "My legs are toast!" Les whined.

"Rest then," Angie replied. "Mehmet, how are you?"

"Well. My legs are tiring, but I can still kick," Mehmet answered. "And you? How are you?"

"I'm good," Angie replied. "I can go further."

"I can help," Les chimed in.

"No," Angie rebuked him. "You rest. We'll need a pair of fresh legs soon, so rest."

The darkness came quickly. Les had fallen asleep and Angie and Mehmet were too exhausted to wake him.

"Can you see the island, Doctor Johnson?"

Angie had given up on getting him to call her by her first name. "No."

"Neither can I. What should we do?"

"It would be foolish to spend all of our strength without knowing where we're going."

"But we may drift further away from land."

"We need rest, too." Angie stretched her legs in the seawater, whose temperature had dropped in the last two hours. "What do you say, Mehmet?"

"I say we rest," Mehmet conceded. "Yes, let's rest."

"Yeah," Angie sighed, "I'm with you. Let's take a breather and hope that the current is kind to us."

"Indeed."

Mehmet and Angie climbed up on the raft and lay down. It wasn't long before they were asleep.

A sudden lurch abruptly shattered Angie's sleep. As she awakened she sensed that the raft's progress had been interrupted. When she heard waves breaking around her, she opened her eyes. "We've landed! We're on land!" she muttered to herself. Then she shouted, "Les, Mehmet! We've landed!"

Les awakened first. "Well I'll be--" He sprang up onto the sandy beach. "We made it! We made it!"

Angie ran and hugged him. "We did it, Les! We did it!" she cheered.

Mehmet jumped forward. "Quiet! Please! Be quiet!"

"What gives, Mehmet?" Les wondered.

"What is it?" Angie added, lowering her voice.

"Do we know for certain we've come ashore in Greece?" Mehmet wondered.

Les and Angie froze.

"We could be back in Turkey. The authorities are still looking for us."

"He's right, Les," Angie agreed.

"What do we do then?" Les asked in frustration.

"Let's check out the beach," Angie suggested. "Maybe there's someplace we can hide."

"In the morning we can see where we are," Mehmet concluded.

"I think we should find out where we are now!" Les disagreed. "If we have landed in Turkey, we need to know now. If we wait, we could be giving the police time to find us."

"But Osman and the Daniels woman are probably dead," Mehmet pointed out.

"The police don't know that," Les countered. "They're still after us and there's no guarantee that they'd let us go, even if they knew Daniels were dead. We've stolen a national treasure; you said it yourself, Mehmet."

"But if we explained to them and gave it back--"

"Still doesn't mean they'd let us go."

"He's right, Mehmet," Angie interjected.

"So let's get off the beach and see what's inland?" Les suggested.

"No. It makes the most sense to stay here," Angie retorted.

"What?" Les groaned.

"We're exhausted," Angie continued. "People make stupid mistakes when they're tired." Angie checked her watch. "It's after eight. We still need rest."

"I've been sleeping for the last two hours!" Les protested.

"You gonna go by yourself?" Angie shot back.

"You are correct, Doctor Johnson," Mehmet replied. "It is best for us to regroup and start anew in the morning."

"Okay," Les grumbled, "I'll go along with you, but I still think you guys are all wet, if you'll pardon the pun."

"Spread out" Angie ordered. "We'll find a safe spot here on the beach and rest till morning."

CHAPTER NINETEEN

April 14, 7:00 a.m.

Angie sensed his presence first. At first she had thought he was the sun shining through the thicket they had chosen for sleep. He looked at her as if he were seeing a strange, wild animal for the first time. He couldn't have been more than three and a half feet tall. She heard him say something but couldn't make out what it was. Angie slowly sat up and the boy stepped back.

"Hello," Angie said gently.

He responded with cautious silence and a step backward.

"Hi." Angie added a friendly wave.

"*Mavri!*" he said softly in amazement.

"What's that?" Angie extended her hand slowly toward him.

"*Mavri!*" he screamed as he ran out of the thicket.

"Wait! I won't hurt you!" Angie tried to pursue him, but her feet slipped in the heavy sand.

"Who was that?" Les groaned as he awoke.

"A little kid," Angie answered. "Probably a native."

"Yeah but a native *what*?" Les wondered.

Mehmet sat up and rubbed his eyes. "You saw someone, Doctor Johnson?"

"A little kid," Les answered.

"He said something," Angie added.

"What?" Mehmet asked.

"'Mahbi…Mahri,' something like that." Angie couldn't fully reproduce what the little boy had uttered.

"Turkish?" Les asked Mehmet.

"Doesn't sound like it," Mehmet replied.

"Greek, then," Les concluded.

"I can't be sure of that either," Mehmet admitted.

"So we still have no idea where we are?" Angie put the question.

"I'm afraid you are correct," Mehmet responded.

"What did he look like, Ange?" Les wondered.

"He was a kid, Les. Three and a half feet tall, dark hair, plain blue T-shirt, short pants--"

"Shoes?"

"I don't think so. I don't remember."

"Does that help, Mehmet?"

"No, Doctor Connery. The boy could just have easily been either Greek or Turkish."

Angie slid her hand over the reliquary.

"So we're still lost," Les surmised. "Well, who's going to come with me?" he added as he stood.

"Where you going, Les?"

"I'm gonna find out where we've landed."

"Agios Stavros," the tall dark-bearded stranger's deep voice announced from the thicket's opening. He spoke excellent American English.

Les abruptly stepped back while Angie and Mehmet sprang to their feet.

"Don't be afraid," the stranger said. He wore the black headgear and cassock of a priest.

"Are you a priest?" Angie asked.

"Yes, I am Father Justin. You are Americans?"

"Father Justin?" Les smiled. "We're in Greece then!"

"Yes. Agios Stavros Island," the priest answered.

Angie, Les, and Mehmet threw their arms around each other and held each other tightly.

"I can't believe it!" Angie cried. "We're here! We're here!"

"We made it, babe!" Les said as the tears started in his eyes as well.

"Are you okay?" the priest asked. "You're from the States, aren't you?"

"Well, two of us are. Mister Yakis here is Turkish, and we're all absolutely fantastic, Father...." Les answered.

"Justin, Justin Phillipos," the priest answered. "Are you hungry?"

"We're famished," Angie answered.

"Please come with me to the village. We have plenty." He grasped Les's and then Angie's hand and gave each a gentle shake. When he came to Mehmet, the young Turk hesitated. The priest extended his hand to Mehmet and added, "You're *all* welcome."

As Mehmet accepted the priest's offer, Angie asked, "Where did you learn to speak English, Father?"

"Chicago. I was born there," Father Justin replied. "My folks still live there."

"Why are you in Greece?" Mehmet inquired.

"I came to Greece ten years ago, vacation," the priest answered. "Met a Greek girl—"

"You're married?" Angie interrupted. "But you're a priest!"

"Orthodox priests can be married," Father Justin explained, "as long as they marry before they become a priest."

"Interesting," Angie added.

"Anyway," the priest continued, "I met Maria in Athens…"

"And the rest is history," Les chimed in.

"Yes," Father Justin chuckled, "you might say that." Father Justin ran his hand over his chin and uneasily posed another question. "Uh, may I ask what brings you to our little corner of the world? We don't get many visitors. This tiny island isn't on most maps."

"Have you got an hour or two?" Angie teased, leading Les and Mehmet to laugh loudly.

"Must be quite a story," Father Justin surmised.

"Oh, it is," Angie replied.

"I look forward to hearing it later. Please, come with me to the village," Father Justin begged again. "It's just a short distance."

"Thank you," the others said together.

"Who was the little boy?" Angie asked.

"Yianni, one of the little boys in the village."

"He said something when he saw me…" Angie tried to remember.

Father Justin chuckled again. "*Mavri!*" he laughed. "It means black woman! He's never seen a black woman before!"

The village was a half-mile's walk away. Along the way, a few introductions were made among the locals. The village glistened in the morning sun. All of its buildings, the houses, the church, the shops, even the post office, were white-washed earthen structures. Some of the roofs were thatched with straw, others with interwoven twigs and branches. The tiny church's hemispheric dome was also whitewashed, as was the diminutive bell tower in front of it. Villagers seemed to come out of nowhere, eagerly gawking at the strangers. Each of them greeted the priest and eyed his guests with insatiable curiosity as he walked them through the town toward his home next to the church.

"*Mavri*," Angie heard several of the little children say as they saw her go by. She waved at them and some waved back and some ran away, but all of them smiled.

Father Justin's house was an earthen bungalow, whitewashed like its neighbors. It contained a bedroom for the priest and his wife, a small study that housed the priest's small collection of books, a kitchen and central great room, which functioned as a sort of dining room and living room combination. Father Justin introduced them to Maria who sat with them on colorful iron lawn furniture in the back yard. Her English was limited, but she performed her duties as hostess with warmth. She quickly brought coffee and orange juice and, a few minutes later, yogurt and sweet pastries. At her guests' urging, Maria took the seat next to her husband.

"Thank you," Angie smiled. "This is wonderful."

Mehmet and Les quickly agreed.

"Please have as much as you like," Justin offered. He turned to Les and Mehmet. "I'd say you've not eaten in quite a while."

Les, whose mouth was embarrassingly full, could only nod in agreement.

When it appeared that his guests were nearly sated, Father Justin sought to satisfy his curiosity. "So, where have you come from?" he asked with a friendly smile.

Les and Mehmet had not yet completed their breakfast so Angie answered, "From Turkey. Yalikavak."

"Did you swim here?" Father Justin joked. "I didn't see a boat."

Angie smiled and gently held the casket in her lap. She ran her fingers over the clear, watertight container and looked through it at the cotton sack that hid it from the world. She wondered how to begin their story.

Les swallowed his last bit of pastry and looked at his wife, expecting her to begin. When she hesitated he prompted her. "Angie?"

"I don't know where to begin," Angie admitted.

"Perhaps I can help," Mehmet asked as he finished his meal with one last sip of coffee.

"Be my guest, Mehmet," Angie conceded.

"I'm certain," Mehmet began, "that you are familiar with most of the Orthodox Church's relics…."

"Yes, as a priest I am familiar with most of them," Father Justin replied.

"Have you heard of the Lance of Longinus?"

"I thought that was a Catholic relic," Justin answered. "Isn't it in a museum in Vienna or someplace like that?"

Maria whispered something into her husband's ear and the others heard him answer her in Greek.

"Do you know its history?" Mehmet continued.

"I've heard a few things," Justin responded. "It is the Lance that pierced our Lord's side during His crucifixion."

"Do you know anything else about it?" Mehmet asked.

"Not really."

"Would it surprise you to learn that the Lance of Longinus was, until very recently, in Turkey?" Mehmet inquired.

Father Justin's visage grew solemn. "You know something about this," the priest said pointedly. "You know where it is, don't you?"

"Father," Angie gently interjected, "this sounds like a good place for us to begin our story."

"Please do," Father Justin encouraged her with an uneasy smile.

It took almost two hours for Angie, Les, and Mehmet to complete their story.

"…and now here we are," Angie concluded.

"That's absolutely fantastic!" Father Justin responded. He and his wife had been eager listeners. He turned to Maria and conversed with her in Greek for several minutes before he turned back to his guests with a sense of intense anticipation in his face. "May I see it?" Father Justin asked. His voice was a little uneasy.

"Of course," Angie answered, "but I would prefer to show you indoors, if that's not a problem."

"Not at all," the priest consented. Father Justin and his wife led the others to the church next door. As they entered the whitewashed building, the guests looked at the many paintings on the walls. "These used to be mosaics," the priest informed them. "The church was completed in April of 1204--"

"Eight hundred years ago!" Les gasped.

"Yes," Father Justin continued. "It was consecrated and used only for three months before the island was seized by the Venetian Republic. When the Venetians came they tore all of the jewels out of the mosaics. The villagers couldn't replace so many precious jewels so they had the icons painted on the walls. As you see, they are a bit worse for the wear. Every twenty years or so the icons get new paint."

"What's up with the ceiling?" Les asked as he peered into the dome.

"An earthquake two days ago damaged the plaster," Father Justin answered. "We had just celebrated Easter the day before. We're trying to get it all repaired."

"Some of it looks very loose," Mehmet observed.

"We thank God that none of it has fallen," the priest sighed. "Look at Saint Michael up there," he said as he pointed to one of the more damaged icons in the dome.

"His sword looks like it's going to fall at any second," Les noted.

"I've called my bishop and he has said that he'll get to it when he can," Father Justin explained. "We don't have the money here. We're a small island."

"It's a beautiful church," Angie declared. "In spite of the help it needs, it makes me feel very reverent, yet very welcome."

"There are no chairs," Les noted, almost complaining.

"Yes that's true," Father Justin replied as he led them forward. "We Orthodox Christians believe that when one is in the presence of God one should stand out of respect or kneel in penitence."

"Whoa, and I complain about sitting through an hour-long service at home," Les muttered to himself.

Father Justin stopped in front of the iconostasis, the screen of icons that separated the nave from the sanctuary where the altar was found. He crossed himself in front of one of the icons then slowly turned back to his guests, saying nothing but trying hard to contain his excitement.

The priest's sudden silence briefly perplexed Angie, but his desire soon became apparent. "Oh," she said as she realized that the priest's actions signaled the time to reveal the relic. She deftly slid the reliquary out of its container and then out of the cotton sack and held it up for him to see.

"It's beautiful!" Father Justin and Maria gasped. Maria added something in Greek and crossed herself.

"Would you like to open it?" Angie asked.

"Me?" the priest shuddered.

"Go ahead." Angie handed him the reliquary, which the priest accepted with trembling hands.

Maria reached over and touched the casket and exclaimed in Greek. Father Justin nodded his head and replied to her. He opened the lid and looked inside. "Oh most Precious Lord Christ!" he gulped as he crossed himself.

Les and Mehmet smiled at each other as they saw the priest's rapture.

Father Justin slowly picked up the Lance, kissed it and uttered a Greek phrase as if he were conducting Sunday liturgy. He brought the Lance toward his wife who crossed herself but then edged back a step. Justin said something that reassured her, and she slowly returned and held out her hands to accept the relic. As it touched her skin Maria shuddered and exclaimed to her husband. He whispered something back to her and she received the relic reverently. She kissed it, inspected it for a minute and handed it back to her husband, tears welling up in her eyes.

"So it's true!" the priest said, trying hard to control his tears.

"Father?" Angie asked.

"The people of Agios Stavros told me about a legend when I first arrived here; a legend about the Lance that pierced Our Lord's side."

"Legend?" Les asked.

"In 1142, the Byzantine Emperor John II Comnenus sent for the Lance to help him with his campaign against the Danishmend Turks in Cilicia, now in southeastern Turkey. John was very successful and the Danishmends were routed. He spent the winter in Cilicia, planning an invasion of Syria for the spring of 1143. However, John's success had gone to his head. He saw his successes as largely his own. Against the advice of his most trusted friends, he sent the Lance of Longinus back to Constantinople. In March of 1143, he was accidently wounded by an arrow while hunting boar in the Taurus Mountains. He ignored the seemingly minor wound. It soon became infected, the infection spread, and he died. On the day the emperor died, the ship carrying the Lance back to Constantinople went down in a storm, just off the coast of this island."

"And the Lance of Longinus?" Mehmet inquired.

"All of the crew miraculously survived the sinking. The captain and some of the crew came ashore in a small boat. The captain held the reliquary in his arms like it was his own child. Those crew members that couldn't fit in the small craft, and chose to swim ashore, counted themselves as honored because they had sacrificed the comfort of the boat for the safety of the Lance of Longinus. The villagers received them warmly and the Holy Lance and this reliquary held a place of honor in the island's church. A month later a Byzantine ship arrived to take the crew and the Holy Lance back to Constantinople. On the day before the crew was to leave, the captain suddenly went into a trance of some kind. When he awakened he declared that someday the Lance of Longinus would return to Agios Stavros."

"Oh good God in Heaven!" Angie blurted out. Les and Mehmet were dumbstruck.

"I couldn't agree more," Father Justin replied. "Really makes you wonder, doesn't it?"

Father Justin peered inside the casket as the others expressed their agreement. He removed the papyrus as he returned the Lance to its home. The priest gasped as he slowly opened the papyrus and inspected the writing. "Latin, of course." He crossed himself and kissed the papyrus and handed it to Maria who duplicated his reverences. "Lord have mercy!" Father Justin declared reverently as he read the document and crossed himself. Angie saw a tear roll down his cheek.

"This is beautiful!" Maria added in broken English as she wiped her tears away.

"I thank God that you have come here and shown us the Holy Lance!" the priest added as he crossed himself again.

"We're pretty happy with God for bringing us here, too," Les interjected.

Justin embraced Maria, and then they both hugged each of the guests.

"So where does the Holy Lance go from here?" Father Justin asked.

"We don't know," Angie answered. "Funny: now that we've gotten it out of Turkey we're not sure where to take it."

"To Athens, perhaps?" the priest suggested.

"Athens, London, Washington…we don't know," Angie answered.

"Where on earth will it be safe from others like the Daniels woman?" Mehmet asked as if he knew there was no good response.

"She's dead," Les replied.

"There will be others," Mehmet declared soberly. "Others who will seek out the Lance for their own desires."

"It's not right for anyone so corrupt to have such a holy thing," Angie added.

"No, obviously not," Father Justin answered. "But where should the Holy Lance go?"

"Into my hands, if you please." The voice came from the other end of the nave.

Mehmet was all too familiar with that voice. He spun his head around and saw Albert Boucher walking toward them, pistol in hand.

"Well I'll be…" Les snarled.

"Well, I see fortune has finally brought me to my prize after all," Albert chuckled. His greedy eyes resembled those of a hungry tiger closing in on its prey. "Doctor Johnson, if you please," he said calmly. When there was no response, he motioned with his gun and yelled, "Hand it over!"

"Don't do it, Doctor Johnson!" Mehmet screamed.

Without thinking Albert raised the pistol and fired at Mehmet. The young man fell to the floor grabbing his chest. The sound of the pistol shot echoed loudly in the dome directly above them.

"Bastard!" Les cursed Albert as he dove to Mehmet's side.

"I've always wanted to do that!" Albert declared in a self-satisfied voice. "I just so happen to have a bullet for each of you!" He cocked the pistol and screeched, "Now give me the relic!"

Angie held the reliquary tightly in her hands as her eyes watched Albert closely. "Les!" she asked without taking her eyes off of the Frenchman, "How's Mehmet?"

"Unconscious but breathing!" Les answered, "He's been hit it the chest! Bleeding pretty bad!"

Father Justin grabbed a towel hanging from the baptismal font and tossed it to Les who used it to apply pressure to the bleeding wound.

"Don't make me do this, Doctor Johnson!" Albert said, pointing the gun at Les. "Just give me the relic and I'll leave you alone!"

Angie stared back at Albert.

The cold look in her eye told him that these crazy Americans just may force his hand. Albert saw that he had to change his approach. "Doctor Johnson," he began calmly, "the world must have such a valuable piece of history. I will risk my life, as you have done, to make certain that it ends up in a very secure place."

"Why don't I believe you?" Angie barked back.

"Pulse is thready!" Les interrupted.

"Father," Albert said as he turned to the priest. "Surely you see the value of such a relic to the Church. Just think of how the Lance of Longinus will strengthen the belief of the faithful! Think of how many converts this relic will bring to the Church! This is bigger that the Shroud of Turin!"

"The Church has done very well for eight hundred years without the Holy Lance," Father Justin retorted.

"But it will bolster the faith of hundreds of millions!" Albert protested.

"That's not faith in God!" Father Justin snapped back. "People shouldn't need a spear to convince them of God's existence or of Christ's sacrifice! What kind of faith is that?"

"Quit thinking like a priest and think like one of your parishioners!"

"I am!"

Albert snorted in frustration. "Father," the word stuck in his throat like a thorny bramble, "Think of the papyrus. It is the oldest document in existence that mentions Jesus by name! It confirms his crucifixion and points very strongly to his resurrection! Why don't you see that?"

"Of course I see it!" the priest answered.

"Then let's show the people of world!" Albert pleaded. "All I ask is that I be allowed the privilege of presenting it to them!"

"He's barely breathing, Angie!" Les yelled as he positioned Mehmet for cardiopulmonary resuscitation.

"Faith in God does not depend on the existence of the Holy Lance!" Justin replied, "It is not an idol!" His thundering retort echoed in the dome.

"Put...the...gun...down!" Angie enunciated each syllable loudly.

"Give me the Lance!" Albert screamed as he pointed the pistol at Les.

"Pulse is real weak!" Les announced. "I'm losing him!" Les added as he began chest compressions.

"The Lance stays here!" Angie's voice boomed back.

As Angie moved toward Les to help with Mehmet, Albert screamed. "No! Stay away from him! Give me the Lance!"

As Les calmly continued to keep Mehmet alive, Angie kneeled down beside the young Turk, placed his lifeless left hand on top of the reliquary and began to pray silently.

"Father!" Albert screamed. "You must show the world the wonders of Christ! It is your obligation as a man of God!"

"I see the wonders of Christ every day!" the priest proclaimed. "His love, given from one to another, His caring shown by His followers to others: the hungry fed, the naked clothed, the sick made well, the hopeless given hope, each and every sinner, no matter how wicked he or she may be, offered salvation through God's grace. These are the wonders of Christ! These are the true treasures of Christianity!"

"Stupid man!" Albert shrieked as he leveled the pistol at the priest.

No one remembered hearing a crack, but there certainly must have been one. As Albert began to squeeze the trigger, the loose plaster from the dome, that piece on which the Archangel Michael's sword was painted, plummeted toward the floor and struck Albert on the head, relieving him of consciousness.

The world seemed to freeze for an instant as Albert hit the floor. Les stopped his compressions of Mehmet's chest, Angie looked up from her praying, Father Justin and Maria looked on in uncertain amazement.

Their dreamlike state was abruptly interrupted by three coughs from Mehmet.

"Oh dear God!" Angie cried as she saw Mehmet turn his head. "Oh dear God!"

"Mehmet!" Les shouted as he saw the younger man sit up. "Whoa! Lay down, buddy! You've lost a lot of blood! My God, you were just about dead!"

"Doctor Connery! Doctor Johnson!" Mehmet cried. "Allah be praised! Allah be praised!"

"Whoa now!" Les warned Mehmet. "That bullet tore a big hole in you," he said as he looked to show Mehmet his wound. "What the...It's gone!"

"Let me see!" Angie interrupted as she nudged Les away from the Mehmet. Mehmet's shirt had a hole in it, but the wound in his chest had vanished. "It is gone!"

Father Justin crossed himself and declared it a miracle with his wife in full agreement.

"Is this really any different from anything that has happened since Mehmet brought us the Lance?" Les whispered to Angie as the priest and his wife embraced Mehmet.

"No," she whispered back. "I guess it's not any different at all."

"So what do we do with it then?" Les asked.

"I think I have an idea," Angie answered. She stepped over to Father Justin and Les joined Mehmet and Maria. "Father," she began, "I was thinking about what you were saying to Boucher over there...." They both looked at Albert as he lay peacefully unconscious. "Why does the world need the Lance of Longinus? Or the papyrus for that matter."

"Yes...." Father Justin urged her to continue.

"Faith is faith," Angie began. "There will always be those who won't believe, no matter what evidence is presented."

"That's true," the priest replied. "For some, there will never be enough evidence to convince them to believe and others already have more than they need. Faith is not an intellectual battle, to be waged with pen and paper, argument and rebuttal. As Saint James says, 'You believe that God is one; you do well. Even the demons believe—and shudder.' Faith is to be lived, practiced, exercised."

"Angie! You're amazing!" Les shouted as he rejoined his wife, his arms out for an embrace.

Angie received him and held him tight. "You're pretty amazing too, Les," she whispered in his ear.

"Father," Les began as he held out his hand, "it's my pleasure to know you."

"Thank you, Doctor," the priest replied.

"I overheard a little of what you two were saying," Les continued. "What have you decided about the Lance? Athens? London? The Smithsonian?"

Angie and Father Justin chuckled together and then Angie announced. "None of the above, baby. None of the above."

"Well, where then?" Les asked with childlike enthusiasm.

"The Lance of Longinus stays here," Angie replied.

"What? After all we've been through?" Les bellowed.

"I have to explain it to you later, Les," Angie smiled as she gently held out her arms and embraced him. "After all, we can't ruin the legend, can we?"

Les was stunned for a second or two but then acquiesced. "Okay. I'm sure you've got a better reason, but for now I won't push it."

Mehmet had overheard Angie's discussion with Les. "Doctor Johnson," He said with a smile. "I think that is a good idea. Where else would the Lance be safer? And its safety is most important, is it not?"

"Absolutely," Angie agreed.

"Safe from those who would tarnish its legacy, abuse its history," Mehmet added.

"Amen to that," Les said resignedly.

"Father," Angie began as she handed the reliquary to the priest, "put it somewhere, anywhere, but don't tell me. Don't tell anyone."

"It must be painfully difficult to relinquish it. You've been its guardian for the last two days. You saved it and it saved you."

"Yeah, you might say that."

"I know of the perfect place--" the priest began.

"Don't *even* tease me, Father!" Angie interrupted with a laugh.

"You can tease me if you want," Les suggested.

Everyone laughed for a minute and then Angie started to cry.

"What is it, Ange?" Les asked comfortingly as he wrapped his arm around her.

"I don't know," she answered. "I don't know." She looked at the priest who held the casket gingerly in his hands.

"It will be safe," Father Justin vowed gently.

"Yes, it will." This voice came from the narthex.

"Lucille Daniels!" Mehmet gasped.

"Give it to me now!" Luci said as she waved a long stick in the air as Osman rushed in behind her.

"No!" Sir Richard Covington-Smith screamed from a door in the north wall of the nave. "That belongs to me! It's a family heirloom, for God's sake!"

Kevin Meeley stumbled in after him, yawning as he echoed Sir Richard's demand, "Family heirloom!"

"Touch the Lance of Destiny," Siegfried yelled from the south door of the nave, "and you die! That is the property of the Knights of the Holy Lance!" Hugo Geissler stood by his side, eating a piece of cheese.

Angie grabbed the reliquary back from the priest and held it above her head. "You want it?" she yelled defiantly. Les and Mehmet jumped to her side. "Well, come and get it!"

Each of the six remaining antagonists sped forward, each of the three teams willing to annihilate the others to possess the relic. When Luci and Osman came within three feet of the reliquary, they suddenly collapsed onto their knees, as if all of the strength in their legs had left them. Seconds later the Nazis suffered the same fate, as did the Templars. They all were immediately silent, unable to utter anything, though they tried. Then Sir Richard fell face first onto the floor, followed by Luci, Siegfried, Kevin, Hugo and finally Osman.

"Are they okay?" Father Justin asked.

"The Daniels woman and Osman are sleeping, but I can't wake them," Mehmet announced after a quick inspection.

"They're unconscious!" Les said as he reached the Germans.

"Same here!" Angie added as she examined the Templars.

Maria held her husband tightly and whispered something to him. He whispered back that everything was all right.

"The Mighty Lance of Longinus strikes again!" Les chuckled.

At nine in the morning, Father Justin sent his wife to gather mattresses and blankets from the villagers as he and his guests carried the seven unconscious interlopers into the parsonage's great room.

"They seem stable, but there's not much we can do for them here," Angie noted.

"Yeah," Les agreed. "We need to get them off the island."

"I'll call the hospital on Leros," Father Justin said. "They can send a helicopter."

"Good thinking," Angie replied as the priest left the room. "What do you think happened, Les? Sudden spontaneous collapse and unconsciousness caused by--"

"Caused by God-knows-what," Les chuckled. Mehmet and Angie did too.

"The phone's not working," Justin said as he returned to the room. "I'll try the village post office phone," he added as he left.

"What do you think happened, Doctor Connery?" Mehmet asked.

"Well, except for the French guy, there's no sign of anything that would explain how they got this way," Les answered.

"Yeah, Boucher's got a large goose egg on his noggin," Angie added. "Hopefully he's got no intracranial bleeding."

Father Justin and Maria returned with many of the villagers. Sheets and blankets turned the mattresses into beds and the unconscious were carefully set on them. Luci Daniels' bed had been placed in the priest's study, next to Angie's bed. The beds of the other six remained in the central great room with Les and Mehmet.

Father Justin reported that phone lines were out all over the island. While there was cell phone service near enough to make some kind of communication, cell phones weren't working either. The islanders had no aircraft of any sort. Some of Agios Stavros' fishermen tried to head out to sea to reach one of the nearby islands, but the Aegean Sea inexplicably would not permit them. Swells rose and the wind gusted *toward* the island, no matter from which side of the island the boatmen attempted to depart. This essentially made any movement away from Agios Stavros impossible.

"So what do we do?" Les asked.

"We wait," Father Justin answered. "At least twice a month, a boat comes with food, fuel oil and other necessities."

"So it won't be long," Angie guessed.

"No, probably just a week or so," the priest replied.

Each morning the villagers would bring food for Mehmet and the Americans. They would chat briefly through Maria, who acted as interpreter. Angie and Les would examine their new patients but come to no new conclusions. Father Justin, Mehmet and Maria would help Angie and Les sponge-bathe the sick ones. After each bath, emollients were applied to the skin, especially the elbows, knees, feet, hands and lips to prevent desiccation. Drops of cool water were slowly, carefully squeezed from a wet washcloth onto the patients' tongues to prevent drying and cracking. However, since the unconscious could not swallow, this tiny amount of liquid was all that could be given. For three days, their conditions did not change.

CHAPTER TWENTY

April 17, 9:08 a.m.

Angie started her rounds as Les finished his breakfast. She picked up Osman's hand to check his pulse. "Eighty-four," she said to herself as she compared Osman's pulse to her watch. When she looked up she saw Osman staring at her. "Les!" she screamed. "Les! Get over here!"

"What is it?" Les asked as he ran in, yogurt dripping from the corner of his mouth.

"He's conscious!"

"Sheez! Look at him sweat!" Les was right. Rivers of sweat poured down Osman's brow.

Angie set the back of her hand against Osman's forehead. "He's burning up! Does Father Justin have a thermometer?"

Mehmet ran into the room as Les ran out. "Osman!" he said as he saw the big Turk sitting up on the bed. "Osman! How are you?"

"Meh—met," he struggled to say breathlessly.

Les returned with a digital thermometer. Father Justin and Maria followed. They were elated beyond words by Osman's apparent progress.

"Praise God! He's awake" the priest cried.

Angie gently slid it under Osman's tongue. "No talking for a little bit," she ordered softly. As she waited for the thermometer to announce the completion of its appointed task, Angie looked over this man who had tried to kill her four days ago. He was indeed a handsome man. When she looked him in the eye, he tried as hard as he could to close one eye and keep the other open. Then he smiled a lewd little smile, something one would expect from an ailing but oversexed teenage boy.

Angie was uneasy with the giant Turk's awakening. She remembered how scared she was when he chased her through the bazaar stalls in Istanbul. Yet she chuckled as she let her guard down. "He tried to wink at me! I think he's flirting," she whispered to Mehmet.

"Yes, that's the Osman I've always known, Doctor Johnson," Mehmet added.

When she turned back to Osman, his condition had suddenly, drastically worsened. Angie didn't think it was possible, but he felt even warmer than before. His eyes were cloudy and he was delirious. The thermometer beeped and Angie removed it from Osman's mouth. "A hundred six! That can't be right!" She stuck the thermometer back in his mouth.

"High fever, yet he's still conscious. I've seen worse." Les kneeled next to Angie and checked Osman's neck, gently flexing it forward. "Supple," he said reassuringly. "Probably doesn't have meningitis."

"Yeah, I don't think so either," Angie agreed. She turned to the priest. "Do you have anything for fever, Father? Preferably ibuprofen."

"Yes, I'll get some."

"That's gonna rip his gut," Les noted.

"I know, but what else do we have? We've got to get his fever down," Angie retorted.

"I don't disagree," Les added, "but I hope this doesn't lead to another problem."

The priest returned in thirty seconds and Angie counted out four two-hundred milligram tablets. The thermometer beeped.

"One hundred seven!" Angie cried. She and Mehmet quickly sat Osman up and delicately administered the medicine tablets to him one at a time with a small amount of water. After he swallowed his last sip of water, Osman's eyes closed and Angie and Mehmet layed him down.

"I'm afraid this isn't going to be enough to bring the temperature down," Angie admitted. "Let's cool him off and let him rest," she added as she applied cool water to Osman's skin with a sponge. "Father, do you have a bath tub?"

"Yes."

"Let's get him into the bath tub. Fill it with cool water."

"Got it," the priest replied.

Two hours later Osman began speaking deliriously in Turkish. He was still in the bathtub in cool water. Mehmet had remained at his side and tried to comfort him. As Angie, Les, Maria and Father Justin rushed in, Osman screamed and began crying.

"He's calling for his mother!" Mehmet noted. "He's crying because he says he mistreated her all of these years."

"Is that true?" Les asked.

"I thought he told me his mother died when he was very young," Mehmet answered.

Angie touched Osman's forehead. "He's as hot as ever!" She slid the thermometer into Osman's mouth and held his lips together. "Can you get ice, Father? We may need to pack it around his body."

"I'll see what I can do," Justin replied as he left the room.

"Did he say anything else, Mehmet?" Les asked.

"No. He only cried about his mother."

"How's his neck?" Les asked Angie.

"Still supple," she answered after she gently tilted it forward. "Still wondering about meningitis?"

"We couldn't do much for him if it were," Les lamented as he stepped forward and examined the patient again.

The thermometer beeped. "One hundred seven point five!" Angie gasped. "We've got to cool him down!"

"He'll be okay, Angie," Les tried to reassured her. "Father Justin is bringing ice."

"What will we do if he doesn't find any?" Angie asked. "More sponge baths?" she proposed skeptically.

"Why don't you use the Lance?" Mehmet asked.

"What?" Les wondered.

"You saw what it did for me, twice," Mehmet replied.

"Yeah, but these guys are the bad guys," Les objected.

"Are we not all the children of Allah?" Mehmet countered.

"He's right, Les," Angie answered as she went into the kitchen where Father Justin had left the relic. When she returned Angie pulled the reliquary out of thecotton bag and placed Osman's hands on it. She bowed her head and submitted a silent prayer. When she was finished, Angie looked up to see Les and Mehmet with their heads bowed.

After twenty minutes Osman's temperature had dropped below one hundred degrees. As the rivers of sweat cleared from Osman's face, Mehmet, Angieand Les sat back.

"Here's the ice!" Father Justin said as he raced in the door, his arms loaded with three big bags of it.

"Sorry, Father," Angie chuckled. "It looks like we won't be needing it."

The priest saw Osman's hands resting on the reliquary and gasped. He dropped the ice and stared in amazement. "Of course we won't." He slowly stepped over to Osman. He looked perfectly healthy. Justin placed the back of his hand over Osman's forehead. "His fever is gone."

"Amazing, isn't it," Angie chimed.

The priest's face grew sullen. "Angie…"

"Yes, Father."

"Were we wrong about the relic?"

"What do you mean?"

"Look what it did for Osman."

"Yeah, so?"

"Well, is it talisman? A charm? A magical tool?"

"What do you mean?" Les asked.

"I see what you mean, Father," Angie answered.

"What? What are you two talking about?" Les wondered.

"When you and Mehmet were looking after Albert," Angie began, "we were discussing whether the Lance itself had the power or was it God's power being delivered through the Lance?"

"And?"

"We agreed it was the latter. That's why we felt it was best for the Lance to stay here."

"So now you feel differently?"

"Les, you saw what happened," Angie added. "Osman's burning up one minute, with a temperature few people, if any, have ever seen, and he's fine the next--"

"After we put Osman's hands on the casket," Mehmet added.

"What we were doing for him didn't change anything," Angie continued. "His skin touches the relic, and he's better."

Father Justin shook his head. "I must have been wrong about the Lance. Maybe Agios Stavros is not where it should remain. Maybe it is God's will that the relic be shown to the world, used to cure the sick. I just don't know. It doesn't make sense."

"I'm confused, too, Father, but I know what I saw," Angie retorted.

"I've got to agree with Angie," Les concurred.

"I as well," Mehmet added.

By evening, Osman was conscious, but he desperately wanted to sleep. Mehmet had not left his side all day. Les and Angie made their rounds, inspecting the remaining six unconscious patients. Father Justin and Maria followed behind them, touching the hand of each patient to the casket and praying.

"Well, one's better," Angie said to Les and Father Justin as they finished seeing the others.

"But why just one?" Father Justin wondered as he cradled the casket in his fingers. He held up the reliquary and asked again. "Why just one?"

The following morning Angie stepped into the great room with Maria to check on Osman. Angie froze when she saw that his bed was empty.

"How are you this fine morning, ladies?" Osman's voice came from across the room.

Maria gasped and exited the room quickly.

Angie took a step back and readied the muscles of her body for combat. She recalled his chasing her through the empty stalls of the bazaar and throwing her down on the pavement. And she remembered the sound of the helicopter rotor whooping overhead, each low-toned pulse punctuated by the staccato of his machine gun.

"Perhaps you didn't hear me." Osman smiled as he spoke. "How are you this morning?" When Angie's stance failed to change, Osman nodded his head. "Ah, yes. I understand your caution."

Angie remained uneasy.

Osman sat on his bed, assuming a posture he felt would be less threatening. "I have not forgotten how we came to be together here. Please forgive me." Again he saw that Angie was unaffected. "I remember what has happened. I remember what I did." His voice grew remorseful. "After all, I did try to kill you and your husband…and Mehmet." He bent his head forward penitently. "Can you forgive me?"

Angie took a deep breath but said nothing. Her posture did not change.

"I understand," Osman said mournfully. "Can I at least thank you? Thank you for saving my life, saving the life of someone who is unworthy of such a magnanimous gesture." Osman stood, as if that would help Angie to speak with him.

"Sit down!" Angie shouted.

Osman obeyed instantly. "How can I reassure you?" he asked gently. "I promise you that I am not the same man that fired at you from the helicopter."

Les and Father Justin rushed in with Maria. They each wanted to speak, but the standoff between Angie and the Turk silenced all mouths.

Osman treated their arrival as another chance to exonerate himself. He turned to Les. "Can you please forgive me for what I have done?" he begged as he buried his face in the floor as diligently as an imam at Friday prayers.

Les looked at Father Justin as if to ask what he should do. The priest's face wore a reassuring smile.

"I forgive you," Les and the others heard Angie say as she softly set her hand on Osman's head.

"Osman?" Mehmet rushed in. "Is he all right, Doctor Johnson?"

"Mehmet!" Osman cried as he rose to his feet. "Mehmet, my friend! Can you forgive me?"

Mehmet was confused. The others seemed very calm, relieved, actually. And now Osman, who had lied to him and nearly killed him, was awake. He wasn't sure how he should feel.

Osman threw his arms around Mehmet and held him close. "I am sorry my friend! Please, please forgive me!"

When Mehmet heard Osman sobbing there could be only one reply. "I forgive you, Osman."

"Thank you, Mehmet," Osman responded. "Thank you, my friend!" Then he turned to Les.

"I forgive you too," Les said hurriedly as he stepped back, not wanting the big Turk to cry over him.

Osman turned to Father Justin, and Maria. "Thank you. Thank you so much. You saved my life."

Angie smiled at Osman and held his hand. "How do you feel, Osman?"

"I've never felt better, thank you." Then Osman looked bashfully at his feet. "Would it be rude of me to ask for breakfast? I'm very hungry," he said, smiling.

The others tittered.

"I will see to it," Maria answered his request.

Angie looked into Osman's eyes. No winking this time and now he wore the smile of a schoolboy, an innocent child. Angie checked his temperature and found that it was normal. She looked him over carefully and shook her head as if she had just witnessed the impossible.

"Is there something wrong?" Osman asked.

"No. No, you're absolutely perfect."

"Thank you, Doctor..."

"Johnson," Angie replied, "but please call me Angie."

"Very well," Osman chirped. "Thank you, Angie."

Maria returned with some toast and coffee.

"This is Maria," Angie announced to Osman.

"Hello, Maria. Thank you for taking such good care of me," Osman said joyfully.

"You are welcome, Osman," Maria responded with equal happiness in her voice.

They all sat with Osman as the grateful man voraciously consumed his breakfast.

"He's a new man," Mehmet whispered to Angie who smiled and nodded in agreement. "You know, I can't wait to tell him how the Lance helped to save his life."

Angie was struck by the irony: that treasure that he was willing to kill for saved his life. "Let's tell him tomorrow," she suggested as she watched Osman pile food into his mouth. "He's got enough to digest for now."

The six others remained unconscious for the next two days, despite the best efforts of their caregivers. Osman happily joined the ranks of Mehmet, the Greeks and the Americans. He was especially attentive and caring, and when the others expressed the least frustration or impatience, he urged them to be constant in their mission.

One day, Mehmet sat with Osman for a bit while the others attended to other things. "What was it like, Osman? Being unconscious for three days," Mehmet wondered. "And then that horrible fever.,."

"I don't remember much of anything," Osman answered. "Except for one thing."

"What was that?"

"The day I ran the fever, I kept having the same dream over and over again."

"Tell me about it."

"I would see the most beautiful women, all shapes and sizes, colors, and nationalities."

"Yes..."

"And then when I felt a desire to seduce them, they would turn into dogs!"

"Oh, my, Osman! That's incredible!"

"And when they turned into dogs, my heart would feel as if someone had just chewed off a piece from it!"

"But now you're fine."

"Yes, I'm fine, Mehmet. And I will never look at another woman that way again, not because I'm afraid of the pain in my heart, but because I realized that by leering at someone lustfully, I change that person from a human being to something inhuman."

"You have become a wise man, Osman," Mehmet smiled as he threw his arm around Osman's shoulders.

That night they all slept as if they hadn't a care in the world, which was not easy because no boats or aircraft had come from any of the neighboring islands and communication with the outside world was still nonexistent.

April 20, 6:10 a.m.

The quietude of the morning was shattered by a piercing scream. Osman leapt out of bed and ran to the source of the earsplitting noise, followed by Mehmet and Les.

"What in the world is that?" Angie asked as she ran into the room a few seconds after Les.

"It's Geissler, the German guy," Les answered. He had recalled the man's name from his passport.

"*Mein Gott!*" Hugo shrieked as he sat up, dropped the bedsheet and pointed to his emaciated arms. Geissler's face was hollowed out. His jaw stuck out and his sunken cheeks made his eyeballs appear as though they might fall out and any minute.

"Holy cow!" Les cried. "What happened to him?"

"He wasn't like this yesterday! He's always been on the plump side!" Angie reacted. She removed his shirt and gasped. Geissler shrieked again and started to bawl uncontrollably.

"The man is a skeleton!" Mehmet exclaimed. Mehmet's description was quite accurate. Hugo Geissler's ribs stuck out like the metal grill of a '57 Chevy. The space under his collarbones was three fingers deep and his stomach was sunken. His torso looked like the hulk of a shipwreck.

"What in heaven's name?" Father Justin asked as he and Maria joined the others. Maria crossed herself and dropped to her knees.

"I'm starving to death!" Hugo cried.

Osman brought him some milk and held it to his lips. The German gratefully sipped some, but it came right back up all over the well-meaning Osman.

"My stomach!" Hugo screamed as he held his upper belly with both hands. "My stomach is being torn apart!" He moaned as he fell backward into bed, writhing in pain.

"Look at him!" Les cringed. "He's getting even thinner! And right before our eyes!"

"How is this possible?" Mehmet pleaded as he held up the SS man's hand and saw the bones of Geissler's fingers beginning to thin. They all ran to his bed and watched in horror as his disease, having already consumed all of his flesh, was now devouring his bones. Hugo's pathetic cries of agony filled the room. Then suddenly they stopped. And when the moaning stopped, his body's dissolution ceased as well.

"It stopped!" Angie declared.

"Yes," Father Justin concurred from the other edge of the bed. "Thank God, it's stopped." In his left hand he held what remained of Hugo's left foot. With his right hand, he pressed the foot against the reliquary, bent his head forward and silently prayed.

The status of the other five remained unchanged, but Hugo Geissler was resting peacefully, awakening occasionally to take sips of broth or fruit juice. He slept well that night and by the next morning he was satisfying his rapacious appetite. Hugo showed that he was truly a jolly soul, and the others enjoyed his jovial company immensely. By evening he would reach a perfect weight and his appetite would be fully satisfied. As Osman had done and continued to do, Hugo helped the others tend to their sick charges, but there was no progress among the others. When they had finished their work, Father Justin went for a walk down to the beach with Hugo.

"You've been through a great deal, Hugo," the priest said.

"I've never been through anything like it in my life."

"Nor would you wish to again, I'm sure."

"No," Hugo answered. Then he stopped and looked back at Justin thoughtfully. "I've never felt better in my life than I do now. I can say that without any reservation. If I would have to go through that torture again to feel this good, I believe I would."

"I'm surprised."

"Well, I hope to God I won't have to do that again, but I can tell you I'm a better man because of it."

"What do you remember about it?"

"I remember most a dream about being in a bakery full of my favorite foods. Of course I was very happy to be there, and I immediately indulged myself. Yet with every mouthful I ate, the hungrier I became. I could see my belly grow as I filled my mouth, but the food did not satisfy me one bit. Then I looked out of the window of the bakery and saw the thinnest human beings I could imagine. I looked back at my huge belly and then out the window again. I looked around the bakery and saw all the wonderful food, and then again I looked out the window. I tried one last small piece of my favorite strudel, but it did nothing for me. Absolutely zero. So I ran to the door, opened it and let in all of those emaciated creatures. As I saw them eat, all of that hunger *I* was suffering went away. My stomach and my body felt wonderful as I saw those human scarecrows turn into normal, healthy people."

"That was a fascinating dream."

"Something tells me, Father, that it was something more than a dream."

Angie quietly took Les aside as the others went for a walk in the village. Angie pointed out Luci to Les. "I don't think she's gonna make it."

Les looked closely at Luci. "What do you mean? She looks like the others. No different, except maybe the old guy. He's turning a little green around the gills."

"I just have a feeling about her. You know? I've asked Father Justin to spend some more time with her."

"I'll ask him to do the same for Sir Richard. It may be the only chance the old guy has."

Angie slid her arm around Les' waist. "You know, it's amazing that Hugo and Osman have bounced back like they have. No food, minimal water and primitive medical care for six days. It's a miracle they didn't die before our eyes."

"'Miracle'. Good word choice."

Angie smiled and held Les close and kissed him. "How are you holding up?"

"Pretty well, considering I feel like I'm living out someone else's nightmare."

She chuckled and kissed him again. "Hang in there, babe. It's going to be all right."

April 23, 8:42 a.m.

"Hey, Angie," Les called across the room. He was examining the Frenchman. "What's with Albert?"

"What are you talking about?" Angie replied as she ran across the room. "Oh my God!" she cried when she saw Albert. "His eyes!" Mehmet, Maria, Osman, Hugo and Father Justin were right behind her.

"It looks as if the eyelids have been sewn shut!" Mehmet gasped.

As the others showed their horror, Albert awoke. "I'm alive," he said softly. "I'm alive!" The volume of his voice grew louder with each statement. "I'm alive! *Mon Dieu!* I'm alive!"

"Albert," Les asked, "Albert, how are you feeling?"

"I feel good," Albert answered slowly. "Very good!" Then suddenly he screeched, "But I can't see! I can't see! Godammit! Why can't I see?"

"Do his eyelids look scarred to you?" Angie asked Les.

"No. It looks like they've just grown together, naturally," Les answered. "However, I must admit I've never heard of eyelids growing together."

"Absolutely impossible," Angie added incredulously.

"I want to see!" Albert screamed as he stood up grabbing for anything nearby. "I want to see like everybody else! Why can't *I* see?"

"Settle down," Father Justin said calmly. "You're going to hurt yourself if you keep thrashing around like that."

"I want to see," Albert whined softly as Justin and Maria gently set him back on his bed. "I want to see."

"Monsieur Boucher," Mehmet said gently, "may I get you something to eat?"

"Mehmet! To hell with eating! Mehmet, you idiot! I can't see!"

"You'll be fine, Monsieur," Mehmet replied. "Let me assure you. Here, eat some broth."

Albert cautiously took a few sips. "Thank you, Mehmet," he said calmly. "You're good." He sniffed a few times because the tears forming under his eyelids could not get past the eyelids to roll down his cheeks, so they ran into his nose. "I want to see," he blubbered. "I just want to see."

The morning passed as all of the preceding nine had. The doctors, the laypeople and the priest ministered as best they knew how. Two patients had recovered; one was showing promise; but four still lay unconscious with no sign of improvement. While Albert slept heavily, Father Justin held the reliquary over his eyes and then made the sign of the cross with it. When Les checked Albert three hours later, he noted that the patient's eyelids had separated a very small amount. Les carefully pulled the upper lids up to inspect the globes beneath. *Still fused together for the most part but definitely more pliable. Eyes themselves look good. Hang in there, Albert!* Albert remained in a deep sleep, not stirring one bit, for the rest of the day.

The next morning Mehmet came to sponge down Albert's face. As the cool washcloth touched Albert's cheek, his eyes opened. Hugo and Osman were tending to Kevin and Sigfreid.

"Monsieur Boucher!" Mehmet said ecstatically. "Your eyes! Your eyes!"

"I can see, Mehmet!" Albert cried as tears rolled down his cheeks. "I can see!" he shouted as he shot up and danced around the room. "I can see again!"

"Welcome back among us!" Osman said as he came over. "I'm Osman," he added as he hugged Albert.

"Albert! I'm Hugo Geissler!" Hugo laughed. "So glad to witness your recovery. This is wonderful!"

"Well look at that!" Les laughed as he and Father Justin came in from the garden.

Maria and Angie heard the excitement and ran into the great room from the priest's study. "Albert!" they cried together.

The celebration was jubilant: another one of the sick was healed. As Osman and Hugo had done before him, Albert immediately set to helping the others in their care of those whom unconsciousness was still master. He impressed the others with his kindness and his willingness to work hard for the others.

That evening Albert walked with Les to the grocer in the village. The others had gone down the beach except for Angie. During the celebrations, Luci's pale skin and sunken eyes would not leave Angie's thoughts. Angie had patients die, more times than she wanted. It was the most unpleasant part of her profession. Now her gut told her that they would not be celebrating Luci's recovery. She knelt beside the stricken woman and ran her fingers gently over Luci's forehead. It was cool, cool as if Luci's failing body had just expended the last morsel of energy it possessed. Angie left her right hand on Luci's forehead and bowed her head forward.

Dear God, I ask you again, like I have so many other times, please heal her! I don't know her at all, but I know you do. I have a feeling that she's really a decent person and if given a chance, she'll come through.

For the next thirty minutes, Angie remained on her knees but didn't say or think anything. She waited and listened patiently, but nothing came. She stood up and took another look at Luci and shook her head.

Les and Albert were but five minutes from the house when Les asked him about his recovery. "That was quite an experience you had," he began. "I've seen plenty of people recover from unconsciousness but not quite like you did."

"I can't thank you all enough for what you and all of the others did for me," Albert replied.

"I suppose you don't remember much."

"Only one thing. And I remember it very, very clearly."

"What's that?"

"A dream. A dream that was *incroyable!*"

"Tell me about it," Les asked. Remembering what he had heard of Osman's and Hugo's "dreams", he awaited the story hungrily.

"I dreamt I was the ruler of a small kingdom. Around my lands were several other kingdoms. Some were wealthy, some were blessed with beautiful lands, while others possessed stunning shorelines. I soon found my kingdom inadequate. I had a thirst for more, so I led my army against one of my neighbors. When I captured the king, he cried that he could not understand why I had attacked him. I merely laughed and sent him away. However, the conquest of my neighbor did nothing to slake this curious thirst I had developed. My troops rode through the next kingdom and then the next. My kingdom was now huge. It was by far the wealthiest and possessed the most beautiful vistas ever known. Yet my desire to enlarge my kingdom only grew. As before, each conquered monarch expressed his or her surprised at my attack: 'Were we not friends?' 'Have we insulted you?' 'Did we not treat you and your subjects like brothers?'

"One day I rode to the eastern boundary of my kingdom with my ministers. As we approached the border, I saw the most beautiful mountains I had ever seen. The tallest of them was particularly magnificent. 'Some day,' I said to my prime minister, 'I will climb that great mountain of mine.'

"'Sire,' the prime minister interjected, 'these mountains are not in your kingdom.'

"'What?' I bellowed. I was very angry. "How could that be?"

"'These mountains lie within the realm of King Andrew.'

"'Not for long! Back to the capital! We are returning here tomorrow with my army!'

"My army climbed up into the mountains and marched through the lush green valleys of King Andrew's dominion. As we progressed my desire to possess this land burned like a fever in a plague-struck man. As we neared Andrew's capital we encountered his army. It was a rag-tag force, not even half as large as my army. The battle would be but a formality. The land was now mine! I ordered my generals to prepare for a frontal assault when a single rider from King Andrew's army rode through our lines.

"'I bear an invitation for you, sire, from King Andrew,' the messenger said as he kneeled before me.

"I read the message and agreed to comply with King Andrew's request. He promised me that he would surrender to me if I would join him for dinner. The only stipulation was that I had to come alone. 'I will return,' I bragged to my ministers, 'with another kingdom!'

"The dinner I sat down to was meager at best. 'We are a poor kingdom,' Andrew said. 'And as of late, we have grown poorer.'

"'What do you mean?' I asked.

"'Yesterday, when we were your friends, our wealth was great. Now that you are not our friends, we are poor.'

"'You are being ridiculous, Andrew! You have beautiful mountains and valleys in your kingdom.'

"'Take these from us if you must but be our friends and both of our kingdoms shall be very rich!' He stood and walked over to me. He extended his hand in friendship.

"Then a very strange thing happened. This thirst I had felt all of these days, this thirst that was unquenchable, this thirst that clawed at my throat and would not go away resolved. Yes, it disappeared. And as my throat felt healed, so did my heart. I stood up and hugged Andrew and vowed to be his friend forever. I returned to my kingdom and released all of the rulers I had captured and returned their lands to them. My kingdom grew wealthy, as did all of the others. Our greatest asset, I discovered, was each other. And when did I come to this conclusion? Why when King Andrew and I climbed that great mountain, together."

CHAPTER TWENTY-ONE

April 26, 5:50 a.m.

Angie yawned as she strolled through Maria's vegetable garden. Albert had made dinner the night before and she was still savoring the cheese sauce he had produced from various cheeses and creams he had obtained in the village. Yet, her ecstacy was tempered by the hard fact that they had now been on Agios Stavros for twelve days, with no communication of any kind with the outside word, essentially marooned.

Angie again thought about Luci and bowed her head to pray when a commotion arose inside the house. She could hear the others yelling and running around. "What's this?" she asked softly as she ran back to the house. When she got there, she saw the reason for the ruckus.

Kevin Meeley ran from one end of the house to the other with Mehmet, Albert and Osman chasing him.

"Stop!" Mehmet cried as he fell over a chair.

But Kevin would not yield. He lept over the dining room table and ran into the kitchen and out the door into the yard, leaving the others far behind.

"He's headed toward the village!" Hugo yelled to the others as he lagged behind to tell Angie what had happened. "He spang out of bed like a jack-in-the-box, Angie! Not five minutes ago! He was unconscious, right next to my bed, and then he was sprinting to the finish line in the Olympics! He hasn't stopped running since!"

"Les, Maria and Father Justin went into town earlier this morning. I hope they spot him!"

"If they don't, he will most certainly die of a heart attack!"

Not twenty minutes later, Osman, Mehmet, Maria and Albert returned with Les, Father Justin and Kevin, who was bound head-to-foot with ropes. Each of the men, except Albert as he was the smallest of the five, carried Kevin by one of his extremities. Their cargo wiggled and fought them, as if he were trying to escape the clutches of hungry cannibals. Earlier, when he screamed bloody murder, ordering them to release him, Les grabbed a napkin from a café table and gagged him. The café owner was happy to donate the napkin to the cause of peace and quiet.

As Kevin lay in bed, Angie looked him over. "Les! Pulse is now over two hundred!" Kevin's legs and arms flailed in his fetters, as if were still running a race, despite his bondage. "Carotid massage and diving reflex failed. Got any other ideas?"

"No. Not unless we can get him to a hospital."

Father Justin stepped into the great room with the reliquary. "How's he doing?"

"No better," Angie answered.

The priest approached and kneeled at the bedside. He gently touched it against Kevin's squirming head. But the ailing man's legs and arms failed to slow down. The others slowly filtered into the room and gathered at Kevin's side.

Father Justin grabbed Kevin's right hand and Angie grabbed the left. He set the reliquary on Kevin's chest and began to pray outloud. Angie bowed her head, as did Les. Soon the others assumed various attitudes of reverence. Kevin's squirming initially intensified as the circle of people closed around him, but as the prayer continued to its end, the patient slowly grew more relaxed. Sixty minutes later, Father Justin and the others finished praying and Kevin was asleep.

"Pulse is down to ninety," Angie announced as she removed the napkin from Kevin's mouth.

Les and Mehmet unbound him and readied him for sleep.

"He should be well by tomorrow," Mehmet ventured. "Don't you agree?"

"So you've noticed a pattern, too, eh Mehmet?" Les asked.

"Awakened from unconsciousness one morning," Mehmet deduced, "totally well the next."

"There seems to be another pattern too," Maria added in broken English. She turned to her husband and continued in Greek.

"That's right, my darling," Father Justin said and then added something in Greek as he hugged her. "Maria has noticed that each recovery has occurred three days after the one that preceded it."

"That's right!" Angie noted. "Osman awoke on the seventeenth, Hugo the twentieth, Albert on the twenty-third--"

"And now Kevin, three days later!" Les added.

"But why?" Father Justin wondered. "Why every three days? And why just one at a time?"

"And why was I first?" Osman asked.

"Why has this island been cut off from the rest of the world since the day we got here?" Les inquired.

"Why was a precious relic found and brought here, to this tiny island, by Angie, Les and Mehmet; to *this* island, where it had been only briefly over eight hundred fifty years before?" Father Justin asked.

"And why are the rest of us here and why are these strange but amazing things happening to us?" Hugo added.

Silence engulfed the room. The priest looked down at the casket he held in his hands and wondered. Around him, the others looked at the reliquary but kept their thoughts deep inside themselves.

"God does move in mysterious ways," Father Justin said.

"That, Father," Les replied, "is a colossal understatement."

The others laughed and moved toward the kitchen for breakfast except Albert, who stepped toward the opposite corner, and Angie and Les, who were moving toward the door. Justin followed them after a brief, thoughtful pause.

"This series of events," he began, "this parade of suffering and recovery following a crippling blow to each of these people, reminds me, in a certain way, of Saint Paul's conversion on the road to Damascus: cataclysm followed by recovery and transformation."

"Transformation?" Les asked.

"A metamorphosis in process," Angie interjected.

"It just may be," Father Justin concluded. "Why else would it be happening?"

Angie glanced at Albert who had moved to the opposite side of the room. He was visibly disturbed. He shook his head and turned away from the others.

"What is it, Albert?" Angie asked as she walked toward him.

"Will the others recover?" he asked when she reached him, tears in his eyes.

The question landed like a rock in her stomach. Angie stepped forward and embraced Albert. "They will, Albert," she rejoined, knowing that she shared his uncertainty. "They will."

"I hope that you are right," Albert replied as he looked doubtfully down at the floor.

As expected, the next morning Kevin Meeley awoke in as pleasant a mood as one could possibly muster. "Good morning," he said to Albert, who was sponge-bathing Siegfried. "I'm Kevin Meeley," he added without hesitation.

"*Bonjour! Bonjour mon ami!*" Albert set the washcloth down and hugged Kevin. "I'm Albert and I'm so happy you are all better! Everybody, come look! Kevin has recovered!"

Everyone came to Kevin and congratulated him on his recovery and introduced themselves.

"Thank you all," Kevin said tearfully. "You are wonderful people!"

They sat him down to breakfast and presented him with delicious food, which he tore into ravenously. Osman and Hugo tousled his hair and Mehmet told him how glad he was to see him doing so well. Kevin was ecstatic about his recovery but only for a short time. He soon grew more quiet as the others continued their boisterous celebration. Most took no notice of Kevin's somber descent, but Angie did.

Les sipped some orange juice and turned to his wife who was sitting beside him. "Four down, three to go," he quipped.

"How's Sir Richard?"

"I don't know. I'm still amazed that the old guy hasn't died." Les took a long sip of orange juice. "What's happening here, Angie? I mean, sure people become unconscious and recover--"

"And some don't."

"Why would God bring them to this island only to strike them down?"

"I think I know why. You can't see it?"

"What?"

"You really can't see what's happening?"

"Well, yeah, they're getting *better* but--"

"You know, I think Mehmet said it best, once Osman had recovered."

"What did he say?"

"He said Osman was a new man."

"You know, the French guy's turned out to be pretty nice too. Not the same snarky character we met in Istanbul."

"Father Justin called it a transformation. Remember?"

"Of course I do," Les answered. He thought for a few seconds and added, "But I don't think they're the only ones being transformed."

Angie smiled at him. "Amen to that. None of us will be the same." She moved closer to her husband and cuddled him. "What do you think will happen to them when we leave the island?"

"You mean if the others recover."

"You don't think they will?"

"I hope they do, but I've learned to be more cautious in my expectations."

"Even after all that has happened? Les, it's been one miracle after another! I had my doubts, but now I know for sure."

"I admire your optimism."

"Do you agree that what we've seen happen is rather incredible?"

Les smiled. "Absolutely," he answered softly as he kissed her lips.

Angie held him tighter and asked, "So tell me what you think will happen to them after we leave the island?"

"Who knows?" Les sighed. "The world is a jungle."

"Will they stay the way they are now? Or will the world change them back to what they were? They're absolutely wonderful people now. I don't think that after all God's put them through they won't remain so. These people were very ill. This transformation is going to stick."

""I hope you're right, but people do change."

"Not this time, Les," Angie retorted. "Osman, Kevin, Hugo, Albert--they're very kind and giving. I could see them caring for the poor, the orphans, the downtrodden."

"And what about us?"

"I feel changed. I feel stronger, better that I ever have. I feel whole, purposeful…happy."

"You didn't before?"

"Well yes, but now more than ever before. I'm ready to take on anything to share this joy, enthusiasm and hunger to help people."

"Don't you already do that as a doctor?"

"I'm not limiting this to a professional context. I mean spreading the love I have experienced here, serving in whatever capacity I can."

Les kissed her again. "You know, I've been feeling that as well, although not as *exuberantly* as you have."

"That's a big word," she teased. "I'm glad to hear that you feel that way, Les."

He winked at her. "By the way, thanks."

"For what?"

"Puttin' up with me through this."

"Oh, Les, you're worth it."

"You're sweet. You know, I think they're all worth it."

"You mean the others?"

"Of course."

"Even those people that tried to kill us?"

"Yeah, babe. I love those people, too."

"So do I, Les," Angie said as she pulled him closer. "So do I."

Later that morning Angie and Kevin walked to the beach where Angie, Les, and Mehmet had landed a little more than two weeks earlier. "How are you feeling today, Kevin?" she asked.

"I'm ready to take on the world, Angie," he answered. "I feel great."

"That's good considering you were unconscious for twelve days."

"I feel as though I've just awakened from just the right amount of sleep in the most comfortable bed I've known, kinda like the one my grandmum had when I was a kid."

"You don't remember anything in particular?"

"Nothing. Nothing except this dream. Not really a dream because it was so lifelike."

"Really? What happened?"

"I was floating through the sky on a king-sized bed. So comfortable. I could have slept for a decade. As I floated over the ground, I saw people running to and fro, running around like they were on fire."

"On fire?"

"It was as if they were one step ahead of the fire. If they stopped or slowed down, the flames consumed them. Oh, it was horrid! And the smell of burning flesh was horrible and so real. The more I tried to ignore the cries of those poor souls below me, the louder their cries became. And the more of them that burned, the louder the noise grew. Of course, the stench became unbearable. There was no way for me to get the sleep I craved so badly."

"So what happened?"

"As I floated over the people, they screamed for my help. Again, I tried to disregard their pleas. I needed my precious sleep. I was so tired! However, their cries only grew more intense. There was no avoiding them, so I reluctantly rose from the bed. I didn't want to look, but something in my heart made me watch the horror below me. There would be no rest for me until I helped them, but I had no idea how I could. I shouted down to them that I had no way of helping, but they replied, 'You have a fire extinguisher under your bed.' 'I do? Good. The sooner I find this implement, the sooner I can stop their wailing and get some sleep!' I landed the bed on the ground and flipped her over and there it was, just as they'd said, a fire extinguisher. I could hear more and more of their screams, so I hurried as fast as I could. After I had defeated the fire and saved the people, my body should have been exhausted. But my soul knew the greatest peace possible, and because of that, my body never felt so good."

"And your bed?"

"I gave it away because I didn't need it anymore. The more I helped those who needed me, the better I felt."

"That's quite a dream, Kevin."

"But it's more than a dream, Angie. Much more."

"I think I know what you mean," she replied. "Kevin," Angie began after a short pause, "This morning at breakfast you looked a little...down."

"I didn't think anyone noticed."

"What's bothering you?"

A tear formed in the corner of one eye. "It's Sir Richard..."

"Of course. I should have guessed that. You're pretty worried about him."

"Oh, he's like a father to me—well, some of the time."

Angie chortled. "He's very special to you." Kevin nodded back. "Les has been keeping a close eye on him. He's concerned."

Kevin gasped quietly. "Is he--"

"He's going to be all right. I know it."

"Would it help if I…"

"If you what?"

"If I said a prayer for him," Kevin answered. "Never really done much prayin'. Wouldn't know what to say."

"Kevin, no one's recovery has had much to do with what Les and I have done. Your praying is as good as, or better than, anything we have to offer as doctors. Say your prayer and then say it again and again. God will hear it. He wants to hear it."

"Yeah?"

"I think you two are overdue for a good conversation."

April 29, 6:57 a.m.

"I think he's choking on something!" Hugo cried as he stood over Siegfried. The gigantic Teuton had been coughing without stopping for the last two minutes straight. A cloud of gray smoke was forming above him.

Angie ran to Siegfried's bed. "Turn him on his side!" She inspected his mouth but could see nothing. "Achhh!" Angie said as she spat onto the floor. "His breath smells like smoke!"

"Like cigarettes?" Hugo asked before he coughed twice.

"No, like sulfur!"

"Sulfur?" Les asked from across the room.

Angie struck Siegfried's back between his shoulder blades three times. With each blow black-gray smoke belched forth from Siegfried's mouth.

"Geez!" Les screeched. "It smells like Yellowstone in here!"

Angie coughed three times and then administered three more blows with her right hand and held her nose with her left. When she finished she inspected Siegfried's mouth and found she had dislodged nothing. Siegfried's coughing continued unabated.

"I don't think he aspirated," Angie said to Les as he approached.

Siegfried coughed again and the smoke that belched forth sent her into a brief coughing fit.

"Smells like he aspirated a volcano!" Les coughed and turned his head away.

With each successive cough, more and more gray and then black, acrid smoke filled the room. Maria had opened all of the windows and doors, but the stench and smoke wouldn't leave the house. It became so bad that everyone was coughing now.

Father Justin tried to wave the darkening smoke away as he stepped forward and layed the reliquary across Siegfried's chest. The priest coughed several times and then started to chant the Lord's Prayer. Every few words were punctuated by a deep cough. As the priest prayed, the others gathered around the bed. By the time Father Justin had finished, Siegfried's cough had diminished only a little and the smoke that filled the room had not dissipated. The priest started the prayer again, this time he didn't chant but spoke the prayer, and soon Les and Angie joined him, each line punctuated by fits of coughing from each of them. An hour later they stopped praying. Siegfried's health had again improved a little, and the odor of sulfur and the smoke that accompanied it began to clear. Justin started the prayer again with Angie and Les. Maria joined them but in Greek. Hugo soon joined in, followed by Albert and Kevin. Mehmet and Osman prayed as they knew best: they lay prostrate on the floor and prayed as their fathers had taught them.

Thirty minutes later, when this last prayer ended, Siegfried coughed very violently three times, smoke and occasional flame, as well as sulfur, spewing from his mouth and nostrils. Then he stopped abruptly. The others were silent, waiting for Siegfried to spew more foul gasses from his lungs, but he didn't. What they did hear was even, comfortable breathing as Siegfried fell asleep.

All were gathered around Siegfried's bed expectantly the following morning. He had begun stirring about ten minutes earlier and with each minute that went by, he became more active. Finally, at 8:10, he awoke to the cheers of all those around him. Hugo hugged him and kissed his head a dozen times. Siegfried couldn't help but smile, and as he did so, he looked as meek as a lamb. Soon the others joined Hugo, surrounding Siegfried and welcoming him back to consciousness. He didn't say much, and when he did, his voice was soft and mild and his breath was as sweet as rose petals. The celebration that ensued surpassed the others. However, the participants were not only celebrating Siegfried's recovery. They were commemorating the rejuvenation of all who had been afflicted, and they rejoiced at the growing possibility of the recooperation of Luci and Sir Richard.

That evening, as the sun went down, Siegfried sat with his father, Mehmet, Maria and Father Justin. They sipped coffee and nibbled cookies that Maria had made that afternoon. Les and Angie went for a romantic stroll on the beach, and Kevin, Osman and Albert walked into town.

"Are you feeling well, Siegfried?" Father Justin asked.

"I feel fantastic," Siegfried replied. "It is so wonderful to be here with all of you. I shall remember this for the rest of my life."

"Tell them about your dream, son," Hugo suggested.

"My dream?" he asked shyly, his cheeks blushing.

"Yes," Father Justin said, trying to encourage Siegfried to share with them. "Each of you had a dream that came before regaining consciousness."

"I did have a dream. It was so real, Father, yet so strange. My dream was fantastic. It was incredible. Are you certain--"

"Please," Mehmet begged, "we would love to hear it."

"Okay. I will start," Siegfried replied modestly in his thick German accent.

"Thank you," Maria said.

"I was a handsome stallion and I could race like the wind," the brawny German began. "Of course, I was the fastest of all of the horses, and they all looked up to me. I grazed in the greenest of meadows. The lush grass was so wonderful. My life was quite good. Our meadow had a pond whose surface was clear as glass. I would see my reflection in the pond and remind myself how good life had been to me.

"One day, while I was racing Walter, another stallion, I injured my hoof. Oh, it was so painful! I had to stop racing for six weeks. During this time I could only watch the others run up and down the meadow. I would listen to the other horses praising the winners of the races: 'He is such a great racer!' 'She is surely the fastest!' 'Amanda is a very graceful runner!' 'There has never been one as great as Walter!' It seemed as though nobody remembered me.

"I quit going to see the others race. I would sleep or walk somewhere else. My friends would come by to ask why I had not gone to see the races. 'This new mare is quite good, poetry in motion!' 'That new Arabian looks promising.' 'Walter is unbeatable! He broke your old record!'

"As I listened to my friends, my anger burned in my stomach. 'Go away!' I yelled. 'Leave me alone!' Well, my friends could not believe what they were hearing. 'Are you well?' 'Can we help you?' I reared up on my hind legs and screamed as loud as I could, 'Leave me alone!' I screamed angrily. My friends ran away for I had truly frightened them.

"Six weeks went by slowly. My hoof had healed, but my contempt for my friends had only grown. I would show them who the greatest horse was. I strutted proudly over to the meadow where the day's races would be. 'Prepare to meet the new winner!' I mumbled to myself as I saw the other horses getting ready far off in the distance. As I drew closer, I could not help smelling a most sickening odor. At first it smelled like hot springs, but it worsened as I went further. 'Rotten eggs,' I thought. Where would these be coming from?

"As I approached the racing field some of the horses saw me. While I did indeed wish for them to be in awe of me, these horses reacted most peculiarly. They whinnied, turned and ran. Soon every horse in the meadow was in retreat. 'Wait!' I cried. When I called to them, I could see why they had all run. When I cried out, my words were accompanied by a stream of fire. The stench I smelled on my way over to the meadow was coming from me. 'What is wrong with me?' I cried. I had to find out so I galloped to the reflecting pond and looked. I shuddered at what I saw, for there was no longer a handsome stallion looking back at me but instead a horrible dragon. My anger had turned me into a monster. 'What have I done? I have destroyed my life!' My tears flowed into the pond and blurred my reflection. 'It's just as well; such a horrible thing to see!' I cried. When my tears stopped, I looked again. The horrible dragon was still there, but this time it was joined by a handsome stallion. 'Walter? Walter, why are you here? Am I not a horrible thing? Go away! Save yourself!'

"'I am not one to desert my friends,' Walter answered me. He rubbed his fine, silky mane against my scaly neck. Come with me, my friend, and be a stallion again.'"

Sigfried stopped and wiped a tear from his eye.

"And then?" Mehmet asked politely.

"Then I awakened!"

The others burst into laughter and Hugo held him tight. "That was a wonderful dream, my son. A wonderful dream."

CHAPTER
TWENTY-TWO

May 2, 11:23 a.m.

"Les! I need you in here now!" Angie shouted.

Les ran in to see Maria and Angie trying to help Luci. All of the others had left the house hours before. The poor woman was suffering from extremely violent tremors of all four extremities. She thrashed about so forcibly, so ballistically, that she struck herself many times in the face. Angie held down Luci's arms and Maria her legs, but the tremors were so strong that Angie and Maria were nearly thrown about when Luci's limbs flailed violently. To make matters worse, Luci's head started shaking uncontrollably as Angie and Maria held her down.

"My God!" Les said. "What I wouldn't give for ten milligrams of Valium right now."

"Grab her head before she hurts herself," Angie ordered.

"Or *you*," Les added.

As Les stabilized Luci's head, she shrieked directly into Les' ear. "My ears!" Luci cried. "The noise is killing my ears!"

"Oww! My ears don't feel so hot either!" Les protested. "What noise is she shouting about?" Les asked.

"I don't know, Les. There's no noise," Angie replied as Luci's tremors accelerated.

"Don't you hear the thunder?" Luci screamed as the tremor subsided briefly. "Oh, God! It's so loud!" The convulsion again accelerated.

Les could barely control Luci's head. "Where's Father Justin?"

"He went into the village," Maria answered as Luci's legs began to thrash more wildly.

"Do you know where he put the casket?" Les asked.

"In the bedroom. He put it there after we prayed for Luci and Sir Richard earlier this morning."

"Angie, I can get her arms if you can get the feet."

"Yeah, sure," Angie agreed. "Maria, you need to get the relic from the bedroom, and bring it here. Les and I can take care of her."

"That noise is deafening!" Luci screamed again.

"Okay, I go." Maria jumped up to run to the bedroom, but as she did, Luci's thrashing became more violent than before. Her legs kicked explosively, and Angie was soon on the other side of the room.

"Angie!" Les cried as he struggled to hold down Luci's arms.

"Her legs are as strong as a horse's!" Angie yelled as she hurried back. "Maria, grab the left one, and I'll hold the right!"

As Maria joined Angie, Luci's nearly threw Les off to the side.

"What about the Lance?" Les asked.

"She could kill herself or one of us by the time we get it!"

"What are we gonna do?"

Before Angie answered, they both heard Maria saying something in Greek, her head bowed, her eyes closed. As the words continued from Maria's mouth, Angie felt the legs relaxing very slightly.

Angie looked over to Les who grinned back, "We should have though of that." But he didn't act on his comment. Instead he looked to Angie to take the next step.

"Dear God," Angie prayed aloud, "please help us! Luci must live! Please, God, heal her as you have healed the others!"

"Please, God! Be merciful. Heal her!" Les added.

Luci convulsed violently and her legs nearly threw off Marie and Angie. The women held on tightly, mouthing the words to silent, desperate prayers.

"Please, God!" Les moaned. "Heal your child, Luci!" Les closed his eyes and leaned his head forward in hope.

Within thirty seconds Angie shouted, "Hey, her legs are slowing down a little! They're not as bad!"

Les relaxed and one of Luci's flailing arms struck him violently across the forehead.

"Oww!" he whined. "Well, her arms and head are still workin' overtime!"

Maria had not said much or moved since she had started praying. Her grip on Luci's leg had not diminished one bit. Her vigil was continuous, without regard to Les and Angie. Now her voice grew louder but without any conscious effort on her part. Her prayer, still in Greek, sent a wave of warm comfort through Angie's heart. Angie looked over at Maria and smiled. She had no idea what the woman was saying, but her spirit was soothed by Maria's melodic prayer. Angie closed her eyes and began a silent prayer of her own. As she prayed she felt her heart take flight from her body. Slowly upward it went. With increasing altitude came growing peace and serenity. Yet her prayer did not cease. She felt Luci's legs tense and seize, but this didn't slow her heart's ascent. Now she barely felt her hands on Luci's legs. Her complete attention was on her prayer and to the one to whom the prayer was directed.

Les glanced at his wife and saw the affect of Maria's prayer. He could only guess what was causing the glow on Angie's face. He felt Luci's arms beginning to relax, but he didn't trust her. He was dealing with a medical unknown. He wasn't about to risk another smack in the head. His arms were past tired, but he held on, saying to himself under his breath, "Come on! Hold on!" After another ten minutes, he drifted off, his arms still restraining Luci. He awoke when his head bobbed forward, but he drifted off a second time not five minutes later. Luci's right arm jerked outward, and Les awakened. A more active plan was needed. He saw that Maria was still praying in Greek. Angie was still mouthing words with her eyes closed. *Should I join them?* Luci's arms grew more ballistic. Her left arm nearly struck his nose. Les was convinced that that punch could have laid him out. He sighed and closed his eyes. *Time to begin. God, I'm not very good at this, but I'm doing my best. I want you to help Luci here. I know she's not a very nice person and probably not first on your list of those deserving special favors. But she needs your help. You're probably the only one who can heal her. Please give her a chance to be a decent person. I think if she sees how kind you are, she'll change her ways. Please, God, talk to her like you talked to me. Touch her heart, and let her feel your love.*

Luci's situation changed little over the next two hours. Her body was still racked by wild paroxysms, but they were less frequent. Les furtively opened one eye and peaked at the others. Maria's prayer had not stopped or even hesitated. Angie remained transfixed on something outside the room, outside of the physical world. He sighed deeply. *Let's try it again, God.*

After another two hours, Luci drifted off to sleep. Her body was still. Her breathing was regular and calm. Her face was peaceful.

"I think that's a new record," Les sighed as he opened his eyes, exhausted after the ordeal. Angie opened her eyes and smiled at him. Maria had fallen asleep next to Luci and was dozing comfortably.

"How long has this been going on?" they heard Father Justin say from a corner of the room.

"Father!" Angie gasped. "How long have you been here?"

"We didn't hear you at all!" Les added.

"I've been here just a few minutes".

Les saw the reliquary resting on Luci's chest. "We could have used that a few hours ago!"

Father Justin asked his question again but in a different way. "When did all this start?"

"Just before six thirty," Angie answered. "What time is it now?"

"Almost midnight."

"We've been praying for over five hours?" Les groaned.

"Yes," the priest answered. "What was happening to her?"

"You should have seen it, Father," Les began. "She was convulsing uncontrollably: arms and legs flying here and there! Even her head was jerking!" Then he thought for a few seconds. "And you just set the Lance against her chest a few minutes ago?"

"Yes."

"It worked really quickly!"

"No," the priest said. "I don't think it worked much at all."

"What?" Angie and Les cried in unison.

"You're joking, right Father?" Les wondered.

"She was moving her arms and legs some but not like you're describing. I have a feeling it was your prayers that did this."

"We pray for five hours and nothing happens! And you lay the Lance on her for a few minutes and she's cured," Les retorted. "No way could I be convinced it was anything but the Lance!"

"I have to agree with him, Father," Angie added.

"Hmmm," Father Justin said out loud. "Well, I guess we'll see," he added under his breath.

May 3, 10:48 a.m.

The next morning came and Luci continued to sleep peacefully. The mood about the house was somber after morning rounds. Morning was reaching its end, and Luci was still asleep. Her failure to recover quickly completely left everyone wondering.

"It's almost eleven, Angie," Les noted as he walked over to Luci's bed and patted his wife on the shoulder. Angie had not left the bedside since five that morning.

"I just want to stay a little longer."

"Sure, babe. I'm going to sit in the yard. Beautiful morning."

"I'll be out in a little."

Les kissed her on the top of her head and left.

Angie looked at Luci sleeping so peaceably. She couldn't help wondering what such a woman was like when she was younger. What had happened in her life that finally led her to Istanbul in April of 2004? Did circumstance shape her or was she destined to become this "dragon lady", as Mehmet had once called her? Luci was a beautiful woman. She probably had a great deal of good qualities in her somewhere.

Angie stood up to stretch her legs. "I hope you make it, Luci," she said outloud as she turned and walked to the door.

"Please don't go," the voice said softly.

Angie spun around to see Luci looking at her with soft, beautiful eyes. "Did you say something?" Angie asked hopefully.

"Please stay with me." Her voice was precious and sincere.

"You bet! I'll sit down right next to you!" Angie replied with a big grin as she reclaimed her seat. "I'm Angie, Luci." Angie reached out her hand, and Luci readily accepted.

"Angie," Luci said with a smile, as if she were saying that name for the first time, "You know my name. I've felt you near me for a long time."

"I've been here most of the morning."

"No, even before that."

"Really?"

"I don't know. I can't really remember much."

"You've been unconscious for over two weeks."

"Oh my goodness!"

"Nineteen days to be exact."

"I-I had no idea."

"What's the last thing you remember, before you woke up?"

"I remember a place, a place very different than this. I'd call it a dream but a very real dream."

"Can you tell me about it?" Angie asked excitedly. She had a feeling it would be a fascinating dream, as all of the others had been.

"Sure, Angie," Luci answered. "I was a bird," she began with a little laugh. "A very beautiful robin. It was springtime, and I was ready to lay my eggs. Of course I needed to build my nest. So, I flew far and wide gathering all that I felt I needed for my nest. I rejected twigs, feathers and mud, things that other robins were happy to use. No, I found the most beautiful things for my nest: silver combs, gold rings, diamond earrings. Oh, I was so proud of my nest. It was the most beautiful, the most precious any robin had ever made. But it needed more. I flew for hundreds of miles, bringing more jewels and trinkets. When the time finally came, I squatted on the bough that held my nest and gently laid four eggs into it, one after another. I smiled when I dreamed of how beautiful my nest would look. I turned around to adore my eggs only see that they had fallen through the nest and had shattered on the ground far below."

"How sad!"

"I guess I built my nest with things I thought were important, things that had great value but things that, in the end, did me no good."

"No twigs and mud."

"No. None of the basics."

"Luci, that was some dream."

"I'll never forget it, not in a million years. It was so real!"

"I'll bet it was," Angie said as she remembered how the others had reacted to their dreams.

Luci's upper lip quivered as she reached to wipe a tear from the corner of her eye.

"Hey," Angie offered compassionately, "what's this? You're fine. You're—"

"I'm so ashamed," Luci cried, looking away from Angie.

Angie recognized contrition in the woman's voice. She gently stroked Luci's black hair and listened gracefully to a familiar catharsis of guilt.

"Why do you treat me so well?' Luci wept. "I did my best to kill you!"

Angie smiled back at Luci.

"My God, I remember looking at you from the helicopter, hoping that Osman would put a bullet through your heart--" Luci suddenly sat bolt upright and grabbed Angie as if she were going to shake her to make her understand, but the tension in her muscles faded. She threw her arms around Angie's neck and wept again. "I'm so sorry! I'm so sorry!"

Angie held Luci gently. "It's okay. It's okay," Angie answered, trying to overcome falterings in her own voice. "It's okay, Luci. Really, it's fine. We're okay, you and me."

Luci pushed Angie away. "But I wanted you dead!"

"That's in the past. We're good right now." Angie gave her a reassuring smile. "I forgive you."

Luci pulled Angie close. "Thank you," She whispered softly in Angie's ear. "Thank you."

When the others returned they were again jubilant. Their disappointment from earlier in the morning vanished. At dinner Les looked around the table. He smiled and felt his heart flutter a bit when he remembered what had happened to each of them, even Mehmet. He smiled at the young man as he remembered performing CPR on the dying youth weeks ago. Now if Sir Richard could pull through...Then Les chastised himself, and right he was to do so, he thought. Was there any reason to believe that the old man wouldn't pull through? Where was his faith? For once in his life, he was sitting in a church every Sunday and enjoying it, even though he didn't understand Greek. Whether he was just dreaming or really *was* listening to God, he was learning something sitting in the little church on Sunday morning.

How can I doubt my purpose here? Think about it. This is The Lance of Longinus we're talkin' about here: the relic that had saved my life and Mehmet's and the lives of six of the other nine people eating dinner with me.

Sir Richard's time would come soon enough. Les took a sip of wine and looked out the window at the sky. There was still no change in the communication situation. It looked like God wanted them on the island a little longer, and he could deal with that.

May 5, 11:58 a.m.

Sir Richard's cries were muffled, so they remained unheard for a few minutes. Then Kevin alertly heard something coming from the corner where Sir Richard's bed lay. He ran to his master and cried when he saw the old man laying face down with a huge mass on his back.

"Oh, my Lord in Heaven!" Kevin screamed. "Help! Help! It's Sir Richard!"

Osman and Siegfried arrived first, followed by Les, Maria, and Angie.

"He has a huge stone slab on his back!" Siegfried cried as he clawed at the mass. He tried to pull off the huge slab. It was six inches thick and ran from the top of his head to his tailbone. *Mein Gott!* I think the stone is fused with Sir Richard's skin!"

The slab's width was six inches wider than the Grand Master's torso on each side so the ends of the slab hung over like ledges. He looked like a tombstone with arms, legs and a head.

Osman tore off Sir Richard's shirt. "This stone is growing out of his back! There is no way to remove it from him! It must weight five hundred pounds!"

"He can't breathe; he'll suffocate!" Kevin wailed.

"If it doesn't crush him first! Lift the slab!" Les ordered. "We're going to have to hold it so he can breathe."

Each of the men grabbed a corner and each woman lifted in the middle of a long edge. "Hold it for a few minutes so he can catch his breath!" Angie commanded. "Is he conscious?"

"I can hear him breathing, a moan here and there, but that's all. What will we do after he catches his breath?" Kevin gasped. "We can't hold this forever!"

"Lay him on his back," Les suggested.

"On his back?" Osman growled. "How can we do that without hurting him?"

"This thing's getting very heavy and if we don't do something soon, he'll be stuck face-first on the floor!" Les protested.

"If we kneel, we can each rest it on one knee," Siegfried offered. "He will still be able to breathe. We can do that longer than we can holding him like this."

"Good idea!" Angie said. "Maria and I can get the others and the Lance!"

"Okay, on three," Kevin started. "One...two...three!"

The women released their grips as the men struggled to lower the massive carapace onto one of each of their knees. Maria ran into the bedroom to find the casket.

Hugo, Mehmet and Albert rushed into the room from the yard.

"Is it Sir Richard?" Mehmet asked excitedly.

"Yes," Angie answered, "but he's not doing well. We need you to help hold him."

"I cannot find it!" Maria cried as she came back from the bedroom with Luci. "It is not there!"

"No!" Angie cried back. "It's got to be there!" She ran into the bedroom only to confirm what Maria and Luci had found. "Where in God's name is it?"

"Is Sir Richard awake?" Father Justin huffed as he ran in.

"Father! Where is the Lance?" Angie begged. Sir Richard needs it now!"

The priest looked at the old Templar and saw the others gathered around him. Siegfried's plan to rest the weight on their knees proved unsustainable. The mass was too great. Mehmet, Hugo and Albert set several short, two-foot long wood posts under the massive slab on Sir Richard's back so Osman, Sigfried, Kevin and Les could get out from under the heavy load. Once Sir Richard's position was stable, Les gathered the others around Sir Richard and they bowed their heads.

"He doesn't need it, Angie," Father Justin replied soberly. He could hear Les and the others softly praying.

"What? Are you crazy?" Angie retorted. "Father, he's gonna die without the Lance!"

"No he won't," the priest answered calmly. He listened to the others praying and he closed his eyes and silently joined them.

"Where is it?" Angie demanded as she stepped forward, her face not six inches from the priest's. "I'll get it myself!"

Father Justin opened his eyes and patiently replied, "I've hidden it."

"Dear God, Father! You've just condemned him to die!" Angie angrily thrust her arms into Father Justin's chest, pushing him away. "He won't live without the Lance!"

"Yes he will!" Father Justin insisted. "You saw what happened with Luci!"

"We prayed for hours and nothing happened. You touched her with the reliquary and she was fine within minutes!"

"That didn't happen with the others," Father Justin reminded her. "Remember? It took much more than a few minutes contact with the Lance for the others to be cured. Remember Siegfried?"

Angie was silent as she replayed the events in her mind.

"Your prayers! You, Les, and Maria! God healed Luci through you! The Lance did nothing!"

"But the other times!"

"Maybe it did; maybe it didn't. Didn't we pray at those times as well?"

"Yes, but they were all so different."

"I don't know why things are turning out like they are. But after Luci's experience, I really questioned whether God brought you here to take a two thousand-year old relic back to the world or something much more powerful."

Angie paused thoughtfully and then replied. "I don't know, Father."

"I don't know either, but Sir Richard needs our help right now." The priest left Angie and went to the Grand Master's side to pray with the others.

"Right," Angie admitted as she followed Father Justin. She could hear their prayers reverberating off the walls. Angie looked at Sir Richard and saw that the mass on his back was about three quarters the size it was before. "It's working!" she cried. "Hallelujah! It's working!"

"Without the Lance?" Les asked incredulously.

"Just look!"

"Well I'll be--"

"She's right!" Mehmet declared. "It's getting smaller!"

Father Justin winked at Angie, as if to say, "I told you it would."

Three hours later, the massive carapace on Sir Richard's back was half of its original size. The wooden posts had outlived their usefulness thirty minutes ago.

"Let's lay him on his back," Angie commanded. "He needs to rest, but that mass on his back is still big enough to stop his breathing if he lies on his stomach."

"Hang in their, old fella," Les whispered to the Templar. "You're gonna make it!"

As the hours of praying continued, the Grand Master's condition continued to slowly but steadily improve. It was decided that Angie, Albert, Hugo, Mehmetand Luci would continue to attend Sir Richard: some praying and others making him comfortable and keeping his lips moist. Some would rest, except for Father Justin, who would give comfort to those tending to Sir Richard. He encouraged them, brought them food and drinks and helped with their needs.

Les and the others replaced the first group three hours later. The massive growth on Sir Richard's back was smaller than the last time, as expected, but only by ten percent. However, they were far from discouraged. The task was difficult but not impossible.

At nine o'clock that evening, Angie and her group returned. The mass on Sir Richards back was a third of its original size. The old man was breathing well and he had more color in is face. By midnight, the stony slab on his back was a fifth of its original size.

"How's it going?" Les asked Angie as his group arrived.

"He's getting' there," she answered. Her exhaustion was obvious.

"Get some sleep. See you at three."

At three o'clock the next morning, when Angie and her group arrived, Les was asleep sitting up and the others weren't much better.

"Les!" Angie cried as she looked at the Grand Master's back. "Les, look! It's gone!"

"Huh?" Les grunted as he awoke. "What are you saying?"

"Look at Sir Richard!"

"It's gone!" Mehmet chimed in.

"Incroyable!" Albert declared. *"Un miracle, certainement!"*

The others, too, gasped in amazement.

Kevin fell to his knees and held Sir Richard's hand. "Thank you, God!" he cried outloud. "You are healing him. He will be back with us soon. Thank you!"

The others fell to their knees as well and joined Kevin in his celebration. But it wasn't just for Sir Richard. Most of them had witnessed the affliction and healing of the others. Sir Richard's healing would be theirs as well as his.

The rest of the morning was full of anticipation. Finally, the last one of them would soon be joining the ranks of the healed. But that moment didn't come quickly. At noon, Angie checked with Les.

"He still looks as good as he did earlier this morning, Les?" Angie asked.

"Healthy as a horse who just had a five-hundred pound saddle taken off his back." Les smiled. "He's pretty resilient. I'll say that for him. He's looking great."

"I'm just going to get some coffee. Want some more?" Angie asked as she stepped away.

"No thanks. Don't worry. He's gonna be fine."

Kevin came by a few seconds later. "How's the patient?" he asked as he stepped toward Sir Richard's bed.

"He's almost there. I can feel it, Kevin," Les answered.

As Les said Kevin's name, the old man began to stir. "Kevin? Kevin, my boy, where are you?"

Les and Kevin were all smiles as they rushed to help Sir Richard sit up.

"How are you sir?" Kevin asked dutifully.

"Fit as a fiddle!" Sir Richard replied. "Who are you, young man?" he asked Les politely.

"I'm Les Connery."

"Connery...Connery...Where have I heard that name before?"

Les and Kevin exploded in laughter and hugged the old man tightly.

The party that followed was far above the others. With Sir Richard's recovery, they were all complete. They had come here together, and soon, they hoped they would be leaving, together.

That evening at dinner, Kevin and Les coaxed Sir Richard into telling them about the dream that antedated his recovery. Sir Richard rose to tell his story.

"Would you rather sit, sir?' Kevin suggested.

"No, my boy. After what you and these wonderful people did for me, it is my honor and privilege to stand before these people whom God has blessed and who have been a blessing to me."

The others applauded noisily.

"No, no it is I who applaud you, my dear friends."

As Sir Richard bowed his head, Les could see tears forming in the corners of his eyes.

Kevin patted Sir Richard on the back. "The dream, sir," he whispered in the old man's ear. "Tell them about the dream. They truly wish to know."

"They do?"

"They do, sir."

"Well then I shan't disappoint them."

"No, sir," Kevin added as he took his seat.

"My dream was about a man who was fool enough to believe for most of his life that he was descended from the greatest king the world has ever known. This king from whom he fancied to be descended was born a poor boy and lived his life as an ordinary man, if one could truly call him but a man. He was a man who preached truth, love and peace, yet, was to die the violent death of a common criminal and not a king. However, his death did not destroy the kingdom he founded, a kingdom of another world, whose throne is in the heart of everyone.

"And what of this poor fool who was delirious enough to believe the lies he had been fed for most of his life, either by others or himself?" Sir Richard smiled. "He met this king and saw Him take His rightful place on His throne."

The room was as silent as a tomb.

"That's my dream," Sir Richard said with a smile. "Thank you for listening."

The others rose from their seats and came over to Sir Richard to embrace him, to shake his hand, to kiss him as the tears streamed from their eyes.

May 7, 9:59 a.m.

The next morning's activities were suddenly interrupted by the loud ringing of the telephone. Everybody froze for an instant and then Maria answered it. She wasn't on the phone more than twenty seconds.

"I have good news! Of course, the telephone is now working again." That brought a chuckle from the others. "And ferry service to Leros will start again on May ninth!"

Everybody cheered.

"Looks like my work here is done," Les said to Angie with his head cocked back in the air.

"Hey, I helped!" she retorted as she jabbed him in the ribs.

"Owww!" Les squealed.

May 8, 6:08 a.m.

Mehmet rose before dawn. Sleep would not come to him that night. He quietly rose from his bed. Perhaps, he thought, a walk would make him sleepy. Fifteen minutes later he was walking along the beach and was no closer to falling asleep. As the sun rose, he spotted another figure walking on the beach toward him. Mehmet strained his eyes in the dim light but couldn't make out who it was that was coming toward him. *Who could it be?*

"Good morning, Mehmet." Mehmet recognized the priest's voice.

"Good morning." Mehmet's response was cool.

"What brings you to the beach so early in the morning?"

"I couldn't sleep."

"Funny thing, neither could I. Mind if I join you?" Father Justin asked. "We can keep going in the direction you were headed."

"Okay," Mehmet answered softly.

Mehmet remained silent as the two of them walked along the beach. Father Justin tried several times to start a conversation, but he failed to enlist Mehmet's participation. Finally, Justin stopped.

"Something's bothering you, isn't it, Mehmet? You're not yourself at all."

Mehmet's first inclination was to deny any problem, but he was far too honest to continue his act. He knew that Justin was seeing through him. "I'm having some problems…"

"Yes," the priest encouraged him. "What kind of problems?"

"It's the Lance," Mehmet began slowly after hesitating a few seconds.

"The Lance?" Justin was surprised.

"Yes."

"What about it?"

Mehmet hesitated. "You know that I am Muslim?"

"Yes."

"As a Muslim, I see Christianity as a faith that is…well, let me just say that if Islam is the True Path…"

"Then all other ways are…not?"

"I do not wish to offend you."

"No, it's all right. Go ahead. Get it off your chest."

"The Prophet recognized Jesus as a great prophet."

"Yes, I've heard that."

"But there is only one True Path."

"Okay…"

Mehmet sighed and rubbed his forehead with his hand. "I'm so confused!"

"You said this is about the relic, the Lance."

"Yes."

Father Justin could see that Mehmet was finding it difficult to express himself. "You don't understand how a relic of a lesser religion could do so many fantastic things. Right?" the priest asked.

"Yes, but I saw them all with my own two eyes! I saw each of them transformed! I was dead and it brought me to life! I've witnessed more miracles in these past several weeks than in my entire life! Why?"

"I--"

"When we were still in Istanbul, I spoke with my friend, Yasmin, about the Lance. We couldn't decide if it was truly something from God or an idol brought by the devil. And I still don't know! Is the Lance something to be treasured, something that manifests the glory of Allah or is it a stumbling block, placed on Earth by *Shaitan* to lead us all away from the True Faith?"

"Mehmet--"

"*Esh-Hadu Ina La E-LaHa illa Allah wa Esh-Hadu Ina Mohammed Rasoul Allah!*" Mehmet screamed into the morning as he ran down the beach. "*Esh-Hadu Ina La E-LaHa illa Allah wa Esh-Hadu Ina Mohammed Rasoul Allah!*"

Justin had heard the Shahadah many times before ("I bear witness that there is no god but Allah, and I bear witness that Mohammed is the messenger of Allah."). He ran after Mehmet. "Mehmet! Mehmet, come back!"

"*Esh-Hadu Ina La E-LaHa illa Allah wa Esh-Hadu Ina Mohammed Rasoul Allah!*" Mehmet continued as he ran down the beach.

"Mehmet!"

"*Esh-Hadu Ina La E-LaHa illa Allah wa Esh-Hadu Ina Mohammed Rasoul Allah!*"

"Come back!"

"*Esh-Hadu Ina La E-LaHa illa Allah wa Esh-Hadu Ina Mohammed Rasoul Allah!*"

Mehmet's progress was slowing. His screaming at the top of his lungs was robbing him of the breath and energy he needed to continue his run down the beach. Two minutes later, Father Justin caught up with him. "*...La E-LaHa illa Allah...Mohammed Rasoul Allah!* Mehmet was gasping for air.

"Mehmet, are you all right?"

"*...Rasoul Allah!*" Mehmet answered breathlessly as he collapsed into Justin's arms. "Mohammed...His Prophet!"

"Sit down. You're worn out," Justin said reassuringly. "Just sit down. Everything's okay."

"One God," Mehmet continued as he slowly caught his breath. "One God."

"One God," Justin said back to him.

"One God." Mehmet smiled and closed his eyes. "One God."

"One God."

Mehmet didn't answer this time. He was fast asleep.

Father Justin took off his coat and made a pillow for Mehmet. He resolved to stay with him until he awoke. But soon he succumbed to the demands of sleep, and he unwittingly joined his charge, lying next to him, in peaceful sleep.

May 8, 9:06 p.m.

Father Justin closed the Bible and kissed the front cover. He had returned early from a celebration the others were enjoying in the village. He sighed and walked over to an icon hanging on the wall on the opposite side of his study. The Byzantine features of this Jesus appeared simple, almost primitive, when compared to those of a Titian or a Raphael. However, the elongated anatomy and the deepness of the eyes offered a transcendence a realist could not convey. This Pantokrator, Ruler of All, reached out for the soul of the observer, ran it through His long, spindly fingers and left an indelible imprint.

Father Justin crossed himself and kissed the icon. As he backed away he looked into the eyes of the Savior and thought about the events of the last several weeks. *My Lord, You are a glorious mystery. Twelve people, changed forever—*

"I'm sorry, Father Justin," Angie whispered as she stepped forward into the room. "Your door was open--"

Justin smiled as he turned around. "No, no! Come in, Angie! Come in!" He pulled up a chair for her. "Have a seat. Are the others back yet?"

"No." Angie paused briefly as she sat. "Are you okay, Father? I mean, you left the party early…"

"Oh, I'm a little tired." He sat in a chair across from her. "Thought I'd turn in early. Tomorrow's a big day."

"Yeah, we're all really excited."

The priest leaned toward her. "Angie, what's on your mind?"

Angie's face was as bright as he'd ever seen it. Her excitement was overflowing. "I just wanted to assure you that we'll take good care of it."

"Care of what?"

Angie exploded in laughter. "That's funny, Father! That's very funny!"

Justin smiled back innocently. "No, really, I don't have any idea what you're talking about."

Angie guffawed a few more times and then stopped. "You don't, do you?"

"No, sorry."

"What did he say?" Les said as he poked his head in the room. His panting suggested that he had just run back from the village.

"Hi, Les," Justin greeted his latest guest warily. "How was the party?" the priest asked slowly as he looked over to Angie for her reaction.

Angie stood and walked over to Les. "I think we've made some assumptions--"

Father Justin gently grabbed their hands and smiled. "Let's start over. Les, Angie, take a seat." He stood up and retrieved another chair from the other side of the room. "Angie, you start. What's this all about?"

"Father, are you kidding?" Les blurted out. "What's been going on in your life for the last four weeks?"

"Are you talking about the Holy Lance?"

"Of course!" Les continued. "We wanted to tell you that--"

"'We'll take good care of it.'" The priest finished Les's sentence flatly. "Now I get it."

"You don't seem too excited about that," Angie noted unexpectedly.

Justin wasn't giving his full attention to them. "I don't know--"

"What do you mean you don't know?" Les barked. "Didn't you see what that thing did? My God, it has power to change the world! Give me a month and I'll have every bad guy in the world singing a new tune!"

"*You* will?" Justin asked.

Les backed up. "No, of course not. God will."

"What makes you so sure?" the priest asked.

"I can't believe you just said that!" Angie shrieked. "Father, don't you remember what happened to those people: Luci, Siegfried?"

"Sure I do--"

"So seven down and a couple billion to go," Les interjected smugly.

Justin buried his face in his hands and shook his head a few times before he looked up. "So you're going to take the Lance of Longinus around the world and zap villains."

"Yeah--" Les began.

"No, not exactly," Angie cut off Les. "Father, you saw what it did.

What would happen if we took the Lance around the world? What do you think would happen?"

"I don't have the foggiest idea."

"What?" His reply stunned her. "Don't you think—" Angie stuttered uncertainly "—it would change people, for the better? It would make bad people good, just like it did here!"

"Are you sure?"

Les stared into the priest's face. "You're serious! For a minute there I thought you were playing with us. Then I thought you were just trying to be annoying--"

"I'm sorry if you got that impression, but let me assure you that I'm serious. Gravely serious."

"Do you have doubts about the Lance?" Angie asked, with a definite tone of irritation.

"No. I don't have *any* doubts about it. I'm just not convinced that's what God wants to do with it."

"Oh, now isn't that just like a priest!" Les fumed. "Only *he* knows what God wants!"

"That's not what I'm saying, Les," Justin replied calmly.

"Well, why are you thinking this way?" Angie asked. She was impressed by the priest's calm.

"This relic is not a weapon," Justin began. He was surprised that Les was so intently listening to him. "It's not a talisman or a good luck charm. It's a two thousand-year old piece of iron--"

"With powers sent directly from God!" Les countered.

"Yeah, that's right, Les, but I think you're missing the point, even though you just said it: 'sent by God'. We didn't do the sending. God did."

"So we need to use the Lance so God will use more of His powers!"

"Three weeks ago we were agreed that the Lance would stay here," Father Justin began. "What about all that talk about faith?"

"A lot has happened in three weeks, Father!" Angie protested.

"Don't you remember what it did?" Les added.

"What happens if it doesn't work, Les? Let's say you flash the Lance at some terrorist, but he goes ahead and blows up the school anyway. Or you touch it to a little girl dying of cancer, but she still dies a horrible death. Does that mean that God failed? Or did the Lance just lose its juice?"

"That wouldn't happen!" Les retorted. "You've seen this thing work!"

"But what if that did happen?"

"What are you driving at?"

"It's just a piece of iron, Les."

"A piece of iron that I almost died bringing here!"

"And who brought you here, Les?" the priest asked. "Have you forgotten what happened in the church your first day here? You were ready to leave the Lance here. Now you're ready to take it away. What changed your minds?"

Les's silence assured Justin that Les was beginning to understand. He turned to Angie who smiled back at him. She was getting it too.

"Sure, God was working through the Lance, but more importantly, He was working through us," Justin declared. "He changed the hearts of Albert and Hugo and Osman and we became a much more valuable tool than the Lance. Luci was already starting to get better before the Lance touched her. Remember what happened to Sir Richard? The reliquary didn't touch him at all that day, but he was still healed. And he was the most ill of all."

"But it was somewhere nearby," Les retorted.

"Well if you're in New Zealand and the Lance is here, that's probably 'nearby' enough for God!" Father Justin snapped back.

Angie and Les recoiled.

"I'm sorry," Father Justin said. "That was uncalled for."

"It's okay, Father," Angie and Les replied together.

The priest stepped forward and put a hand on each one's shoulder. "Jesus sent ordinary women and men around the world to spread His message. And these poor, uneducated people changed the world. They didn't need a Lance of Longinus or anything else, except for their faith. It was their faith in God that kept them going, even to the point of death." Father Justin paused briefly. "It was through our faith that Luci, Sir Richard and the others were changed. We can't forget that."

Les looked down sheepishly.

"You're right, Father," Angie conceded.

"It will be safe here," the priest assured them. "Churches all over the world house valuable relics. I can store it somewhere safe, very safe. On special holidays it will be displayed in the church. I'll have the village carpenters make a special case for it. You're welcome to see it anytime. The entire world can come to see the Lance and perhaps, this old piece of iron will bolster their faith, too."

"Won't the Greek Orthodox Church want you to surrender it?" Angie asked. "I mean, Saint Stavros is a very small island. Won't they want the Lance to be in a cathedral in a big city?"

"This church and Saint Stavros are as much a part of the miracle that happened here as the Lance of Longinus is," the priest answered. "I'm confident that in light of what has happened here, the Church will leave the relic here."

"Can I see it now?" Les asked sincerely, breaking his long silence.

"Sure, Les," Justin answered as he went to get the relic. "It's in the study now." When he returned, he handed the reliquary to Angie. "You know, relics are great things if they enhance our faith, but they are not to be the reason for our faith."

Angie set the golden casket on her lap and turned to Les, who smiled at her and then softly kissed her forehead. Angie opened the casket and gently unwrapped the Lance from its red silk covering. Both she and Les could feel their hearts accelerating as they looked at the polished iron weapon as it rested on its papyrus companion. Neither said a word as they read the Latin inscription. Angie carefully placed her fingers on the blade and ran them over the relic. She closed her eyes and recalled all of the moments she spent with this magnificent piece of iron: running through the bazaar stalls with Osman on her heels; desperately looking for the reliquary as the old wooden boat sank into the sea; watching seven flawed people metamorphosize into seven new creations. Then she felt Les's fingers running over hers. She opened her eyes and smiled at him, and he smiled back.

"The world's still a nasty place in many ways but it's also a very good place in other ways," Justin added. "God is love and when you love you are living your faith. *That* is what you should take away from this island, not the Lance."

"You know, Father," Les interjected, "in a way, you're wrong. Each of us will take a tiny bit of the Lance with us when we leave. So it will be with us forever."

"I couldn't agree with *both* of you more," said a voice from the doorway. It was Mehmet.

CHAPTER
TWENTY-THREE

Agios Stavros, May 9, Noon

Good-byes are never easy, especially those so tightly wrapped in the emotion of life-changing experiences. Angie, Les, and the others boarded the ferry bound for Leros full of hope but not devoid of anxiety. No eye was dry as Father Justin and Maria hugged and kissed each of their ten guests and sent them on their ways home. Angie looked thoughtfully at each of her new friends and remembered what they had been through together, a spiritual crucible of sorts, that, through fire, produced a renewed spirit in each of them.

An Olympic Airways Boeing 737 flew them all to Athens. Les booked rooms for everyone at the Grande Bretagne Hotel with his VISA card and took the weary travelers out to dinner that night. The next morning they started going in their own directions. Mehmet, Albert and Osman managed to grab the last three seats on a flight for Istanbul. Siegfried and Hugo headed to Frankfurt and Kevin and Sir Richard managed to squeeze aboard a flight to London, coach class, but Sir Richard didn't mind a bit. Luci followed Mehmet's group to Istanbul on a flight that left two hours later.

Needless to say, the good-byes brought tears and promises of continued contact and future visits. However, they would never be alone, the ten of them. They would always have each other. The bonds they formed were unbreakable and boundless, extending over the entire surface of the earth.

Luci met with Turkish authorities soon after her arrival and used her influence, and a little bit of money, to clear Mehmet, Angie and Les of any criminal charges. And, without any prompting, she offered to sponsor three archaeological projects for the Turkish government. She boarded a 747 for New York two days later.

"It's amazing what happened to all of them," Les said to Angie that night over dinner at an outdoor restaurant in Athens' Plaka.

"And to us," Angie added.

"I guess I'd call it a miracle."

"I'd say ten miracles."

"Yeah, right. Ten miracles."

The miracles didn't end there. Angie and Les returned home and, on the surface, you might say they hadn't changed much. However, with a closer eye, one could see that they were kinder, more patient, more giving, more understanding and much more loving. In each of them a seed was planted long ago and this newly consumed nourishment was actively promoting the growth of a young sapling into a great and wonderful tree that would provide wonderful fruit to many. In upcoming years, Angie and Les would spend six months of each year sharing their medical skills with the poor all over the world.

Luci Daniels donated all of her treasures to museums around the world. When she returned to the United States, she built a shelter for the homeless in Philadelphia and ran it by herself. She gave her fortune to hundreds of charities.

Osman married a plain woman and had three daughters. He took very good care of them and worked his fingers to the bone sending them through university. He was a model husband and father and he never missed the call to prayer.

Siegfried left the SS and formed a committee in Munich that sought to help smooth over relations between ethnic Germans, Turks, Pakistanis and others in that city. He once loaned a Jewish community enough money to repair its synagogue after a fire and he remained a true friend of their community until the day he died.

Hugo Geissler, too, left his old SS friends, kept himself at the ideal weight he had attained on Agios Stavros and founded a group to help compulsive overeaters. The weight lost by all he helped exceeded fifty thousand pounds. He helped the poor for free and wrote a gourmet cookbook, which sold millions around the world. He gave all of the receipts to the world's hungry.

Kevin Meeley left the Templars and started his own fitness club. He soon developed a model physique and was an inspiration to all who met him. He became a much sought-after motivational speaker. Kevin was known for his high-energy lifestyle. Friends complained that he never slept. He used the money he earned from his fitness club and speaking engagements to teach people all over the world to take care of their physical fitness needs and help others. His energy knew no bounds.

Sir Richard resigned as Grand Master of the Knights of the Temple and thereafter had nothing to do with them. He gave away his money with joy and started a free service bringing meals to shut-ins, personally. He continued his newfound passion until he could no longer walk, but he remained an integral part of the service until he died.

Albert Boucher would return to archaeology in Istanbul. Strangely enough, he would grow to love it. Later, he would move to Lebanon and marry a young woman from there in a church with beautiful Byzantine architecture. He often described his wedding as a most beautiful experience in a most beautiful church. He spent the rest of his days deep in the study of archaeology. Albert and his wife would frequently travel to Istanbul to visit their friends Mehmet and Yasmin.

Mehmet would stay in contact with Doctors Johnson and Connery for the rest of his days. He returned to Yasmin as he had promised and married her after graduating from the University of Istanbul. They continued to live in Istanbul but traveled all over the Middle East, providing the world with many important archaeological finds. Their encounters with the Lance of Longinus brought many positive changes in their lives, but it also brought conflicts in their hearts between their beloved Islam and the Christian beliefs about Jesus, which were difficult to sort out, to say the least. Mehmet and Yasmin would finally resolve these conflicts one day, but that is different story.

And what of Leslie Connery? You remember, the famous American archaeologist. It seems that she looked up some old friends when she first arrived in Istanbul and spent the evening with them. She returned to room twenty-three at the Ambassador Hotel the next day totally unaware that anyone had been in her room. Later, she would meet a young Turkish student, Mehmet Yakis, and a French graduate student, Albert Boucher. They were particularly attentive to her, which she found a bit peculiar, but she appreciated it nonetheless. Doctor Connery was very busy during her stay in Istanbul. She worked with an abundance of treasures from ancient, Byzantine and Ottoman Turkey. She was a veritable child in a candy store. When Doctor Kemal's return signaled the time for her return to the United States, she felt that her time in this mystical city had flown by far too quickly.

EPILOGUE

Everett, Washington, April 12, 2007, 2:00 a.m.

"The altar!" Angie shouted as she awoke from a sound sleep.

"Wh—wh--what?" Les wondered as he stumbled into wakefulness.

"The altar, Les!"

"What are you talking about, Ange?"

"Father Justin! He hid it under the altar!"

"Hid what?" Les moaned.

"The Lance, I'm sure of it, Les! I just saw it, as plain as day!"

Les smiled patiently at his wife. "Angie, sweetheart, does it matter?"

Angie snuggled up to Les and kissed him. "No, I guess not," she admitted. "But I know it's there, Les! The dream I just had was so clear!"

"Well that's probably where it is then." Les's voice could not camouflage his ambivalence.

"Don't you care?"

"Of course I care. I care about you and Mehmet and Father Justin and everyone, but I don't really care that much about the Lance anymore."

"Les?"

"Listen, that little episode was undoubtedly the most exciting part of my humble existence. I'll never forget the Lance of Longinus and how it changed my life, how it changed me, how it changed all of us, but I've let go of it, Angie."

"That's not true and you know it. The day we left the island you said that we would all take a little piece of the Lance with us. Don't you remember?"

"Yeah, of course I do, but I'm not that concerned about the ancient relic we left behind. I'm only concerned about what has happened to us since we came across it. That was the past. Let's concentrate on the future and the present."

"So the story's over?" Angie asked pointedly.

The question caught Les off guard. "Well, now that you put it that way, no. No, I guess the story's not over. We were part of a miracle. Witnessed God in action. No, that story will never end."

"Aha!" Angie responded playfully.

"However," Les added, thinking quickly, "those chapters concerning us and the actual relic itself are over."

"What?" Angie grumbled.

"I'm saying let's just leave the Lance of Longinus in the care of our good friend Father Justin Phillipos."

"And?" Angie asked, demanding more.

"And…always remember what it means to us." Les smiled at his wife triumphantly.

Angie sighed heavily. "You're right."

"Of course I'm right."

"I love you."

"I love you too, Angie."

"Pity we're so awake now; nothing to do."

"Oh, I can think of *one* thing," Les suggested with a snicker.

Angie giggled. "You're so predictable."

"I consider that a virtue," he said as he wrapped his arms around her and planted his lips squarely on hers.

"And I love virtuous men," Angie added just before she kissed him again and locked him in an embrace that would last until the sunrise and the alarm clock signaled the beginning of a new day.

CPSIA information can be obtained
at www.ICGtesting.com
Printed in the USA
BVHW072028010720
581819BV00001B/14